101 3 | 26

CW01563738

SING THE NIGHT

SING THE NIGHT

MEGAN JAUREGUI ECCLES

PIATKUS

PIATKUS

First published in the US in 2026 by Grand Central Publishing,
A division of Hachette Book Group, Inc.
Published in Great Britain in 2026 by Piatkus

1 3 5 7 9 10 8 6 4 2

Copyright © 2026 by Megan Jauregui Eccles

The moral right of the author has been asserted.

*All characters and events in this publication, other than those
clearly in the public domain, are fictitious and any resemblance
to real persons, living or dead, is purely coincidental.*

All rights reserved.
No part of this publication may be reproduced, stored in a retrieval system,
or transmitted in any form or by any means, without the prior permission in
writing of the publisher, nor be otherwise circulated in any form of binding or
cover other than that in which it is published and without a similar condition
including this condition being imposed on the subsequent purchaser.

A CIP catalogue record for this book
is available from the British Library.

Hardback ISBN 978-0-349-44815-2
Trade paperback ISBN 978-0-349-44816-9

Printed and bound in Great Britain by Clays Ltd, Elcograf S.p.A.

Papers used by Piatkus are from well-managed forests
and other responsible sources.

Piatkus
An imprint of
Little, Brown Book Group
Carmelite House
50 Victoria Embankment
London EC4Y 0DZ

The authorised representative
in the EEA is
Hachette Ireland
8 Castlecourt Centre, Dublin
15, D15 XTP3, Ireland
(email: info@hbgi.ie)

An Hachette UK Company
www.hachette.co.uk

www.littlebrown.co.uk

*For all you phoenixes: may you burn,
may you rise, may you soar.*

And for Paul, always, for everything.

CHAPTER 1

Selene took a half step onto the stage, the staccato articulation of her heart a sharp reminder of what was to come. She sang each precise note and summoned the wind, fluttering the curtains open. Row after row of empty seats shimmered blue and gold in the flicker of stage lights and the chandelier. This was her tessitura: what she knew, what she expected, what she was destined for.

In six days, this auditorium would be filled, and Selene would perform for the wealth of Mondreves and the king. It was the height of opulence and elegance that positioned the kingdom on the cutting edge of art and magic. Dignitaries would travel from around the world to see their latest innovations and offerings. They were allowed in selectively—the king guarded his secrets well. One of the many reasons auditions were kept closed. Selene was mere breaths away from her chance at the stage, free of nerves or concern that she would make it through. She was favored to win in all the papers and knew the scope of her talent and ambition. Competing in L'Opéra du Magician was the only thing she'd wanted for as long as she could remember.

Almost.

There had been a time when Selene wanted to be something

new each day. A pirate, a flower seller, the girl who sang the books back onto the shelves in the library. She wanted to be everything. But that was a long time ago, before she'd come to live in the opera house, before she'd lost her father. She'd traded a menagerie of dreams for this singular purpose. Selene had nothing else. She only wanted this.

Something shifted behind her. A whisper, a flutter, that familiar feeling of solitude breached.

When she turned, the stage was empty. Selene was alone.

The ghost.

A thrill of fear ran through her. The opera house was notoriously haunted. For decades, students swore they saw a face in the mirrors. The rumor was a girl grew so frightened that she threw herself from the rooftop. And so there were no mirrors in all of the Opera Magique—not to protect their vanity, but to protect their souls.

Selene had looked for the ghost in bowls of water and window glass, in any place she could see herself reflected. She wanted ghosts to be real. She wanted to believe that the people she loved and lost were somehow still here. That her father stood in the place between shadow and light, watching her. That somehow, he'd forgiven her for what she had done.

"You're early."

Gigi stood behind her, dark, curly hair swept up in a tight bun. Her cheeks were rouged and eyelids dusted in glitter, lips showing the barest shine. She turned out her long, sculpted legs in first position. She looked like she belonged in a music box, spinning and spinning and never growing weary—the kind of pretty that was meant to stay forever, but never would.

Selene relaxed a little. She pulled her father's watch from the pocket of her dress and ran her thumb over the familiar engraving: a nightingale caught in starlight. It was the only piece of him she had left. "If you're on time—"

"—you're already a minute too late." Gigi laughed through her teeth. "I can't believe we're finally here."

"Nothing left to do but sing."

And Selene was ready. She knew her aria like she knew the rhythm of her own heart. She'd written it piece by piece over the last three years, making sure it was perfect. Every note filled with meaning. Risoluto. Con fuoco.

The door crashed open. Priya stood in the frame, catching the light, an artist's rendering of classic beauty. The hollow of her long neck fluttered with each intake of breath, like a butterfly reposing on a blossom. Her hair was long and lush, her mouth painted in plum. It was a shame that someone so beautiful could be so terrible. That pretty face twisted into a sneer. A flash of cruelty—before it was replaced with a politician's smile.

"I don't know why you two even bother." Priya swung her hips as she walked, each step a performance. "Madame Giroux's talentless daughter and the orphan of the Mad Mage. No matter how you perform, the king will never pick you. What will the papers say?"

" 'Talent surpasses nepotism and bribery,' " Selene snapped. " 'Priya Ankari seen weeping in her lover's arms while her fiancé looks on.' "

Priya's mouth flattened to a thin line. "And what would you know of lovers, Selene?"

"Nothing," Selene said sweetly, trying not to let the barb

sting. Once, Selene had thought she loved someone. But it was the folly of childhood, gone as swift as a sigh. "My only love is music."

"Then I fear you'll be spurned."

"Ignore her." Gigi pulled at Selene's sleeve.

Selene caught the retort on the tip of her tongue. She'd show Priya on the stage. Gigi was right, Priya wasn't worth the wasted words. She wasn't worth the energy hate would expend. Selene needed everything she had today.

Gigi's fingers tightened on Selene's arm.

Priya stood with a poisonous grin. She held a small, silver mirror in her hand.

It caught the light. A glimmer, a glint, a slip of reflective glass. Anywhere else, it would have been a worthless trinket.

In the Opera Magique, the mirror was a knife.

"Selene." Gigi's fingers dug into Selene's flesh. Selene knew the shape of Gigi's nightmares—had been with her through those sleepless nights. The ghost had terrified her since before she could remember.

"The only monster here is the one holding the glass," Selene seethed.

Priya curled her lip. "What do you think it would take to get your mother here, Gigi? Shall you cry, or do you think she'd come quicker for Selene?"

"That's enough." With a few steps, Selene positioned herself in front of Gigi.

"As if you could tell me what to do." Priya bared her teeth. "Are you scared, Gigi? Scared enough to jump from the roof?" She lunged forward with the mirror.

SING THE NIGHT

Gigi staggered back, forgetting the rope that coiled like a snake beside the velvet wing. Selene grabbed for her hand—but she was too late. The sound of Gigi's body slamming into the stage echoed through the auditorium. Selene dropped down beside her.

"It's fine." There were tears in Gigi's eyes. She looked past Selene to Priya.

Selene's heart thundered con furore. She could accept Priya's viciousness on her own behalf—had been for years. But for Gigi, she would let the world burn.

Priya's face was marred with rapture. "What are you going to do?"

The options were endless. Selene could sing the air from Priya's lungs. She could summon fire and spark that fine dress into flames. She could grow vines to wrap around Priya's pretty throat and squeeze until all the light was gone.

Except.

Magic was never to be used as a weapon. Magic was art and entertainment—beautiful, impractical, and privileged. It required years of study, careful attention to technique, and could turn dangerous quickly on a technicality.

And maybe it was hubris or recklessness or the privilege of never living in fear. Selene had been raised on the wild idealism that magic and art existed in the everyday. She had not been held to the standard that magic was only meant for this higher form. Selene didn't understand why magic couldn't be more. Her father had taught her first how to pull water from the sea into a bucket, how to hush out a candle with a breath of wind, how to find the heart of a flower and make it grow. It wasn't until she'd lost her father and been sent to the opera house that she'd learned a fear of magic. Rumors abounded of magicians who tried to light a candle with the power of their voice and instead set themselves ablaze. Ruined for a flame.

Selene knew of ruin. She knew what magic could be. She didn't care about candles or clouds. Those were simple, small things. There was so much worse magic could do. Selene had tasted the sweet poison of destructive power. There was already blood on her hands.

There could be blood on her hands again.

She banished those violent delights, breathing slowly and deeply. Priya wasn't worth it. Selene wasn't one of the silly dilettantes seeking a hobby before they shackled themselves to a wealthy spouse. Those practitioners weren't here to win, not really. They wanted the prestige and stories to tell at parties. This didn't matter to them like it mattered to Selene. Priya—despite her engagement to a viscount—actually seemed to want this. At least she wanted it badly enough to destroy anyone who stood in her way. And because of that, Selene knew exactly how to hurt her.

Her smile was the sharpened edge of a blade. "I'm going to be better than you."

Worry flickered in Priya's eyes before it was replaced with pity.

"It's a shame the Mad Mage didn't finish what he started." Priya angled the mirror to reflect Selene's throat.

The high collar of Selene's dress had shifted, revealing the tips of the silver scars that circled her neck. Without thinking, Selene adjusted the lace to conceal them. She regretted it immediately. Priya's smile curled at Selene's show of weakness.

"Did your father lose his mind before or after he tried to rip out your throat?"

It was all Selene could do not to be crushed by memories of that day. She focused on the music—power building under her skin. She'd pull the moisture from the air and freeze it into a sharp shard. Priya would bleed, all the evidence melting into the red. The placement of the music lifted the back of her throat. High road be damned.

No.

She wouldn't throw away her chance to be the King's Mage for Priya. She wouldn't give everything up for vengeance.

Priya's smile faltered, her motives clear. She'd been trying to goad Selene into action. She'd gone after Gigi first, then Selene's father. She'd wanted Selene to react and get herself thrown out of the competition.

Selene took a deep breath, letting the heat of her fury cool to an icy rage. She brought her hands together in a slow clap.

"Brava, Priya. Though you'll have to try harder to—"

The surface of the mirror rippled.

Selene might have convinced herself that it was a trick of the light. But there was something *there*. A face cast in shadow, all angles and furrowed brows. Cold, blue eyes that cut straight to her soul.

The melody came to Selene before she had the chance to process what she was doing. She sang the wind into a scythe that forced Priya back against the wall. The mirror shot in the opposite direction. Away, away, away. Selene waited for that beautiful breaking sound. It would be freedom. A mercy.

But the mirror did not break.

It didn't even fall.

It hovered there in the center of the stage, catching the lights.

Madame Giroux stood in the threshold, eyes thinned to slits beneath her half-moon glasses. She leaned heavily against her wolf's head cane. Her mouth moved with music, soundless.

Madame had a cat's countenance and a gift for silence, even in song. Magic did not need volume or vibrato; it needed practice and an open mind. Anyone could do magic if they had the pitch and the focus and knew the melody. But not everyone could be a magician. While there were magicians in taverns and carnivals and every rich man's hall, it was a dangerous undertaking. As with all art, talent was not spread evenly. One might be good enough to sing shifting shades of light on a street corner and still be unable to weave an illusion deftly enough to hold the attention of a tavern. There was little unity between mages. The failure of one meant the success of another, which bred contempt as they became more adept. The higher the court, the more the mage had to work and sweat and bleed to get there.

And the King's Mage was the highest one could go. Once every seven years, a mage had the chance to be known as the greatest in the world. It was more than prestige. There was power in it. Doors opened to the whole world, if the mage wanted. There was no more competing for the limited spaces in which a mage could earn a living. It was everything, a guarantee of a good life, a great life.

But it was not without risk. Magic required perfect technique and absolute precision. Few were brave enough to perform without schooling. Fewer still underwent the preparations for L'Opéra du Magician. It took years of training, and more magicians seemed to lose themselves each season.

Selene couldn't be good. She had to be the best. The audience expected grandeur, each competition bigger than the last.

And Selene would give them that, if she made it through the auditions.

All the fire left Selene, replaced by fear. Like Priya, Selene had broken the rules. Priya may have brought in a mirror, but Selene had harmed a fellow magician. Art was not a weapon. It was a soul laid bare, an expression of beauty and pain and all the loveliest things. It was never supposed to be used in violence.

Madame's melody changed, barely audible over Selene's furious heart.

The mirror shattered. Not shards or pieces, but a shimmering powder that drifted down and settled into the cracks of the stage like glittering ash.

"Can you still sing?" Madame looked directly at Priya, her eyes as severe as her voice.

Priya pressed her fingers to the back of her head. They came back slick with blood. Her hand trembled. She clenched it into a fist. "Yes, Madame."

"My office," Madame said. "When the auditions are finished."

"And what about her?" Priya's look of vindication slipped from her face like a mask. "She could have killed me."

Selene braced herself. There was no way she'd be allowed to compete now. Her stomach dropped like a stone. Priya had gotten exactly what she wanted.

Madame's gaze settled on Selene. "You were warming up your voice."

Selene swallowed hard, not letting any emotion show. "Yes, Madame."

"Magic has its risks." Madame Giroux stood very still.

Priya looked like she'd bitten into a lemon. "That's not—"

"Enough." Madame struck her cane against the stage.

Selene kept her breath even, her features empty of guilt or surprise. She'd accept this mercy from Madame Giroux. Gigi struggled up from the floor and Selene rushed over to give her a hand. She tried not to think of what she'd seen in the mirror and how Priya would make her pay for this later.

The door opened behind her. The rest of the students filled in the spaces between Priya, Selene, and Gigi. Benson took his place beside Gigi, catching her fingers in his. He looked to Selene.

"You look like you saw a ghost."

As usual, Benson was impeccably dressed. His clothes were tailored and pressed, hitting all the right lines and angles. Except for the ankles. He'd gained inches over the last few months, and there wasn't any hem left to be let out from his trousers. People in the opera house regarded him with fluttering lashes and bedroom eyes, as if the inches made him a new man. But he was still Benson. All Selene saw was the boy who flooded the practice rooms when he first learned how to sing for water. Who cried when he learned that meat came from things that had once been alive. Who still tore the crusts off his sandwiches because he swore they tasted better that way. She'd vowed never to let childhood friendship turn into something more. She'd never be that foolish again.

Gigi was not afraid of those feelings. She'd loved Benson since he was spindly and strange. She'd finally gathered the courage to tell him a few months ago. He loved her, too. Selene had volleyed their affections back and forth as a confidant for both, never knowing if it was the right thing to encourage them into each other's arms or encourage them to let those feelings die. The rules for the King's Mage were clear: your first loyalty belonged to the king. Marriage was banned. And though discreet romantic entanglements were ignored, the kind of love that both Gigi and Benson had would not be allowed. If either of them were to win, they'd have to put their feelings aside for the next seven years.

Still, Benson pressed his lips to her forehead. The pain in Gigi's face dissipated.

Selene made her face as smooth as glass, flattening out every ripple of emotion.

Benson raised an eyebrow, his mouth quirking into half a smile. "You know that trick doesn't work on me."

Selene thought of those pale blue eyes from the mirror, like sapphires set in silver. Perhaps she could write that off as a trick of the light.

"She used magic against Priya." Gigi spoke barely above a whisper.

"Did she deserve it?" When they were younger, Priya had filled Benson's only pair of shoes with honey. He'd worn only socks for weeks. Needless cruelty was her hallmark, now heightened by L'Opéra du Magician. "What am I saying? Of course she deserved it."

"Are you going to be okay?" Selene whispered.

"My hip." Tears choked Gigi's voice. "I don't know if I can perform today."

"You should have killed her." Benson wrapped his arm

around Gigi, helping her keep the weight off her injured hip. "I'll kill her."

Gigi relaxed against Benson. "She's not worth it. She'll never be worth it."

On the other side of the stage, Priya held court, garnering sympathy from her friends. The twins—Camille and Cecile—gasped at Priya's tale. Revelio dragged his lips down the line of her neck. She held on to him, the weight of another man's engagement ring clearly not enough to keep her hands off.

Madame Giroux held up her pocket watch by the chain. The second hand settled over the twelve and she struck her cane against the stage. Selene took her place in the half-moon around Madame.

Frantic footsteps of students desperately trying to make it before it was too late echoed in the hall.

Madame sang a few crisp notes that made up the motif for metal, slamming the door to the stage shut. Locks clicked into place.

And like that, those students' chances were gone. Selene heard sobs. Shouts of protestation. Fists against the door and melodies wrangled through frantic throats. But it was too late. In the next hour, they would be ushered out of the opera house, condemned to normal lives. A dream, a wish, a lifetime of work, gone. There was a possibility they'd find work as magicians, but it wouldn't be easy. There were so many hopeful mages willing to risk life and limb trying to carve out a reputation in the city and garner patronage. Some noble houses wanted the next best thing and some houses preferred someone loyal, someone who would last. Foreign courts would gladly open their doors to a talented magician who'd trained in the Opera Magique.

But without the prestige of L'Opéra du Magician, it might not be enough. They'd be lucky to find a place with a high enough wage to sustain a life, a family. There were plenty of street magicians, singing tableaux on the street corners, hoping to catch a few coins. And there were those who did magic—not magicians, per se—singing the fires lit in noble houses and sweeping up rooms with a collection of notes. Practical magic, nothing more than utility. Not music, not performance, nothing but a vessel for quick and basic tasks. There was still some risk, but those mages rarely pushed themselves. To Selene, it seemed like a fate worse than death.

Those who'd been born into wealth would be fine. They'd fold back into their fancy dresses and horse-drawn carriages with little thought for the years they'd spent in the opera house. Those without titles and wealth—like Selene, like Benson—would look back on the wasted years with endless regret as they tried to make up for the time they'd lost working a trade. If they were lucky, they could find a steady gig, but those seemed few and far between. Talent seemed a minuscule measure of success.

Selene didn't concern herself with that kind of stress. She was confident about her chances, and even when the barest sliver of self-doubt crept in, she remembered she had her name. She was the daughter of the great Giuseppe Dreshé. That was enough to get her through any door, and her voice would keep her there. She could go anywhere.

But there was only one door that mattered. Only one place she wanted to be.

"You know why you are here." Madame took out a deck of cards. She discarded three, flinging them out and singing them gone. A burst of fire, and then nothing—Madame used practical magic without fear of scrutiny. She was a teacher; she had to teach. "You are the brightest mages in the land. And your time here has made you the best. L'Opéra du Magician is not about memorization or mesmerization or even the music. This is your chance to show what magic can do." Her dark eyes slashed through them all. Selene felt the cut, hope welling inside her like blood to a wound. "Each of you will perform your audition piece. Your years of training come down to a single aria."

A ripple of uneasiness moved through the remaining thirteen competitors. Madame Giroux didn't have to explain what that meant. They had all seen it firsthand: when the magic went wrong. Selene didn't think of her father, but of the many hopefuls she'd studied with over the years who hadn't made it to this point. One wrong note and their dreams—and sometimes limbs—were shattered.

"Once auditions are finished and the competitors are named, you will be announced and presented at the Unmasking Ball. Then the end begins—with L'Opéra du Magician as your final performance as my students. And one of you will be named the King's Mage."

Madame's eyes rested briefly on Selene. The hairs on the back of Selene's neck rose. This was it. This was her moment.

Madame struck her cane against the stage and took her place in the third row. Monsieur Fenrir, the manager of the opera house, had slipped in. He slumped back in his seat, looking frazzled, like someone had told him that the sun would continue to rise and it was too much for him to take.

"He'll quit before the end of the week." Gigi leaned against Benson as they descended the stairs to the auditorium.

"He can't. We're too close," Selene said.

Gigi smiled with the wisdom of a girl who'd grown up inside the opera house. "Bet on it?"

"The usual?"

Selene reached her hand down to Gigi and discreetly shook before taking her seat a few rows back. Monsieur Fenrir flinched when the palace representative settled beside him. The man was young and handsome, moving with the ease of someone who knew his worth. It was a familiar confidence. For a moment, Selene held on to a spark of hope. But it died when she saw the man's face. Stupid, to feel this way after all these years. It was not Victor. It would never be Victor.

"And now..." The cards moved like water between Madame Giroux's hands. "We begin."

CHAPTER 2

Let it be me, Selene thought.

She wanted to be first, needed to be first. Her hand rested on her folio. Music was a language, with each sentence holding the potential for magic. Selene had carefully crafted each motif to tell her father's story. She'd copied and recopied her aria, burning the pages in between. He was the only mage in history to serve a second time when that season's mage lost her mind shortly after her debut. Before he was the Mad Mage, he had been someone respected and loved. Someone whose art had meant something. It could mean something again.

Madame drew a card. Selene closed her eyes and imagined her own face there. Willed it to be true. Madame Giroux spent a moment scrutinizing the card, then turned it around.

It was the perfect depiction of Revelio.

Revelio looked a little stunned, like he couldn't believe his luck. He kissed Priya full on the mouth. She whispered something to him and a smile spread across his face.

Selene tensed in her seat, the delicately carved arms of her chair biting into her skin. Gigi reached for her hand and squeezed it apologetically.

Revelio handed the maestro his music. The orchestra sight-read as an attempt to prevent sabotage or the arias being leaked to the press. Selene wasn't worried about that. She had her own ways to protect her music: locks and keys, secret places, pages curling with fire.

Revelio strutted across the stage. His puffed black silk pants gleamed with strips of gold. He'd left his shirt open halfway down his chest, revealing a swath of dark hair and the glistening skin beneath. He must have tanned on the roof, spread out by the copper dome, to turn his olive skin into such a rich bronze.

That was one way to prepare for L'Opéra du Magician.

He flourished dramatically with his hand and nodded to the maestro. The maestro tapped his baton against his music stand. This was it, the moment of silence that always made Selene feel like she was home. The pause for breath before everything was sound.

The baton sliced through the air. The first chord struck— a clever inversion of the tonic, followed by an all too familiar chord progression. The hum of the cello and the weep of the violin resonated through her. Selene knew this melody, down to her bones.

She knew it, because it was hers.

No, she thought.

Her heart beat tumultuoso, disbelief warring with reality. This couldn't be happening. It was an impossibility. She should do something, say something, rise up and stop him. But the music played on and there was little Selene could do without facing steep consequences. Interrupting another mage's audition was strictly forbidden.

Selene reached into her pocket, feeling the worn edge of her leather sheaf of sheet music. She knew it was all there; she'd checked it before she'd left her room. How had Revelio gotten her music? She'd been so careful, paranoid even. She dug her nails into her palm, hoping that she'd wake up from this nightmare. This was too terrible to be real.

Revelio disappeared in a puff of purple smoke. Not the stuff of extinguished candles and green boughs bent by wildfires. This was a glittering vapor, more for ambience than anything else, though it was the most dangerous part of the piece. It was difficult to sing since it filled the lungs with something other than air. It smelled of burned sugar—sweet and bitter. Selene had meant it as a transition and a screen for casting her illusion, beautiful and elegant and seamless. She hated the way Revelio popped in and out of the smoke—each time taking a huge breath of the clean air—like it was some cheap sleight of hand. He had her music, but none of her artistry. This was not his story to tell. He'd sped up the tempo, blasting through the delicate lines like they were meant to be shouted instead of sung.

From his shimmering plume of smoke, he cast her a glance.

Dared to wink.

Violence built inside of Selene. How much would it take for her to sing the smoke into poison and watch Revelio choke on his own breath? She could think of a dozen ways she could invert the melody, how she could let it be a whisper or a scream. The louder the better, so he would know exactly who was to blame.

Selene wouldn't. She couldn't. There were too many witnesses and too much at stake.

Besides, it would be wrong.

Priya leaned forward, humming the next line. "Brava, Selene. You'll have to try harder next time."

Selene flinched. Priya looked like a viper satisfied with its strike. She had done this. Stolen Selene's music. And she had put it all on Revelio—letting him take the blame, should things go wrong.

Gigi squeezed Selene's hand tighter, face flushing with anger as the pieces fell into place.

They locked eyes, conveying the rage and pity and despair now shared between them. Gigi glared at Priya with murderous intent.

Revelio's lyrical tenor crescendoed. He emerged from the smoke, pursued by a dragon with slick scales and wicked eyes. Her dragon hadn't been this creature of darkness. It was meant to be an homage to her father guiding her to this place, and a nod to his winning performance. Revelio popped out his notes in short staccato. This part was supposed to be soft and lyrical, and then sforzando with the dragon spreading its wings to fly over the auditorium. Lifted by her voice, rising up to meet her father wherever his soul rested.

But Revelio wasn't a good enough magician for that. He slipped from his illusion to the corner of the stage, still sustaining the dragon, and wrapped himself in a clumsy illusion of armor. He burst back onto the stage accelerando. The dragon's long claws reached for his throat. He ran toward the dragon, dodging and weaving and finally—with one sustained note— struck the dragon through the heart with his lance.

Stars and smoke settled around him. He took a desperate breath and raised his hand up in triumph. Sweat beaded on his temples.

He bowed. His smile was a lance aimed at Selene.

There were no words to match the devastation. She'd written that piece over years, carrying it in her heart from the first time she'd heard her father's aria. She'd worked so hard to craft every line, every note perfect, perfect, perfect. It was a piece of her very soul.

Good artists borrowed, better artists stole. Revelio was mediocre at best. He'd taken her structure, her melody, her magic, and cheapened it.

But he'd done it first.

Monsieur Fenrir was on his feet, clapping furiously. The palace representative applauded beside him, pausing to take notes. Madame Giroux did nothing but reach for her deck of cards.

It wasn't over yet.

Selene had fallen onto the sword of Madame's mercy once today. It might happen again. She could recover from this. She'd write a new piece or adapt an old one. She would not sleep a wink tonight. Her whole life would not come down to this stolen piece of music.

The shuffling stopped. Madame picked a card, and disappointment creased her face. She held it up. Dark curls, wide, haunted eyes, a set of determination in the mouth. In this depiction, Selene looked like a shadow of her father, without any of the joy Selene attributed to him. Was that how Madame saw her?

"Oh, Selene," Gigi said. "What are you going to do?"

There was only one thing she could do.

"Sing."

Selene brushed her fingers against her collar to make sure

it covered her scars. She walked up the stairs like a march to the scaffold, taking mental stock of the arias she had in her sheaf. Most of them had been taken out this morning. They had weighed down her pocket too much. She'd left in her audition piece and her strange, experimental work in progress: a tempest aria. But it wasn't ready. It wasn't safe. She wasn't even sure it was possible.

What choice do you have?

Selene handed the maestro her sheet music. The first chair magician sang duplicates of it onto the blank sheets on the rest of the musicians' music stands. Selene watched them skim over the key and motifs, preparing to play it for the first time.

She took her place at the center of the stage.

CHAPTER 3

First the breath.

Selene relaxed her shoulders, relaxed her jaw. She cleared her mind of everything and let her body fall into muscle memory. The breath was the root of all music. Selene often imagined the magic as silvery wisps she'd catch in her throat and convert into something marvelous. She was but an instrument, a focal point to channel magic. She could manipulate the key, vary the motif, play with tempo, but she could not perform without breath. Not just hers, but the magic that filled her the moment she gave it air and purpose. This was her chance. She looked up to the golden scrollwork of the chandelier and the pale light cast from its many glowing candles.

When Selene's father, the great Giuseppe Dreshé, had stepped onto this stage twenty-eight years ago, he had been a young man—not yet Selene's father. Back then, each mage chose a single motif and sang its variations. It was a display of vocal talent, imagination, and ingenuity. The motif could only be pushed so far before it lost its shape and with it, the magic, but that was the game. Fire would burn in various shapes and colors or water crystalized to ice and melted again or buds burst into bloom around the mage, hopeful that it would be enough to entertain and catch the eye. Each note was embellished and inverted and melismatized until it was nearly beyond the point of recognition. Giuseppe wanted to be more than a collection of lovely notes and sustained motifs. He wanted music to tell a story.

He chose the motif for illusion and used light as a counterpoint in the orchestrations, allowing him to channel two different motifs. The violin picked up the melody for light and carried it like a voice, striking the notes while her father maintained the magic. There was no real explanation for why this trick was possible, it simply worked. The magic responded to the music and the will of the magician as long as the intent and the motif aligned. His sung dragon flew through a series of scattered stars, landing on the chandelier and then soaring over the auditorium, leaving a shower of sparks in its wake. No one in the world had seen magic like this. He'd won L'Opéra du Magician and changed the course of history, reshaping what the world knew was true of magic.

But that's not what people remembered when they said his name.

Mad Mage.

They only spoke of the sensational tragedy. Plenty of magicians succumbed to injury or madness. It was the cost of their art, the perilous chance they took to charm an audience. But few lost their mind with such a horrendous display of blood. Her father was supposed to be different, to be greater than the madness. His fortitude had allowed him the opportunity to serve the king a second time but had left him in infamy. People didn't remember him as the talented magician; he was the fool who'd pushed himself beyond his craft. The madman who'd lost his mind within a week of ceding as the King's Mage. They forgot about his brilliance, his kindness, his easy smile. They only spoke about the way he'd tried to tear out his daughter's throat with his bare hands.

She swallowed, feeling the movement of the fabric against her scars. She wore a reminder of his madness on her skin—of her sins and secrets. For too long Selene had only been seen as a cataclysm. This was her chance to change the world. To remind people what a Dreshé could do.

Be with me, she prayed. Wishing for a ghost, for *his* ghost.

Selene nodded to the maestro. She pulled her starting note from the violin, listening to the liquid movement of the opening bars. The violin slid its melody, countered against the haunting echo of the bassoon. She pressed her heels into the stage.

And breathed.

She sang the motif for illusion and formed a tableau of the sea, focusing on her breath and letting the magic fill her. Illusion was the favored motif for most magicians. It was merely a variation of light, adopted and directed to bend and project an image. There was no inherent danger or mess to clean up after. But it required an intensity of focus that was often challenging. The music was easy enough to sing, but the vision of the tableau had to remain perfectly clear in the magician's mind to maintain its projection. One deviation and the whole thing would fall away.

Which made Selene's aria even more impressive.

The water lapped against the edge of the stage. She stood in the foam, the image of water moving around her. An illusion this complex took more than singing the line; Selene needed to feel it in her soul. But that wasn't hard. Her father loved the ocean. He'd built their home there, before he'd accepted the king's request and they'd made a home in the grand suites of the palace. Selene had only been eight. Young enough to be excited about the adventure and old enough to realize that something was being taken away.

She held the music there, like a sweet memory: a fermata.

Then she sang the water out of the air, letting it froth and foam at her feet. It splashed over the orchestra to the audience. Gentle, for now. The calm before the storm.

The tempo moved accelerando. Her indigo dress churned with the sea. The waves rose up and crashed down. The magic caught her rage and projected it out to the auditorium. Water fit in easily with the illusion, the two melodies piecing together like old friends. She could stop here and let the audience get caught up in the ambience of the storm—the image of the sea and spray of water and ebb and flow of her orchestrations all knitting into something beautiful and easy.

But Selene didn't want easy. She wanted to be great, like her father. She wanted to rewrite history.

A third motif.

It was more theoretical than practical. Her father had been the first to bring in a second element. Since then, magicians had tried unsuccessfully to incorporate a third element. Those who tried wrought damage on themselves and others in their attempts. That wouldn't be Selene. It wasn't enough to fold the melody into the orchestration; both had to be sung. Selene had worked out variation after variation, lining them up until they fit together. To an untrained ear, it would sound like another embellishment.

Until the lightning struck.

Selene wouldn't just emulate her father; she would surpass him. She would remind everyone what a Dreshé could do.

And so she would sing real lightning—let it sunder the air and sweeten it. Ozone resting against her tongue like a sun-ripe berry. She'd take the worst thing that had ever happened to her—the worst thing she had ever done—and turn it into a triumph.

There was a moment when the notes coalesced—illusion, water, lightning—and then split into three, all striking notes in the elaborate melisma, rising to a sustained high note that worked for all three motifs. Selene only needed to hold that note and maintain the illusion and water, with the melody sustained in the violin and cello. Then she would have her storm.

She'd practiced and practiced the vocal line, but never had the proper accompaniment to prove her theory. Until now. This should work. It had to work.

Selene sang the note, loud and clear, like the toll of a bell, and readied herself for the new thread of magic.

The magic pulsed through her. Power surged, all three motifs coming together, just as she'd wanted.

This was it.

The edges of Selene's mind stretched; the magic channeled through her. The storm—a hurricane—pulled into the air. It was a thing of terrible beauty and infinite power.

Her father was in the center of it all. She imagined him sitting at their little piano in the cottage, plucking out melodies for her to imitate. Remembered his praise when she sang the salt out of the seawater to sprinkle over their dinner. His eyes lit up when she sang, how he'd say again and again: *Sing for me.*

She felt where it went wrong, slipping from her fingers like the memories of her father's voice, the brightness of his laughter. There, and gone, replaced by Father's face when he realized what he was about to lose, his features contorting with fear. Then his pupils blown black. Musician's fingers tearing at her throat. Making sounds no human should make.

There was too much magic.

It tore through her, its own kind of storm. Selene could not accommodate the breadth of power. It pushed against the limits of her mind, threatening to break it.

For one, wild moment, Selene considered letting it take her. The magic was intoxicating and endless. She could be endless, too, if she just gave in; she could go on forever: power and magic and bliss.

She knew better than to let the magic have her.

Selene let go of the illusion, hoping to compensate with the water to carry the elements. The magic unbalanced inside her. She tried to pool her focus, but it was too late.

Everything else fell away.

Except.

Lightning volleyed through the auditorium. It struck one of the golden statues that clung to the walls. The gold shuddered and dripped, turning the carved angelic face into a monstrosity. It struck again, setting a seat in the auditorium on fire. The orchestra halted; musicians flattened in the pit with shouts of protest and alarm.

Selene gasped for air, tasting electricity on her tongue.

What had she done?

Monsieur Fenrir and all the students curled under their

seats. Only Madame Giroux stood, her cane in the air. Singing for control. It struck a final time, hitting her cane like a lightning rod.

And then there was nothing but the saccharine taste of ozone, the scent of burning velvet, and the destruction left behind.

Madame regarded Selene from over the rim of her glasses, her mouth a tight line, eyes lit with something more than disappointment. Monsieur Fenrir lifted his head above the seats. The representative made a quick note on his papers.

"That is all for today," Madame said. She sang water out of the air, sending it to the burning chair. The orchestra mages stood below the twisted statue, singing the molten metal back into shape. Drop by drop, calling back the damage Selene had wrought.

Shame crackled through her like residual lightning. This was a disaster—more than the damage, more than the ruined song. She'd ended the auditions with her calamity. Sure, they'd continue tomorrow. But she'd be remembered for shutting them down on the first day. The papers would have their fun with her. The thought made her sick.

Gigi half dragged Benson up the stairs, still leaning on him for support. She looked like she was made of lightning and about to strike. "You have to tell Madame. This isn't right. We can fix—"

Madame Giroux's cane struck the stage. Gigi hesitated for a second, still determined. Selene shook her head sharply. After what had just happened, she doubted it would do any good. Gigi sighed and went with Benson out of the auditorium.

"Selene." Disappointment crept over the edge of Madame's voice. "A moment."

"Yes, Madame."

Selene grasped her trembling hands against her skirt, breathing through the aches in her mind, which had pushed further than it was meant to. She'd tried impossible things before and had felt the effects of too much magic—but nothing quite like this. She'd been close to something. If she'd held on just a moment more, perhaps she could have had it.

But at what cost?

Madame Giroux sighed. "Do you know why I took you in?"

"You knew my father," Selene said cautiously. She had pieces of the story, but not the whole. Madame had been a new teacher when her father was a student, before he took the title of the King's Mage. She'd been young and ambitious and had been appointed as head before Selene's father started his second tenure. The papers noted she'd been handpicked by the king.

"When you were dropped on my doorstep, orphaned and still bleeding from the cuts on your throat, I asked you to prove yourself."

Selene had only been thirteen—too young to train at the opera house—when she'd been unceremoniously tossed into that tiny carriage with a trunk and a satchel of gauze and salve for her neck. The palace had disappeared behind her like a dream she couldn't quite hold on to. Victor's screams still echoed within her. She'd been deposited on the snow-dusted steps of the Opera Magique with her whole life lost to her. The driver argued at the door for long enough that Selene bled through her bandages, staining the lapis blue of her cloak. She'd waited and waited, until, at last, the door opened.

There was nothing in the world like seeing the inside of the opera house for the first time. Selene let it steal her breath and had never quite gotten it back. Everything was gilt and gold and grander than even the palace. There were chandeliers and golden statues holding candles at every turn. The grand staircase split in two and curved like a beckoning hand. Balconies nestled in every arch, so that everyone could see and be seen. The Opera Magique was the seat of splendor and a font of dreams. Selene knew excess and luxury—she had spent so much of her childhood in the marbled halls of the palace. This could not compare. There was something endless about this place, like stepping into a memory.

And there was, of course, the ghost of her father. He had been here. Her father had made a name for himself on this stage. He sang in these halls and slid down these banisters. In a way, that made it home.

Madame appraised Selene like she was something she couldn't wait to forget and led her to her office. There were no notable exceptions to early admission for the Opera Magique's conservatory. Even the most talented young artist had to wait until they were at least sixteen. Madame had asked Selene to show her what she could do. Selene knew what she'd expected: a pretty song with a light illusion. The safe kind of party trick young ladies were taught. But Selene wasn't that kind of girl. A fire raged inside her. It was so much easier to feel passion and anger than grief. She'd taken a rose from Madame's desk, sung it into rot and back into bloom, and then into a seed.

Madame Giroux had looked at her then like she looked at her now: with reverent expectation and hunger. She accompanied it with a sigh. "I had never seen someone with such raw talent."

Selene knew what was coming next. She could feel the pull of the despair, gathering and ready to come down on her like an ocean wave. Good, but not good enough. Close, but not close enough. Something always missing.

"Your performance was technical, but poorly executed."

Madame kept speaking. Saying all the things Selene already knew. Selene had to tell her what had happened. She couldn't let this be the end. She could show Madame. Lay out the pages of sheet music and prove what had been stolen.

"Madame, my music—"

"Selene," Madame snapped. "I don't want to hear excuses."

"But Revelio—"

Madame Giroux's gaze was sharp enough to cut Selene into silence. The knuckles on her cane were bloodless. Selene anticipated her strike, like she was facing down a predator. She would not win this fight.

"Yes, Madame."

"I expected more from you. You are so like your Giuseppe." Madame shook her head. The bitter disappointment etched into the lines of her face. "Some stars burn bright. Some stars burn out."

CHAPTER 4

Selene took each step up to the dormitories like it was a gallows march, her body heavy and listless. She'd failed her audition. In a few days, when the lineup for L'Opéra du Magician was announced, Selene would be out on the streets. She knew that she'd have little trouble finding a patron. Even if Monsieur Fenrir and the representative from the palace told the sordid tale of her audition, it wouldn't make a difference. They could not attempt to sully her name without speaking it first, and that's all that mattered.

But it wouldn't be the palace. She wouldn't be the King's Mage. She wouldn't fulfill the only dream she'd had for so long. Sure, she could have comfort and security in another house. But she didn't want another house. It was more than the title, the prestige. She wanted to step where her father had stepped, to breathe where he had breathed. If she did that, she could make him real again. She would be less alone. If she failed to reach it, she might as well not reach at all.

She meditated on the final memories with her father, a litany of last things. All the candles in their suite had been burned down to nubs. Sheet music dusted the floor, melodies scratched out in ink and blood. Selene had known that he was pushing himself too far. He had, too.

They'd sat together in the dim light. Selene had tucked her quail beneath a tumulus of seasoned rice. She couldn't fathom eating the poor thing. She'd been out in the palace bailey where the fowl were kept. They were little things with sharp bird eyes and speckled eggs. She and Victor—the youngest and least important prince—had cradled the tiny chicks in their hands. Selene had never held anything so small or soft in her life. And now its mother or father or friend was dead on her plate. Her father's meal had grown cold, untouched. He was hunched over in his chair, tracing musical notes onto the tablecloth with his finger.

"Father?"

He snapped to attention, eyes wild for a moment before they settled into exhausted fondness. "This can't go on, Nightingale."

"Can't we just leave?" She covered her plate with her napkin.

"I have to see this through. One more week, and I'll be free." His hand rested briefly on the pendant he wore as the King's Mage. The stone was onyx, swirling and endless. "No more talk of sad things. Sing for me."

Selene sat up straighter in her chair. "What kind of magic?"

"You choose."

Selene shivered with excitement. She wanted to show what she could do, what she'd been working on all day. Father leaned in, catching the notes. Selene hadn't let in the magic yet. It waited at the edge of her mind. She knew what her father anticipated. She'd carefully embellished the line so it contained the motif for fire. His eyes moved to the little flames that now danced in moats of wax. Selene smiled and focused on the magic. Not fire at all, but air. She blew out each of the candles one by one, and with a breath, stoked the dying embers of the fire back to life. They sparked blue and green, like they'd been starved out. Father's eyes—still heavy with exhaustion—reflected back the brightness of the flames.

"Brava!" He applauded uproariously. "Well done, Nightingale. You're going to do great things with that voice, Selene."

"Thank you, Father." She let her dark curls fall in her face, hiding her blush.

Even when all seemed wrong in the world, Selene had this. Music and her father and Victor.

She only had one of those now.

Her father never warned her of the danger. He didn't talk about the way magic could go badly. Beyond the madness, she hadn't ever seen a magician burst flowers from accidentally swallowed dandelion seeds or slice off a hand with too strong of a wind or remove all the iron from their blood until she was at the opera house. Her life before had been limitless. The Opera Magique was all edges and glass walls, showing her every limitation.

Today was no exception.

Selene slipped her key into the lock. It stuck, as usual. She leaned into it, listened to the familiar groan, and pushed open the door to the room.

Gigi's half was, as expected, an unmitigated disaster. Tutus and ribbons and tights and worn-out pointe shoes littered the floor. The duvet was piled on the rug. There were hairpins and sewing supplies cluttered on the nightstand. Her dresser was a mess of cosmetics and jewelry and rumpled sheet music.

Gigi was a perfect, pristine ballerina. The epitome of grace and poise. And she was a total slob.

Selene's half of the room was the exact opposite. The bed was made. Each article of clothing was folded and carefully put away. Her closet was organized by color and occasion. Her cloak hung neatly on its hook—not a thing out of place.

Except.

There was a big, white box sitting on her bed.

Selene's heart pounded in her throat. This was the last thing she needed for the competition. Her dress for the Unmasking Ball had arrived a few days ago and was tucked in the closet. It was a pretty thing, but *this* was so much more important. Weeks ago, she'd sat with Gigi on the floor of this room. They'd giggled over hot chocolate, spreading their dreams over pieces of paper like it could be that easy. Gigi had helped her sketch and design a dress for her performance. Selene had picked out the fabric and the thread. Everything was going to be perfect.

Selene lifted the lid.

Embroidered gold lace glimmered in the low light. Selene ran her fingers over the silk. She'd layered the sleeves to appear like armor. The décolletage was open, with a swath of delicate lace enclosing the throat to conceal her scars. The bodice gave way to a generous skirt, the shimmering lace and embroidery folding into a cream silk. This was the dress she'd wear when she became the King's Mage.

And now she'd never have the chance.

Selene wanted it to burn, to see the cloud of smoke rise bitter and charred, so different from the magical smoke Revelio had conjured. That smoke had destroyed her dream. This would swallow up the air and destroy everything else. The melody was on the tip of her tongue. Beautiful ruin.

All because of Priya and Revelio. Because good was not always good enough. Because some stars burned bright, but Selene's had gone out.

The fabric was too lovely against her fingertips.

Selene tore at the buttons around her throat and down her back. She didn't care where they flew or what ripped. She let the indigo dress fall into a heap on the floor, casting off her failure like a second skin. She put on her performance dress, carefully tightening the silk ribbon up the back. It was utter perfection, everything she could have ever wanted.

She glanced out the window. Down in the narrow, cobbled streets below, the lamplighters sang fire into their globes. Had they once hoped to sing on a stage as grand as the Opera Magique, only to succumb to the reality of domestic magic?

The tangled map of Songerie overwhelmed Selene. It was no wonder. Mondreves' royal city was the most populated and prosperous in the country, far from the remote seaside cottage she'd grown up in. She didn't remember the bright, adoring sentiment for the king while she lived there, but perhaps it was the innocence of youth. She was sure there was no ruler as beloved as their king in all the world. The labyrinth of attached shops with wide, peaked windows and cramped apartments above each boasted a token or portrait of the king. They were lucky, it seemed, to be in a city rife with joy. At its center, the Opera Magique stood tall. It had been a while since Selene had seen the opera house from the outside, but she remembered standing in its shadow that first time.

And now she'd stand in its shadow again. Not a lost little girl, hoping to catch a dream. No, she'd be a woman trapped in

SING THE NIGHT

her worst nightmare: stolen songs, lightning strikes, and everything she'd wanted behind her. Once again. The pit in her stomach deepened, pulling her mind to places she did not want it to go. It couldn't end like this.

Selene's room was dark as a broken dream. Soon the worst of the city would crawl out to gamble and drink and do things not meant for the light. Against her better judgment, against any sane thought, and desperately in need of a distraction, Selene looked—as she did almost every night—to see if Victor was there, waiting on the steps of the opera house to fetch her, as he had promised.

Prince Victor, the third son of the king. The prince no one wanted. They'd sat on the cushioned palace chairs and listened to her father sing so many times she'd lost count. Victor was the last vestige of her childhood, the only remaining tether to her life before. He had known her when she had a father.

She knew he was back in the city. His name was in the papers over and over again with blurry pictures of drunken escapades. If she was thrown out of the Opera Magique, would he recognize her, after all these years? Would Victor even notice her at all?

She'd heard that he'd been sent as a living peace treaty to the mountains of Erramasque. She knew that he'd gone from there to the military, serving as he was expected to serve. And now he was drinking and debauching and gambling away the jewels of the state.

In the deepest, most secret part of her heart, she wondered how things would have been different if he'd come for her like he'd vowed. They'd only been children, with no power or control over their own lives. For so long, she'd looked forward to the moment when she would step out onstage for L'Opéra du Magician. When he would see who she'd become without him. When the weight of his broken promises would crush him.

It was supposed to happen in this dress, with the aria she'd written for her father, and the voice she'd nearly lost all those years ago. And then Selene would be back in the palace—the last place she'd seen her father.

In the place she'd seen him die.

The door creaked open. Gigi stood on the threshold with a cup of hot chocolate in each hand. The worry on her face turned to wonder and then to grief. "Your dress came."

"What do you think?" Selene tried to hide the bitterness and dismay with a twirl.

"It's perfect." Gigi leaned against the door frame, favoring her injured hip.

"A perfect waste." Selene bit the inside of her cheek until the welling of tears was replaced with the welling of blood.

"You don't know that." Gigi offered a cup of hot chocolate in supplication. "It all depends on the other auditions."

In any other circumstance, Selene could have held on to the hope. She'd showcased her voice and her capacity with magic. But this wasn't any audition. Perfection was a requirement for Selene to make it into the competition and perform for the king.

"I melted the face off a statue."

"What did Madame say?"

Selene took the hot chocolate from Gigi's hands and took a sip. It was a comfort she didn't deserve. She didn't know what to say. Didn't know how to sum up the events of the afternoon without weeping. The awfulness of Priya and the loss of her music and the catastrophe of her aria and the breaking of her dream. Her head still ached from the magic, pressing up against the edges of her sanity, trying to tear through. Gigi looked at Selene like she was staring into a well of sorrow and seeing the depth of her disappointment.

"Some stars burn bright. Some stars burn out."

A little of the hot chocolate splashed out of Selene's cup and onto the pale silk. The stain spread over the fabric. Gigi winced. Selene knew the melody to lift the chocolate from the cloth but decided against it. Let this be another thing she'd broken. Let this be ruined, too.

"I'll talk to her. She always stresses the rules. This is such a violation."

"You know how she is when she makes up her mind about a situation."

"How did they get your aria to begin with?" Gigi rubbed her temples. "You've been so careful."

Selene checked the drawer where she kept her music. The lock hadn't been tampered with.

"Could they have stood outside your practice room?"

Selene made a face. "You saw them in our dictation class. Besides, I made a change to the coda three days ago. He sang the final version."

"Then how—"

"Does it matter? It's done," Selene snapped.

Gigi's features shone with indignation. "Priya and Revelio can't get away with this."

"They already have."

"You're so talented, Selene. There are countless courts and halls that will want you as their mage. You could go anywhere."

"I don't want to go anywhere," Selene cried. "I want to go home."

The words tumbled from her mouth before Selene knew she was saying them. She wished she could gather them up like little stones and hide them away. She wasn't sure why she'd said them, where the feeling had even come from. The palace wasn't home. Selene's home had been her father and he was gone.

"*This* is your home."

"This," Selene said. There was so much she could say about the Opera Magique. It was an opulent cage. A shackled opportunity. She so desperately wanted the glorious burden that came at its end. She wanted to be the one to win, no matter what it cost her. She crossed her arms over her chest, a chill creeping through her veins. "This is only temporary."

"It doesn't have to be," Gigi pleaded.

So much was changing. Selene thought of the way Gigi had cowered when she saw the mirror. Did Gigi really think this was the result of the ghost stories they'd been told as children, meant to frighten them into submission? There was nothing in this opera house beside memories and music and disappointment.

But Selene had seen something in that mirror.

Eyes like the heart of a flame.

Selene didn't want to think about that. She didn't want to think of anything. "It doesn't matter now. What's done is done."

"It does matter, Selene. We have to do something."

She couldn't stay here. The walls were pressing in. Shadows crept up like spiders. Soon the others would come up the stairs and talk and laugh and prepare for their auditions. Gigi's dark eyes were sympathetic and kind, which was the worst thing. Selene wasn't ready. She couldn't do this right now.

"I have to go." Selene pressed the cup of hot chocolate back into Gigi's hands.

"Selene, wait!"

Selene sang the door shut behind her.

CHAPTER 5

The architect for the opera house must have loved secrets. There was a set of stairs at the end of the dormitory hall, tucked behind a tapestry as old as the opera house. It wasn't the only secret passage, but it was Selene's favorite. She stood before the tapestry, hands trembling. It was too dusty and thick for even the moths to chew through. King Renard sat on a throne, a sword in one hand and three gold pieces in the other. His mouth formed a tight-lipped smile. Renard had been in some sort of an accident and all the teeth had shattered out of his mouth. They'd replaced them with pearls: only the best for the king. He had founded L'Opéra du Magician. The opera house even bore his name—Palais Renard—but it hadn't stuck and was quickly nicknamed the Opera Magique. He looked a little like Victor. The same nose and strong jaw. But there was something hollow and empty in his eyes.

Clever of the weaver to capture that in the stitches. She'd seen that same look in Victor's older brother, Henri. He'd tormented them as children, until Selene had had enough and sang the vines up from the ground and wrapped him in thorns. She still remembered the look of pure hatred he'd given them. Pretty face, with nothing inside. Soul black as black.

If only she knew how to carry her heart in a steel case and just take and take. Maybe, if she had burned brighter, she would be hollowed out and strong enough to do what was necessary.

Selene glanced behind her. Gigi hadn't followed. She lifted the corner of the tapestry and slipped through the wooden door behind it. They'd discovered many of the secret passages together when they were children, including this one, which led down five flights of steps below the opera house.

Selene sang softly, repeating the melody for light over and over. She'd never felt the imminent danger of most motifs. Though they were sometimes temperamental, they were predictable. Fire burned and wind blew and light shone. She should have known better than to try lightning today, but it was too late now. A ball formed in her hands, low and pulsing, like the heartbeat of a dying star. Without an instrument to maintain the melody, the light flickered, casting her into darkness each time she paused to take a breath.

Students were not permitted to access the subterranean floors. It was treacherous, a web of set pieces and dusty costume boxes that did not belong to the conservatory. In the years leading up to L'Opéra du Magician, magical operas ran season to season on this stage. Selene and her fellow students had picked up the extra roles here and there, and had learned the art of the voice and performance from some of the greatest magicians. Many of them had even grown up here, too, and competed in L'Opéra du Magician. The company was on tour now in Erramasque, leaving the space available for the competition. As much as Selene loved that stage, she could not abide the thought of returning as a failure.

Selene wove through the debris of set pieces and trunks and forgotten treasures, appreciating the movement of her dress. Gigi was such a talented designer. Gigi was good at everything. She could be anything when she left the opera house, if she ever left. Each gold stitch caught the light and dimmed with a puff of grime. This was where memories were wrapped in old drop cloths and left to gather dust. Selene would be one of these things, too.

Selene ran through the movements of the tempest aria, looking for all the places it had gone wrong. The piece was theoretically perfect. She should have pushed herself further, opening her mind up to the magic. She should have performed her original aria, been grander than ever before. She should have screamed the song out of Revelio's lungs and watched the blood pour from his mouth.

Not that.

But why not? She'd followed the rules. She'd played fair. She was the better singer. The better mage. She hadn't engaged in any sort of subversion. Selene had focused and focused and shaped her dream with little worry of anyone else. And for what?

Selene let the light go out.

She knew better than to scream. Her voice was all she had left. She picked a note, ran it up to the top of her range. No magic, just music. All her fury distilled into the G6, bright and clear as a bell. Her vision swam. She closed her eyes, focusing on only this. She took a breath and kept singing until the sound lost all meaning.

She wished her father were here to help her navigate these next steps.

Selene let herself slide into one of the precious memories she kept of him. Not those final days. Before, when his cheeks had been wide with smiles and there was no darkness beneath his eyes. When he could win her with a wink and whistle. They'd lean over the piano together, chipping away melodies and dreaming up songs.

She imagined the timbre of his voice, warm and rich. Imagined what he would say, if he were alive.

Take your broken heart, turn it into art.

All she'd wanted was to prove that she was worthy of his name. To make him the hero again. She wanted people to remember him the way she remembered him. A good man, a brilliant man, a man who deserved more of a legacy than that last, terrible day. She could still feel the blood on her hands, smell the copper and the sugar and hear the awful sound his body made as it struck the floor.

No.

Not that memory. Anything but that horrible day. She sang higher, high enough that she could feel the earth tremble. Too much, too far. The music floated out of her, carried by a power other than magic. She could push a little bit higher, a little bit farther. That's what her father would do. That's what he'd done. And she'd watched him break.

Shatter.

It was the music of breaking glass, deep and vast and bright. At first, she thought it was her imagination, until she heard the echo.

"Hello?"

No one responded. She focused, listening for the sounds of breath, for the patter of another heart. A chill of terror rose up her spine, the quiet all too much.

There was nothing.

She thought at once of the opera ghost. Had Priya brought the phantom in with her contraband? Had Madame released it with her song?

"No," she said out loud, to no one.

Because no one was here.

Selene sang the melody for light, illuminating the shapes in the dark. They loomed a little too close in the moment before her light struck them. Her heart raced. She was being childish. There was nothing down here but the detritus of the stage. Each shape was something forgotten and locked away, another friend long lost to the dark.

There, tucked against the back wall, leaned a stained-glass window, either a set piece or some early architectural marvel of the opera house. Jagged teeth of broken glass still clung to the frame. She shifted boxes and crates out of the way.

The stained glass fractured the light in her palm. When it had been whole, this window must have been breathtaking. She should have been devastated to destroy such a beautiful thing; sundered by what she had done with the power of her voice. There was some small satisfaction in that. She'd made her mark on the opera house. If she was cast out, she could remember the lovely, broken thing she'd left behind.

She put her hand through one of the jagged panes, letting it rest on the stone wall. A shard caught the fleshy part between her thumb and forefinger, bleeding in a way only hands bleed. She watched the drops fall, heavy and dark against the floor.

The stone was damp beneath her fingers. Except it wasn't stone at all. It was wood, painted to look like stone. The paint crumbled beneath her fingers.

This was a door.

CHAPTER 6

Selene pushed the window out of the way, careful of the colored glass that littered the ground. Someone had gone to great lengths to conceal the door. Even the hinges—now dark with rust—had trace amounts of paint. There was a lock but no handle.

There was never a question of what she should do.

Selene brought her light up to the mechanism, heart racing. There could be a key somewhere in this chaos. She inspected the shape of it and how it was cut into the door. It was no ordinary lock; it had to be sung open, spun with magic to give the melody enough weight.

This lock was meant for her.

She touched the lace around her throat. Her fingers brushed against the scars. Her father loved musical locks and put them every place he could. Selene sang the low melody into the keyhole. The mechanism groaned and released. The door cracked open.

Selene pressed her fingers into the space between the door and the frame, fear and curiosity sparking inside of her. She imagined the world that hid beyond the door. A king's treasure, jewels and riches in heaps. A whole new universe, where the spiders were as big as horses and there was a round eye in the sky instead of a moon. A cathedral of bones, from singers who'd lost their way in the fragile dark.

Turn back, something inside her whispered.

It was too late for that. She couldn't leave the last of the opera house's secrets unturned. What did she have to lose? Selene worked the door open so she could get her shoulder in, leverage the frame, and use her whole weight against it.

Selene sang the light back into her palm.

Stairs disappeared into an expanse of water, lit turquoise by her voice. Stone arches faded into dark. Each of the pillars was adorned with a chandelier sconce—miniatures of the grand chandelier in the auditorium. They were rusted and warped, some of them swallowed up by the water. The door was slick and swollen at her back.

This had *been* something.

Victor would have loved this. He would already be in the water, dauntless and fearless and ready for anything. Selene had been that brave, once. Now she wasn't sure if she could be that girl.

She didn't have the chance to find out.

The stone beneath her boot gave way. Her fingers slipped against the door, against the frame, against the stair. She was falling.

Down, down, down into the deepening dark.

Fear had claws and teeth and it tore through her. She could have screamed. There was a split second where she thought she would.

But she was a mage first. And the song was there, beneath her skin. Waiting for her to open her mouth and her mind and let out her voice.

Selene landed against the floor of the cavern. The water had split for her. She was dry and trembling against the stone. Bioluminescence lit the water bright and impossibly blue. Little silver fish darted behind the churning light. Something twisting and dark clung to the shadows of the water.

Selene took a quick breath. The water moved a fraction of an inch closer to her. She sang it out a little farther, to make sure she'd have room to breathe. Behind her, steps led to the door, back to the safety of the opera house.

Selene was tired of playing it safe. She was tired of being the girl who did everything right. She'd been that girl, and she'd lost. She clenched her hands into fists, her nails biting into her palms. She wasn't going to go back now.

She pushed a path through the water—just a few feet. The light rose and followed her. The stone floor had been worn by underground currents into ripples and waves. There was only water and the slither and shimmer of the things that lived here now.

Who else knew about this forgotten space? Was this why they'd been urged away from the underground floors? Or had this secret died with the last person who had braved its depths?

A voice rang from out of the darkness. Silky baritone, warm and robust. It was the sound of coming home after a lifetime of being away. She leaned into the beauty of it, dark and free and effortless. Oh, she should have been afraid of the voice that called to her in the dark. But she was lured by its loveliness, tantalized by the richness and complexity. She knew it was foolish to follow that sound, and a part of her screamed at her to turn back. But then he leaned into the dissonance, resolving at the very last second. He caught her rhythm and fell into the offbeat. It was so clever and improbable, and there was no way she could leave without seeking the source of that.

There was someone on the other side of the water. He matched her melody and split into a counterpoint, adding depth and dimension to the motif for water. He did brilliant, unthinkable things, contrary to her training and somehow perfect. His voice was so beautiful, lovely enough that she could close her eyes and let herself drown.

Selene had to find him.

But Selene was at the bottom of an underground lake, water flung out by the power of her voice at all sides. The stairway back was half-formed, worn to rubble beneath the water. There was no guarantee there was another way out.

She should let the water fall around her, lift her up, so she could swim her way out. That was the logical thing to do; it was what Madame would have wanted from her.

Yesterday, Selene might have turned back.

But she wasn't that girl anymore. Maybe she was never that girl. Either way, she'd been made new. She took a step on the slick, uneven ground, pulled to the voice as if by a string. She focused the magic, cutting through the water. It glowed brilliantly around her, lighting her hands and catching in the gold thread of her dress. It was like walking through the night sky, the bioluminescence casting constellations all around her. She'd remember this and use it in performance, someday. It was far more beautiful than she dared to dream.

There were remnants of a life lived down here. Fallen wall sconces dark with algae, a set of chairs that barely held their shape through the rot, something that looked like chains, now flaked with rust. She pushed toward the back of the cavern. A tiny fish fluttered on the stone for a few frantic moments before it was swept up by the water in Selene's wake.

Selene sang louder, changing the key. The stranger met her, matched her. He danced around the motif for water, playing off her notes. This strange duet enraptured her, pulling her closer and closer to the source. His voice was elegant and grounded. She was used to baritones anchoring her lyric soprano, but this was more. She inverted the motif. He was quick to respond, catching the wisps of melody and shaping it into a story. She could feel his loneliness and loss, his curiosity and hunger. She wanted to know the ending. Wanted to be a part of it.

The water swirled away from her, revealing a second set of stairs, this one still fully intact. Selene ascended, illuminated by the constellation of bioluminescence. The water folded on each step behind her, splashing up and darkening her hem.

She tried not to let the timpani roll of her heart or the cymbal crash of the water distract from the sound of his voice, growing closer with each step, echoing in the dark. Until they were matched, sound for sound. As if he were singing right beside her.

But there was no one. Nothing.

She let her voice taper off. The water churned behind her.

Selene sang the light back into her bleeding palm.

A great, beveled mirror stood in the center of the flat stone. The frame was molten gold, shifting and moving in strange patterns around the edge of the glass. It was as if lightning had struck the frame and it had failed to settle into a solid state.

Fear and fascination warred inside her. She should run, turn back and forget about this place. But she was afraid if she left, it would be the end of the dream.

She stepped closer.

She saw herself inside the mirror, and the magnificent dress, damp and blood splattered. It had been years since she'd truly seen herself. Selene rarely left the opera house, which meant her opportunities to catch her reflection were limited. She undid the buttons around her throat. The scars had faded silver, the grooves not as deep as she always imagined. She swallowed and watched them tremble. They were a choker of memory. A spiderweb of sorrow.

The blood from her cut palm dripped onto the hollow of her throat. A dark jewel against her fragile flesh.

The mirror rippled.

A shift in the shadow. A face in the dark.

The ghost.

It was like looking through a veil of smoke. Broad shoulders, wide chest, tall, and strong. Not a monster, but a man. He was all shape and shadow, except for his eyes. They were a clear, bright blue, like frozen mountain rivers and the turn of froth on the sea.

Pleading. Hungry. Beautiful.

If eyes were the window to the soul, then she knew all she needed to know about this ghost. She knew the depth of that loneliness and the weight of that loss. She wanted to share in the sorrow that seemed to plague them both. It was like meeting an old friend, someone her soul inherently knew. She could call it fate or providence or magic.

Selene sang the melody for light. He matched her, note for note, then broke into a discordant harmony.

Mournful and wanting, more than any wolf in search of a moon. He came into clearer focus. The edges of him were still blurred by darkness. But his eyes. Oh, they were like water falling over pale sapphires. Blue fire opals beneath a sea. Precious and bright and pulling her in to drown.

If he were a song, she would have sung him until the world was filled with his music. If he were magic, she would have opened her mind and let him flood her until all the world was remade. If he were real, she could have loved him.

She shivered, the strangeness of that last thought drawing her back into herself. She'd pressed herself to the mirror. The tender wound on her hand throbbed against the cold glass.

Blood against the mirror.

Red and silver and gone.

CHAPTER 7

It was like falling into water. The absence of air, the loss of gravity, her limbs heavy and weak. It was like slipping into a dreamscape. There was shadow and movement and her sense of self but nothing else. She was dead or she was dying or she had never been alive at all.

All at once, up was up, and down was down, and dark was dark. The inky shadows were living, moving, all-consuming. They roiled at the edges of her vision like knots of snakes. It was a wonder she could see anything at all. The place she stood—not earth or stone but something flat and supple, like the stage—was a shade lighter. Like her mere presence brought in light. Not light exactly, something that had been light once and wasn't anymore. An echo of light. A memory of what light should be.

But that wasn't what felt so strange about this place. It wasn't the colors or the shift of shadow. It was the absence of sound. No drip of water or whisper of breath. No wind or creak of wood. No swish of skirts or tap of boots. Not even the beating of her heart.

This place was wrong.

Just behind her, she could see the whirl of the bioluminescence before it stilled into watery dark. Tarnished, like she was seeing it through a dusty window, or from the inside of a mirror.

"Hello?" Selene said.

"Hello."

There was a person at the edge of her vision. He was half in darkness, like he was being formed from it.

There and not.

The ghost stepped toward her. His movements were disjointed, like his limbs were a little too long. Like he'd forgotten how to be human.

Wake up, she begged herself.

Selene sang for light.

It was blinding, penetrating the darkness. The ghost threw up his hand to shield his eyes.

Selene was sure this was a dream. She'd fallen asleep below the opera house. There was no door, no underground lake, no secret mirror or creature trapped inside. Her subconscious had taken all her burdens and spun them into a vicious web. This was a culmination of the pressure of the competition, exhaustion, and Madame's words ringing through her head.

Some stars burn bright, some stars burn out.

He came into the light.

Not completely, not at first. Half of his face was still cloaked in shadow. But it was enough for her to see him. There was a wildness to him, an unchecked beauty and power that was too familiar to be made up. She'd seen artist renderings of faces like his, carved-out angles and thick-drawn lashes, like some monument of youth and pulchritude and the insatiable mystery of the unknown that must be discovered. His linen shirt was wrinkled and thin, torn in places. There were stains on the sleeves. If the colors had been right, she might have guessed it was blood. The trousers had been black, now a faded gray.

It was more than his unearthly beauty, more than the siren song of his voice, more than the impossibility of the moment. This was someone her soul knew.

She reminded herself how to breathe, steeling herself for a sudden influx of darkness without an instrument to help her sustain the motif. Preparing for what might happen in the dark.

The light stayed. It was not snuffed by breath, or the end of her song.

The sphere of light was strong and unbreaking. She pulled her hand back like it might burn her. It hovered in the space before her. This was not the way the magic behaved. This was something different, something more, like a full moon on a cloudless night. The edge of the light hardened and rose, no longer a glowing orb. It transformed into a tiny moon. The magic worked without song or concentration, living solely on intent.

It wasn't supposed to be like this. Magic needed more than just wanting, didn't it? Selene measured all her years of training, of spending countless hours in practice rooms curating her talent, memorizing motifs, learning how to twine them together to form a song. She was sure she understood it, sure she could hold it inside her and transform it with her will and the direction of a motif.

And yet.

Curious, she willed the light apart, scattered it into constellations. The darkness shattered into a cluster of stars.

"Clever." Half of the ghost's mouth lifted into a smile.

Selene caught her breath at his expression. It was like being sliced by moonlight on the darkest night, that smile.

"How is this possible?" Selene lifted her hand and the stars danced. Magic was not for everyone. It required talent and study, a willingness to lose everything for the sake of a song. It couldn't be this easy.

"Everything is different here." His voice was a rumble of thunder dipped in honey. It was a timpani roll, an articulation of the cello.

"Where are we?" She tracked the shadowy edges of the light. They looked sketched, smudgy graphite marks that fed into a greater darkness.

"My prison." The ghost brushed the dark hair from his eyes, face still cupped in shadow. "My tomb."

Panic crawled up Selene's spine.

"Is there a way out?"

His eyes unfocused. "I didn't know there was a way in."

What had he done to deserve a place like this? There was blood on his sleeves, that knife's edge of a smile.

"Who are you?" Selene whispered.

Silence. Selene counted breaths until the quiet stretched so long that her skin rippled and crawled. She'd made a terrible mistake stepping into nowhere, this nothing. She ran arpeggios through her head, trying to calm her frantic heart, then took a step back. Looking for the way out.

There was nothing but shadow and shadow and shadow and him.

"I am a thing best forgotten."

Selene swallowed the sharp side of a scream.

He turned his head, catching all the light and shadows. His cheekbones were high and sharp like the cut crystal of the chandelier. His jaw was strong and straight. There was a scar nicked into his eyebrow. That full mouth quirked up as to smile with a secret.

How could someone so beautiful be bad? There was some intangible quality to him that drew her in like the soft part of a song. She could see a light in his eyes, marred by a well of sorrow. It wasn't like looking into the dead eyes on the tapestry of Renard or Prince Henri. The prince's mere presence had made her skin crawl. She didn't feel like that with this lovely, haunted stranger. There was something so familiar about him. Against all odds, something safe.

"A name, then," she said.

He regarded her through his thick, dark lashes. "You are used to getting what you want."

Selene's stomach tightened. She was no worthless dilettante, with her space in the opera house bought and paid for, like Priya. "I'm used to working until what I want is mine."

"Relentless." He raised and lowered his wide, strong shoulders. "And perhaps foolish."

There was a shape and sound to his words that was foreign to her. He spoke like most people sang. Each consonant crisp, each vowel pure, no laziness or carelessness.

"A gentleman would honor the request of a lady."

"I am no gentleman." He brushed a hand over his shoulder. "And you, my lady, are in a place far from polite society."

"You're deflecting." Selene quelled the brittle fear inside her. She didn't know where she was or what he was or who he was. And she needed to. She needed more of him the way she needed music and magic and air. "Your name, sir."

"Will you stop at nothing to have it?"

Selene put on her best performer's smile. "Better tell me now and save yourself the trouble."

The laugh rolled from deep within him, like distant thunder. And that's when Selene was sure. He was real. However stars burn, Selene knew the difference between real and dreams.

"I have no name."

He was toying with her. Selene could play this game—and part of her wanted to—but she was unsettled by the way the darkness pressed in.

"Everyone has a name."

His brow furrowed with concentration, then broke with mourning. "I have forgotten."

Selene prepared a rebuttal, until she saw his face. The sorrow in his eyes was a beacon of truth. There was something so honest and tragic about him, as eerie as a worn stone statue guarding a forgotten grave. She thought of a riddle, a callback to childhood. Victor loved to try and catch anyone he could in riddles and word games. *What belongs to you but is used more by others?* A name, a name. She wondered if names, like the voice, were lost from disuse. Like the door that led her here, rusted shut.

"What *can* you remember?"

He closed his eyes. His hands laced and folded in front of him. She counted the scars overlapping his forearms, following them until they disappeared beneath his sleeves. There were too many. She imagined what it would be like to trace those scars with the lightest touch. She reached for her own scars, the familiar grooves soft against her fingertips. It was another sharp reminder of the difference between her and her peers. Selene knew pain.

So did he.

When the ghost opened his eyes, he looked bewildered. Afraid.

"Nothing."

But that couldn't be true. A person couldn't just be lost entirely. Even the dead remained, clinging to the edges of memory, kept until the last person forgot, until every book and story rotted into dust. But this man wasn't a fading memory. He was speaking to her. He had sung her here.

Music.

He remembered music.

Selene sang the light doloroso. All the melancholy in the world: for want of a name, for the loss of it. For the stranger inside the mirror who had lost so much of himself.

She turned the constellations brighter, grew a distant star into a moon that waxed and waned. He listened for a moment, head tilted in concentration, then joined in. Selene sang the counterpoint, turning her magic into illusion. She grew a forest around them, trees yearning toward the light. Already, she mourned the loss of this beauty. It would all fall away the moment her song ended. That was the trouble with illusion and tableau. Nothing stayed.

He pulled the stars down, letting them hang from the trees like ripe fruit. Selene sustained her motif in wonder. He was changing her magic. She didn't know it was possible. For all the duets she'd sung, they had to maintain their own motifs and choreograph the magic separately. This was something else entirely, as if music here yielded a different magic. She caught his eye and they let the song fade. The magic stayed. The forest—which outside the mirror would have faded with the final note—stayed lush and full and too close to real.

"That was…" She didn't have the words. She'd never sung with anyone like this. It was more than a duet; it was two souls crashing together, raw and wretched and open.

"Incredible." He collapsed against one of the trees, hands splayed against the bark. It held, like it was solid and not an illusion.

Selene pressed her fingertips against one of the trunks. She did not pass through, as she would with an illusion. She reached up and plucked one of the perfect fruits. "It's real."

"Why wouldn't it be?"

Selene broke it open. A hundred golden seeds gleamed up at her. A pomegranate made of light and song. She crushed one of the seeds against her teeth. It tasted like that last day of summer, a sweetness marked with grief.

Selene offered him the other half. He took it. "Outside the illusion is just an illusion. You can't make a real tree out of nothing. You need seeds."

He peeled back the skin of the pomegranate, tearing into the jewels inside. Some of the juice glowed on his fingers. His expression shifted. "Things are different here. The magic is closer."

Selene leaned forward, eager for some crumb of memory. "You remember?"

"It's hard to put it to words."

"Try."

"I have language and music and magic and pain. The rest—who I am, where I come from, my name—is inside me, under the surface. I have the sense that I deserve this. That I'm being punished for something terrible." Those blue eyes were resolved, intensely fixed on Selene. "Singing with you is like the first breath after drowning. It brings back pieces of who I am—who I think I might have been."

Selene's heart skipped, heat rising through her, feeling more than the magic of his voice or the cold blue of his eyes or the darkness that surrounded him.

"Is it the magic in the music?"

He shook his head, wisps of dark hair falling into his eyes. She wished she was brave enough to smooth them away. "It's you."

She drew in closer to him, aware of the rise and fall of his chest, the flicker of his pulse along the lines of his throat. Singing with him was a union of souls, so much more than any duet had ever been for her. Maybe that connection could make him whole.

"All I do is sing." Selene was quiet. "From the moment I wake up until I go to sleep. I dream in treble clef and wake up knowing the key in which the birds trill. Every part of my brain is made for music. But what we did is different from anything else. It's more."

"You are music and you do music and you have nothing except music," he mused. "Are you a prisoner, too?"

Selene did not think about the great doors in the foyer that were forbidden from being opened or the strict curfews or the brilliant summer days that passed with the students of the opera house locked inside. She thought of her father, bent over his piano with trembling hands and exhaustion so deep it curved his spine.

"No," Selene said, too quickly. The ghost seemed to take note. "If the music helps you remember, why do you stop singing?"

"Because I'm afraid." His voice was pianissimo. One of the snakes of shadow reached for him. He dismissed it with a look.

"Afraid of what?" Selene looked around at the opaque, whirling dark.

"You ask too many questions."

"You give too few answers."

He laughed again—that rich, musical sound. She wanted to fold herself inside it, let it make her new. That surprised her. Being here, being with him filled her with a headiness like drinking too much wine.

Selene focused on the stars she'd created. The stars that shouldn't exist, bright and glowing like living gemstones. There was music in them. She could feel the brightness of the notes, the motif cut through each facet like it was captured within. A remarkable experience, something she couldn't fathom in the light of day. She felt for the dark. There wasn't music there. It was magic and something *else*.

The ghost watched her, waiting.

"This goes against everything I've been taught," Selene said.

"Perhaps you've had the wrong teachers."

She thought of her father. Of Madame Giroux at the piano.

Of the various voice teachers she'd run out of the opera house. Not on purpose, at first. She was relentless. They couldn't challenge her and she'd had no problem correcting them. After that, Selene had studied exclusively with Madame Giroux, who loved rules. She wrapped them around Selene like a shield, while still pushing her to be the best. Selene dove deep into the history and the theory of music and magic, filling herself with every possibility. Once she knew the rules, she could break them.

This was different. Selene could feel the rules fracturing around her, shattering like stained glass. What else could magic do if it could create a place like this?

A tendril of shadow threaded toward her. She could feel the pulse of it, like a beating heart. It called to her, wanted her, *needed* her. Selene took a step forward, the weight of all these years of magic and music and untapped sorrow heavy on her.

"Can you wield the dark?"

Selene reached out her fingers, like she might touch it. If she let the darkness have her—just for a moment—she might finally feel at peace. The darkness purred, drawing her in and blurring her thoughts. Wasn't this everything she wanted? Wasn't the lure of the dark sweeter than the promise of prestige? Selene could have that. She could finally rest. She could forget all the terrible things she'd done.

"Don't." There was power in his command.

Selene pulled her hand back, suddenly aware of where she was and what she was doing. The darkness slipped back into the void. Selene turned sharply to the ghost. His hand was stretched as if to pull her from her reverie, long fingers curling into a fist to fall to his side.

The ghost's chest heaved. His eyes were weighted with memory. "The dark takes things from you."

Selene traced the edges of the prison. There was no reprieve here, no place that offered the barest hint of shelter. "How do you fight it?"

His smile was half-mad. "Sometimes I let it have me."

"You remember?"

"When you speak the words, it's like waking up from a dark dream to the fresh light of morning and feeling unworthy of the sun."

He turned his face up as if remembering what that was like, as if the existence of the sun had just returned to him. He was so beautiful, impossibly lovely. She could sing a tableau of this moment and no one would believe it was real. She understood what it was to emerge from dark into light. The familiarity of that web tangled her, guilt and grief and ambition coalescing, only ebbing when she disappeared into music.

"I know that feeling."

"We are alike, then. Prisoners, in our own way." The ghost's cold eyes softened. "You haven't told me your name."

"Selene Dreshé."

"Selene." He said her name like a prayer, a plea, a song. "How did you find me?"

"I heard your voice and followed it into the dark."

"Hasn't anyone told you not to talk to strangers?" There was humor in his voice. "And not to walk into places when you don't know the way out?"

"Relentless." She didn't tell him that there was something about him, a deep knowing in her that made him unstrange.

SING THE NIGHT

"There's never been a door that can keep me out. Even doors that do not exist."

"There was a door?" The ghost leaned in, hopeful and intrigued.

Selene shook her head. "I saw you in the mirror and put my hand against the glass. And then I was here."

"A mirror." The ghost closed his eyes, as if he was drawing something from the darkest recesses of his mind.

Selene ran her teeth over her lip. If she kept talking, maybe she'd trigger another memory for him. "It's the only mirror inside the whole opera house. Deep below, in a cavern of water and stone."

His eyes snapped open. "The Palais Renard is finished?"

He spat out the name Renard like it was a poison. Selene could feel the anxiety build around him, buzzing with the electric energy of a thunderstorm. Even the trees around him seemed to quake.

"That name never stuck." Selene tried to lighten his tension with a smile. "We call it the Opera Magique. Home, to me. It was built a century ago."

The air changed the moment she said it. Everything colder and cold. The look on the ghost's face was that of absolute devastation. What little color had been in his face drained away. Selene wished she could take it back, wished it could be different, somehow.

He pressed his hands to his forehead, then through his hair. "I've been here for more than a hundred years."

A single, dark tear—like ink—slipped from the ghost's eye and down his cheek. He sank to his knees. There was something terrible about it: to weep darkness, like something out of a nightmare. Selene took a step back. She should run. Go back to a place with a little more light.

But he was so beautiful and broken. A hundred years had passed with him trapped in a mirror. How could she let one more day go by? She knelt before him. Her fingers were close enough to feel the heat of his skin. Flesh and blood and more real than anyone she'd known. Not a ghost at all.

He looked up at her with wild eyes, flinching away from her. "You can't touch me."

"I didn't mean—"

"Never touch me."

He had a knife in his hand. The blade swirled like an oil slick, the most color contained in this place. He pressed the blade to the inside of his forearm. Selene reached forward to stop him.

Blood, then shadow, unfurled from his wound. It ran up his arms, gathering swirls of black around his back like thunderclouds. He shot her an anguished glance, those inky tears still on his cheeks.

The darkness spread like wings made of black spider's silk and tendrils of poisonous vines. The rush of those wings, the force and violence of their exit, pushed her back. It was all she could do to keep from falling out of the light. His wings shuddered and lifted him up until he hovered above the ground, crowned by the stars Selene had created.

She should have been afraid. She should have found the way back through the mirror and never returned. But he was so hauntingly beautiful. His sorrow so close to the skin that it hurt her to witness. She couldn't live with herself, knowing she'd left him here.

He hovered there—winged in darkness and haloed by false stars—like a vengeful god. There was no music to this magic. This wasn't controlled by breath or voice. This magic was wild, living. It had taken his blood and made him monstrous and lovely.

Something sparked, feral and hungry inside Selene. Whatever he was doing, whatever dark magic this was, she needed it. If she could harness this, she would have magic like never before. They'd have no choice but to crown her the King's Mage. To write the Dreshé name down in all the books. She would be unstoppable.

"Selene." His voice was all the thunder but none of the honey, dissonant and dark and somehow still a siren's song.

He flapped his great, dark wings. The force of it shattered the air, pushing Selene back, back, back. The ground slid from beneath her feet and she was floating, falling into the shapeless nothing that was the dark.

CHAPTER 8

All the rumors were true. The myths, the legends, the lies. There was a mirror in the opera house. There was a ghost in that mirror, who was not a ghost at all but a man who might be a monster. And the churning, roiling dark. The impossible, living shadows that enraptured her and made Selene feel watched.

But that wasn't the half of it. What he'd done in the mirror went against everything she'd ever learned.

He'd bled shadow into wings and fury and taken flight. In Selene's wildest dreaming, she could not invent a magic so beautiful and terrible.

Selene looked over her shoulder, to the door she'd concealed behind a discarded set piece. She thought of the girl who had leapt from the rooftop because she'd been so afraid of the mirrors. She was the reason they had been banned—the final straw after years of whispers. Had the girl seen the ghost's ethereal beauty and been unmoored? Had she seen him first as a monster? Did she know what his blood could do?

Selene shivered. She had to tell Madame Giroux. And maybe, just maybe, that would be enough to give her a second chance.

A whisper of guilt wove through her. What would happen

to the man trapped inside if Madame found out? It was hard to imagine something worse than the mirror, but at least he had magic there. She could be taking him from a prison and placing him into a nightmare.

You can't help him if you're not here.

Selene walked to the true entrance to the upper floors of the opera house, not some secret place. It was a risk, but one Selene was willing to take. She had little left to lose. The stairs were wider and there was a lift to allow for the rise and descent of sets and costume boxes. Stepping onto the landing in the hallway off the grand foyer was like stepping out of a dream. From out of the shadowy depths and into the glittering expanse of gold. Madame Giroux's office was down one more hallway. A dozen steps, and Selene could guarantee a place in the competition.

Gigi was slumped on the floor by Madame's door, head in her hands. There was music scattered around her. Selene cleared her throat. Gigi looked up. Her eyes were red from crying.

"What happened?"

"Not here." Gigi's voice was thick with sorrow.

Selene helped pick up the sheets of music and gave Gigi a hand. Gigi led her down the hallway, to the little nook they'd used as a meeting spot for years. She tipped against the wall.

"Why are we doing this, Selene?"

Because we want this. Because we need this.

"Because we don't know how to do anything else?" Selene took her place next to Gigi, handing her the remaining sheet music.

"I tried to talk to her about the sabotage. Someone slipped oil under the door of my practice room. I brought up your music, too." Gigi flexed the toes of her left foot and dragged them up the wall before she dropped down, defeated. "It did not go well."

"I appreciate the effort." Selene took Gigi's hand. "I'll fight my way back in."

"She asked to see my music." Gigi held up the rumpled pages. They were marked with so much red. "And her official opinion is that my piece isn't good enough to steal."

Selene took a deep breath, releasing the tension in her jaw. Madame Giroux had always been cold to Gigi, but this was cruel.

"May I see?"

Gigi's smile was thin. "It won't make a difference now. I won't have time to rewrite it. Besides, we're supposed to be independent."

"We're also supposed to perform our own songs, and Madame turned a blind eye to that." Selene took the music. A cold feeling rippled over her skin. Madame had told her the rules mattered. But when they were broken, she didn't care. She wouldn't even listen. What good would telling her about the mirror do? What use was the mirror to her at all?

Unless she had the magic within it.

What he'd done—cut himself and bled the magic—it was far beyond what she knew was possible. Selene always looked for doors. If magic existed beyond song, then it was more than a door. It was the whole building knocked down.

Resolve settled over Selene. "Can you dance? How's your hip?"

Gigi extended her leg up to the ceiling. "Just needed some ice."

Selene examined the swell of Gigi's hip. She'd hit the stage hard enough that Selene was sure she wouldn't be able to dance today, tomorrow, or even the day after. But Gigi knew her body better than anyone else. Who was Selene to say what hurt and what did not?

"Your dress." Gigi appraised Selene, no doubt looking for wounds.

Selene kicked the stained hem forward. The gold threads were frayed and smudged. Blood splattered the silk, darkened to something that could be mistaken for rust. She didn't know if she had the words to describe what had happened. She'd stumbled into the darkness and found what should have been impossible. A ghost. *The* ghost. The fear was warranted. The ghost was real.

His voice still resonated in her bones with a music like night. She could feel its magic without magic, drawing her back to the mirror like a fire-starved moth. His beauty unraveled her, his very presence enraptured her beyond her endless pursuit of power, her drive to win. There was something about him that made her want more.

"Are you okay?" Gigi's voice was tentative.

Selene had gone too long without an answer. She thought of the way Madame had looked at her. *Some stars burn bright. Some stars burn out.*

She could tell Gigi everything: spill out her new secret the way shadow had spilled from the ghost's skin. She should tell her about her life before the opera house. Her life at the palace remained locked away—Victor and what she had done to her father. But she didn't know where to begin or how it would end or if it was even worth the words.

"Let's go."

"Do you want to change?" Gigi's face was a mask of calm, no doubt disturbed to see the dress she'd designed destroyed.

But Selene liked the feel of it on her skin. She liked the beautiful ruin. She'd earned this wreck. "It's fine."

They crossed through the public spaces of the opera house. Here everything was polished marble and shining gold: lush and lavish beauty fit for a king and his mage. It was arches and balconies and the grand staircase splitting like a serpent's tongue. Selene had grown desensitized to its beauty. It struck her now. It was another thing she could lose.

This could be the last time she walked through these halls, beneath this ceiling, across the veins of marble. Those who failed to make it through the audition process were packed up and sent away. But where would Selene go? She had no home, no family to return to. There was this or nothing.

The farther they moved from the front of the opera house, the uglier things became. The statues gathered dust, the marble lost its luster, the floors turned to wood. The walls here were just walls. The hallway was lined with private practice rooms. This part of the building faced an inconsequential side street. Most people did not even know this section of the opera house existed.

Gigi bent at the waist and sang a complex melody into her lock. It released. She pushed open the door.

Unlike their bedroom, Gigi kept this space mostly clean. There was a pile of broken shoes in one corner, but the rest were carefully hung up. She had a ballet barre against one of the walls. The floors were different in here than the other practice rooms. This was a dancer's space.

Selene placed the marked-up sheet music on the piano. She sat at the bench, tucked in the corner. It was a wildly different setup than Selene's practice room. She'd made a shrine to her piano, centering it in the room. Everything else was secondary to the music.

Gigi stood in first position. The opening chord took shape beneath Selene's fingers.

The music reverberated through the upright piano in a way that made Selene crave the muted dark. Gigi's voice was soft and gentle, striking each note with perfect intonation. The practice of singing words had long since fallen out of fashion. It had no effect on the magic and sometimes muddied the line and pitch. The mages were trained to keep their vowels round and their tones pure—the voice was just an instrument, after all. The better the imitation, the more likely the magic would carry through the orchestrations. The magic did not care about the size of the voice, but the openness of the singer and the precision of the technique.

Gigi's heart was open and her technique was flawless. She kept her voice light enough that she could maintain the magic while her body moved through the dance. It was not an entirely new concept: pairing movement with magic. Her voice would float softly above the orchestration, with barely more impact than the second violin. Any more would distract from the dance. It was the exact opposite of Selene's approach. Her voice was part of the magic, part of the performance. For Gigi, it was just a means to an end.

A diaphanous man appeared beside her. There was something familiar about him, stretched a little too tall with thin limbs. He looked like Benson. Gigi blushed and grinned. She changed her illusion into a dancer. Not quite as tall, strong with dark skin, and a sophisticated face. This was the entrée. The two of them moved closer and closer together, circling the space. The music was simple, with variations on the illusion to allow Gigi her breath without a secondary element. The dancing was the portion the audience wouldn't expect. There had been previous attempts by magicians to dance while singing, but none of them held a candle to Gigi. Her strength and control was unparalleled. And her voice—clear and resonant as a bell—folded into the piano as if she were striking the keys. Finally, they were close enough to touch. Gigi took his hand.

Gigi stepped through the adagio slowly, each movement graceful and elegant, showing her strength and control. Her partner held his poise, offering her support as she needed it. It was strange, knowing that he was not real and that his offered hand was nothing more than air. When Gigi balanced, she did it alone.

The music picked up. Gigi and her illusion went through a series of leaps and turns, each more powerful than the next. Gigi had put work into her partner. He was close enough to flesh that his muscles bunched and released, sweat beading between his shoulders. Gigi had poured everything into this illusion.

They moved into the coda. There was a second element subtly written in. Gigi had written the motif for air in the bass, tucked neatly away. Selene played the music, but her heart beat at a different tempo. If Gigi pulled this off, she wouldn't just be dancing.

Gigi leapt.

There was a brief moment when her partner held her in the overhead lift and Selene was sure Gigi had done it. But the wind wasn't powerful enough to sustain her, and Gigi quickly lost hold of the illusion. She was alone on the stage. Falling with a ballerina's grace. She landed, quickly picking up the melody for the man, and the two of them bowed.

Selene was drawn back to the man in the mirror and his dark wings. He'd stayed in the air like a dark angel waiting to pass judgment on her soul. Selene let the final notes resonate from the piano.

"Say it." Gigi sat hard against the floor. She dropped her face into her hands. "I can see it all over your face."

Selene did her best to still her features. "It is pretty."

"I thought we promised not to lie to one another."

Selene wasn't technically out of the competition yet. There was a chance she would make it into L'Opéra du Magician. A mediocre audition from Gigi would be the best thing for her. All Selene had to do was say nothing and smile and let Gigi believe that her piece was good enough.

But if she did that, she'd be like Priya. And Selene was so, so much better.

"If the audience wants to see a pas de deux, they will go to the ballet." Selene was already deconstructing the melody, thinking of ways to make it soar. "You are giving them something they already have. Where is the magic?"

Gigi's dark eyes rippled like the water beneath the opera house. There it was: acceptance. "I don't want to take advantage of you."

Selene rolled her eyes. "This is your work. I'm just helping you make it better."

Selene inverted that first chord, changing the sound. Gigi closed her eyes, no doubt envisioning the stage spreading before her. Her smile went wide with delight.

Selene played the second chord, adding a minor seventh. Gigi's movements synched easily. Selene reshaped the music, pausing briefly to make notations on the page. Gigi danced through it, not adding the magic yet.

"No partner illusion." Selene tapped the page. "Any ballerina can dance with a man. Who can you dance with?"

"Ballet is about uniformity and conformity." Gigi went onto her toes and then back down again. "A perfect performance would be identical versions of myself."

Selene struck a chord. "Excellent. And what else?"

Gigi sang the illusion of herself and moved through a few steps. She brought her leg up over her head; the duplicate Gigi did the same. Selene sustained the melody for illusion in the contralto. The two dancers moved across the floor. Gigi took a deep breath and caught the overlap, singing the second motif to bring in the wind. It was tricky to hold the magic like this—willing the illusion while singing another motif, tracking the combination of both in the piano. Made more impressive by the movement of the dance. But the audience didn't know that. To them, it was all just performance. Only a trained magician would know just how technical and impressive Gigi was. Selene's fingers moved through the chords, her mind racing to translate just how incredible this all was.

Gigi needed wings. Not terrible and black and made of

blood and shadow. She looked down at the keys, something beginning to take shape. She wrote down a few notes, a line. Selene saw it like it was the first time. They were almost to the coda now. Selene moved the illusion into the bass and the wind motif up to the voice. She sang the line, hoping that Gigi would catch on. Of course Gigi did.

All at once, Gigi was not just a girl. She was winged and wild and poised in the air. Arms extended; toes pointed. She was an angel of music, made of perfect angles and bathed in light. She was the opposite of a ghost. Her wings trembled as she descended.

Selene was on her feet, rapt with applause. "That was amazing."

"I've been trying to nail the lift for months. I thought I was going to have to cut it." Gigi was giddy. "Can we run it again?"

"This time, drop the illusion of yourself a measure earlier, to build up the tension."

"Brilliant." Gigi was already in position to start again.

They ran the whole thing, and then the coda. Again and again. The air lifted Gigi and held her there like a human fermata. There was magic in her form, the extension of her arm all the way down to the smallest finger.

She landed perfectly and soundlessly.

Selene notated music and Gigi danced.

"This is it." Gigi held on to the sheets of music like they were the last good thing in her life. "It has to be one of us."

Selene lifted her hands from the piano keys, trying to absorb the shock of the blow. Because what Gigi meant was: *it has to be me.* Selene had her chance.

The sun cast colors of gold and burgundy, stretching the

shadows until they took the room, inch by inch. Selene smiled fieramente. She wouldn't fight harder; she'd fight smarter. The rules no longer applied.

Selene would have everything she wanted, even if that meant begging magic from a ghost.

CHAPTER 9

When Selene stood in front of the mirror again—clean and dressed in a lapis lazuli gown—she knew exactly what she wanted. She clutched a shard of glass in her hand and pressed it onto the pad of her thumb. The ghost had made such a little cut—merely a drop of blood.

She slid into the mirror. This time, she knew where she was going and what she wanted. The dark was just as disorienting, but it had a purpose.

She sang for light the moment she felt something solid beneath her feet.

He was crouched in the dark, head bowed against his chest. So lovely, he looked like he could be gilded and placed in this opera house. Perhaps it was the sharpness of his cheekbones or the cut of his jaw, the width of his shoulders or the curl of his fingers. Her breath caught in her throat, made a mockery of all her years of training. The tendrils of darkness scattered from him. Some of the shadows were still in his eyes, breaking up the clear blue. He blinked, and his eyes were back to winter skies, as if they'd never been touched by the dark.

"You came back." He looked as if he had hoped for this but couldn't believe it would come true, like she was the North Star on a cloudy night, enough to guide him home. No one had ever looked at Selene like that before. "Aren't you afraid of me?"

"I'm not afraid."

"But you saw what I am. What I become." There was a tremor to his voice.

"I'm not afraid of you."

She'd never been less afraid of anything in her life. She wanted to know more. She wanted to know everything. She reached for him, fingers close enough to touch. They both stood perfectly still, as if waiting for the other to pull away or push forward.

"You became something new."

"A monster."

How like Selene he was, and yet she could see all the wonder in him that she forgot in herself. He was pure magic—an impossible, lovely thing.

"It was incredible."

He looked at her strangely then. "Magie du sang is an art unto itself."

"Magic of blood?" Selene shivered.

"Magic of pain. Blood is a small necessity."

"If I had known I could bleed magic, I would have saved myself a lot of time in the practice rooms."

He cocked his head. "What kind of magic do you have in your world now, after all of this time?"

"There is only one," she said, tasting the soured truth on her tongue. She knew now that was a lie; she just wasn't sure how big of one. The shadows whirled around her with a magic of their own, different from what the ghost had performed. "Music."

The ghost made a small cut into his arm. The blood became shadow and the shadow swirled around him, forming a chair. "Someone has been lying to you, Selene."

"It could have been forgotten," she said.

"It seems a lot to forget in a hundred years."

"They forgot you." Selene swallowed. It had only taken a single act for the world to forget Giuseppe Dreshé, for them to replace him with a madman. But the ghost wasn't wrong.

"And what of the Council of Mages? Surely they could not let all other magics be lost."

"If you can't remember your name, how can you remember a council?"

He closed his eyes. "I remember things with you."

Selene considered what she had said to spark this memory, how she could repeat the process. "There is no council."

"Who governs the magics?" Distress crossed his beautiful face. It should have made him less, but somehow it deepened his loveliness.

"No one." Selene brought her hands up in supplication. "Magic is art. There's nothing to govern."

He turned his palms up. She watched him curl his fingers into fists and open them again. They were strong and calloused. Not the hands of useless wealth. Who had he been a hundred years ago and what did she need to do to help him remember?

"Who governed you?" she said at last.

"I don't remember the names or the faces, just the feeling," he said, as if it didn't bother him in the slightest. He was distracted, focused on something else. "What is the purpose of your art, Selene?"

"To entertain." She shivered at the sound of her name on his lips.

"That's it? That's all it is to you?"

"As if that's not enough?" Fury rose in Selene. "I've spent the last seven years studying to compete in L'Opéra du Magician. To win and be the King's Mage."

He flinched and tried to hide it with the sweep of his arm up and into his hair. "To be a servant of the king is something you truly wish?"

"It's the highest honor."

He pressed his head into his hands. It was more than the grief of a hundred years' captivity. There was a depth to this Selene did not understand.

Selene wanted to change the timbre between them, to change the key into something brighter. He was too beautiful for this profundity of sorrow. Perhaps if she asked the right question, he would have an answer, a memory.

Selene lit the space with her most dazzling smile. "Did they have horses when you were young?"

"Horses," the ghost said. There was a twinkle in his eyes. His smile was haunting; he'd play this game with her. "As big as elephants."

"Oh?" Selene was coy. "They're much smaller now, the size of teacups."

"Our teacups were the size of soup bowls."

"Then they're the size of thimbles," Selene said. "And what of cakes, did you have those?"

"Alas, no cakes," the ghost said. "Merely cubes of sugar stacked high, sometimes spun into webs."

"To catch flies?"

"To catch boys who want things above their station."

There was something chilling about that assertion, something too close to home. "And what of the moon?"

"It was close enough to touch," the ghost said, his musical voice taking her in for a story. "And every night the hungriest of us would bite along the edges, little by little, until there was nothing left. And then we'd wait for it to grow again to something big and round and full."

Selene leaned into him. "What does the moon taste like?"

"The same sugar they catch us with."

A chill traced up Selene's spine like a finger. The playfulness of the mood had turned and the ghost's pale eyes were downcast and stormy.

"Why did you come back?" he said.

"I couldn't leave you," Selene said. "Alone in the dark."

"Surely there is more reason than that?"

There was so much she could say. She'd run possible questions and answers through so many times it almost felt like she had lived them. She knew exactly how to appease the papers or a crowd, to garner adoration or sympathy. It was harder to find words for the truth.

"My father was the greatest magician that ever was," Selene said. "And when he died, people seemed to forget. If I win, I have a chance to right history. To give my father the legacy he deserves."

The ghost held up the knife, watching the colors change in the light. Selene couldn't look away from the set of his jaw or the shadows cast by his long eyelashes. He was the kind of beautiful that seemed like a lie. "And this is truly what you want?"

"More than anything." She didn't know who she was without this. Losing her chance was like losing herself. "It's been every part of me for longer than I can remember. Haven't you ever wanted something so badly you'd do anything to have it?"

"I want to see the sky." He tilted his head up to an imaginary sun. "I want to breathe the salt air. I want my name, and everything else that was stolen from me."

Selene sucked in her bottom lip. With all that she knew, with all the resources at her disposal, there had to be something she could do. "I can help you."

The ghost's dark brow furrowed. "Why would you do that?"

"Because." Selene stood a little straighter, channeling her best Madame Giroux. "You're going to teach me your magic."

He held out his hands, showing his scars in their fullness. He pressed his fingers against the line on his arm. A silver scar where there had once been a wound. It matched a hundred other marks. She wondered if he remembered each one, or if they'd been stolen like his name.

"Why would you want this?"

"I need to win."

"That's not enough."

The dark slithered like a quiver of snakes. It frightened and calmed her. How could she tell this next part of the story without betraying her heart?

"Then what is? I am here, in this impossible place, asking, begging you to change my life. This is all I want. This is all I have."

He regarded her. She let him assess her, as she'd been weighed and measured by so many teachers, and waited for him to somehow know. She was worthy. She would fight for this.

He must have sensed that in her.

"Magic has a price." His voice was soft and low, sweet and soothing, as if she were a wild thing.

"Of course it has a price." She swallowed, aware of the movement of her collar on silvered scars around her throat. "I've been paying my whole life."

"I need to know that you are sure."

The memories came to her in a terrible rush of blood red and sky blue. She swallowed them down like sickness and licked her lips. Slowly, she undid the buttons around her throat. Her pulse fluttered beneath her fingertips. She'd gone to such great lengths to conceal this part of herself. Everyone knew how it happened, but few knew the reality.

"When my father went mad, he tried to rip my throat out. This is my only chance to clear his name, to remind people who he was. Not the madman, but the mage."

The ghost took a step closer. Brought his hand up, as if to trace the network of scars that circled her throat. He never touched her but was close enough that Selene could feel the heat rising off his skin. There was a spark of something in his eyes. He knew what it was to bleed.

Selene fastened the buttons around her collar. The ghost ran his thumb against his forefinger, warring with the idea. She watched him, tried to keep herself from falling to her knees and begging. She needed whatever would give her an edge. Madame Giroux wouldn't be able to say no to this kind of power.

No one would.

"Please." Selene let the desperation creep into her voice, real and raw. She had to have this.

His exhalation came so softly, but this close, she could feel warmth and the resignation. "You have to promise me that you won't teach anyone else."

That was easy. Selene wouldn't give any more fuel to her competitors. "I promise."

"There is a price."

Selene didn't even try to count the beats of her heart. She'd worked for years to be good enough with music, and even then, it wasn't enough. This magic came as easily as breathing. She didn't care what it cost. "I'll pay it."

"You don't know what you're saying." He turned away from her.

For a moment, Selene was sure she'd seen a glint of something dark in his eyes that made her wonder. She'd fallen through the mirror with this beautiful, monstrous man who could teach her impossible magic. It was all too strange, too convenient, too *right*. She should be questioning it, fighting against the ease with which this bargain appeared.

But Selene was decided.

"Then tell me."

"The magie du sang requires your pain."

Selene laughed. "It can have it."

"More than that." The ghost smoothed his dark hair. She counted the scars on his hands, wondered if she'd soon share in that tapestry. "If I am to teach you, there are things you must agree to. There is a magic older than pain. I'm bound to it; I don't know why or how. I just know what must be done." All these magics secreted away. There was a part of her that doubted him, doubted the realness of the magie du sang and whatever this older magic was. In her world, there was only music. But how much of her world had she actually seen? Selene could count the cities she'd been in on one hand. She could count the days she'd spent out of the opera house in the last seven years on two. What did she know?

"I'm not afraid."

He regarded her thoughtfully. His eyes were so blue, they seemed to glow, like gems caught in the light. "Every day I will ask of you three things. One for the magic. One for you. And one for me. If you cannot answer these three things, you cannot come back."

Selene took a breath. "How do I know that you won't ask me something impossible?"

His smile coiled like a serpent. "You don't."

"All right," Selene said. "I'll do it."

The ghost took out the little knife. Selene was drawn to the kaleidoscope of colors, comforted by the vibrancy. At least there was color in this place, some proof that he might have been real.

"We must swear to it." He made a shallow cut down the palm of his hand and then offered the knife to her, hilt first, careful to keep his fingers from touching hers. "Swear on something that matters."

His blood still warmed the knife's edge. Proof that this wasn't a dream, proven again when the blade sliced into her skin. The pain was nothing compared to the elation. "I swear on the soul of my father that I will do all you ask of me."

"I swear on my name that I will teach you magie du sang."

His name.

The drops of blood that ran down her hand onto the ground stopped their descent. They lifted to the space between them, mingling with the ghost's blood. They twisted and twisted together until they evanesced into shadow.

"Let us begin."

CHAPTER 10

"First," the ghost said. "What is it you want?"

Selene sighed, her patience waning. "You know what I want."

"This is the first thing I ask of you, Selene."

Selene straightened, chastened by the edge to his voice. "I want to learn the magie du sang so that I can perform in L'Opéra du Magician and become the King's Mage."

The ghost rolled back his shoulders. "This I have asked and you have answered."

She quirked her head. "So formal?"

"There are no shortcuts in magic. Blood is the seed. Magic is energy. It is not creation or destruction. It can only be gathered and directed."

"Like with music."

"A candle compared to a moon. Your music requires exactness. The notes must be sung properly and in the right order and offered with intent. Pain is merely felt and focused. It is far more powerful." He drew the knife across his forearm. "Once you've felt the pain—really felt it—the magic will be yours to command."

Selene counted the hours she'd spent in the practice rooms, the nights she'd gone to bed with her fingers cramped and her throat raw from singing. "It's that simple?"

The ghost smiled all the way to dark. He offered her the knife. "Is anything ever that simple?"

Selene pierced the tip of her finger with his borrowed knife. "Is this enough?"

"Blood is the beginning. You have to use the wounds within you."

Selene exhaled and focused on the pain. She'd cut too deep. Blood splattered around her like fallen cherries. She thought of awful things: of the views from her window, the narrow, meandering streets where the rich used the poor like stepping stones, the sickly-sweet scent of decay, lesser magicians gathering up coins in stained silk hats. She focused that all into wanting.

Color leached from her blood. The splatters on the floor faded, growing more faint with each moment. She was doing it. The whole world was at her fingertips—like a rose waiting to be plucked. But then it was gone, the burn of magic she'd felt beneath her skin dissipating. The tip of her finger healed into a thin line. Disappointment sliced through her, sharper than any knife.

"That's not enough. The memory—it has to be black. A cut to the soul."

"How will I know if it's enough?"

"You'll know." He turned his head into a hanged man's tilt, brushed his fingers against his exposed throat. "Tell me something true."

There were so many things she could say. She shifted through them, like riffling through sheet music. She could tell him about the last time she'd seen Victor, but that didn't seem right. She could spill out the first cold night she'd spent in the opera house, orphaned and miserable. She could describe for him the first time she'd sung alone after her father's death.

"I killed my father."

She clapped her hand over her mouth. She hadn't meant to form the words. But it was the truth, always waiting there inside her. The secret that had sundered her world and set her on this path. It was the truest thing about her, who she was at her core. A killer. She'd destroyed the person she'd loved the most.

"That is a terrible burden to carry," he said.

She tried not to think of her father's body, prone on the floor. Still sizzling with the melody of lightning. Bending, broken, gone. She swallowed a sob. "You are the only person who knows other than the king and Victor—the ones who were there."

"It is an honor to be in your confidence." There was such determination in his gaze, an ease of power. "Use it."

She braced herself and brought the blade down again on her already healed thumb. A shallower cut but a deeper pain. She let the onslaught of memories cut her more than a knife ever would. They were too sharp, too real. She couldn't hold on to them.

The magic slipped away before she had a chance to grasp it.

"Talk me through it," he said.

"He had his fingers in my throat. Tearing, like he was trying to rip out my voice." Selene closed her eyes, fighting to remember and wishing she could forget. "Do you know the sound a body makes when it's struck by lightning? There's the flash, the heat. The sound of flesh against stone. And then the boom. Thunder, at last."

Selene shook the image from her head of smoke rising from his body, tossed across the room like a broken doll.

"Who killed your father, Selene?"

"Please don't make me say it again."

"It is the second thing I ask of you." There was a softness to his eyes, like he didn't want to make her face this.

"I did." Selene forced the words out. The words she had never spoken out loud before today. "I killed my father."

"This I have asked, and you have answered," the ghost said. "Go back to that place. Live that pain. But understand: the pain is a currency that can be spent."

Panic crashed like cymbals inside Selene. He'd said there would be a price. Would Selene lose the precious few memories she had of her father? Was this the true reason for the ghost's lack of memory?

"Will I forget?"

There was a moment of hesitation, a measure of rest that unnerved her. The ghost's expression tightened, then relaxed, as it had when he'd remembered.

"The memory should stay but the pain associated will be gone, like the letting of a wound."

It was worth the risk. Selene closed her eyes and took a measured breath.

Like many terrible things, it happened on a day far more beautiful than it deserved. Selene settled into the memory, each step, each breath. The colors were so vivid. Her pale pink dress was a primrose's delight, the white pinafore so bright and clean, like it had been made from starlight. The blue, blue, blue of the sky like a jay's wing in spring.

SING THE NIGHT

Her father stood by the piano in their suite. His hand hovered over the keys; his violin tucked under his arm. Selene remembered this excitement, this joy. Her father was going to perform for the king today. It was one of the last performances, the finality marked by the boxes and boxes with their things stacked around them. Selene rushed to his side.

"What are you singing today?" She reached up and took his hand.

"Something new." His smile didn't touch his exhausted eyes. "You have to stay here, Nightingale. I promise I'll be back soon."

He paused at the door, drew her in for an embrace. His fingers were cold and trembling. The skin under his eyes bunched in a way it hadn't before. He reminded her of the anatomy drawings she'd studied with Victor's tutors. Skeletal, held together with wires and strings.

He kissed the top of her head and slipped out the door. Selene crossed her arms over her chest. She'd never missed an opportunity to hear her father sing.

She found Victor exactly where she expected him: lying beneath one of his mother's famous damask rosebushes. When he saw her coming, he broke a rose from the bush and held it out to her.

"You look very clean," he said, studying her. "And pretty."

She tried to ignore the way his compliment made her cheeks heat. It wasn't always like this. Something had changed, folded between the years of thirteen and fourteen. She quickly explained the situation to him, with a twinge of guilt. Her father rarely asked anything from her, and yet he'd asked her to stay.

"I overheard my father this morning. They're in the conservatory." Victor dusted off his pants. "Secret passage?"

"Secret passage," Selene said without hesitation.

"Your dress might get dirty."

"So?"

"That's my girl," Victor said, and kissed her cheek. It was only a peck, something they'd always done.

Selene turned her face away, that feeling of elation and embarrassment creeping in again. She couldn't let him see.

They raced across the palace grounds, ducking between a pair of columns that looked flat against the wall, offset enough for a person to slip through. Another part of the palace made for spying or quick escapes. Selene and Victor passed dozens of similarly hidden exits, rooms they'd both slipped in and out of without warning over the last five years.

"I hope we haven't missed it."

"Never better late," he whispered. It was a silly inversion of the line, something that infuriated the king, which was exactly why he did it.

Selene followed behind Victor closely, nearly colliding with his back when he stopped at the conservatory. He held a finger up to his lips. Selene slowed her breathing and bid her racing heart to still. He dropped to all fours and crawled toward the light, Selene at his heels.

Her father stood at the center of the room. It was all glass and columns, showing off the green of the palace gardens and the glint of the sea. The light refracted in endless rainbows. Selene loved this room. It was one of her favorite places to come and sing. The glass caught her voice and reflected it back in such lovely ways.

Her father didn't look prepared for loveliness. His face was creased with worry. The king was saying something, too low for Selene to hear. He sat in a wide, regal chair, facing the palace grounds—away from Selene and Victor. It was unlikely that he would see them. Her father, on the other hand, might. She hoped that his violin would consume his focus, as it usually did.

"Is he going to do the dragon again?"

"No," Selene whispered, suddenly aware of how close Victor's face was to hers. They'd done this so many times, been like this so many times. And yet this time it felt different. Everything made new. "This is something else."

There was a knot in her stomach. She'd thought it was excitement at the time. Father had worked late into the night. She hadn't been able to sleep, so she'd watched him, wondered what melody drove the frantic movement of his pen. He'd hit a few notes on the piano and then gone back to scribbling. The candles had all burned down.

"I've done it," Father had said at last, putting down his pen. Ink splattered his fingers and the corner of the page.

Father was laughing, laughing, laughing. He'd taken his music and cast it into the fire before Selene knew to stop him. She ran to the fireplace, ready to snatch the pages out of the blaze. But it was too late. The center blackened and spread. Selene read the melody just before it turned to ash. It was strange and unfamiliar, lifting and lilting in a way that seemed impossible for the voice. Dissonant, with octave leaps and modulations.

Like the writings of a madman.

Or a genius.

"Father?"

He picked her up and spun her around, once, twice, thrice. "This is it, Selene. This is the end."

And she'd foolishly thought that it meant they would go home, back to the cottage by the sea. She'd thought it was all over.

She'd been right, in a way.

Father stood before them, his dark hair smoothed back. He wore his favorite suit. Silver and blue. There was a determined peace in his countenance. The king tapped his foot on the ground expectantly.

Father placed his fingers on the neck of the mahogany violin and ran his bow over the strings. It was a little sharp. He adjusted the tuning and played another note. Selene loved when her father played the violin. It paired so well with his voice, almost like a duet. It brought her back to moonlit nights in the cottage, where every lullaby was accompanied by faeries and falling stars.

Selene reached out and grabbed Victor's hand. He wove his fingers between hers.

"When this is finished," he whispered, "let's have an adventure."

"This time," Selene said, "I get to be the pirate."

She prepared herself for the usual banter on who got to be the pirate and who got to be the general, an argument that usually ended with the flip of a coin.

"I'd follow you across the sea." Victor looked at her then like he was seeing her for the first time. Selene took a controlled breath, trying not to lose herself in the light of his eyes. He brushed his thumb against the hollow of her throat. "I don't want you to go."

Selene thought of the things she could say. She didn't want to go, either. She didn't want to burst the bubble of this idyllic life of wayward adventures and endless summers. Victor wasn't just her best friend. He was so much more. And maybe she was bridging that gap between a child and a young lady. Maybe she was okay with things changing. Maybe the butterflies that fluttered inside her meant something.

Selene didn't have a chance to say any of those things.

The violin shrieked.

That first chord straightened Selene's spine and made her skin crawl. It was ugly and dissonant and almost painful to hear. The slide of the violin was anything but beautiful.

And then Father started to sing.

It was the strangest thing, how all the minor seconds and unresolved fifths and sevenths and sharp ninths could sound right under her father's voice. That warm, endless baritone filled the whole room. Like this whole place had been built simply to contain the divinity of his voice.

Selene marveled at how beauty could remove her from her own body. She felt herself lifted, the warmth of Victor's hand fading to nothing. She hadn't even realized how much her shoes pinched until the feeling was gone. The rose in Selene's hand shimmered, as if with heat. Selene's very skin seemed like it was made of glass, like something was happening inside her that she couldn't understand. There was only light and dissonance and Father.

Until.

From one heartbeat to the next, Father went from singing to screaming. The music continued on the violin. Desperate and jarring, like silver against glass. Cutting, breaking, screeching. He wasn't even playing anymore. The violin floated in the air, moving of its own accord.

Father's back was arched like a bow pulled too tight. His movements were disjointed. Joints popped in and out of their sockets, moving at impossible angles. He pressed his lips together, still singing, still screaming. Blood ran from his mouth. Broken teeth, bitten tongue, throat in ruins.

Selene flew to her feet. He'd warned her that music could open up channels, how the music could find each bruise of the soul and press and press until it yielded anguish. But it had never been like this. She had never seen him like this.

Victor grabbed her arm, but she wrenched herself free.

"Tell me what to do. Tell me how to help." She was beside her father, wiping at his bloody face with her pinafore.

His neck popped. His head turned at an odd angle, eyes fixing on her. She did not recognize those eyes. The pupils were blown. Blood vessels burst. Dark against dark. Black against blood. All the laughter ironed out. All the light gone.

His hands shot out like a viper. His fingers—long and strong from years of playing—burrowed into the skin around her throat. She didn't even know how to scream. How to make a sound when the man who had once been her father tore at her flesh.

Scratching deeper, trying to gain purchase, trying to get in.

He was going to rip out her throat.

Selene was never sure how it happened. Music had always been a part of her life, and the magic, the magic was there, waiting for her. She didn't remember singing at all. She didn't know how it started or how to stop it, just that it was there. Sudden and perfect and exactly what she needed, even though she didn't want it.

Lightning cut the air, the smell of it sweet at first, and then burning.

The violin clattered to the floor; the bow splashed in the spreading pool of her blood.

Father crumpled on the ground, smoke rising all around him, a black burn mark at the center of his chest, below the onyx and gold of the King's Mage necklace. He wasn't moving. He wasn't breathing.

Selene's vision blurred. She brought her hand to her throat. It felt like a sun-ripened pomegranate, cracked open on a rock. The fragile seeds burst sweet around her fingers. The king's eyes were wide, his mouth working around words she couldn't hear. Victor stood at the edge of the shadows, the ruined rose at his feet. Thunder cracked like great applause.

She looked into the pale blue eyes of the ghost and grounded herself in them.

The blood on Selene's thumb deepened, darkened into black. It ascended like smoke from her thumb, spectral and new. She wished it, willed it, coaxed and called it. The heat of it swirled beneath her skin, like her blood was hungry to do more. To be more. All she needed to do was want.

She would start with a rose.

The flower took shape in her hand. She didn't want just any

rose. She wanted something that hadn't been seen before, something indomitable. The petals formed, bright white as newly fallen snow. The thorns pressed sharp against her palm.

And then it bloomed. The inner petal was such a dark, rich red that even this place could not steal the color away. The fragrance was sweet, intoxicating. She brought it up to her face, brushed her lips against the soft petals to know that it was real. She tried not to think of Victor. Selene offered it to the ghost.

He took the rose from her, careful never to touch her. He turned it in his palm, dragged his fingernail over the waxy stem. The rose bled, as all living things do, dark and red as its petals. She'd done it. She'd made something real.

"Pain is meant to be felt." His lips curved up into a sickle moon. The light in his eyes was brighter than the cascade of false stars. "Take your broken heart, make it into art."

A chill ran up Selene's spine. "My father used to say that."

"Show me what you can do," the ghost said.

CHAPTER 11

"Once more." Selene stood in the wake of what she'd created. A fantastic, impossible garden. Flowers of every color. Ivy that tangled with the dark. Lilacs hung down from the constellation of stars and brought their own glowing light. "It hasn't lost its power."

"It will. Remember, the magic is closer here." The ghost leaned against a giant, phosphorescent mushroom. "You have to rest."

Selene knew he was right. Despite the exhilaration of what she had learned, she was wrung dry. Her limbs tingled with exhaustion. She was too tired to even cry.

"Isn't there a magic for that?"

"Sleep is a sort of magic," the ghost said. "Close your eyes, and when you open them again, the whole world is new."

Selene looked at every corner in the dark and imagined waking up to this. There was no crime worth being trapped here for a hundred years. She wanted to tell him that. She wanted him to know that she believed that he was worthy of light.

Instead, she said, "Where do you sleep?"

"Wherever the dark won't touch me," he said.

"And what happens when it does?" She suppressed a shiver.

"It takes something from me." He rolled the words around in his mouth like cherry stones.

Selene reached up and plucked a glowing blossom. "I thought the light might stay."

"The moment I find rest, the magic leaves and the light goes, and it's just me in the dark."

Her heart might break, imagining the ghost fighting for a moment's rest in a hundred years of this. Her thoughts were interrupted by the roar of her stomach.

"What will happen to my magic, when I go?" She hoped the light would stay and it would shield him.

"It fades when you wink out. Everything goes back to black."

"I'm sorry."

"Don't be."

The ghost smirked and plucked one of the fruits she had created—a pear with silver skin. She caught it and bit the tender flesh. The inside was red and dark as blood. Cold juice washed down her fingers. The ghost held a golden apple in his hands. He watched her, even as she ate through the core.

"Aren't you going to eat?" Selene wiped her mouth with one of the velvety leaves, feeling suddenly bashful.

"I don't need it. I am in some sort of stasis. My heart beats, but I don't change."

"Is that why I can't touch you?"

The ghost wet his lips. "Do you want to touch me?"

Selene inhaled sharply, heat flooding to her cheeks. He was beautiful like the fading light of a winter day. Of course she wanted to touch him. "I don't like being told no."

"Relentless. I remember that."

"You're mocking me."

"I would never." His smile was sweeter than the fruit she'd dreamed up. A flash of light, and then gone. His brows furrowed with the effort of remembering. "I don't know why I can't be touched. I just know it's important."

Selene worried her bottom lip. She let the silence lengthen between them. With each passing moment, her head grew heavier. If only she could fall into his arms for a bit of rest and the magic of sleep. It was not hard to imagine the weight of him, the rush of his skin. She leaned against one of the giant leaves she'd created from blood and misery, a poor substitute. If she closed her eyes for a while, she'd be ready for more magic. She didn't have to go back to a world where all her dreams were waiting to be crushed.

"Why can't you bleed yourself free?"

"You ask so many questions."

"You give so few answers."

His laugh was deep and resonant. She could trace the left-handed melody. God, he was beautiful.

"If I have tried it, I left with only the shadow of certainty that it won't work." The ghost shifted, his hands tracking the scars on his forearms. He looked at her with an intensity even she couldn't match. "Before you return, find a piece of sky. Bring it to me."

"That's not a question."

There was something binding in his words. The air shivered around her, heavier and heavier, like a violent wind. Pushing her out, out until she could fulfill what he asked of her. She dug her heels into the ground, bracing herself as if standing in the way of a storm.

"You did not swear to answer questions." The ghost's blue eyes were fire bright. "You cannot return until it is done."

"What does that mean?"

"Quickly." He shook his head. "The other way out is one you would not like."

Her feet slipped on the shadowy floor as the darkness ripped her from the ghost's light. Like the pull of a tide, threatening to suck her into the darkest part of the ocean. This was not like her magic. This was gravitational, so much bigger than music could ever be. Like a candle to a moon, he said. She wished she knew more.

She didn't want to be forced out of the mirror by the tendrils of shadow that swirled around her. She bit down hard on the pad of her thumb. This time, she pulled the magic from the terrible reality that waited for her outside. Her things could be packed up and she could be out on the streets. And what she wanted, what she wanted was to stay. But she trusted the ghost's warning. She needed him to be true.

Let me out, she thought.

And then she was crouched against the cold stone in front of the beveled mirror. The bite she'd made in the mirror still bled. The rest of her cuts had healed, like she'd made them years before.

The water around the platform shifted and churned, the bioluminescence glowing with each underwater movement. She was too tired to sing her way out. She closed her eyes and imagined another way, piecing together the darkness inside of her to propel the magic forward.

For a moment, she was afraid it wouldn't work. Then the threads of shadow poured from her wound. She exhaled her relief. It was easier than music, but not quite as effortless as when she was inside the mirror.

Selene wove a boat together, desperate to see if the magic would hold outside the mirror, made from nothing but blood and desire and sorrow. Still, she wasn't sure it was real until she placed her foot against the wood. Solid and safe and exactly what she needed. A lantern hung in the front. A great oar sat in the center. Selene stepped inside and pushed her way across the water.

The water churned bright blue. Dark things slithered beneath the surface. But none of that mattered because Selene had crafted this boat from only her desperate longing and pain. She glided between the arches, past the rusted chandeliers and dripping walls.

Back to the stairs, back to the door.

She closed it behind herself, shifting a set piece to block it, in case someone happened to wander down. She looked toward the staircase that led to the dormitories. She'd have to creep through the whole hall to get back to her room. Everyone would be asleep in their beds, and Selene didn't trust the silence of her steps. Instead, she took the stairs that went up to the grand foyer.

She slid off her boots and padded across the marble floor. The dark wasn't quite as dark as she'd always thought, now that she'd seen inside the mirror. This was all shapes and shades of gray. A hand reached for her, but it was just a statue. The golden faces along this hallway observed each and every transgression.

There was a light on in the library.

Benson was there, surrounded by books. He wrote furiously, no doubt finishing his composition for the auditions. There was ink splattered on his nose and chin and all over his hands. He paused for a moment and cross-checked something among three open volumes, then went back to writing.

Selene pushed open the door. The noise startled Benson out of his seat, knocking over several of the books and nearly dumping ink over his pages.

"Sorry," Selene said. "What are you still doing up?"

"Rewriting my music from scratch." He rubbed his temples. He looked dreadful, like a candle burned down to the nub.

Selene was sure she didn't look any better. "That's bold."

"Like doing an entirely new song for your audition?"

Selene held very still. "How'd you—"

"Your practice room is next to mine, Selene. Why didn't you tell Madame that Revelio took your music?" He leaned forward, resting his elbows on his knees.

Selene slumped into one of the chairs. She was tired, down to her bones. "How do you think *that* went?"

Benson made a face. "I can—"

"Don't you dare." Selene didn't want to think of what Madame might do. "It doesn't matter now."

"For what it's worth, you were brilliant with that tempest piece. I bet you still make it in."

Selene shook her head, thinking of the way Madame had looked at her. "It'll take a miracle."

"Or a disaster." Benson's grin turned into a yawn. "It's going to be us, Selene. You, me, and Gigi."

Selene was so tired; she pressed her head against one of the books in his stack. A miracle, a disaster, all out of her control. What if she could make her way back into the competition? Who would stop her if she went to the stage and layered song with sorrow? Madame may say no, but if the palace representative saw what Selene could really do, there was no way they would keep her from performing before the king.

It might be delusion from the lack of sleep or it might be her salvation. She wouldn't know until the morning.

"And what will you do if you win?"

Benson grinned. "I'll sing for seven years and then marry the beautiful ballerina mage, who will undoubtedly be changing the world on her own."

Selene fought to keep her eyes open. "And if she wins?"

"Then I will be but a humble servant to her until I can make her my bride." He bowed his head with a flourish.

"Hmm." Selene could sleep in the library. It wouldn't be the strangest thing that happened tonight. "And if I win?"

"I'll marry her next week."

Selene sat up. "Really?"

Benson's eyes were full of stars. He was genuine. "I've loved Gigi since the first day I saw her, Selene. I won't waste another day."

Selene smiled wickedly. "You should definitely forfeit, then. Make that dream happen faster."

"I'll consider it." His laugh turned into a yawn. "What are you going to do?"

Selene considered the words she could string together like smoke. She'd met a man in a mirror who taught her how to bleed shadows. She'd found a ghost with untold secrets, even to himself. She'd fight her way back in.

Instead, she scanned the room, eyes grazing the familiar titles of the books for something that would give up secrets of the ghost. She found exactly what she expected: nothing. In the last seven years, she'd read almost every book in this room. They were mostly music and magic theory, history, and scores and scores of sheet music. There was nothing here that would explain the boy trapped in the glass or what he could do.

"I don't know what I'll do."

"You do know." Benson found the shape of the silence and filled it. "Gigi asked me if this was all worth it. Years off our life. Tears, sweat, blood."

Selene absently ran her finger along the raw edge of the wound on her thumb. "Of course it's worth it."

"That's what I said." Benson leaned back in his chair. "Even without the competition, I'm not sure I'd do anything else."

"Not even with a needle and thread?"

"That's my father's passion, not mine. Writing music, shaping magic, it's like living a dream. It's the best and worst thing I've ever done. I can't imagine my life without it."

"I've tried." Selene took one of the books from the stack and flipped through it. It was a collection of sheet music from competitions past. She paused briefly at her father's. "I don't like who I am without it."

Benson put his chin on his hands. "That is a different problem, Selene. Who you are and what you do are not the same."

"That's easy for you to say." Selene traced the notes on the page, the music taking shape in her mind. That feeling—the push and pull of passion and the overwhelming need to be part of her art—consumed her. "You've had a life outside of this."

"Are we going to talk about it?" Benson's voice was gentle.

Selene stilled. 'Talk about what?"

"That doesn't work on me, Selene." Benson reached for her hand. "This must bring up a lot for you."

Selene exhaled. Benson had no idea how much, though he clearly sensed it. Selene's mask must be slipping. "It's a lot for all of us."

He gave her a look too close to pity.

"Now, off to bed with you."

"I need a few more minutes." Benson tapped his page. "I'll see you in the morning."

Selene rose and paused at the door. "It's already morning."

By the time she reached the top of the stairs, she was out of thoughts. It took all of her will to drag her feet the remaining steps to her room.

Dawn crept up through the scattered rooftops and buildings, shattered into fractals until the light broke through her window. Gigi's snores were soft and elegant. Her foot hung over the side of the bed, bandaged, like any dedicated dancer's.

Selene wrapped herself in her quilt. She was so tired, the exhaustion almost crushed her.

Sleep was quick and heavy, the pull of a curtain, and into dreams.

CHAPTER 12

The street was shadowed with afternoon by the time Selene awoke. Gigi was long gone. She'd attempted to make the bed, throwing the down comforter over the rumpled bedsheet. There was a cup of coffee and a plate of eggs, toast, and bacon on their shared table, with a note beside.

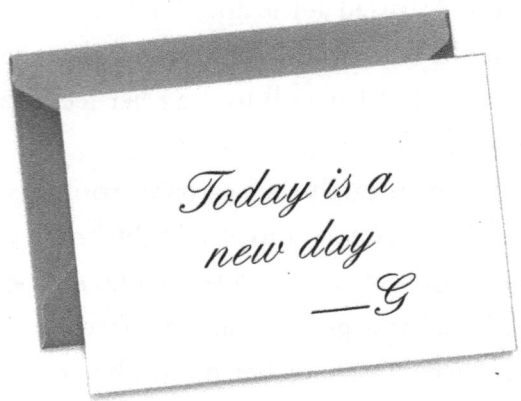

Selene smiled and folded the note and placed it into her top drawer. Her stomach was unsettled, and there was nothing appealing about cold eggs and the now-soggy toast. The cream in her coffee had congealed.

Selene could have sung it warm. She could have used music

for practical magic, as she had so many times before. But she didn't need music. She just needed to want, and then she could have it all.

The exhaustion that clung to her like cobwebs swept away. Selene rifled through the basket on top of Gigi's dresser. It was an unmitigated disaster, but Selene found what she was after. The needle was shiny and sharp like a tiny rapier. Every few days, Gigi would sit on the edge of the bed and stitch the ribbons into her pointe shoes—as evidenced by the stray threads that clung to her comforter. She wouldn't miss a single needle. Selene pricked her finger and squeezed to make the drop.

She took the first memory that came to her. Her father, sitting with her on the beach. She didn't have much from the seaside cottage days. Those memories were precious. Part of her was afraid that the magie du sang would burn through the best and the worst of her and leave her as empty as the ghost. But if what he said was true, she wouldn't lose the memories, just the ache associated with them. That seemed like a gift. She wanted to remember her father without the pain of his loss. She centered herself around that sorrow.

Except magic was different outside the mirror. Memories of that terrible day swirled in the back of her mind. After so much time not remembering, it seemed strange to reach for it again. It was still there, but softer. The colors were less saturated, blurred around the edges. And that was fine. She could live with that.

The magic pulsed through her veins.

She focused it on how the coffee should taste, sweet and creamy and hot, with a touch of bitterness on the back of her tongue.

Selene brought the coffee to her lips. It was hot and good, the heat of the cup bringing out the ache of her fingertips. This was so much easier, hurting and wanting. She didn't have to worry that a minor slip in precision would turn the cup bitter or burn through her hands. The ghost's magic had an unimaginable ease to it. If she hadn't already promised that she wouldn't teach anyone, she would be shouting it to the whole world.

She took a moment to enjoy her coffee and consider what it would be like when the ghost was freed. Would the curse that kept space between them be lifted? She could imagine the feel of his scars beneath her fingertips, rising up his forearms to the corded muscle of his biceps, his shoulders, the flutter of his heartbeat in his neck, the edge of his jaw, the crest of his lips. Was his mouth as soft as it looked?

"Selene."

Gigi stood in the doorway, eyes wide with worry. She was in her best tutu. She looked like a morning glory hung aloft, waiting to bloom. Her hair was slicked back out of her face. Rouge dusted over her lips and cheeks and lids. She was dressed for an audition.

Auditions.

"There's a new rule, posted in the hallway, as of this morning. All students must attend auditions or forfeit. You have to move. Now."

Selene's heart skipped a beat. She placed the mug onto the table carelessly. The hot coffee sloshed over the side. "That seems...pointed."

"It is."

Selene gaped. "Help me."

Gigi was already there, pulling a black raspberry organcy gown from the closet. Selene saw immediately why she picked it—no buttons. Selene drowned herself in the dress. Gigi pulled it down, adjusting it as best she could. The window reflection showed the grooves of Selene's scars, visible above the neckline of the gown. She reached for a scarf to tie around her throat but grabbed the wrong one. She'd intended to grab the black lace, but she'd reached deep into the drawer. It was too late to correct the mistake; Gigi was already halfway out the door. Selene wrapped the faded blue scarf she'd bought with Victor, years and years ago.

"Come on." Gigi held out a pair of slippers.

Selene took the stairs by two, thinking of what she could do with the magie du sang. How with a drop of blood and pent-up misery, she could fold the floor in front of her and be in the theater in a half step.

But she couldn't do that now, not without spilling her secrets. There was a sign on the door, growing clearer with each step.

ALL STUDENTS MUST ATTEND AUDITIONS.

The sign seemed deliberately written for her, but why? The rule must have come from Madame or the palace or some combination. It was unnecessary. Why would someone assume that she'd be curled up, wallowing in woe, deep into despair? Let them count her out. Let them think she had nothing left to give.

They made it through as the door started to close and Selene settled into a seat in the auditorium. There was a blank space—conspicuous as a missing tooth—where the chair Selene had struck with lightning had been.

At the front of the auditorium, Madame shuffled the deck slowly, her eyes resting on Selene for a moment too long. She plucked a card from the deck. Turned it to face the gathered singers.

Beautiful, treacherous Priya. She kissed Revelio and walked lazily onto the stage. The stage lights caught her engagement ring and refracted her infidelity.

Priya nodded. The orchestra swelled in the pit below. Priya's painted mouth began to move.

In another life, Priya might have actually been a singer. Her voice was powerful, large enough to fill all the space in the theater. A dramatic mezzo-soprano with a flair for acting. Had she taken care with her vocal training—solidifying pitch and rhythm and dynamics, learning how to control that big voice— she could have been great. And she'd had the opportunities, of course. The best voice teachers in the world at her disposal. But Priya's father hadn't wanted a daughter who could sing. He wanted a daughter who could do magic. So she'd fought her voice lessons, leaning into the pageantry and the magic. Selene watched the way Priya sashayed her hips, the way she unfolded her hands like they had anything to do with the magic. Every step part of the performance.

The air crackled with magic. Priya brought her hands out. There were tiny seeds stuck to her palms—undetectable to the audience. This was a common practice. Magicians could not create something out of nothing. If they wanted flowers, they needed seeds.

But not Selene. Not anymore.

The addition of seeds was a puzzle that was easily rectified. Often the simplest solutions were the best.

Selene had always accepted that as fact, never worrying too much about the mechanics. Idly, she pondered more deeply. Where did the magic come from? How did it channel through the magician to transform into something other? And why hadn't she wanted to know this before? Perhaps it was unknown. She'd read all the books in the library and knew the answers were not contained there. The power centered around Priya. A roar ripped through the air, loud enough to drown out even Priya's voice. Vines burst from her palms. Sweet autumn clematis, based on the shape of the leaves and the structure of the buds. That was a mistake. No one cared about clematis or baby's breath or lilacs. They wanted drama and passion. They wanted sunflowers and lilies and roses, flowers that *meant* something.

Priya didn't have a handle on this magic. She closed her eyes, her song changing shape. The vines twisted and rolled into the orchestra pit. Half the orchestra cut out, tangled in vines, trying to save their instruments and sheet music.

Priya kept singing. Her face reddened with frustration.

The flowers didn't bloom.

Selene didn't even try to fight the growing sense of glee. Priya was power, not finesse. Flowers were a delicate work. They needed the right breath, coaxing, and shaping. Raw power wasn't enough. But Priya—always the performer—ended her piece with flair, grinning as if she'd meant the vines to go unbloomed, meant for them to fall into the orchestra and disrupt the music. She bowed and strode away with false triumph.

Monsieur Fenrir's mouth tightened. The palace representative didn't seem displeased. He clearly didn't know any better.

Madame cast Priya off with a look. There was something smug in the corners of her mouth. She burned the vines and sang a gust of wind to sweep away the ash.

Priya sat down and entwined herself in Revelio. "At least all the statues are intact."

Selene didn't feel the need to rise to the occasion. She may have wrought destruction, but at least she had *done* something.

Madame drew Cameron's card next. He was another legacy competitor, though his mother hadn't won and had instead used her knowledge to put on parties instead of real magic. His piece was entertaining—a play on court drama, with deference to the royal family. He was precise and thoughtful, if a little bland. He bowed and stepped off the stage.

Cecile came after. Like Priya, she wanted flowers. With less subtlety than needed, she scattered them over the stage. Her aria was a lament for beautiful things, each of the flowers bursting from buds to bloom around her. She'd woven in the motif for fire, no doubt intending on igniting each of the flowers and setting the stage ablaze.

But her flowers were too green and she didn't put enough power behind her fire. Instead of flames, plumes of white smoke formed around her. This was a pretty mistake, allowing her to keep the artistry of the flowers with the drama of the smoke. But Selene had known Cecile for long enough to know that she wouldn't play it off like a choice, as Priya had. Cecile's eyes went wide. She breathed in deeply in preparation for the coda—the worst mistake. The smoke filled her lungs, leaving her gasping and choking. She cut off her aria with a quick bow, eyes streaming as she coughed her way offstage.

And it was wrong of Selene to feel the elation at Cecile's failure, selfish and unkind. But it was the truest emotion: petty and ugly and honest. Selene needed her fellows to be mediocre so she could have the chance to show the world her greatness.

Carefully, Madame shuffled her deck. She held the card up to the light.

Selene felt a bubble of rage rise up inside of her. It was a little girl dressing up in her mother's costumes and ballet slippers. If the card had been a knife, it would have hurt Gigi less. Judging by Madame's gaze, Selene knew what she expected. It was hard to imagine a mother being so cruel to her own daughter.

"Show her," Selene said.

Benson took Gigi's hand and kissed it. "Be everything I know you can be."

Gigi took first position in the center of the stage. She was up on relevé, arms extended. Her mouth moved almost imperceptibly. Her voice was barely audible above the orchestra, but Selene knew what to listen for. If Gigi had been anyone else, she would have gone home years ago. But she—like Selene—was relentless. And she had found a way.

Selene could see the notes on the page—written in her own hand—as Gigi moved through the pas de quatre with three versions of herself. Turning pirouettes before moving in step. So perfect, it was hard to tell who was Gigi and who was imitation. Gigi started a series of fouettés. The imitations spun with her, moving closer and closer until they *were* her. Toes pointed, ballet slippers a perfect extension of Gigi's long, dark legs. The magic moved into the clarinet. Gigi chasséd across the stage, grace and power and beauty.

Selene held her breath, ready for this next part. She didn't watch the stage—already knowing the way Gigi would spread her wings and fly. Instead, she watched the audience—especially Madame Giroux—for the collective intake of breath, eyes dazzled with delight. It was nothing they'd ever seen before. A complete reimagining of how music and magic could intersect.

Magic as *more*.

The wings fluttered on Gigi's descent. Gigi had done it. She'd pulled off a flawless routine. Madame Giroux's face rippled with horror before she settled into dubious approval. She brought her hands together in the same polite applause she'd offered every other student. But there was something behind her eyes. Selene wanted to believe that it was pride and love for her daughter. What else could it be?

CHAPTER 13

"I'm having cake tonight." Gigi practically leapt through the threshold.

Mikael and Hugo had followed Gigi's audition. Mikael's had been passable—he'd darkened the auditorium with illusion and grown forests, delighting the senses with scent and sound—but it was nothing compared to Gigi's wings. Hugo's nerves had gotten the better of him and he'd brought in a wind so powerful that it whipped the curtains and nearly knocked him into the pit. Madame had ended the auditions after that. Truthfully, she should have ended after Gigi. Anything following that triumph would appear as failure.

Which was why Selene had not burst onto the stage and taken her audition back. This was Gigi's moment. Besides, Selene needed more time to consider the aria. It felt dull to use the tempest aria again, but perhaps that was the best choice. She could show exactly what she intended to do and get it right.

Selene offered a genuine smile. She was happy for Gigi, despite the way her stomach ached and her fingers curled. This was the razor's edge between being a good friend and a good competitor.

"Please, it's not like she'll win. She barely sings." Priya was holding court around the corner.

"And you barely do magic," Selene snapped. "How does your garden grow?"

Priya reddened, spinning her ring around so it dug into her palm. She closed it into a fist. Camille and Cecile sped briskly down the hall. Priya lingered a moment, as if she had something more to say. But she followed the twins, Revelio close behind her.

Benson took Selene's hand and shook it. "Selene did not come to play."

Gigi rolled her eyes. "Not even Priya can ruin my day."

They walked past the dormitory stairs and into the hallway alongside the auditorium. This was one of the supposed perks of the final stretch in the Opera Magique. They ate their meals in one of the opera house's formal dining rooms with one of the best chefs, sent by the king, with several courses for each meal. Nothing but the finest for the future of Mondreves' magical lineage.

The room was set to be a small version of the auditorium. Everything was decorated in navy and gold, meant to be rich and elegant. The tables were little stages with thick velvet tablecloths that ruched and draped and soaked up spilled wine like sponges. It almost hurt to look at—taking the extravagance of the theater and miniaturizing it somehow made it tasteless and tacky. A chandelier dripped down from the center of the room.

Selene nodded to Milton, the former palace guard who had been reassigned to the opera house. He'd been at the palace when she'd lived there and she found his presence to be a comfort. There were more ways to get ahead through the audition process than performing well. He watched the preparation and consumption of the food carefully, after a near-fatal poisoning in the last cycle. Selene got in line, passing the choice cuts of meat and an array of butter-drenched vegetables. She paused momentarily at the desserts. Tartes and crème puffs and custards topped with burned sugar.

But her stomach was tender. Selene filled her bowl with soup, took a piece of warm, crusty bread, and poured hot water into a porcelain cup over tea leaves. She set her bowl down at the table in the corner where Benson was perched—far from Priya and her kin. Camille sat down with an extravagant, glistening berry tarte. The sight of it made Selene a little sick.

The teacup was hot against Selene's aching fingers. She drank it down. It was oversteeped, bitter and dark. She relished the way it burned against her tongue.

Benson busied himself with a potato that he had mashed and rearranged into staves. The potato song was abstract, either brilliant or mad. Anyone who could turn a potato into music was a kindred spirit. He stopped, briefly, to run his finger around the rim of his glass. A note resonated from the goblet—it was real crystal. Nothing but the best for the future King's Mage. Benson wrote the note into his potato masterpiece.

He was the perfect person to help her with this puzzle.

"Benson, if someone told you they needed a piece of the sky, what would you give them?"

Benson tapped his fork against the table, carefully considering. "A jar of air."

Selene weighed the idea and found it wanting. "Something more tangible."

Benson took a long drink and put down his cup. "A raindrop."

Selene caught the edge of a smile with her teeth. It was so simple, but effective. "I can do that."

"Do what?" Benson's eyes narrowed. "You're scheming."

"Just trying to solve a riddle."

"I hate riddles." He missed his mouth with his fork. Buttery potatoes dropped down his shirt and into his lap. "What's yours but used mostly by others?"

"A napkin?" Selene arched an eyebrow.

"Are you okay?" Gigi plopped down beside them. Her plate was an orchestra of cakes.

"Don't worry about me. I'm just tired and thinking in songs." His smile was dreamy, eyes half-lidded. He kissed Gigi's forehead and rested his head on her shoulder. "Today is about you."

"Thank you." Gigi closed her eyes and leaned her head against his.

Victor had leaned on Selene like that, seven years ago, when they'd sat together on the palace floor or in the gardens or in the servants' hallways. The brush of his lips against her cheek was the last good memory before her life turned upside down, and that didn't feel like nothing. But he hadn't come to find her.

There was a wet, choking sound and a scream. Selene jumped up. Blood bubbled from Camille's mouth. It stained her teeth and the front of her pale silk dress.

Milton sprinted across the room, shouting for someone to call Madame Giroux. She was there before they finished saying her name.

Madame sang for light. She held it up to Camille's bloody lips. "Call the doctor."

She turned to Camille's plate.

At its center sat the beautiful tarte. The plump berries glistened with sugar. Madame touched a blackberry with a gloved hand.

"Glass."

"My gods." Selene fell back into her seat.

Someone had taken the time to grind glass small enough to pass it off as sugar. Someone had sprinkled it on those beautiful tartes. This wasn't just stolen music or a cruel trick with a mirror. Camille could die.

"Who would do this?" Gigi looked at her own plate, heaped with countless desserts. She pushed it away, stood like she was going to do something about it. Benson reached for her hand and shook his head. Gigi sat back down.

Selene glanced around the room. Each face was a mask of shock and horror, even as Camille was taken. Even as the blood was wiped up from the floor. Even as the plate with the doomed tarte was carried away. This was worse than stolen music. So much worse.

Madame Giroux circled the room. Her eyes were dark, discerning slits. She scrutinized each one of them.

Madame stopped in front of one place setting. Cecile— Camille's twin—kept her eyes downcast. The horror and guilt were clear on Cecile's pretty face. A mirror to Camille's, save for the blood and the agony and the terror. Selene didn't understand. Cecile had performed well today. What had she been thinking? Selene wanted to win, but not if it cost her friend her voice, her life.

Madame stood beside her, fingers wrapped around the wolf's head on her cane.

"What have you done?"

Cecile burst into tears. "I didn't know she'd take such a big bite."

Gigi reached under the table and took Selene's hand.

"Pack her things," Madame said to Milton. "Someone will fetch her within a quarter hour. And notify the king. It's gone too far this time."

Milton took Cecile by the arm. Her sister's blood splattered on her sleeve.

"The rest of you are dismissed. There will be food available direct from the kitchen if there is anything you need."

Selene looked for Priya. But Priya was distressed and ashen. Blood had splattered onto her dress and she didn't seem to notice.

Selene tossed her napkin over her untouched bowl of soup. She took the crystal goblet with her, a fitting vessel. When it was empty, she could catch a raindrop in it. A piece of the sky.

"Did that really happen?" Benson said. "Or am I trapped in some terrible nightmare?"

"If we are trapped in some collective dream, I wish someone would wake us up." Gigi's font of joy had run dry.

"Maybe we all belong someplace else. A place people can just be happy." Benson draped his arm around Gigi.

"I already found that place." Gigi burrowed into Benson's side, adoration bright on her face.

Selene tangled her fingers in her hair. Camille and Cecile were gone. Two less people vying for spots in L'Opéra du Magician. A few more misfortunes and Selene wouldn't need the ghost or his magic or a way to set him free.

It was a terrible thought, and she banished it as quickly as it came. No one should be harmed for the sake of art.

Except.

Selene ran her thumb over the crisscross of scars on her fingertips. Pain had a purpose. Even this pain. Selene could feel the burn of magic from standing witness to Camille and Cecile's downfall. The truth of it left its mark inside her like a brand. This was the worst of her, the ugliest part.

"I almost grabbed that tarte. I was behind her. It had the ripest berries." Gigi shivered. "Why would Cecile do something like that?"

"To win." It was a drive Selene knew well. "At any cost."

"It sounds so cold when you say it like that."

It wasn't cold. It was the heat and pressure needed to turn coal into diamond. Wanting something so badly that all the lines blurred into an arrow pointing straight to the goal. Selene knew Gigi was just as ruthless, even if she dressed it up in glitter and bows. There were no other ballerinas in the opera house. Gigi had put in the work to be the best—bloody pointe shoes and aching muscles. A different sort of rancor.

"What do we do now?" Benson looked to Selene like she was their guide through tragedy.

"Go upstairs and go to sleep." Selene pushed him in the direction of the upper dormitories. "Or you'll be no use when your name is called."

"How am I supposed to sleep after seeing that?"

"Chamomile and honey. It's good for the voice."

"Go on." Gigi nudged him gently.

Benson kissed Gigi and sighed his way up the stairs, leaning against the stone wall for support.

"What do you think will happen to them?" Gigi popped up onto her toes, an anxious habit.

"If Camille lives, she'll likely never sing again. Wealth will keep Cecile out of prison, but she'll never be allowed to do magic." Selene inched toward the staircase to the roof. "She'll likely be sent to live with some distant cousin until the papers have moved on, and then married off to someone twice her age."

"Bleak." Gigi was on her toes again. "Do you think either of them had anything to do with your music?"

"No." Selene wished it could be that simple.

"This isn't right. The way we're pitted against each other until we break. When did magic and music stop being fun?"

"Has it ever been fun?" Selene had loved doing magic with her father, but that was different. She wasn't a performer, then. She was just a girl enraptured by the endless possibilities of the world. Once they'd moved to the palace, everything was different. This had always been for a purpose.

They stood in the hallway, neither of them looking at the other. Selene couldn't scrub the bloody image from her mind. She didn't want to. She needed to hold on to it while she searched for her piece of sky. She'd bring both to the ghost and have the magic necessary to win.

"Selene, wait." Gigi's footsteps pattered behind her. "I think there's something more going on here. We've seen sabotage before, but it's never been like this."

"I need fresh air," Selene said tentatively. "Do you want to join me on the roof?"

"Yes?" Gigi had never liked the rooftop. Too much sky and not enough railing, and the lingering fear that somehow she'd be pulled off the edge of the roof like the girl who'd seen the ghost.

They started up the first of many staircases. Selene kept her hand flat against the banister. Each time her cut thumb pressed against the wood, it served as a reminder of what she wanted. She glanced at Gigi, who took the stairs two at a time, flexing her toes on each of the landings. Always in motion.

"Do you remember that short, dark time in which Maestro Naron insisted we form a choir?"

"Ha," Gigi said. "That poor man. To think that a group of cutthroat soloists would have the ability to blend."

Selene remembered the bright cacophony of voices. "Ensemble work is not our strong suit."

"Speak for yourself," Gigi said. "If I recall, I was the perfect choral specimen. Mother—Madame—even tried to use that to get me barred from the competition."

Selene put a hand on Gigi's arm. Madame Giroux had never been particularly motherly, but the movement toward L'Opéra du Magician had created such a chasm between her and Gigi. "Perhaps she's creating distance so as not to manufacture conflict should you win. That way it's your merits, and not hers."

"Then why wouldn't she say so? Why instead look for reasons to have me removed?"

"She's a peculiar woman."

"I've been thinking about your music." Gigi moved up the many flights of stairs with an elegance Selene admired. "I've narrowed down the timeframe Priya and Revelio could have been in our room based on our rehearsal schedules and when I know one of us was in the room."

Selene nodded for Gigi to go on.

"Three days before auditions, you finally took a break from rehearsing. I remember you locking your music in the drawer, and we went to dinner. It's the only time in the last few weeks that you were away from your music."

That had to be it. She'd tweaked the coda a few days before—and Revelio had performed the newest version. It wasn't like they could have used an old copy. "The only problem with that theory is that both Priya and Revelio were at the same dinner with us."

"I know." Gigi looked at Selene with a sort of resolute horror. "I don't think they stole the music. I think it was given to them."

An unease came over Selene. There was only one person that could be. Selene didn't want to imagine a world in which her mentor could do such a thing. Madame could be cruel, but this was beyond that. "Why would she do that?"

Gigi pushed the door open. "There isn't anyone else."

The sky was a bright, endless blue. The city below cut into shapes and patterns, buildings crossmarked by the bustling streets. Everything cramped and forced together. The opera house was the heart of Songerie, towering over most of the city. Selene's stomach clenched as she looked over the edge of the railing, imagining the brief and overwhelming feeling of slipping from this roof. There was no way the girl who'd seen the ghost could have survived her fall to the cobbled streets below. Selene could imagine her body there—broken and bloody. It was hard for her to fathom that the ghost was responsible for such a death. There had to be something more to the story.

Just beyond the tangled city, in the place Selene yearned for but could not reach, was the sea. She imagined herself growing old in the little cottage, everything the same as it had been when she'd lived there as a child. Sandy footprints and seashells in glass jars. On a clear day, she could see the line of the horizon. But today there was a haze above the shoreline. The farthest she could see was the palace. It glistened in the distance, wrapped in its familiar white walls. Rainbow light glinted from the glass conservatory. The gardens and menageries formed a barrier between the castle proper and those shining gates. The difference between those it kept in, and those it kept out.

How many summer days had she spent trying to scale that white wall with Victor by her side? They'd wanted so badly to be free, and yet now Selene would do anything to be back there. They'd only managed to escape once. Victor had bought her a scarf from a street vendor to commemorate the event. They hadn't even made it down another street—nowhere near the opera house—before they'd been caught. Victor had been whipped mercilessly by his father for endangering himself. His shirts wept blood for weeks.

"It's my fault," Selene said, after Father had spoken to her about the danger she'd put them both in by crossing that wall. "I wish the king had whipped me instead."

Father shook his head. "Be grateful the days of whipping boys are over, Selene. It's terrible to carry the burden of someone else's sins."

She took the scarf off her neck and handed it to Father. "Take this, I don't deserve it."

Father kissed her on the top of her head. "Enjoy this gift, Nightingale. Let go of your guilt. Life is too short for sorrow."

She hadn't worn this scarf in years. In the days when she had still held out hope that he would come for her, she'd worn it every day. Dreaming that he would come and take her past the edge of the sea and free her from her sadness. After a while, she'd folded it up and put it at the back of her drawer. Her only hope in forgetting.

Selene leaned against the stone guard. The air was crisp and cold up here. Selene took each breath slowly, savoring the scent of smoke from the chimneys that rose from the city like seedlings.

"It's beautiful." She glanced back.

"Is it?" Gigi had pressed herself against the copper dome, as far away from the edge as she could manage.

"You made yourself fly today." Selene raised an eyebrow. "And now you're afraid to fall?"

Gigi laughed. "It's not the same, and you know it."

Selene moved to Gigi and rested against the dome. The sun-warmed copper felt good against her back.

"This is it." Selene intertwined her fingers with Gigi's. "The beginning of the end."

"It's already begun." Gigi squeezed Selene's hand. "It's been here, for a while."

A different sort of ache permeated her chest. Not fractured love and jealousy, but the finality of this moment. Soon enough they'd leave the Opera Magique. Their lives would go on separately. Selene wouldn't settle for anything other than the King's Mage. Gigi could end up in a noble house, singing lovely distractions for those who could afford it. Their art could take them all over the world. Mondreves was the center of magic, creating trends and precedent for the other nations. Every history book she read boasted their influence and power over the known world. Did any of them have beautiful boys trapped in mirrors who bled power? Selene shook the thought from her head. After all of this, Gigi would marry Benson and have beautiful, talented children. And all of this would fade into fond memory.

Like the way things had happened with Victor. She'd thought for so long that he'd find her here and return her to the life she'd had before. That she'd have another chance at mischief and joy. That things could go back. But time was fluid. It slipped between her fingers, always changing, flowing forward with little regard to what was left behind.

Selene's head spun, suddenly dizzy. Maybe it was the view of the palace. Maybe it was the altitude. Maybe it was the clear, cloudless sky.

Selene looked up sharply, the weight of the goblet against her palm. There wasn't a cloud to be seen. No hope of rain or mist or anything she could capture and take with her down below. Her heart sank quicker than a girl thrown off the side of an opera house.

"Where do you think we'll end up?" Gigi said.

They'd played this game a thousand times. Wondering about what life would be after this was all over. Selene had always been so confident. Sure that she would be the one in the palace. She wasn't so sure about that now.

"If it's not the palace, I don't want it."

"Do you think you'll make it into L'Opéra du Magician?" Gigi said gently.

"There's still a chance." Selene would make a chance. A door where there was not a door. "Priya's audition didn't go well, either."

"I'm just worried about you." Gigi sucked in her lower lip. She was holding something back. Keeping secrets, like Selene.

"Say it."

"Your audition. Your obsession. I know it wasn't what you meant to do, but the magic got out of hand so quickly. Is it really worth it?" The words rushed out of Gigi. "Selene, you could have died. You could have *killed* someone."

Selene tried to forget the way the lightning had volleyed across the auditorium and what lightning had done to her father. There was blood on her hands and in her head and in her heart. Would Gigi still love her, if she knew? Would anyone? The only person who hadn't run from her was the boy who lived in the dark.

"I had it under control."

"After all we've been through." Gigi pressed her hand into Selene's shoulder. "Don't you think I know the truth? I don't want to see you get hurt."

Selene counted her breaths and the measures of silence that stretched between them. Didn't Gigi understand? There was nothing else for Selene.

"This can't be the end," Selene said.

There was a screech and the violence of wings. Gigi gasped and stumbled toward the door. It was a bird. A pair of birds, fighting for their space in the sky. They fought and thrashed and tore at one another, caring little that Selene was there. There was a familiarity to the violence, to the scraping and scratching and screeching. They used talons instead of music and glassed berries, but it was all the same. A want so deep that it could only end in blood. She sang for air, spinning it around herself and pushing the birds away. They startled and broke apart, into the bright blue. One following the other, claws outstretched.

Selene let her song end. Her heartbeat slowed to a more reasonable tempo. The dust settled around her. The dust, and a sleek black feather.

"Are you okay?" Gigi said breathlessly.

Selene picked up the feather. Held it up, catching the golden rays of the sun on its slick dark surface. There was something special about it. It hummed with energy, the ache of loss and being left behind. The bird that dropped it was long gone, a speck on the horizon. He'd left part of himself behind.

A piece of sky.

CHAPTER 14

The boat was still there, still whole, and still carried her across the underground lake. She drifted on the water, imagining how the ghost might look at her when she made her triumphant return. Stepping in front of the mirror was like stepping into a tangle of moonlight. Selene leaned into its glow, hoping she'd see the shape of him on the glass. She sang the opening lines to the melody they had shared. He didn't come. Had she failed to answer what he had asked?

Be enough, she thought desperately. *Please.*

She took the pin from her pocket, her fingernails ringing against the crystal. Something struck her. Cradling the goblet, she caught its reflection, hoping against hope that this might work. She rapped her fingernails from glass to glass. The mirror's pitch was the same. Excitement welled in her, quick as blood to the newest pinprick on her finger. With each passing moment, Selene could feel her heart beat accelerando, punctuated with doubt. The feather wouldn't be enough. She traced the deep circles beneath her eyes and the tangled curls of her hair. What was she doing here? There were no guarantees that she would make it back in. She was wasting time, chasing a ghost.

The mirror soaked up the blood, hungry for her offering,

washing away her uncertainty. She pushed through the shimmering surface and into the dark.

The relief was cut by the dizzying effect of going from one world to the next. It was a thousand pirouettes while being tossed beneath the churning waves and the space between dreaming and waking all at once.

She gasped, desperate for purchase. It should have been easier to adjust, knowing what to expect. But it was a little worse. She breathed in the shadow. The light she'd placed the night before was gone. There was a flicker, just beyond her. A candle guttering in a storm. Selene moved toward it, but it seemed more distant with each step. The darkness roiled around her, coiling in like snakes, closer than before.

She sang the melody for light, letting the magic flood through her. The darkness rushed away. She changed the light into a chandelier, like the one that hung in the theater. It was too big for the space, twinkling and blinding and suffocating her. She shrank it down until she was no longer overwhelmed by its glow.

"Samuel?" If she found the right name he might remember. "Gaston? Theodore?"

"Names." He came from nowhere, extinguishing the wish of light he held in his palm. "None of them mine."

Selene felt a fleeting slice of terror. She wasn't afraid of him, but how could she contend with the years of warnings against the ghost? His beauty grounded her, his dynamic presence pulling her closer and closer, treading a dangerous line between touch and not touch.

Selene put on a smile. "Here I am."

"Have you brought me what I asked?"

Selene took the feather from her pocket and held it as an offering on her open palm. "A piece of sky."

"That will do." The ghost took the feather gingerly between his fingers, a smile playing on his lips. Not enough to reach his eyes. But enough to set her teeth on edge. "This I have asked and you have answered."

He brushed the fringe of the feather against his skin. Eyes closed, like he was waiting to remember something. Or maybe he was imagining her fingers, too.

He dropped the feather and watched it spin down and down. A tendril of inky darkness crossed into the light. Then another. Then another. Until a wave of liquid black moved around the ghost. Violent and vicious, this was the predator she had grown up to fear. Not the man, but the blackness that contained him. The feather was consumed before it even hit the ground. Swallowed into the merciless dark.

The tendrils crept back, sated. The dark seemed to hum with pleasure, like a cat after a kill.

"My gods," Selene said.

"Don't let it see your fear." The ghost rolled his shoulders back. "As long as you're in the light and don't let it in, the dark can't hurt you."

"Let it in?" Selene centered herself in the light.

"With fear, with doubt, with curiosity. The dark will find any crack." He shrugged as if it was a mundane inconvenience like a spider or misplaced key. "What is it you want?"

"To win L'Opéra du Magician."

"This I have asked and you have answered."

"What would have happened to you if I didn't come back?"

"Something terrible, I'm sure," the ghost said. "And I could not fulfill my vow to teach you."

Selene held the crystal goblet aloft. "I think I know a way to free you."

He leaned in, a hunger crawling up into his face. She remembered him to be monstrous, then. Something beyond human. Her breath caught, but she released it quickly.

"Hold the glass"—she gestured to the narrow window through the mirror's face—"and stand there."

"As you say."

She took a step back to give him space to move, their paths crossing as if this were some sort of dance.

"Ready?"

He held up the goblet.

Selene sang her highest note. It rang, sharp and clear, piercing in its clarity. The glass trembled. For a moment, Selene was sure she could feel the floor shift.

The ghost's eyebrows went up, and then settled into understanding.

"No!" he cried. The glass shattered in his hand, shards spraying across his face. "If the mirror shatters, there'll be no way out. There'll be nothing—for either of us." Freckles of blood formed over his cheeks and began to weep. "The mirror is the window. It is the anchor. Without it, there is nothing."

Selene went cold. She hadn't considered what would happen if the glass broke. She'd be trapped in here forever, or worse. "How can you be sure?"

"There are things I seem to know." Blood ran down his face. The broken glass fell.

And so much he did not know. Selene caught a tremor in her hand, fighting the urge to wash the blood from him. Somehow, the brutality of it didn't make him less lovely. There was something wrong about all of this that she had yet to unpuzzle, some sense of uncertainty that plagued her. Perhaps it was the door painted to look like nothing, or the steps someone had carved from stone.

"Has this happened before?"

"I don't know for certain." All levity was replaced by dark consternation. "Of this I am sure: I could never forget you, Selene."

If there had been darkness in his eyes, it was gone now. They were bright as twin moons, looking at her with an audience's admiration. Countless people had looked at her father like that. No one had ever looked at her this way. She felt all at once undeserving of his adulation.

Selene had been forgotten. And the ghost had, too. He'd been abandoned here for a hundred years, his life and his mind stolen from him, because he had slipped from the consciousness of the world.

"I won't forget you," Selene said softly. Her heart beat con ardore, the disparate longing to close the space between them and brush fingertips almost too much. "Do you already know the way to escape the mirror, somewhere, down deep?"

"It is certainly forgotten. I would have used it."

"I used blood to escape the mirror before," she said. "Can you try?"

His cold blue eyes cut to her soul. He exhaled and the cuts on his face and hands—some of which had healed and some of which still bled—shifted from red into black, blood into shadow. Selene marked the tempo of her heart. This was the simplest solution, the easiest way out.

The magie du sang stuttered.

The shadows that had lifted into the air twisted, as if strangled. The rest of the ever-present dark churned with a sudden violence Selene did not expect.

And the ghost was not freed.

Selene was almost embarrassed by her disappointment. "I'll keep looking."

"I know you will." He waved his hand. "Has the magie du sang proved its worth?"

"I love it. I love getting what I want."

"And will it get you into the competition?"

"I have a plan."

She sang the opening of the tempest aria, the illusion forming easily around her. She didn't need the orchestra to hold the motif like she would on the stage. It stayed easily. The waves lapped at her feet. The tableau was a shade off the ghost's eyes, near enough that the undulation of the waves was close to distraction. Selene focused on the next motif. The water's soft spray turned harsher as the music picked up. Selene pricked her finger with a pin and let the blood fall. She used the same memory from this morning—her father by the sea. The memory was still there, although it felt like there was a veil over it, colors muted. Still, the air around them crackled with heat. A sprig of lightning danced weakly across the water. Selene stopped singing. The sea's illusion stayed, the air thick with sung moisture.

The ghost stood in the midst of her half magic, enraptured by the sea. "I remember this."

"It's supposed to turn into a storm."

He ran his fingers through one of the waves. There was a gentleness to his touch that filled Selene with an impossible sense of longing.

"What went wrong?"

She looked up at him, frustrated. "I don't understand. I used this memory earlier and the magic worked."

His brows knit together, like they had before. He was remembering. She watched his expression shift, his eyes still closed. She couldn't have dreamed him more beautiful. The strength of his jaw and the height of his cheekbones and the little cut below his chin. He was a study in the way flaws made perfection, from his broken nose to the scar in his left brow to the shadow of a beard.

He opened his eyes—that shock of blue. "The pain slips away when you reach for it, like untangling a knot. Embracing it makes it hurt less."

"What happens when I run out of terrible things?"

The ghost moved behind her, close enough that she could feel the whisper of his breath on her shoulder. "There is always more pain, Selene. Even without memory, I find pain to draw from. It lingers in the body, in the soul."

Selene hesitated. "There is so much I don't understand about this magic."

"Magic is a well that we draw from and shape to our will."

"No," Selene said sharply, unease building. "That's not..."

He regarded her carefully. "How does your music work?"

"Is this another one of your questions?"

"You'll know when it is," the ghost said.

SING THE NIGHT

Selene pulled up her father's watch. He'd explained it this way to her once. "It's like the mechanism of a clock. Each piece must fit together, just so, to make the magic work: the right notes, the right order, proper pitch, an openness to the magic, intent. Put them together and the magic flows through you."

"Those are the mechanics. I need the soul of it."

But...that was it. Music was rules and order and precision. It was calculations put to page and then made beautiful. And it moved her; music always did. She didn't know how to give him what he asked.

"I've never been much of a teacher, not like my father."

"So how did he teach you?"

"He filled a glass and held it up to the sun. Showed me the patterns that broke against the floor." Selene closed her eyes, sinking into the memory. She could almost hear his voice. "He said: 'The light is everywhere, like magic is everywhere. We are the glass; the music is the water. They exist separately, but together, together they can hold the magic and make it stronger.'"

She remembered the way her father had made the light dance on the table. She'd forgotten that, until now, as if the ghost had drawn out the memory with the right question. In all her years of studying, she'd been so focused on the clockwork of magic, she'd buried the light. She wished she could hear his voice, just one more time. She wished she could tell him she loved him, that she was sorry. That she was ready to follow in his path.

"He showed me how to hold the light."

The ghost dropped his head down to his chest, his cold eyes burning up at her. "Who killed your father, Selene?"

She pulled away, as if he'd struck her. "You know who killed him."

"You have to say it."

Already the dark seemed to press in, hungry for her hesitation. Would it be like music, pouring through the center of her with magic like breath? Could she hold its power? Or would it spread like madness, consuming every part of her?

"I killed my father."

"This I have asked and you have answered." He brought his head up, looked at her with those cold, blue eyes. "Show me what you can do with music and pain."

Selene sang for fire. It coiled around the ghost, all passion and fury. He stood coolly in the center of the flame, hands in his pockets. He took out his knife and let a drop of blood fall to the ground. The fire turned black and slick as a snake. It slithered around them, eyes catching and swallowing the light.

Selene pierced the soft part between her forefinger and thumb and watched the blood form like pearls. The snake bit down on its tail, shrinking the circle and forcing Selene and the ghost closer together. Drawn in, the threat of their near touch imminent. She wanted to see what he would do.

He moved so quickly, wanting and bleeding and singing two elements all at once.

The serpent burst into flowers that were caught up in a brief tornado before they fell around them like snow. She was close enough to him that she could reach out and brush the flecks of dried blood from his face, make a constellation of his scars. Flowers drifted down around them like forgotten dreams. He was so much taller than she was. The linen shirt pulled up, revealing the bare skin of his hip.

His eyes never left hers.

She tilted her head up. "The glass cannot break. You cannot bleed yourself free. You cannot walk out that door. What am I missing? What is the key?"

"I would tell you, if I knew."

"How can I save you?" she said, her voice soft as summer rain. "I've never seen anyone do what you can do."

"Sing your tempest and bleed it true."

Selene exhaled her frustration and focused on the music. This time, the sea rose up around her darker and grander than before. She didn't waste time on its gentleness. She funneled her frustration at the unanswered questions and twisted mysteries and endless secrets into the song. And when it came time for the lightning, Selene didn't think of her father. She thought instead of the unfulfilled promises that had led her to this competition, that had trapped her in this opera house, that had made her the girl to follow a voice into the dark. The lightning sundered the darkness, crackling down around Selene in a hideous halo of heat and light. Selene looked at the ghost, heady with triumph.

His face was dark with consternation.

"What have you remembered?" Selene's voice was whisper-soft like the midnight hush of waves against the shore.

"Something I wish to forget."

"Tell me."

He closed his eyes. "There is a reason I created magic from pain. I had an excess."

An ache permeated Selene. "Someone hurt you."

"And I was resourceful enough to use it."

"How can I help?" Selene kept her hands in tight fists, sure that if she forgot, even for a moment, that she was not allowed to touch him, she would. The misery on his face could unravel the world.

"The dark will take it away."

Selene opened her mouth to say something—anything.

"I know your problem, Selene."

"Tell me."

"You have to get out of your own way. You have to want it enough." The ghost was back to himself, all of that sorrow tucked away.

"When is it enough?"

"Bring for me a heart that does not bleed. You cannot return until it is done."

"Wait—"

The dark came swiftly.

CHAPTER 15

Selene sat cross-legged on her bed, singing through her warm-ups. Her voice cracked and stretched, waking up as she moved it through arpeggios on different vowels. Finally, she lay down on the floor to release the growing tension in her shoulders and sang through her favorite aria. This one had no magic to it. Without the intent and precise alignment of motifs, it was just a song. Pretty and ambitious, taking her all the way up to the top of her register and back down again. She didn't have to think. The music came to her with the relief and ecstasy of bleeding. She repeated it, until she felt like she was floating outside of her body, free from all the sorrow she'd trapped inside. Her father had taught her this one. Singing it was like coming home.

She'd been to the library this morning, combing through the familiar tomes to source some hint of magical mirror prisons for beautiful ageless boys. There were no leads, no explanations, nothing about magic that was older than twenty years. Most of the books were only a few years old, marking her father's musical triumph as the beginning of a new era. Everything before that was irrelevant. Selene had never questioned that before. But now she wondered how so much history could be forgotten.

I could never forget you, Selene.

The velvet of his voice, saying her name with such earnestness and intensity, was sweeter than any music. It felt like a promise he could not keep. Oh, but how she wanted him to. She wanted this to be real. She wanted to see him in the light. The magic of the mirror made little sense to her and she was asking all the wrong questions.

A heart that did not bleed. What did that mean? The ghost's magic was all about blood; it was hard to consider things without it. A heart was the core of something. The essence. The center. But how could she make that tangible? How could she make that matter?

She took out the pocket watch. It was later than she realized. Stripping off her simple day dress, she turned to her closet, overfilled with gowns. At the bottom were twin boxes from the couturier, each containing a dress and mask for the Unmasking Ball. They were all required to attend, with the places in the competition revealed dramatically and publicly. Selene reached into the box, fingering the pale yellow silk.

Why had she chosen this fabric? It was all wrong. She held her stolen pin to the pad of her thumb, but there were already too many scars there. She took it to the back of her wrist. Blood welled immediately.

Selene took stock of her tragedy, of the spaces inside her that ached. There was little magic in her worst memories, the face of her father farther away. There were things she could afford to forget. The first thing that came into her mind was Victor splayed across the doctor's table, stripes of blood crisscrossing his back and legs from where his father had whipped him. But even now, even when she needed it, she didn't want to think about him.

The magic burned in her veins. Selene leaned into it. She wouldn't second-guess. She wouldn't get in her own way.

Her blood lifted from her finger, turned into shadow. She willed it into the fabric of the dress: a dark, amaranthine purple with black lace at the cuffs and collar.

She dropped the lid back over the dress she'd made new, filled with a new confidence. She would wear something to pull her from the line of singers, to remind Madame and Fenrir and whoever else was there that she was the one they wanted. That she was the one who mattered. And when the moment came, she would reperform her aria, all three elements guaranteed.

She pinned back the top of her hair, letting the rest fall down her shoulders in ringlets. For today, she chose a gown of vibrant cerulean. Black lace circled her throat, secured with a thin silk ribbon. She dusted a bit of rouge over her lips and cheeks. Instead of her boots, she chose a pair of thin satin slippers. Pretty, useless things. They would move softly against the stage, allowing her to steal her moment.

Everything needed to be perfect.

Someone wept in the hallway. Selene bled the door open. It was Priya. Even sobbing, she was beautiful. She collapsed against the landing, clutching a letter in her hand. Revelio must have heard, too.

"Amore, what's going on?" He ran to her, wrapping her in his arms.

"He says even if I win, I'll have to forfeit. That this marriage is not negotiable." She tore the massive engagement ring from her finger and threw it.

Revelio caught it, looking at the ring like it was a knife

aimed at his heart. "Your fiancé will have to take that up with the king."

"This isn't fair. I don't want to be his wife. I don't want to be a mage. I just want to be with you."

He kissed her head, sliding the ring back on her finger. "I know. We will do what we must, amore. We will do whatever it takes."

"Let's run away. We can go now. Forget this place, forget everything but each other."

Selene wanted him to say yes. She wanted Priya and Revelio to ride off into the sunset, never to be seen again. She wanted to live a life without them.

Revelio paused.

Priya pushed him away, tearing down the hall.

"We can go!" He ran after her. "We can go now."

But Priya had already found her answer in his hesitation. Selene would have felt sorry for her, but she couldn't muster it.

She wound down the stairs like an unraveling thread, trying to catch sight of the heart she needed. All she saw were the empty eyes of the statues and the flicker of candles and the rows and rows and rows of chairs.

Behind her, the door slammed shut.

Benson looked better than he had yesterday, which meant he'd managed to catch a few hours of sleep. His hair was combed back. The dark circles beneath his eyes were gone. Magic or makeup or sleep, Selene wasn't sure. His smile was easy and confident.

"I figured it out." He handed her the crisp white pages of his music. There was a slight tremble to his hands.

"Have you?" Selene held the music like it was a precious thing.

"With this line," Benson began. He tapped the first sheet. "And this below it, I can do it. I can do all three at the same time."

"Which will allow you to add the illusion." Selene kept her fingers very still. Turning water into mist was no great feat. Adding an illusion through the water and the mist at the same time was nearly impossible.

But he would do more than that. He'd swallow up the moisture from the air and make water and mist simultaneously, enough to fill the whole house. And while the audience swam in his magical mist, he'd cast a tableau in the sphere of water. He'd tell a story while his beautiful voice would entrap them completely.

Three elements.

"I wouldn't have been able to do this without you. Your piece was brilliant, Selene. It changed the way I thought about music."

Benson had written the perfect piece. Clever and technically challenging with enough fanfare to capture a crowd. Selene wished she had written it.

And yet.

She could sense the danger of it. Could feel the razor-thin distance between brilliance and madness. Mages had lost themselves for smaller songs, stretching their minds beyond their capacity to hold the magic. She'd experienced it, in the moment when the magic grew too big for her and she had to choose between ruin or ruin.

"This is..."

If he did this, he would win. The blood she'd shed would be for nothing. If he did this and didn't go mad in the process.

"Amazing."

He breathed in relief. What had he expected her to say?

"It has to be one of us." Benson's smile was genuine. The sleepless bruises beneath his eyes tucked and folded away. "Whatever happens, I'm glad we were here together."

"Me too."

And it was true, for now.

"You look lovely, by the way." He dropped into a bow.

Selene bowed back. "As do you. What's the occasion?"

"Today is my day."

"You don't know that." Gigi emerged from the wings, already rolling her eyes. She walked with a confidence she had earned. No tutu today. Her dress was a deep fuchsia that cut above the calves and looked like an inverted flower. Selene recognized the design from Gigi's sketchbook. The skirt moved around her strong legs like petals drifting in the breeze. The neckline was modest. The back dropped low beneath her shoulder blades, showing off her dancer's strength.

"My hair is far too amicable today. It's a sign." Benson tousled it to offer proof.

Selene smirked. "Last time your hair looked like this, the practice rooms flooded."

Benson held up a finger. "Not all the practice rooms. Just mine, yours, and Gigi's. If I recall, that kerfuffle is what made us friends."

"We've always been friends," Gigi said.

Benson's laugh was short and sharp. He took Gigi's hand and kissed the palm. "Please. You're my competition. It's actually a shame that I love you so much."

Gigi's eyes went wide. "You love me?"

"I love you."

"You're just saying that because it's a good hair day."

Benson took her in his arms. "I mean it, but I didn't mean to say it. I was going to wait to say it until after auditions."

Gigi folded herself into him, her face against his chest. Selene should have looked away. This was a moment far too intimate. But she wanted to mark this as something beautiful that had come out of this experience. Real love. What Priya and Revelio had was an escape, a self-sabotage. It was nothing like this: light and joy and simple, unabashed truth.

"I love you, too." Gigi tilted her head up.

Selene turned away, letting them have this moment.

Priya and Revelio burst onto the stage, fingers tangled together. They'd made up enough that Revelio had a dark purple mark below his collarbone, but not enough to leave.

The rest of them trailed in, spreading out into the seats of the auditorium. Someone had replaced the seat Selene had struck with lightning with a new chair. It shone too brightly, its colors untouched by time or dust.

Madame took her place in the front row of the auditorium. She waited a few minutes. Fenrir entered, looking annoyed. They exchanged words—short and sharp. Selene wasn't close enough to hear. Madame must have won. She shuffled her cards and pulled the first one out.

Tatiana.

Selene looked at Benson expectantly.

Tatiana was generously curved for her short stature. Her hair hung down in dark waves. Her gown, a rich purple, perfectly complemented her brown skin. She sang something simple and elegant, pouring different colors of sand from glass vials and forming a moving, vertical painting. Tiny bits of sand shimmering in the light. A mother held her child for the first time. Watched the child grow and leave her. The magic in this was not in the motifs, but in the power of Tatiana's voice. Her rich alto was so luscious and heartbreaking, it was more magic than the shifting, colored sands.

She took her bow and moved back to stand with the other singers. Madame raised an eyebrow, the barest hint of a smile on her lips.

Ramin went next, rumbling out an aria with his true bass. He used fire and illusion to construct hell, centering himself as both the punisher and the punished. It was riveting, but far from the melodic expectations for the competition.

Gerard's performance was beautifully sung, but the magic was weak. He couldn't sustain two motifs at the same time. He sang illusion and then wind and then water in a mismatched jumble, as if he'd written the song first and then thought of the magic.

"Just wait," Benson said. "It'll be me next."

And then me, Selene thought. They were almost finished with auditions. She would crash the stage after Benson's performance and make them rethink everything. She would force them to see her as a contender. There was no way they could ignore her.

Selene studied the adjudicators. Madame was implacable, as always. The representative from the palace was missing, which was unusual. Monsieur Fenrir didn't have his notebook or pen or anything useful. He wouldn't stop looking over his shoulder nervously. Like he was afraid. Like he was waiting for the ghost.

The ghost isn't there, Selene thought. *He's beneath your feet.*

Madame cleared her throat and drew a card.

Of course it was Benson. His picture didn't capture the good hair or the rosy glow of new love, but it was clear enough. He winked at her and stood.

Benson stepped up from the other side of the stage. His suit was immaculate. Pressed and tailored to fit. He stood straight and tall as a birch tree. There was a slight tremble to his hands. He clenched them into fists and took one step into the light.

"Pardon," Monsieur Fenrir burst out. His dark hair was pulled back with a white ribbon, making the gray threading from his temple more prominent. His hair had been perfectly black three years ago when he'd taken the management position of the theater. "I have an announcement."

"Can't this wait?" Gigi's eyes didn't leave Benson.

Selene shrugged. "Monsieur Fenrir has never had good timing."

Fenrir swept into the center of the stage. Benson took a step back.

"I am sad." He cleared his throat, wiped the glee off his face. "Sad to announce that this is my last day as part of Opera Magique. I have urgent business to attend to in the countryside."

"He's lying," Gigi whispered.

"Does it matter?" Selene said.

There were scattered gasps and curious looks throughout the auditorium. A few gold pieces caught the light of the ornate chandelier as they exchanged hands. Bets laid and won on the tenure of their manager. Somehow, all that gold ended up in Gigi's pocket. Gambling had come back into fashion since Victor had poured a fortune into all the darkest places of the city. Fenrir didn't seem to notice—or at least, didn't care.

Gigi looked abundantly smug. Selene wouldn't hear the end of this. She had lost, and grimaced thinking of the piles of tutus and old shoes on Gigi's side of the room she'd have to tidy.

"Please welcome Monsieur Avile, your new manager."

"Call me Marcus."

From the darkness of the house, Marcus emerged. He walked with a limp, leaning against a polished wood cane. She recognized him. He'd trained to compete in the last L'Opéra du Magician, seven years ago. He hadn't made it through the auditions. His hands were calloused, and his body was thick with muscle. Whatever life he'd found, it was very different from the one he'd made here.

Some of the girls shifted, adjusting their hair, puffing out their chests. Marcus was handsome. Anyone could see that. But looking at him made Selene long for the ghost's cold blue eyes and the cut of his smile. She didn't want handsome; she wanted unearthly beauty that made her question her very existence. She wished she could have him here, outside of the mirror. She wished he could see her on this stage. His freedom was another riddle to be solved. She could not bleed or sing him out. This was not a matter of wanting; the magic of the mirror was something beyond her understanding. She didn't even know if it was the same magic. The thought unsettled and thrilled her. The possibilities were endless. And that was the problem. She needed time, which was something she did not have.

"Thank you, thank you. All of you." Marcus gestured widely. "I am so pleased to be part of this momentous event. I cannot wait to see the talent you possess. Monsieur Fenrir has told me marvelous things."

Monsieur Fenrir had stepped aside, fading into the back of the auditorium. Selene could practically hear the slap of his shoes on the marble as he ran from the theater. Already gone.

Marcus centered himself behind his cane. He looked so collected, so different from Monsieur Fenrir. Still, he searched the mezzanine of the theater like it was haunted and he was waiting to catch sight of the famous ghost in the opera house.

"My first act as manager is to introduce you to our new patron: His Royal Highness, Victor Chastain."

A ghost indeed.

CHAPTER 16

Selene forgot to breathe. She forgot what breath was. She forgot everything about who she was or what she wanted or what she was trying to do.

Victor was here.

He emerged from the sea of blue velvet and gold gilt like a thief with the key. The buttons on his military jacket were misaligned and his hair was windswept and wild, the chestnut brown bleached copper and gold by the sun. There was a scar on his cheek that hadn't been there when Selene had known him. His tea-dark eyes were bright in the stage lights. He brought his hands together, joining in his own applause.

Not the boy she remembered; not a boy at all. Victor was a man.

The glow of the chandelier's candles reflected in his dark eyes. The ground beneath her feet shifted. It was like coming home: not to the palace, not to the opera house, but to the little house above the shore where she'd been close to a dream. It was like the golden light on the water at the end of the day.

Victor moved with the grace of a man born into wealth, like a cat with his claws out. She remembered the way his brow arched up, independent of the other. His jawline hadn't been so strong then. Nor had he been quite so tall. So much of him had changed. But she'd know him, even in the dark.

His deep brown eyes swept the row of performers. He was here, but not for her.

"Hello, gorgeous," Gigi whispered. "Like something out of a painting."

"He's grown up well," Selene said begrudgingly. She traced his uneven gait, the place he'd missed shaving below his jaw, the trail of mud he left on her pristine stage. Looking for flaws, hoping for flaws. "But it's been ages."

Damn him.

Careless, reckless, insouciant boy. The devil might care, but Selene could not. She begged her heart to stop racing. Willed the bird or bat or whatever foolish creature fluttered inside her stomach to die.

Victor Chastain had always had that effect on Selene. When they were children, he only had to smile and wink, and she'd follow him into trouble. Staining the queen's dresses with burst pomegranates, filling the sugar bowls with beach sand, releasing all the horses to see how fast they'd run. Selene lost a bit of herself when she was with him, swept up in his charm and easy smile. He'd been the bane of her existence and the balm of her soul. Her first real friend.

And the only person here who knew what happened to her father.

Selene tempered her expectations. "I'm sure he does not remember."

Gigi's eyes slimmed to slits. "No one forgets you."

"Sorry to interrupt," Victor said in that easy voice. How many cakes had she stolen from the kitchens at his bidding? "I am thrilled to be a part of this great competition."

Madame Giroux arched an eyebrow. Selene could practically hear her thoughts. She allowed the manager his short-lived glory—as long as he didn't interfere with her performers. There was something about Victor—his coat askew, his dark eyes twinkling in the low lights, the confidence in his broad shoulders and the swagger in his step—that betrayed him. He would not leave anyone in peace.

But who could say no to a prince?

Even the third son, boots laced in scandal and coat buttoned with debauchery. He'd only been back a few weeks and his name was a staple in the papers. Selene tried not to look. But she had seen it, alongside hers and the other performers.

"Welcome." Madame Giroux bowed her head, not low enough for his station. Victor didn't seem to mind. If anything, he seemed intrigued. "Shall we continue with our auditions?"

"Please." Victor flourished with his wrist. He moved down the stairs, disappearing into the sea of seats.

Monsieur Avile followed Victor like a shadow.

Focus, Selene thought. *A heart that does not bleed.*

A heart that does not bleed.

A heart.

Benson was already at the center of the stage. The tremble had left him. This was his space. He discarded all pretense for the sake of his art. Practice made perfection.

The music began. Benson was a mellow baritone, voice lilting and lyrical and easy to get lost in. He started with water:

summoning it from the air with the familiar motif. It formed a shining ball in his hands—reflecting the fire of the stage light. His hands were steady and still. All focus and perfect concentration. He was going to turn the water to mist, weaving illusion into the water and the rolling clouds of gray.

It was in his eyes, the way they reflected the flicker of the stage lights. The confidence near mania. He wasn't going to just fill the stage.

It rolled down into the pit and beyond, forming around the chairs. It was beautiful. But there was something else to it. More than art. It struck Selene that this could be used to conceal ships at sea or secret lovers or soldiers preparing for ambush. It wasn't just the scuffed military buttons in her purview. Selene had pondered this before: the fine line between art and war.

Victor leaned forward. Selene could see that look in his eyes, the mischief and fascination. It was the same way he used to look at an unreachable pomegranate after summer had turned into fall. Somehow, his fingers always ended up stained with it.

Benson's voice surged, summoning more water. It sapped from the air, from the floor, from Selene's skin. The ball of water expanded. The story inside grew bigger. It was the story of a tailor and the dancer he made tutus for, falling in love stitch by stitch. This sort of thing pleased a crowd. It was exactly like her father had done, turning the song into a story. Behind it, she could see his reflection in the shimmering water. She knew he could see when it started to go wrong, too, because something in his expression shifted.

Selene formed her fingers into claws. The skin above her

clavicle—which had healed into thin, pretty scars—ached and itched. Memories and nightmares summoned like water unto mist, unbidden by song or chant.

The music stopped.

The magic did not.

Benson's mouth moved without sound. His body twitched and jerked. The ball of water expanded. Edges faded into mist. Growing and growing until it *was* the stage. The lights hissed out, steam swallowed up by the great ball of water. The orchestra fled, protecting their precious instruments. The mist swallowed Selene. The water drenched her outstretched hands. Reaching like she might stop it.

There would be no stopping it. She knew, like she knew the frantic rhythm of her heart. Like she knew the burning of her lungs from the wall of water. Like she knew the moment it was finished.

The bubble popped. Water sprayed all over the stage and auditorium, drenching the curtains, the musicians, the seats.

Shouts of joy, of rage, of relief.

And then a mournful keening. The sound was its own magic, spraying sorrow over the stage with more force than even the water had carried.

Not this, she thought.

Selene ran to him.

Gigi was there, caught up in the arms of her mother, fighting to get to him. Madame Giroux held Gigi in a vise grip. She knew how dangerous it was when a mage lost their mind.

Selene didn't care.

Benson was curled on the stage, head in his hands. His whole body shook with a violence Selene expected but that made her sick to witness. She dropped down beside him, nearly slipping on the slick stage. It was all dark around them, the few remaining candles casting strange shadows over his face. One by one, her competitors sang for light. It rose from the theater like a moon, growing brighter as they stood at the edge of the stage—pure and beaming, untethered by fire. It would have been beautiful, had it been close enough to reach her. But they kept their distance. They knew enough to do that.

Selene focused on Benson's hands. They were pressed to whiteness on the dark wood.

"I'm here." She brushed her fingers over his. Gently, gently, like touching a feral, wounded animal. He flinched at her touch, then relaxed into it. He rested his face against her knees.

"Careful," Madame Giroux said.

Like she needed to tell Selene. Like Selene didn't already know. Madame stood a few feet away, arm held up. Protection for the other students. Protection for herself.

"Benson," Selene whispered.

He pushed himself up slowly; it was a good sign. If he knew his name, there was hope. There was a possibility. He could come back from this.

Then she saw his eyes.

They were frantic and wild. The warmth was gone. His pupils were blown wide. Endless, black, haunted caverns. Music echoed from the bottomless dark. His lip was split. Blood dripped down his chin.

All the hope emptied from her, the way all of Benson had emptied from his eyes. He was gone. She knew. She knew it in the way he wrenched back. In the way his fingers danced across the puddles on the stage with a frenetic energy. In the way his lips curled, showing all his teeth.

He snarled, winding back like a spring.

Somewhere, someone screamed.

Benson lunged.

Selene shouldn't have done it. This was her secret, the weapon she needed to win. But it was Benson, and she didn't want to see him hurt. Didn't want him to be shot down like a rabid animal. Didn't want to be the one to have to do it.

She could grow vines around him, like a rabbit in a trap. It would be as easy as breathing. If only she had a seed.

You don't need one. You have so much more.

All it took was a drop of blood, emptied of everything except the pain of this moment, of moments passed. But that wasn't enough. She was, after all, a performer. And she needed to protect the magie du sang and all her secrets. How quickly she strung together the notes, the words forming on her tongue without hesitation.

The thorns twisted up and around Benson. Sinuous vines thick enough to trap his hands and torso, then his legs. He thrashed, quickly realizing that stillness held the least amount of pain. Selene was careful; the thorns only pierced him when he moved. She constructed this prison to do the least harm.

His head dropped. The keening returned. Subdued, but not Benson. Not that bright, ambitious boy. Her friend. Her competitor. No. Before her stood a wild and broken man. Cracked wide. Defeated by the madness of magic. Consumed.

Selene took a step back. Her breath was even. Her heartbeat—though steady—pulsed an ache through her body that she could not contain. She should have done more. She should have stopped him. Would he have listened? At least she could have said she tried. She spun around, looking for relief from the shadows. She struck something. Someone. She looked up.

Victor.

Victor with his tea-dark eyes and broad shoulders and clever fingers. He gripped her shoulders, looking past her to the thorns. She knew that hunger. It was the same way she looked at new music. The same way she tracked the progress of her friends. The same way she looked in the mirror.

"You are dismissed," Madame Giroux said curtly to the gathered crowd.

There was a murmur. Hesitation. Madame Giroux slammed her cane into the stage. The others scattered like frightened doves. Her eyes didn't leave Selene, appraising her like she knew what Selene had done. It wasn't possible, was it?

Selene pulled back. She couldn't stand the tightness of Victor's grip. The warmth of his hands. The taste of his breath as it mingled with hers. Salt and pomegranates and a hint of champagne. She should have known. Victor didn't move. He held her there, captured like Benson was captured.

She whipped her head around. The movement caught him off guard. At last, he stepped back, looking at her for the first time.

"How did you do that?" There was no recognition in his eyes. "Did you know you'd need the seeds?"

She couldn't answer him, not without lies. She had no problem weaving half-truths or falsehoods, or even staying silent. But she didn't think she could lie, not to him. He'd seen her broken and bleeding, everything she'd loved stripped away. Even though he didn't seem to remember. She couldn't bring herself to smile and piece together a lie.

Selene dipped into a quick curtsy, ignoring the blood and water that stained her skirts. The cerulean dress was ruined. "Pardon, Your Highness."

Selene moved like an arrow, cutting through the crowd. Victor wasn't the only one asking those questions. They swarmed around her like bees.

She would not blink. She would not turn her head. She would not acknowledge them in any way. If she did, there'd be more questions than answers. She slipped her hands into her pockets, rolling her fingers together, feeling the ache of the cut she'd made with the pin. It had only taken one drop. The wound was already healing into a thin line that no one would notice.

Let them believe what they wanted.

CHAPTER 17

Selene did not cry. Not when they cut the thorns off Benson's wrists and replaced them with cold iron. Not when they dragged him off the stage, down the expansive grand foyer, and out the front doors. The carriage had bars on the window. She was sure the Asylum would have more of the same.

She held Gigi, anchoring her in the storm of her grief. There was nothing she could say to make it better, no magic she could sing to stop time and bring him back. The devastation of his loss was too deep a cut to be offered something as useless as words. But she could be here. That was enough.

Selene had been dragged away in a carriage once and taken to the opera house. At the time, she had felt smothered by the beautiful marble floors and immaculately carved columns that stretched up and up. She had wanted the room to be ugly. She'd wanted it to be as terrible as she felt inside.

Even now, the beauty of this room seemed at odds with the monstrosity of grief. Each of the entryways in the grand foyer opened into balconies that looked out, little stages of their own. There were gold figures throughout with glossy eyes and hands so real they could have reached out and touched her.

Selene pressed her hands over her eyes. The marble stairs

were cold beneath her. She couldn't worry about the ghosts of her childhood. Not when everything had gone so wrong.

"This feels like a dream." Gigi shuddered involuntarily with the aftershock of her sobs.

"A nightmare."

Just outside the grand doors, carriages rolled by. Women walked with their cloaks drawn tight. Men gripped their cravats. Concerned about the wind and upcoming winter, with no thought to the tragedy that had occurred mere meters away. It would hit the papers by morning. Just a line, so that those making and taking bets could strike Benson's name from their rosters.

She thought of Benson's blown pupils. The curve of his hands. The way he'd looked at her when he'd lunged.

Someone had brought them mugs of hot chocolate. Gigi's eyes were red and swollen. They'd been through the best together, and now the worst. Selene wrapped her arm tighter around Gigi. It was only the two of them now, huddled on the magnificent stairs of the grand foyer. Everyone else had gone back to their practice rooms or dorms.

"Did you know?" Gigi asked.

"Know what?" Selene took a drink and set the cup beside her. She willed her hands not to shake.

"What Benson was going to do."

Selene waited a beat too long, and that was enough for Gigi. Instead of fury, she was met with sorrow.

"Promise me you won't push yourself that far. I can't lose you, too."

Promises, promises, strung up like pearls. Meant to be

broken. When they were younger, they'd promised not to keep secrets. Not just Selene and Gigi, but all the King's Mage hopefuls. There'd been so many of them then. Rows and rows of narrow beds in the cramped lower dormitories. Slowly, and then ever so quick, the beds disappeared. Students who didn't make the cut. Students who got hurt. Students who couldn't take the rigor of living and breathing and dreaming music and magic.

"What do you think it's like at the Asylum?" Gigi spun her cup between her fingers.

Selene suppressed a shiver. She'd heard terrible things. It housed mad mages from all over Mondreves, on the outskirts of the city. It was white and cold and empty. A place to store the refuse of magic. And instead of going home to see his family, instead of finding a position worthy of his talent, Benson was going there to rot.

She should have killed him and called it mercy.

"They'll take good care of him." Selene rubbed circles on Gigi's back. "He'll have a safe place with people who know what to do and how to help him."

Gigi took a deep breath. Tears caught in her lashes. "Do you think he'll ever come back to himself?"

Selene wiped away one of the tears with her thumb. "I wish I could say."

"I know magic has its limits. But what if we could sing him whole?"

It was a flight of fancy, a dream without mooring. Selene had imagined it more than she'd ever admit. She'd conjured up a world in which she'd struck her father with a cure instead of lightning. Enough to bring him back. But it was all fantasy.

Better magicians had tried over the last hundred years. The madness was absolute.

Or so they'd been told.

Selene wondered how much blood it would take to restore Benson. What kind of pain she'd have to relinquish to dispel the madness. Selene took a deep breath, elated and terrified by the possibilities.

"Maybe."

Selene looked up, catching the dregs of sunlight as they passed through the windows. They glistened on the edge of a gilt frame. She'd passed it a thousand times. She'd never looked at it, not really. It was part of the background. Another beautiful thing in this beautiful place.

It was a painting of Prince Renard, standing in the space that would become the Opera Magique. He had a jewel-encrusted shovel thrust into the earth. His teeth had been painted without a sheen, so it must have been when he was young, before they'd been replaced with pearls. The king had his hand on Renard's shoulder. Adrik, the famed mage and theorist, stood to his right. The rest were inconsequential. Faces forgotten to time.

Except for one.

A boy with dark hair and a sharp jawline and eyes so blue that the artist had taken the time to thin out the paint he'd used for the sky.

She knew that face. That stance. The way his lips tilted up into half a smile. Daring her.

Selene stood up.

"What is it?"

"That painting." Selene pointed. "I never noticed it before."

"That's when they broke ground on the opera house."

"Do you know who that boy is, the one with the bluest eyes?"

Gigi shook her head. "All I know is that the Opera Magique was a gift to the prince. Can you imagine? No trinkets or books or colored paper, but a whole opera house."

Victor would have been grateful for trinkets or colored paper, she thought.

But how could she say that? It wasn't her sorrow to share. It wasn't her pain. She wondered what magic Victor could conjure from his gilded neglect, all that abuse wrapped in pretty packaging. She'd seen the bruises, tended the wounds. More secrets, more parts of her she didn't know how to share. She looked down at Gigi, huddled on the stairs, the cooling cup of hot chocolate in her hands. Selene could do with one less secret.

"When my father went mad, it felt like the end of the world." Selene sat down beside Gigi. "It feels like this. And I'm sorry we're both here. I wish none of this had happened."

"You don't talk about him. Or any of your life before."

"What happened with my father—it's all tangled up. Victor, the palace, the king. It's hard to unravel part without unraveling the whole."

Victor had pressed his fingers against her skin. He had looked into her eyes. Spoken to her. And he had not known her. She was a stranger to him, and she supposed he was a stranger to her, too. He was no longer the boy who'd known how to make her laugh and fill the hours with mischief. No longer the boy who'd been her escape from her worries about her father, a refuge in the complicated world of palace life. He'd been everything to Selene, once.

And now, he was nothing.

The rhythm of Madame's cane sent Selene's heart racing. Gigi pulled away from her, smoothing her hair. Posture perfect. Eyes bright with hope.

"Girls," Madame Giroux said. There was a weariness to her that Selene had seldom seen. This was her loss, too. "It's time to prepare for the Unmasking Ball."

"Oh."

Anguish washed through Selene. She hadn't taken the stage by storm, as she'd planned. If anything, her capture of Benson hurt her chances. That was magic used beyond the scope of art. What little hope remained came at the cost of her friend.

"I can't." Gigi pressed her hands to her face. "I don't think I can do this."

"You must." Madame's voice was fierce, almost violent. "You all know the risks. I taught each of you."

There was a moment of deep despair in Madame Giroux's face, before the curtains closed and she seemed like stone.

"Come on." Gigi fought a losing battle against her tears.

"First." Madame put her hand on Selene's shoulder. "A lesson."

CHAPTER 18

Selene tried to keep the startled expression from her face. "Yes, Madame."

"You'll have time enough to get ready."

Gigi cast a long, lingering glance at the two of them before disappearing with the empty cups of hot chocolate.

Selene followed Madame to her office. They'd stopped their regular lessons in the last few months, allowing Selene to focus on her aria. Madame could not help her write her performance piece. It was all up to Selene.

She stood beside the piano. Back straight, heart pounding in her chest. Madame struck a chord.

"Sing through E."

She nodded and began, moving up the scale, and then chromatically through the next key. E was a tricky vowel. It was unforgiving, revealing every weakness and break in the voice. They worked up, up, up to the G above high C, and then came back down.

"Messe di voce."

Selene matched the note played on the piano. She crescendoed and decrescendoed on that same pitch. Moving up the notes of the scale and back down.

Simple, easy warmups she did almost every day to wake up

her voice. Would she miss this, the way she missed her days at the palace? It was bittersweet. She loved music; she loved the push to greatness and the endless possibilities in between the notes. She would not miss feeling like her life was about to start and she was doing it all without her father.

She wished she could talk to him, wished she could ask him why he'd pushed himself so far. He already had everything. The title of the King's Mage and a second tenure, a daughter, a life. What could have pushed him to the edge? Selene could answer that for Benson, but she didn't have answers from her own father.

Her eyes caught on a tiny brown speck, marring the black lacquer of the piano.

A seed.

A few hours before, she'd gone without one. She'd made a seed out of blood and sorrow. But magicians needed more than that. They carried seeds and sang them into trees and flowers and other beautiful things. Her father had often marveled over the whole of creation captured in the tiny hull. A seed was a whole world. It contained everything it needed to live.

A seed was a heart and a whole and it did not bleed. That was all she needed. She could go back in the mirror and offer the ghost a seed.

Selene reached down between arpeggios. She wasn't sure what compelled her to take it. She could offer him one that she made, a drop of blood and the truth of this moment. It would be her heart, then.

But the seed was waiting there, like a mirror in a place that should not be. Like it had been put there for her. Selene stopped singing. She looked up at Madame. "Do you know what my father was trying to achieve before he died?"

Madame stopped playing for a beat. She continued on to the next chord. "I've been waiting for you to ask me that question for a long time."

"Do you know?"

"Nothing is as simple as that."

Madame kept playing. Moving away from scales and into a D minor sonata.

"When a king asks something of you, it is nearly impossible to say no. He has asked a great deal of my predecessors. To train up young magicians and present them like lambs to the slaughter."

"I don't understand."

Madame's fingers drifted over the keys. "Whatever it was, the king still hasn't found it. Every mage since your father has lived but has given up magic entirely since their tenure as the King's Mage. They won't tell me what happened and perhaps that is for the best."

"Why are you still doing this, then?" The words tumbled from her affannato. "Why bring the lambs to inevitable slaughter?"

"Sometimes young girls make foolish promises." Madame's mouth flattened into a thin line.

"And what of your promise to us? As our teacher, as our protector. Where was that promise when Benson was going mad?"

"There is one every year." Madame picked her words carefully, like she was sharing a secret.

Selene counted the students she'd seen go mad. There were a few, but certainly not one a year. "Who?"

"You think you are the only mages in the kingdom? The Asylum fills with or without the Opera Magique. I do all I can to keep you safe. But these things do happen."

Selene pondered that, her eyes drifting to a small portrait on the desk. She hadn't seen it before. It could have been Gigi, but it wasn't. A young Madame Giroux standing in the grand foyer with a look of light and wonder on her face. It was before the cane, before the years had carved a darkness into her face. Selene knew she'd been here, the cycle before her father. She was both singer and ballerina, blending the crafts much like Gigi. But she hadn't competed in L'Opéra du Magician. Selene and Gigi had often wondered about what happened—settling on an injury. Madame caught her looking and quickly turned the picture over.

"If it were just me, I'd leave."

"Gigi would go wherever you go." The finality of the moment made Selene brave. "She wants your approval. Your love."

Madame struck the wrong note. "Soon, this will all be over."

The words rang through the room eerily.

"What do you mean?" Selene said.

"You're asking the wrong questions, Selene." Madame struck a chord with her left hand, the piano rumbling with music. "Haven't you figured it out by now?"

Selene's heart raced. Did Madame know about the ghost?

Madame shook her head, straightening at the piano. "There will come a time when all is brought to light. Until then, I am bound to my silence by our sovereign."

"Who can say no to the king?" Selene said softly.

Her father certainly hadn't. Selene had never considered that Madame's role in their lives might be a burden, that she might not want this. It didn't change anything for Selene. She couldn't simply shift her goals, this close to the end. Could she? Madame played a few more arpeggios. Selene sang with her. She put her hand into her pocket, brushing her fingers against the seed. There was magic in it, she could feel it.

"Sing the aria."

Madame played a chord, and then another. Selene tried to hold the notes in her head. But they kept slipping away. This wasn't the song she'd auditioned with. This was the aria she had written for her father.

"You're like a daughter to me, Selene."

Madame knew.

She knew that Revelio had performed her piece, like she knew that Selene had pushed herself to the edge with a song that was never meant to be sung.

And that wasn't the worst of it. Selene knew she was good. And that wasn't a trip of ego or delusion. It was a fact. Selene Dreshé was born on a clear, cloudless night and she was good at magic. She knew what she was capable of, and it was so much more than this.

Devastation burned beneath Selene's skin like the magie du sang. All this potential and talent left to rot, like a ripe plum burst against the earth. She didn't know how to make herself known. She didn't know how to be more. But then, what if that wasn't enough? What if she was never enough?

Selene steadied herself on the music stand. She wished the edges had been sharp enough to cut away the terrible ache in her fingers and toes and head. It wasn't enough to be good. It wasn't enough to be great. She needed to be ruthless.

Some stars burn bright, some stars burn out.

The violence of a light so powerful, it shone from millions of miles away. A fire so hot, it created its own mass, own gravity. She needed to be a force of nature. A star, a star, a star. And if she went out, she'd take them all with her.

She sharpened her words into points.

"You know I am the best mage here."

Selene waited for admonishment. She'd spoken out of turn.

"I want what is best for you, Selene." Madame kept playing. "That pretty little prince of yours would take you away from here. You could have a life outside of this opera house."

"I don't want another life." Selene could scream, but she wouldn't. "He doesn't even remember me."

"Make him remember."

Selene drew in a breath. Victor didn't matter to her. She had moved on. But the ghost? She could help him remember. Then she could fulfill her promise and get him out.

Resolve burned through her. "Stay out of my way."

Madame faltered on the note and recovered quickly. She did not speak. Selene's rage moved from a boil to a simmer. She counted the measures, tapped the rhythms on the inside of her palm. The magie du sang bubbled beneath her skin. It rushed with her blood, pulsing and pulling to be let out. She wanted to. She longed to prick her fingers and build a dragon out of shadow and wanting. Big enough that she could climb on its back and fly away—straight to the palace where she belonged. Madame worked her way through the last movement of Selene's aria. She leaned into the end, closing her eyes and letting those final notes resonate.

"There is a bird," Madame said. "That lays an egg so beautiful that it is sought out, hollowed, and displayed. It is treasure to kings and emperors."

Selene knew of this. She had seen the eggs lined up in the palace. That same bird was engraved on her father's pocket watch. "The silver-breasted nightingale."

"Only a few remain. The shell is beautiful. But unless it breaks, you have nothing but a pretty, empty thing."

"Am I the bird or the broken shell?"

"That is all for today." Madame looked up from the piano. "Go prepare for your ball."

CHAPTER 19

Selene flew down the stairs, crossing the lake with urgency. The water seemed to know, churning and bubbling to the same cadence as her stretto heart. She stood in front of the mirror and took the seed from her pocket. The outside was ridged. She brought it to her mouth, feeling each of the contours against the softness of her lips, like a kiss. It had to be enough. She needed this one thing to feel like a victory. Just one good thing.

She couldn't save Benson and she couldn't heal Gigi and she couldn't steal back the time she'd spent believing Madame Giroux was on her side. But she could watch the blood well; she could press her thumb against the glass of the mirror. The red soaked in. Selene quieted her heartbeat until it was barely more than a whisper, slowed her breathing adagissimo.

With her heart nothing more than the echo of an echo, the mirror gave way. She pushed through the cold, silvery film into the dark.

The light shocked her. There were great wings of golden feathers stretching above her. Like angels had descended to scare away the dark. Each of the feathers was perfectly articulated, the rachis bright white and the veins a softer light.

The ghost stood at their center, bathed in golden light. He'd rolled up his sleeves so they tightened around his thick, corded biceps. She wished she was a different kind of artist and could render this image permanent in paint on canvas, capture this unearthly beauty and show the whole world its wonders. His cold blue eyes met hers.

"Welcome back, Selene." He banished the wings, replacing them with spinning orbs.

"Joseph? Ambrose?"

"No," he said.

"Martin."

"What have you brought me?"

Selene reached into her pocket. The darkness seemed to lean in, eager for her spoils. She dropped the seed into his open palm. "A seed is a heart that does not bleed. It is the center. It is the whole."

The ghost's eyes lit up with surprise. He held the seed up, examining all its edges. He brought it to his lips, just as she had. Then he tossed it into the air. The darkness shot out, struck like a serpent. The heart was there, and then gone.

"This I have asked and you have answered."

Selene's eyes filled with tears. This seed, the smallest thing, had worked. She wished all her troubles were so easily answered. She wished a seed was all she needed for those, too.

The ghost's brow furrowed in confusion. She wanted him to ask her what was wrong. She wanted to say it, and then have him tell her everything would be okay. That Benson wasn't her fault. That there were good things left in this world. But she knew what his next words would be.

"What is it you want?"

Selene breathed out slowly. There were so many things she wanted. But only one she knew she could fight for. "To win."

"This I have asked and you have answered." He took a moment, worrying the scars on his bicep with the tips of his fingers. "Are you all right?"

Selene was not. She might never be again. And yet she couldn't stop, she couldn't take the time to grieve. "Is that one of your questions?"

"You matter to me, Selene. Every time you leave, I hope for your sake you don't come back." His eyes were endless pools of woe, like all his promises were meant for breaking.

"I want to be here."

"That's the trouble."

"My friend." Her tongue stuck on the word. She wasn't talking about Victor. She wasn't thinking about him. He wasn't her friend. He didn't even remember her. This was about Benson. "Today, he—" Selene tried to fit the right words together. He wasn't dead. He was here, but not. Hollowed out. Gone. "He was too ambitious and paid the price."

The ghost tilted his head, like he was trying to remember what that might mean. Something settled in his eyes and he exhaled slowly. Selene could feel the warmth of his breath on her skin, even at this distance. It rippled over her and made her shiver.

"Use the pain."

Selene closed her eyes. She was running out of time. She sang for water, like Benson had. Let it slide into mist, tableaux of what had happened projected all around them, bought with blood instead of madness.

When she couldn't stand to look at it anymore, she sang it all into ice. The images shattered against the ground.

The ghost picked up the end of her melody and matched her, grief for grief. He knew the depth of her mourning. She wished she could share his burden, like he shared hers. But he was all scars. His voice was warm and deep, musical to its core. He could have sung off the face of the moon if he wanted to, like her father. She joined him, their voices twining. The music was stronger when they were together. They sang flames without heat, casting light into all the dark spaces. Everything was bright and burning and blood and song.

She wished she could bottle this feeling and take it with her everywhere. She wished she knew how to get him out of the mirror and take him, too. He would take the world by storm with the power of his voice and the cold fire of his eyes.

"What happens now?" He bled a tiny horse that pranced around her. "Did you give them your storm?"

"No." Selene reached for the horse. It yielded to her touch, the illusion bending around her. "The decisions have been made for L'Opéra du Magician."

The ghost's cold eyes glistened. "Is it you?"

"I find out tonight." Selene should be upstairs putting on her dress and laughing away the nerves and sharing this moment with Gigi. But she wasn't sure there was any laughter left between them. "In a few hours."

"Then you should go."

"What if I can't come back?"

"I'll know you've stepped into your dream."

"I had to see you, to see if there was something more I could do." Selene worried her lower lip. "I don't know how to save you. I need more time."

"Isn't time a fickle thing? I've had a hundred years and all you need is one more day." The ghost's voice was rich with understanding. "I will not hold you to your promises."

There was something about the way he said it, as if this had all happened before. As if hapless girls had wandered into his prison for a blink and were then gone as quickly as they'd come. A shiver of jealousy surged through her. She didn't want to be one of many. She wanted to be the one. She shook her head, hard enough that she lost purchase for a second and had to breathe in slowly.

"I saw you," she said. "There's a painting in the opera house, the day they broke ground. You were there."

The ghost's face cracked into a smile. "Prince Renard had that ridiculous golden shovel. It bent as he pushed it into the earth."

"You remember!"

"I remember a little more, every time I see you."

Selene's heart beat vivace. Could this be enough to get him out? "What were you doing there? Were you part of his retinue?"

"No. I was there, but I was not. Something in between." He smiled. "A ghost then and a ghost now. I've always had a talent for slipping between the cracks."

Selene was close to something. She was asking the wrong questions.

"How do I unravel the magic that binds you?"

Something rippled in his eyes—not quite a memory. He opened his mouth.

"You must—"

Shadows shot like arrows from the churning dark and wrapped around his mouth. He fought against them, but something terrible happened with each brush of them against his skin. His pupils dilated all the way dark and then moved back to that pale blue. They were taking parts of him. Stripping away his hard-earned memories. Taking everything he had left.

Selene sang the light. She brought it all around him, her voice near enough to a scream that she felt that burn of pain. The shadows shuddered and faded into the beam.

The ghost fell to one knee, his chest heaving.

"I'm sorry." She fell beside him, leaving more space between them than she wanted. "I'm so sorry."

He looked up at her with vacant, searching eyes, his remarkable beauty matched with a hollowness. He could have been carved from stone in that moment, a monument to some long ago with no remnant of today. Beauty for the sake of beauty, but nothing else. Selene was gutted. He'd forgotten her, after all. He'd lost her to the dark. A tear cut like a knife down her cheek; she didn't bother to wipe it away. This was her fault. She couldn't lose him, too.

"Selene?" Recognition lit in his eyes.

Her heart lost its tempo, erratic and unsure and far too hopeful.

She moved as close to him as she could allow. "I didn't mean—"

He pressed his hands into his forehead. "It isn't your fault."

"I don't want to hurt you."

"Pain is inevitable."

"What did it take from you?" Selene was afraid of the answer.

"Everything." His voice was quiet. "Except you."

I could never forget you, Selene.

He pushed himself to standing. Selene was still on the ground looking up at him. A statue, indeed. His chest rose and fell raggedly. Selene wished she could hold him, wanted to brush the dark strand of hair that fell onto his brow, damp with sweat and something darker. Wanted to trace memories into his skin with her fingertips. She wanted to protect him from the shadows that kept him prisoner in an impossible, living cage.

"You can't save everyone." The ghost seemed to sense the weight on her shoulders, the guilt and grief all bound up in her body.

He summoned a violin out of shadow and held up the instrument. He coaxed sound from the strings, even though they were merely wisps of smoke. "When a violin is played too hard and it breaks, is it the fault of the bow, the bout, or the hand that played?"

"I'm not sure what you're asking."

"Who killed your father?"

Oh, that question. That knife between her ribs. She'd hoped it would get easier to answer. But it was the same pain every time. Worse, even, with time to fester.

"I did," Selene said.

"This I have asked and you have answered."

The ghost looked apologetic. She took a deep breath, searching for something she could ask him that wouldn't drive the dark to him.

"What happened when a mage lost themselves to magic before?"

"I don't know." He closed his eyes, as if trying to pull the memory from the darkness.

"You don't remember?"

His eyes opened, bright as a winter sky. "It never happened."

"How can you be sure?"

"There's no gap there. With some things, I just know. Like the sky is blue and there's salt in the sea. I've seen a magician spent of their power. I remember a bone-deep exhaustion and days of sleep and ravenous hunger. But I don't remember why I did the magic, or for whom. It's like knowing the names of things but not the faces."

It made sense why he wouldn't remember the Asylum. It had been built after he'd been locked away. And perhaps L'Opéra du Magician and time had pushed mages to their edges. Tried to make them better. Opened them further to the magic.

It was an easy explanation.

Too easy.

Like the books in the library. None of them were older than she was. There were new editions each year to be studied when it came to music and magic. Selene had always assumed that was a mark of innovation. But what if it was more sinister? What if the very nature of magic was being wrought from them? In all her years of studying magic, Selene was sure of how magic happened. It was music, and nothing else. She had never questioned if there might be anything more.

But there was.

She had been lied to.

What had Madame meant about bringing lambs to the slaughter?

Selene didn't have time to worry about any of that. She could feel the press of the darkness, knew that the ghost's request was coming. He could feel it, too, she was sure.

"What happens if it's not me?"

His smile was half in shadow. "I thought you were relentless, Selene. Making doors out of nothing and finding your way into mirrors."

The words held weight and resonance.

"Were there libraries, a hundred years ago?"

He laughed. "We had the greatest library in the world, just north of the city."

"There's nothing there now, save the Asylum."

"That's—" His eyes went dark—just for a moment. He focused on her, the intensity in his gaze growing. "Find me a song that sings itself."

Selene pressed the pin into her skin, not ready to leave but too afraid of the consequences to stay. "Wish me luck?"

"You won't need it," he said.

She lost gravity, slipping out of his stasis and into the cold dark below the opera house. She thought she heard the echo of his voice from the glass. A word, a whisper.

Luck.

Real or not, Selene would wear it like armor. She'd let the sound of his voice bring the strength to face what came next.

CHAPTER 20

Selene dusted a dark, shimmering powder over her eyes, longing for the presence of a ghost on this momentous evening. She could use some of his darkness with her, a reminder of all the secrets magic still held.

Gigi helped her wrangle her curls back in an elaborate knot at the nape of her neck so that they didn't distract from the mask and dress. Selene had never understood the point of the masks. Their identities weren't a secret. The nobility was notorious for using the ball to solidify an agreement with one of the mages for their house—with the understanding that no contract held above the king.

Still, Selene couldn't help but love the way the lace mask made her feel. It was another layer of performance, pageantry for the sake of pageantry. The masks were made by a palace-appointed artisan. Selene was pleasantly surprised by the craftsmanship, the delicate turn of the lace, intricate as a song. She'd chosen black even before she knew of the shadows. Now she hoped that she could emulate the ghost from that first time—when he was both man and monster. She painted her lips a dark, claret red.

"What did Madame want?" Gigi dusted a finely milled shimmering powder over Selene's cheekbones. "You were gone a long time."

"A voice lesson," Selene said hollowly. She tried to make sense of what Madame had said and whatever promise she had made, what it meant for the coterie of magicians she raised up from children. Selene wasn't sure it mattered. The tangle of truth and lies was obsolete. What was Selene missing? Was it too late to find it? "You were right. She had something to do with my music."

Gigi dropped the glittery brush onto her dresser. "And she just came out and said it?"

"She played my song." Selene took off her dress.

Gigi rushed to the closet to pull out their gowns. "I don't understand why she would do this now, and to you."

"She said she trained us up like lambs to the slaughter." Selene's voice was low, still unsure what it meant.

"If there's something she's trying to avoid, something she's trying to keep me from…" Something passed over Gigi's face. "I wish she would talk to me, to us."

Selene thought of the dark holding the ghost's memories hostage. "Maybe she can't. Maybe there's something keeping her silent."

"I'm her daughter." Gigi's anger seemed intertwined with the grief of the day, with the grief of a lifetime. "You'd think that would matter."

Gigi closed her glittering eyelids for a moment. Selene had seen this before—Gigi was bottling up the ache and heartbreak and putting it into a safe place inside, where it would still exist, but it would no longer hurt her. Selene wished she could tell her about the magic in it. That her wounds could be made into wishes. That her broken heart could remake all the magic in the world.

Gigi's shoulders rose and fell with the sharpness of her breath. "Benson would want us to go and live this for him."

Selene put her hand on Gigi's shoulder. "It's all right if you need to grieve."

Gigi's eyes shimmered for a moment before she blinked back the tears. "I'm moving forward because of him. Because it's what he would have wanted for me."

"Okay." Selene sighed and put on the dress.

It was a masterpiece. Not the original yellow gown, meant to shine like a dragon's treasure, with a wide full skirt and a simple bodice. This dress had been made new, sleek and slender, tracing down her curves and into a train. The bloody plum of amaranthine melted into the elaborate black lace. She pricked the skin above her wrist and twisted the lace into thorny vines. She allowed a single damask rose at the back of the hem, for Victor and what they'd had. He was in her past now. He was behind her.

"That is not the same dress I designed." Gigi had her hands on her hips.

She was dressed in a pale green gown with slits cut around the legs and up to the thighs. Her talent came from her long dancer's legs, and tonight they were on full display. The back cut low, showing off the lean muscles of her shoulders. Flowers dripped from the shoulders in a capelet down the length of the dress, ending in a garden of a train. Her mask matched the flowers at the hem. She'd twisted her tightly curled hair to one side and left her makeup simple. Selene could see why: her eyes were dew damp with tears. She looked like the goddess of spring, like someone who had a heart intact.

"There must have been a mistake at the couturier." Selene brushed her fingers against the material.

"You were meant to look like the sun, but this is better. You look like a lunar eclipse." Gigi's smile was bright and sad.

Someone knocked on the door three times.

Gigi looked at Selene, unsure of who it could be. She stepped toward the door.

Milton stood there, dressed in court finery. Selene hadn't seen him since he'd carried out Cecile. He looked deeply uncomfortable.

Milton muttered something, handed a box to Gigi, and shut the door. Gone as quickly as he'd come.

Gigi turned around. There was a wooden box in her hands. "It's for you."

The box was heavier than Selene expected. There was a note on the top with her name on it.

This felt like a trap. The box could contain anything—poison, serpents, all the sorrow in the world. The possibilities were endless, but the reality was less treacherous. It was probably the gift of a hopeful patron come early. The beginning of the fortune she'd reap for her entanglement with L'Opéra du Magician.

"Aren't you going to open it?" Gigi slipped on ballet flats that matched her dress.

Selene's fingers grazed the fine wood. It was polished, but the edges were scuffed. A little scratched, a little worn. It looked

SING THE NIGHT

like it had traveled around the world and back. Perhaps it was an answer to the ghost's new riddle, a music box of sorts.

She opened the box cautiously.

A single damask rose nestled into the blue velvet. It was the softest, palest pink, like the beginning of a sunrise. It was so lovely and fragile Selene was afraid she'd break it with a touch. There was an envelope tucked against the lid.

She broke the royal seal, her heartbeat in the hollow of her throat.

> Dearly Selene,
>
> Shall I sing you a song? Shall I spin you a tale? Or shall I meet you out at the garden at midnight when the fullness of the moon will be our only spy?
>
> Warmly, coldly, and all else in between,
>
> Victor
>
> P.S. Never better late.

Selene's hands trembled. He remembered. More than remembered. She thought of all the silly rhymes they'd put together. The adventures they'd had: tea plates shattered while attempting ancient games, indignant geese stripped of their best feathers while they attempted to form wings for flight, damask roses strewn about her room for her birthday, for apologies, for a reminder that things hold a moment of beauty before they fade and die.

She picked up the rose. It moved the way flowers moved. If she hadn't known it was glass by the translucent edges and the coldness of its flesh, she would have thought it was real. The glass so delicate she could feel it warp from the warmth of her hands. If she hadn't touched it, she wouldn't have known.

He'd brought her a flower that would never die.

There was a part of her that wanted to watch it shatter. A part of her that wanted to take it down below the opera house and watch it sink into the depths of the water. A part of her that wanted to plant a garden of this glass and spend the rest of her days marveling at the beauty.

She let that coldest part of her win. Indifference made easy, followed by disappointment and resentment. Victor was here, but it was too late. She put the rose back in the case. It was the first of many gifts, no more consequential than the dresses and furs and jewels that would soon consume her side of the room—attempts to woo her into a noble house, should she fail to win L'Opéra du Magician. He was merely a man who had the advantage of memory. A man, and no more.

"Who is it from?" Gigi said casually. As if she hadn't seen the seal.

"Victor." Selene held out the note and showed it to Gigi. "When I left the palace, he promised he'd come for me. I suppose this is his way of apologizing."

Gigi smirked. "I told you he remembered."

"I am difficult to forget."

Selene thought of the way the ghost had looked at her. Even now, it made her heart move: stretto, presto, and all the things a heart did when it felt too much. She forced herself to take measured breaths.

"What was he like?" Gigi eyed the flower.

"Victor was impetuous. Impossible." Selene shook away the memories. Shook away the tightness crawling up her throat.

Gigi adjusted one of the flowers on her gown. "If the stories are true, nothing has changed."

One thing had changed: Selene was no longer a part of his story.

"I wish him all the best." She shut the box and put it on her dresser. She palmed her father's silver watch and put it in her pocket. She needed his spirit with her tonight. "He's the least of my concerns now. Shall we?"

Gigi twirled. "We shall."

CHAPTER 21

The last time Selene had been in a carriage, she'd been ripped from her life at the palace and foisted into a new one. There was a strangeness to this reversal: going back to the palace with a sense that she was already sundered. She had been fortunate enough to be placed in a carriage with Gigi. There her luck had run out. Priya and Ramin shared the carriage with them as well. Poor Ramin looked miserable, nearly smothered in the amaranthine, floral, and gold gowns that overwhelmed the space.

Priya wrinkled her nose and fixed her eyes on Selene. "I'm surprised you had the audacity to even come, Selene. Especially considering you only have a chance because what's-his-name lost his mind."

And it was like lightning. A flash of movement, and then the crack of sound. Gigi lowered her arm back into her lap. Priya's lovely cheek was red and getting redder.

"His name is Benson." Gigi's voice was a deadly whisper.

"You slapped me," Priya said incredulously.

Gigi's warm brown eyes were so reminiscent of the dark of the mirror that it made Selene's fingers ache. "That's not all I can do."

It wasn't even half of what Priya deserved, but it was

something. It was enough in this moment. Selene did her best to contain a smile of satisfaction. Ramin didn't even try. His grin was wide and silly. He looked to Selene and Gigi with an unearned solidarity. He'd run with Priya's crowd, knocked sheet music out of their hands and laughed when they tripped on outstretched legs. Perhaps he'd finally grown up, tired of her unnecessary cruelty.

Selene only managed a half smile back. It was too late for him to make this right, to turn the tide. Perhaps there was redemption, but where was redemption without contrition? Where had he been during the countless times Priya and her ilk were making everyone else's lives miserable? Where was he when Benson was losing his mind?

The carriage wheels clattered as they moved from the cobblestone street to the white marble road. Selene knew the change in sound and what it marked. She held her breath.

The palace's white marble walls were bright in the starlight, brighter because of the new moon. The lack of it made Selene long for the magic and the music of the mirror and for the ghost. He was a bright spot in the darkness, a single star in the darkest part of night. Even without his memories, he'd know how to help her feel this. She imagined the warmth and musicality of his voice.

What is it you want?

This. She wanted to be the King's Mage and spend the next seven years in the palace. She wanted to sing magic and push its boundaries. She wanted to be the best. She wanted to be everything.

Outside, hired magicians volleyed orbs of light over the big, arched doorway. Rows of footmen clad in crisp white and gold livery waited in a perfect line. They were completely indiscernible from one another, as if they'd been hired as a matching set. The coaches before them unloaded heaps of jewel-toned attendees. Ball gowns and velvet suits and silk dresses that hung on the skin like spiderwebs. They were all masked and fighting to get inside. Selene had seen her share of parties at the palace, but nothing like this. The air shivered with magic; melodies carefully intertwined as the various mages sang individual magics for different effect. Offra—the current King's Mage—would have orchestrated all of this. She was a talented composer, and it showed.

There was nothing guaranteed. Not her life, not her mind, not her place in the competition. There was no more she could do. She'd either proven herself, or she hadn't. Selene let herself bask in the splendor.

All of this was for her.

She should have been over the moon, heart beating allegro. She should have been overwhelmed with emotion—of any kind—following in her father's footsteps. But her mind drifted: to Benson, to the ghost, to Victor. She felt the oppressive crush of time. She had so much to do—find a song that sang itself, free the ghost, win this competition—and yet she wanted to settle into this grand debut.

"Selene, are you coming?" Gigi was outside the carriage, being led up the steps by one of the many footmen. Madame Giroux waited at the top of the stairs.

Selene took the footman's hand. Let him lead her out of the carriage. How many times had she run up and down these stairs with Victor? How many times had she crossed this threshold with her father? She imagined him beside her, taking her hand and leading her toward her destiny. She was doing this for him.

The footman took Selene by the arm and whisked her away toward the ballroom.

The palace was as she remembered. Everything crisp and white and clean. She and Victor often made a mess of the walls and floor and furniture with sticky fingers and muddy shoes. She narrowed her eyes at the pillar to the right of the entry. She thought she could make out a dark smudge from where they'd burst a pomegranate in an unfortunate game of catch.

And this was where her father used to teach her about acoustics, singing all around the room to show how the dome caught his voice. In this hall, she'd skipped after Victor and, on one of the white rugs, skinned her knee. She'd bled all over the floor. The servants had rushed to clean up the red, leaving Selene crying and bleeding until her father found her and swept her away. Down that wing would take her to their suite.

Selene stepped into the ballroom.

The air was sweet with the scent of perfumes and cakes. Selene was dizzy with the swirl of dresses, the endless towers of champagne, the bodies that spun and moved in a kaleidoscope of colors. Masks ranged from simple black silk to elaborate horned monstrosities. A woman with a mask made of grape leaves and real fruit plucked one and popped it into her partner's mouth. A man in floor-length burgundy tailcoats and a mask with exaggerated features kissed a beaked girl in a dress made of pale pink feathers. She spun away from him, her feather skirt puffing out. They laughed and laughed and laughed until the sound was dissonance and distortion, and it was all Selene could do to keep from pressing her hands to her ears.

There was a mage stationed every few feet in elaborate palace finery, softly singing illusions of light and stars over the ballroom. The king and queen sat in their ornamented thrones. Beloved, as always. The king's benevolence was evident in the teeming hall of adoring subjects—a mix of subjects from every class and creed, only marked by a difference in dress. Anyone could enter and be entertained by the king's court, regardless of station. It was something that set Mondreves apart from other nations. Victor looked so much like his father. Those same dark eyes and bone structure, though the king kept his silver speckled hair cut short and maintained a beard. He was handsome and regal and everything a king should be. The queen was dressed in ceremonial white. Her copper hair was streaked in gray and she slouched in her throne, clearly bored. She'd never taken much interest in her kingdom or children—save for Henri.

On the king's other side sat the reigning King's Mage: Offra. Her onyx necklace caught the light. The last time Selene had seen that necklace, it had been coated in her blood, around her dead father's neck. She wondered if the stone still shifted, as if liquid inside, or if that was the workings of her overactive imagination.

Alexandre, the heir, was conspicuously missing. Henri was there. He looked so much like Victor. There was less gold in his hair but his eyes lacked the light and laughter. Selene hoped she would not run into him tonight.

Victor's chair was empty.

Good. It was better this way. Selene did not have room for

him in her life. She had a dance floor to command, a song that sang itself to find, and a competition to win. Victor could bring her all the roses he liked. He was nothing to her.

"Isn't this amazing?" Tears glimmered in Gigi's eyes. "We're finally here."

Selene squeezed her hand, her stomach still sick from Madame's words. "At long last."

Gigi pressed the tips of her fingers into the corners of her eyes to catch and stem the tide of sorrow. "Benson wouldn't want us to be sad. We have to make this the best night—for him."

Selene put on her best smile. "I can do that. For Benson."

For you.

She centered herself. She'd enjoy every single moment of this—being beautiful and young and full of promise. Selene would be the centerpiece of the event—gleaming like the chandelier over the auditorium. She'd make sure the world knew she was ready to win, that the king knew.

Or the prince.

Selene suppressed a shiver. Could he guarantee her spot in the competition? She forced the thought from her mind. She wouldn't need him. She had the magic of blood and shadows, the power of her voice, and the legacy of her name.

Above the dance floor, the illusion of a clockface counted down the minutes. A little more than an hour before the unmasking. Selene took a deep breath. Until then, she'd make the most of the next ten minutes. And then she'd find her song that sang itself. If she was lucky, she'd find something more than that, something to give her answers on how to free the ghost. No matter how tonight ended, she needed to see him again.

The moment she stepped onto the dance floor, someone took her hand. A man in a spiderweb mask spun her around, taking her through the complicated motions of the dance. He was finely dressed but a little careless with his dance steps. Selene dazzled him with a smile.

"Sing for me, darling. Just a little, so I can guess who you are." There was elderberry wine on his breath.

"You'll know soon enough."

"It will be our little secret."

Selene showed her teeth. She had enough secrets. He spun her out, and she used the momentum to break away from him.

Another man caught her hand and took her through the next motion of the dance. He was old enough to be her father.

Giuseppe Dreshé should be here. He should be dancing with her on this floor. He should be up on the dais with the retired King's Mages, enjoying the splendor, looking handsome and happy and proud. The ache of it would be enough for her to spin this whole room into darkness, letting the power of the magie du sang bring them all into the black.

"What will it take for you to be the jewel of my home?" the man whispered in her ear.

Selene repressed a shudder, keeping the hint of a smile on her face. "I am here to win, sir."

"I'll be your consolation prize."

Selene didn't wait for a spin to break out of his arms. But the moment she was free of him, she was caught up with another stranger. And another, and another. She could not take a step without finding herself in the arms of some would-be patron, offering her whatever she wished, if she would sing for them.

The wealthy loved to ornament their halls with the best of the best, as if the excess of talented mages proved their status in society. For her competitors, a patronage like that would offer security and prestige and a place for their art for years to come. There was an allure to Selene that belied all the others: she was the Mad Mage's daughter. She was wanted for her talent, yes. But also for the potential for a most sensational tragedy.

The darkness of her mask showed her true self; her smile was the part of her that played pretend. She would belong to none of these people. She would be the King's Mage or she would be nothing. Someone pressed a glass of champagne to her lips and Selene drank, hoping the bubbling burn would fill her emptiness. She moved from one dancer to the next, spinning and spinning and spinning. Selene closed her eyes and imagined herself alone—almost alone—in the mirror. Just her and the ghost. A dangerous place that somehow felt safe to her. Selene could already feel the magic building in her skin. Something to stop the endless turning and touching. Something to keep her still.

And then it happened.

Selene gasped and opened her eyes.

A man held her firmly in place. He snapped his fingers and the music slowed. The whirl of dancers stilled around them, some of them vacating the dance floor, no doubt exhausted and parched from the bacchanal.

Selene took a deep breath and let him guide her through the steps of the dance. The vertiginous nature of the last song ebbed, allowing her to settle into the movements. She'd been trained as a dancer, as they all had, and following the steps was easy enough. The man led her with a gentle strength, with none of the false flirtations or press of ownership of the others. Selene relished the respite, listening to the orchestra weave through the melody.

Her dance partner turned her again and dipped her. Above them, the hired magicians set off little bursts of light that scattered and skipped in the air. They made it look effortless, despite the intense concentration it took to create a tableau like this. To her left, one of the displays broke and dissipated. The magician responsible sank to his knees with exhaustion. Another magician stepped forward to take his place. The lights went up as if they'd never been lost. As if someone hadn't just collapsed under their weight.

Her partner brought her back up, closer this time. Curious, Selene met his eyes.

She would know those tea-dark eyes anywhere, brimming with mischief and satisfaction.

"Hello, Selene."

CHAPTER 22

Victor's hair was swept back and free of its wildness. He was dressed in a military suit of white and gold, with intricate navy embroidery on the collar and sleeves. His mask was a rippled deep blue, reminiscent of the sea in the dead of night. It offset the copper in his hair and the sunned warmth of his skin perfectly. It took all her power not to reach up and trace the scar on his cheek. To see if he was real, to be sure this wasn't a dream. She stumbled in the next step of the dance, accidentally striking his foot with her heel. He winced.

Real, after all.

"Did you get the rose?"

She could say yes and let that be done. There was a way for her to come out of this with minimal pain and engagement. A glottal stop for their relationship. An end and a beginning. She could let this go.

And maybe it was the dizziness of the previous dance. Maybe it was easier to speak with a mask covering up who she was. Maybe the weight of the years had built up in her like champagne bubbles and the pressure of Victor's hands on her skin was like a cork popping free.

"You think that a single gift makes up for the years? How

dare you, Victor. How dare you come to me now after seven years of silence." They were still dancing, moving to the slow rhythm of the song. Selene knew how to put on a performance.

Victor did, too. He took her through the steps of the dance with grace and charm. She didn't want that from him. She wanted him to react.

"You said you'd come for me."

"I'm here now," he said quietly.

"It's not enough." Selene tried to pull the tremor from her voice, tried to be stoic and devoid of emotion. "You were all I had left and then you were gone, good as dead. You were supposed to be different."

Victor's eyes softened with sadness. Selene felt the cascade of it, and it made her want to lean into him and tell him it was okay. But it wasn't okay. Nothing he said could make it okay.

He spun her out and pulled her back in, as the dance demanded. "Didn't you get my letters?"

Selene's mouth dropped open, the fury leaving her. "What letters?"

He pulled her closer than the dance required, his voice low in her ear. "I wrote to you every day, Selene. I wrote you letters until I was good at writing them. I sent you letters from Erramasque, from the mountains, from each port. Thousands of letters, Selene."

He searched her face. Selene wondered what he was looking for. She didn't have the letters. She didn't have anything from him. Had he been waiting for her the last seven years, like she had waited for him?

"After years of silence, they stopped being for you and started being for me. You really didn't get them? Not one?"

"No."

Victor slid his hand from her waist to interlace with her fingers. His skin was rough against hers. He led her effortlessly through the steps and she let him move her. "The rose—that rose. I had that rose made for you weeks after you'd been sent away. I've carried it with me across the world, waiting for a chance to see you again."

"You've been in the city for weeks."

"I thought you didn't want to see me." He brought his hand up to brush away an errant curl from her face. "I didn't want to disrupt your glamorous life."

Selene's laugh was short, all the fight drained from her. "I've lost hold of my righteous anger."

"Shall I do something to bring it back? You know I can be a scamp." He winked.

Selene looked up at him, fighting back tears. She was tired of the lights and the sounds and the bodies. She needed rest she could not have.

Victor regarded her carefully. "May we have a moment alone?"

"I'd like that."

He took a few spun steps to the corner of the room and then pulled her behind a tapestry. She knew this passage. They'd used it a hundred times to slip into the king's events and steal fruit tartes and cream and centerpieces. Turn right, and they'd go straight into the kitchens. Victor took her to the left, and then to the left again. The passageway was unmarred by cobwebs or dust: perfect and clean like the king preferred.

Once upon a time, Selene would have followed this boy anywhere.

She followed him, again.

Despite the years, he still knew the right place to take her. He guided her through a discreet door and into the night.

Selene breathed in the salt of the sea and the sweet fragrance of the garden: fresh-cut grass and the subtlety of the damask roses and petrichor. This was the Queen's Garden, separate from the sprawling grounds peppered with guests. They were alone in this space: Selene, Victor, the roses, and the stars. He still held her hand, his fingers rough against hers. He was not a boy anymore. And she wasn't that girl. Selene took a step away from him, giving herself the space she needed.

Victor collapsed onto the grass, tossing his mask into the nearest rosebush. He was flat on his back, eyes glittering with stars. His white uniform soaked up the green. "That did not go as expected."

Selene sat on one of the marble benches, letting her dress spill around her. She kept her mask on. "What did you expect?"

"That you would hate me."

"I do hate you," Selene said.

And part of her wanted to. But she could feel that slipping away from her. The resentment she'd carried for most of a decade replaced by the familiarity of their friendship.

"But only a little." He smiled at her, unguarded and deeply relieved.

"Certainly not as much as I'd like."

Victor undid the top few buttons of his military coat and turned onto his side, head resting in his hand. "Now what do we do? Are we friends again?"

"I don't know," Selene said, and wished she did. "How do you make up for seven years?"

"We could steal all the cakes." He pulled himself up, a creature of perpetual motion. "No, we've done that before. We can do better."

Selene looked over her shoulder, trying to get a glimpse of the magical clock hanging over the ballroom, counting down the minutes to her fate.

He reached to the nearest rosebush, plucked the husk of a rose from the dirt. He put it in his pocket. "Someone would be whipped for that. Mother and her roses."

Selene had forgotten about the casual cruelty of the queen until Victor mentioned it. She had a catalogue of memories of the queen's incivility that she'd tucked away in the corner of her mind. Victor's mention was like the unfolding of a piece of paper, memory after memory caught in the creases. Once it had been Victor whipped for mischief in the garden.

"Do you want to feel the anticipation, or will you welcome a distraction?"

Selene was caught off guard by the question. Victor was paying attention.

"Distraction," Selene said. "And someplace quieter."

Victor nodded. He stood and placed his hand at the small of her back, guiding her through the Queen's Garden and out to the main grounds. Enough had changed that Selene would have had trouble navigating alone in the dark. But she knew where he was taking her. Where she was *letting* him take her.

He bent down, whispering in her ear: "This will be in the papers tomorrow."

Selene's traitorous heart trilled. She would not let herself fall in love with this boy. For years Victor had been a sputtering candle in her heart. Now she was here and he burned like a torch. She had to refocus her attention. Victor was one step closer to the king, a way to secure her path. It wasn't that she liked the heat of his skin through her gown or the way he felt like home or the brine and summer scent of him.

All at once, they were at the strand between the sea and the shore. The grass tapered into sand. The tide was high with the new moon and the stars were bright as magic, sung into their constellations with a rapturous fervor. The light reflected down to the shimmering water, dark and shadowed as the inside of a mirror. A dozen steps and her feet would be in the water. A dozen steps and she'd be close enough to drown.

"Do you want to—"

Selene already had her shoes off, was already sliding down the dunes to the water with Victor's laughter at her back. He caught up to her in a few strides, tossing his boots behind him. She held up the edge of her skirt just as the icy water foamed around her ankles.

Victor hadn't bothered to roll up his trousers. They were soaked, darkening the grass-stained white.

"How many tides did we follow, up and down, until we were practically fish?" he said softly.

"Enough." Selene fought the ache in her chest. "And far too few."

"I'd do it all again just to be with you."

Selene breathed in the sweet, salted air and stared into the distancing endless dark. She couldn't tell him that she had wondered and dreamed, too. In her mind, they had lived a thousand lives, each one more fantastic than the next. Until they didn't. Until she'd traded her dreams for her ambitions. She had given up on him. And who could blame her? Seven years seemed like a lifetime. She could see him looking at her from the corner of her eye, features earnest. She couldn't stand the silence. She needed to fill it—and maybe puzzle through the ghost's request.

"Ask me a question, and I'll ask one of you."

Victor's eyes widened with surprise—but only for a moment. He smiled, always ready for a game. "Do you really want to be the King's Mage?"

What is it you want?

"We all want to win," she said carefully.

"I didn't ask about *we*. I asked about you."

"Of course I do." That hunger, that endless want seemed like too much to share. It left her vulnerable. She cleared her throat and leaned into diplomacy. "Though I'd be happy with any opportunity."

Victor's half smile was lazy and all-knowing. "Ah, Selene. You lie to your friends, and I'll lie to mine. But let's not lie to each other."

She buried her feet in the sand, pulling her dress up to keep it safe from the oncoming wave. She looked at him with naked determination. "Winning is my only option."

"There she is," Victor said. "Is it worth the risk, after what happened today?"

"It's not your turn." Selene arched an eyebrow.

Victor's sheepish grin was reminiscent of any time he'd been caught, hand in the cookie jar. Selene was transported back, back, back to another time when she was another girl—just for a moment. Victor didn't notice. He tossed something no bigger than her thumbnail up into the air. He tossed it again, this time almost losing it to a sea breeze, and held it to his body, cupping his hand toward the starlight to make sure it was still there.

"What *is* that?"

"Terrible use of your question." Victor lifted his palm up to the light so she could see. "It's a nautilus shell. Unusual for these parts."

Something about it tugged at Selene. She couldn't quite put her finger on it.

"Listen." Victor held it up to her ear.

Selene could hear the song of the sea echoing within. The melody was simple and sweet and familiar. She'd done this with her father, shell after shell, identifying the pitches with him. He'd used it to teach her about resonance. The shell had no song of its own; it captured the shallow sounds outside of it and amplified them.

A song that sang itself.

Selene shivered.

Would this be enough for the mirror?

"May I have it?"

Victor brushed his calloused fingers down the length of her forearm, cupping her hand. He placed the seashell in the center of her palm.

"It's not your turn to ask questions, Selene." His voice was low and playful. She dared to look into his eyes. He watched her like she was the sea. A wonder and a force of nature and something deadly to behold. She thought he might kiss her. She was very sure he would.

A wave splashed up. Victor wrapped his hand around hers, protecting the tiny shell and shielding her against the water. She was speckled with it, but he was soaked. His laugh sounded like bell tolls. He released her and took a step back, deeper into the water.

"What do you think my father will say?"

"Nothing," Selene said. "But he'll make you—"

She swallowed her words. She didn't want to say it, even though it had been true their entire childhood. She couldn't say it. There was so much unspoken between them about the way the king had treated Victor. She hoped it wasn't true anymore.

"He'll make me pay for it later," Victor finished. The lightness of his voice did not meet the void of his eyes.

"Does he still?"

The great clock in the great hall struck. The sound of it was amplified, and it nearly startled the shell out of Selene's hands. She looked to him, eyes wide. This was it. This was the moment she'd find out if she was enough. If all her dreams would coalesce.

"You don't have to do this, you know." Victor reached for her hand. "We can be fish again, back in the sea. You can live a different life."

She pulled her hand away. "I've worked too hard for this, Victor."

"There's a whole world outside your opera house, beyond this city."

She wondered then, about the wideness of the world and the magic within. Did they have opera houses filled with ruthless and hopeful magicians who'd do almost anything to win? She didn't think so, but couldn't say for sure. Any simulacrum of L'Opéra du Magician in other places could be no more than a shadow. But she hadn't paid enough attention to anything besides her music and magic to have even a sense of that. "I don't want the world. I want to win."

He put his hands in his pockets. "You'd better run, then."

The bell of the clock tolled, counting down the moments before the competitors were unmasked. Selene picked up her skirts and sprinted, Victor close behind her, carrying her shoes. The crowd gathered in the ballroom, spilling out the expansive doors. All manner of masks and extravagant colors marred the usually sparse ballroom. Selene slipped through a secret entrance and followed the passageway. It would deposit her at the edge of the dais—right where she needed to be.

Victor caught her hand, just before she entered the room. His skin was wet and sandy but warm.

"Keep your eyes open," he whispered. "It'll be worth it, I promise."

Promises, promises. She didn't have a chance to ask him what he meant. She was swept up into the line of her competitors. They made a half-moon at the back of the dais. Gigi was on the other end of the stage, the beginning of the line. Selene was the end. She cast a glance at Selene's bare feet, one eyebrow lifting above the mask. Selene flashed her a smile, glad to focus on that rather than the raucous beat of her heart.

The past King's Mages shared the dais with them, sitting in a row behind the thrones. Offra looked worn thin. She was pale and pinched, not at all the bright, bronzed girl who had taken the title seven years before. There were gaps between the mages, leaving space for those who were now gone. For her father. And for Maris, who had gone mad a year into her tenure. Her departure was the reason why Giuseppe had been called back. It was a sort of déjà vu seeing these mages again now, each of them adorned with enough jewels to make a king's ransom.

Selene had thought of this moment a thousand times. Thought of seeing these faces, being with the people who shared the same title as her father. Looking at them now, it was no wonder that they hadn't been the ones called back. It was as if all the color had been drained from them, the light gone from their eyes. Her father hadn't been like that. He had still been bright and effervescent, until the end.

The king stood. The queen and Henri did, too. Victor had managed his way around the back of the dais and was dripping on the velvet cushion, looking endlessly pleased with himself. The king flashed him a dark look, a muscle working in his jaw. He put out his hands and the crowd hushed.

"Tonight," he said, his voice slick, "is the beginning. Tonight, we unmask the magicians who will have their chance to win L'Opéra du Magician and be *my* mage."

A chill ran up Selene's spine at the way he said *my mage*.

"Only the greatest magicians can serve this court," he said, glancing to the pointed edges of the half-moon. Selene and Gigi. Selene cast a glance to Madame Giroux, standing just out of the light next to the dais. Her hands were tight on her cane. "Which of you will serve me? Step forth, and we shall find out!"

One by one, her competitors moved in a line. Ramin's hands trembled. Priya looked smug, despite her lackluster audition. Revelio's eyes were downcast, refusing to make contact with Selene. There were only ten of them now, down from thirteen. How many more would be cut tonight? The number varied from year to year, with only the best going on to perform for L'Opéra du Magician. Selene reminded herself to breathe.

Let it be me. She wished her father could hear her.

There was a great flash of light.

Selene wanted to shut her eyes and block it out, but she remembered what Victor had said, only moments before. She kept her eyes open. Her mask burst with a blinding flash of luminescent color. The orchestra swelled, timed with the symphony. The stage magicians sang the light and bent it to new spectrums, turning it into a kaleidoscope of color on her skin. The crowd roared, drowning out the sound of the music.

Selene reached up, just to be certain. Her mask was gone, leaving her face bare. Those still masked were ushered off. Revelio looked at Priya with shock and seething rage, just before he was ripped from the dais.

The king put up his hands again. They looked older than they should, with papery skin and age spots. The room went silent.

From the corner of the stage, Selene could see Madame Giroux. She expected to see pride or joy or pleasant surprise. But

Madame's eyes were wide, mouth gaping. She looked like she was trapped in a nightmare, like this was the worst thing that could have happened.

But only for a moment, a slip of the mask. And then she had a vague smile on her lips. Her hands gripped her cane tight enough to snap it.

And then there was Victor. His dark eyes were lanterns, lighthouses. He looked at her like she was just out of his reach and he'd stop at nothing to reach her.

"Introducing the talent for L'Opéra du Magician: Gigi Giroux, Priya Ankari, Cameron Garnier, Ramin Mondego, and Selene Dreshé."

Selene closed her eyes and listened to the music of the applause.

CHAPTER 23

Selene had been the last one to the carriage, guests still reaching for her, trying for another dance, another drink, another entreaty. Selene barely registered the sights, the sounds, the rush of bodies. She hadn't found Victor again after she'd been named. Everything was a blur until she was settled inside. The colorless silence let her thoughts regain purchase.

Grief and exhaustion had pulled Gigi into sleep, her head resting on Selene's shoulder. Adrenaline coursed through Selene; she could barely sit still. It was only the three of them: Selene, Gigi, and Madame Giroux. Madame did not look at her. The night rolled by, the weight of their earlier conversation hanging between them, made heavier by the secrets. Selene cleared her throat.

"I saw you." Selene looked at Madame. "I saw your face, right before the names were called."

"There is more to life than titles and jewels, Selene."

"Why can't you just be happy for us?"

"Know when you're being used." Madame's eyes flicked to Gigi. "Do you think this is all there is? Songs and sorcery? There's a whole world out there."

"I don't want the world."

Madame Giroux sighed. She kept her eyes on the road.

"When Monsieur Avile and his patron declared the auditions complete, they asked about each of my students. When they asked about you, Selene, I told them no."

Selene's skin went cold. This betrayal should have been more of a surprise, but the certainty of it settled on Selene. Madame had known about Revelio and had said nothing. Madame had witnessed sabotage after sabotage and done nothing. She'd treated Gigi like an afterthought for the last seven years, dismissing her daughter's talent and dreams. She was not the hero Selene had thought, not the brutal and honest teacher and mother figure Selene had kept so high on a pedestal. She was just a petty woman in a position of power.

"The king insisted you be allowed to compete, like he insisted you be brought here to train."

"Not Victor?"

"You think Victor has that kind of power?"

"Yes," Selene said, without thinking. She couldn't afford to be unguarded around Madame anymore. "Why not me?"

Madame regarded her carefully. "Giuseppe wanted more for you."

"More than this?" Selene swallowed, her stomach coiling like the endless shadows in the mirror.

"He'd want you to be safe."

Selene chose her words carefully. "And that is difficult when the person who is supposed to be looking out for me, for all of us, has done nothing to stop the sabotage."

"You'll understand someday." Madame's eyes stayed trained on her. "You're like a daughter to me."

The carriage rolled to a stop. The driver jumped from his

seat. The movement shook Gigi awake. She yawned and smiled woefully. "I had the most wonderful dream that Benson made it, too."

Madame was out of the carriage first, already up the stairs and gone through the great, gilded door. Selene followed slowly behind her. The grandeur of the opera house seemed dark and muted compared to the brightness of the palace. She lingered near the dark statues, falling out of step with Gigi. She knew what she should do: go upstairs and change and get some much-needed rest.

Selene reached into her pocket and brushed her fingers against her father's pocket watch and the seashell. She must hurry, now. Selene had crossed the first threshold. She was in the competition. That impossible hurdle seemed like a small, easy step. Selene now had to prove herself to the world. And she had no song to sing. She needed to go below ground to write her music in the secret dark.

"I'll be right up," Selene said to Gigi.

Gigi waved her off, too tired to argue.

Selene turned down the hallway, stopping first in one of the empty rooms to get a stack of sheet music and a spare fountain pen. With Priya still in the competition, Selene couldn't write anything out in the open. She needed the promise and the secrecy of the dark. She needed absolute caution.

She needed the mirror.

Selene rounded the corner, close enough to the door leading beneath the opera house that she could smell the dust and damp and sweetness of the earth.

Madame Giroux's cane tapped on the floor behind her.

Selene spun.

Madame darkened the end of the hallway, eyes boring into Selene.

"Shouldn't you be in bed?" It was shaped like a question but was an accusation.

Selene held up the sheet music. "I was going to use the adrenaline to write something new."

"Not tonight."

Selene was too tired to argue. Too tired to think before she spoke. "Where are the letters Victor wrote me?"

Madame sucked in a breath, the truth written on her face. Another betrayal.

Anger that simmered inside Selene—the music, the coldness, the stars—boiled over.

"On second thought." Selene smiled. "I think I will turn in. Goodnight, Madame Giroux."

Madame opened her mouth like she had an answer, but Selene did not wait for her to speak. The seashell weighed down her pocket. It would have to wait just a little longer.

Gigi's breath had already settled into the evenness of sleep. Her dress was added to the pile on the floor. Selene took the sheet music and the seashell and her father's pocket watch and put them on the top of her dresser, next to the box with the glass rose. Selene carefully removed her dress and hung it up in the closet. It still smelled like brine and champagne and the woodsmoke scent of Victor.

She would lie down—just for a minute—and then go into the mirror.

But the minute her body sank into the mattress, she gave up

on that dream. Her limbs were heavy, weighing her down. She barely registered the door opening. Madame Giroux sang light so softly into her palm and stood there for a beat before she shut the door behind her.

Selene dreamed of places she could not get to, of things she could not have. Restless, troubled sleep. The cry of the mourning dove woke her right before the dawn. Gigi was still asleep. And Selene wanted to fall back into dreams. She wanted to go back to that place, but she knew better. She needed to start writing the aria for the competition. Gigi and her competitors would use an adaptation of their audition piece. They would each perform a single song, one aria to determine the rest of their lives.

Selene had certainly planned for that—she would sing her father's name back into the mouths of the city with her homage. But it had been taken from her. And she couldn't bring herself to perform the disastrous tempest aria—even with the magie du sang. The music was rife with humiliation and failure.

She needed something new. She could not afford to rest.

Selene took a quick bath, washing away the salt and sand from the night before, scrubbing the last of the glitter from her skin. She listened to music in the stir of the water, in the birdsong outside the window, in the patter of her bare feet against the hall floor. She needed a song without experimentation, something sure. The king's insistence had put her into the competition, and she had to prove to him that she was worthy of that faith. More than worthy. She would be the best.

She dressed quickly and quietly, slipping her sheaf of sheet music in the front of her dress, hoping to keep it safe from the splatter of water. She had some ideas, but she could already feel the knife of a migraine pulsing in her jaw. The music had to be perfect. She wanted it lacrimosa, a blend of fury and weeping. If she could sing the night, capture each burning star and the razor's edge of the moon, the longing so pure and pervasive that she'd bring the audience to its knees, she was sure she could win.

She'd go to the practice rooms first. Her time with the ghost was limited. She wanted to gather herself and get the best of her ideas down before she sought his intercession.

Everything needed to be perfect.

The halls were quiet—mostly. She heard the soft sounds of weeping behind some of the doors. She caught a glimpse of Priya outside Revelio's door, whispering something against the wood. Those who had not moved into the next round of the competition would be expected to pack their things and be out by noon today. Their lives here were over. Most of them would move on in society, with their years of magical training no more than a party trick.

Selene settled into her practice room, fingers resting above the keys. She traced out dozens of possibilities. Music reverberated, rife with promise and empty all the same. None of them were right. She could feel the wrongness of it. No matter what order she put the notes, she couldn't seem to coax out a song.

Take your broken heart, turn it into art.

But there were too many pieces, the shards too sharp. They cut away at her, leaving the music disjointed and fractured. She didn't know what story to tell or how it should be shaped.

Everything was grief: her father, Benson, Victor, the ghost, her own perilous ambition. No matter how many ways she approached it in song, she couldn't seem to capture it. She was close to something. But it wasn't quite right.

There were three days until L'Opéra du Magician. Three days for her to compose and perfect this song, along with the magic. Three days for her to master the magie du sang.

She couldn't do this alone.

Selene passed through the silent halls of the opera house, past the portraits and the statues and the library. Benson's seat was empty.

She didn't want to think about him now. She didn't want to think about anything but what came next.

And for that, she needed a song that sang itself. She reached for it in her pocket, silently cursing herself. The shell was upstairs in her room, sitting on the dresser next to her father's pocket watch. She rolled her shoulders back and started the journey back upstairs, feeling the stab of every lost second.

A pair of young girls—no older than sixteen—whispered at the bottom of the steps. Selene recognized the awe and naivety in their faces. These were the next generation of King's Mage hopefuls, eager to take the space in the upper dormitories and continue their training.

Selene rushed past them. There was nothing left in her to be shared, even though it would be a kindness. She had to focus.

Gigi slammed her pointe shoes on the floor. She got them custom from a shop that worked with the Opera Magique during the regular season. They'd been dyed to match the umber of her skin. Now they'd be broken and cracked and made perfect for Gigi's nimble feet.

"Can you believe it?" Gigi hit her shoe against the floor again and again. Her eyes were rimmed red. "How can the worst thing and the best thing happen in the same space of a day?"

Selene thought of the bright, brilliant blue sky and her father, dead on the floor. "Sometimes that is how it goes."

Each pound of the shoe brought a shock of pain behind Selene's eye.

"I thought you just broke in new shoes."

Gigi held up the pointe shoes she'd carefully broken and sewn. She turned one of them over, showing the wooden block her toes rested on. Someone had driven a razor blade into the wood. "I knew something was off before I put them on."

"This has to stop," Selene said furiously. "These stupid, petty attempts to ruin one another."

"It won't," Gigi said. "It's only begun."

Selene knew it by the new lock on the door. She knew it by the last few days of misery while she held on to the hope that she still had a chance in the competition. "I confronted Madame last night."

"And?"

"And nothing. I don't think she sees what she's doing is wrong."

"The people who think power is best won by a knife in the back are never truly punished. They just wait for you to turn around." Gigi slammed her shoe down again.

"Do you think that's what happened to the girl who jumped? One sabotage too many?" Selene leaned forward, hoping against all hope that Gigi would know something, anything.

"If that's it, then why did Madame remove the mirrors and enable the sabotage?" Gigi hit her pointe shoe one more time, then held it to the light, satisfied.

Selene thought of the ghost. Of what he might have done to deserve being trapped in the mirror. The possibilities were endless. If she could find out who the girl was, it might lead her closer to finding out the reason for his imprisonment. If she could find something terrible enough to warrant that punishment, she could find out who he was.

There was a part of her that didn't want to know, her imagination run wild with what he could have done. She knew what Henri did and now that merited a crown. What sin was so great that it warranted a hundred years trapped in a mirror? Or was there some other trick to it, some explanation she couldn't quite reach? She didn't want to mar her vision of the ghost.

"She doesn't want us to win. She might not want anyone to win."

"We're still missing something." Gigi shifted the contents of her sewing basket. "Have you seen any of my needles?"

Selene had one in her pocket. A tiny sword waiting to spill her blood. She wouldn't give it up.

"Have you checked behind the dresser?"

Gigi sighed and dropped onto her stomach, shifting the dust that lived beneath.

"Benson would have made it," Gigi said. "Don't you think?"

Selene closed her eyes. She didn't want to talk about Benson.

Didn't want to think about what they had lost. She needed to save that pain and make use of it. It did no good to bleed here without purpose.

"Yes."

"Aha!" Gigi came up with a handful of ribbons, a knot of thread, and a slightly bent needle. "It'll have to do."

Yes, it would.

Gigi made a few attempts to sew on her ribbons and then tossed the bent needle aside. She looked like she was going to cry again. She pulled her knees up to her chest and took a few steadying breaths, exhaling the frustration.

"Are we designing dresses?" Gigi retrieved her sketchbook, clearly in need of distraction.

It still seemed surreal to Selene that they had a whole team of seamstresses at their beck and call, ready to sew whole dresses based on their sketches and dreams. This was part of the privilege of the competition. They could have what they wanted because it was what the king wanted. All Selene wanted was to close her eyes to the world and wake up to the setting sun and the hope of tomorrow. But Gigi needed this. She sat up and patted the bed beside her.

"Absolutely."

Gigi flipped through a half dozen designs. She talked about fabrics and their movement and how they took the light. Selene tried to listen, but her head was full of bees.

A royal carriage rolled by on the street below. Selene followed its movement until she lost sight of it. They could not see the palace from this vantage. She'd always been grateful for that.

Until now.

Victor was not supposed to be here. He was supposed to be off doing whatever third princes did. Starting wars or sending ships or losing the crown jewels in an illicit poker match. This was her space, her life. He wasn't a part of her anymore.

Her heart fluttered against the lie. She wished it were true. She wished she could look at him and feel nothing. She wished that she could take the painful hope of those memories and bleed them out. Make a magic out of them and use it to forget.

He remembered her.

Maybe she should let the darkness have her. Let it take and take until there was nothing left.

"What colors go best with your piece?" Gigi said. The look on her face told Selene that it wasn't the first time she had asked.

"I haven't written it."

"I thought that's what you've been working on. All these late nights."

A lie bubbled in Selene's throat. She borrowed enough truth to assuage the guilt. "Nothing has been good enough."

Selene had been given a yes. The door had been cracked open enough that she might slip in. All she had to do was be the best. Show everyone that she was made of stars and shadows and a power so great she'd break them all. She would be the bird, not the shell. She would be the thing inside with a voice and wings. Not left on a shelf. Not an end, but a beginning.

"You have to go and write your aria." Disappointment crept into Gigi's voice.

"Yes. But if you need me..."

Gigi rippled with emotion, no doubt wrestling with the

options. Selene could stay, but at what cost? They both knew what was at stake.

"Go."

Gigi turned the pad of paper around. She had sketched a preliminary dress for herself. The gown was blue taffeta, soft embroidered flowers up the bodice. It was a spring day over a crystal-clear lake. It was a promise of new life, of new magic. That's what Selene needed. Something new.

"Draw something for me? Make it red as blood."

CHAPTER 24

Selene held up the seashell, pressing it to her ear one last time. It whispered the music of the sea, transporting her to that moment last night, with Victor by her side. His presence was a complication. As much as she'd missed him, as much as she wanted to fall back into old habits, she knew she was borrowing trouble. He'd always had a gift for distraction. He wanted her to go and she needed to stay.

The mirror soaked up her blood.

Selene stepped through the glass, closing her eyes to ride the wave of disorientation. The coils of darkness shivered with pleasure, inching closer and closer still. She sang the light and cast a halo around herself. They buzzed around her impatiently, as if waiting to have her.

No matter how many times she saw the ghost, his beauty still overwhelmed her. He faced away from her. He reached up, his thin linen shirt pulling up to reveal the low dimples at the base of his spine. The skin on his back was marked with the silver strips of long-healed scars. He was singing softly to himself, making patterns with light. Selene saw this for what it really was: keeping the darkness at bay. She understood that need. She wished she was better at it.

"Back so soon?" He looked at her over his shoulder, eyes bright with the false light.

There was a shadow to his smile, a worry Selene did not understand. She was afraid to ask. She knew what the darkness would do to him if she said the wrong thing. Instead, she held up the shell.

"A nautilus." His brows furrowed. "Unusual for these parts. You really are a girl of impossible things."

She smiled and dropped it into his palm. She didn't tell him that the shell was not hers. Didn't tell him that Victor had scooped it from the shore. Where it came from didn't matter as long as it worked.

The ghost held the seashell up to his ear. For a moment, Selene worried that the resonance wouldn't exist in the mirror. Seashells, after all, were only echoes. But he must have heard something. His face turned to rapture. The light played on his cut-glass cheekbones and broken nose, highlighting the scar above his eye and the stubble on his chin.

Selene held her breath, not wanting to change the sound. Not wanting to move, lest she trigger the tendrils of darkness that were pressing against the light. The ghost did not heed them. He was enraptured by the music of the shell. When he opened his eyes, they were like a clear summer day.

"This I have asked and you have answered. Thank you. It has been too long since I heard the sea." He held out the seashell with more reluctance than she'd ever seen from him. The darkness did not hesitate. He pulled his hand away right before the shadows touched his skin. "What is it you want?"

"To be the King's Mage." A bubble of excitement rose within her. Here in the dark, she could finally let herself be happy. "I made it. I'm in."

The ghost's smile was bright and genuine. He took a step toward her, as if to embrace her. Selene leaned closer, wishing that he could. "Congratulations. It is well deserved."

"It was at the king's insistence."

"Who killed your father, Selene?"

"When will you stop asking me that?"

"When you give me the right answer."

She pressed her fingers to her temple and massaged. The migraine still pounded behind her eye. "I killed him."

The ghost took the oil spill knife from his pocket. He peeled open his shirt and cut the space above his heart. The cut was deep. The blood soaked his shirt, his pants, and then the floor. There was so much blood. An unreasonable amount, far more than the pinpricks Selene had offered with tiny beads of blood like precious jewels. This was a travesty, a waste. She wanted to press her hands against his chest and hold the wound closed.

"What are you doing?" Selene cried.

The blood congealed into shadow, lifting from the floor. It shifted, rising, and then burst into a dark red mist. The mist surrounded her, filling her mouth and nose and eyes.

She gasped and thrashed, drowning in shadow. She'd been waiting for this moment for so long, for the sins of her past to catch and consume her. There was a stark relief to this penance. Father killer, breaker of rules, betrayer of friends. She'd been a fool to think that her life was worth anything more than the waiting dark. She had known he was a monster when she'd stepped into the glass and she deserved whatever terrible thing happened to her.

All at once, the shadows left.

And with it, the throbbing pain in her head.

Selene wasn't sure whether to express gratitude or regret or horror—none of them seemed like the right emotion.

"My migraine is gone."

"I know." His smile was polite, tired.

"How?"

The ghost lifted his shoulders. The cut above his heart had healed into a thin line. The blood that had soaked his clothes had been spun into shadow and away. "Magic."

"Magic doesn't work like that."

"Of course it does."

The ghost ran his finger over the pink scar on his chest. She longed to do the same. He was tall and strong and looked a hundred years younger than he was. Standing here with him was like standing out in a thunderstorm, the air damp and electric. Like that first sip of sweet wine. Like trying to hold on to a moment before it slipped into memory. Familiar and true. "Healing takes more. Blood, pain, and wanting. More of each is required."

"Could magic like that heal those who've gone mad?"

"I don't know," he said. "I don't know your madness or its cause."

"But I could try."

If Selene could undo what was done to Benson, to all the mages trapped in the Asylum, what would the world be? What would magic be if there was no more threat of being lost to madness?

"Be careful." His voice was low. "Whatever this madness is, it is something we could not have imagined a hundred years ago."

Selene thought of her father's feral eyes. The color of that day had left with the pain. Selene was unnerved by the sepia-toned memory. Was this the cost of the magic?

It wasn't forgetting, not quite. It was something else. Something she'd have to worry about another day.

With her head clear and without the sharp stab, she remembered what she'd wanted to ask.

"Do you remember a time when you weren't alone?"

"Pieces. A little before, and a little after. For a time, I could see out into the world. Instead of all this black, there were windows in all shapes and sizes. I can't remember, exactly, but I think there was something more to them."

"Mirrors." Selene knew every ghost story, every hint of the unusual. There had been sightings of a ghost in the mirrors. That's why they'd been banned. Because the ghost was real. "Do you remember someone else coming inside the mirror?"

The ghost stood very still. "Tell me what comes next for you and your tournament of mages."

Selene took out the sheaf she'd tucked into her dress. She opened it up to the first page. It was a mess of phrases and half-finished thoughts. Each of them written with the same intent: capturing the devastation of grief and ambition and the terrible cost of it all. The ghost shook his head. Selene pulled out a blank page. Just the clef and the staves and requiem written in fine, black ink.

"Set it in D minor." The ghost cut the tip of his finger and used the blood to mark the key on the page. "It is the most melancholy key."

Selene hummed the first note, the beginning of an aria taking shape in her mind. She pricked her finger with the pin. She didn't bother pressing it to the page. She merely wanted the blood to be there.

"This will not do."

The ghost dragged the tip of his knife against his pale skin. The blood swirled into shadow and then took form. Solid wood and familiar keys, all of them black. It was an inkwell of a grand piano, cool beneath her fingers. A bench—long enough for them to sit beside one another without touching—spread between them.

The ghost took his seat. "What if you went up to A here." She sang the note. He met her voice and carried it down in steps. "And brought down the bass?"

"Yes," Selene said. Her heart beat pressando. The ghost seemed to know what the song needed just as she did. Their shared minds stitched together an aria. There was something intimissimo about sharing breath to sing the same note.

Each one was carved out of her soul. All the darkness, a little of the light. She needed both. It wasn't enough for her to sing every dissonant and melancholy note. Even the minor scale was dappled with major chords. The ghost concentrated on the keys. His long fingers traced the black and the black with such tenderness.

When he sang with her in anticipation of a line, it was as if her very essence had been extended to another person. Their voices lifted, entangled. They were like two hands on the keys working in tandem to create something greater than themselves.

Selene could trace the history of him in the way he stacked the chords and the way he wrote the rhythms. She met him, note for note, and brought in a hundred years of growth and knowledge. He lit up as she showed him something new. What could he have done, if he had lived outside the mirror? What greatness could this man have achieved?

Perhaps if she unraveled his crime, she could free him. What had he done to deserve this? What had she done to deserve him and his magic? She was lucky to be here. In his prison. In his tomb. She took that feeling and wrote it down. There was a melody for all types of sorrow.

"Sing for me," he said.

Selene looked at what they had written, committing the notes to memory. She wove them together into a mournful melody, leaving out the magic. She needed the music first.

And oh, this aria. She glanced down at the sheet music— written in their combined blood—and let her voice caress the line. It was gentle and wanting, like a bandaged-up broken heart, a thin scar on a once-open chest. She wanted to carve this music into her skin and keep it there. She wanted to sing it until her throat was filled with blood. She wanted to stay here in the dark and forget, forget, forget.

Selene shivered and focused on the music.

It was only twelve measures. Not quite a song. But a start. It highlighted the strengths of her voice, pushing it into perfect clarity. This piece was the best of her.

When she was finished, she looked at the ghost. This piece was the best of him, too. He made her better. He made her want to be more.

There's nothing else for me, she thought. But she wasn't sure she believed it.

"I will hold on to the memory of your voice long after I've forgotten every other part of me."

"You'll remember everything," Selene said, "when you step into the light."

"You are the light."

For a moment, she thought he might kiss her. They were close enough for it, a sixteenth note of space between them. They couldn't touch; they were never supposed to touch. That didn't change this want, this *need*.

"Selene." His eyes were wide and wet and so very blue. Not as cold as she once thought. The heart of a flame could be as blue as ice.

She knew this part was coming and hated it.

"Bring me a fragment of what once was."

And for the first time tonight, Selene was sure. She would complete this task and come back to him. She would be here again with this beautiful man and listen to the warm lull of his voice. More than a vow. She wanted to set him free, like she wanted to win.

CHAPTER 25

"There you are." Gigi was waiting on the edge of her bed when Selene slipped into the room. She jumped to her feet. "Come with me."

"Why are you still awake?" Selene said coolly. She pressed her hand to the sheaf of music tucked into her dress.

She knows.

Panic rose like wisps of shadow inside Selene. She needed her secrets kept for a little longer. This could ruin everything.

"I found something. I think I know what's going on with Madame." Gigi grabbed Selene's hand, pulling her out of the room, down the stairs, and into the near-perfect dark of the sleeping opera house.

Selene practically ran to keep up with Gigi, moving as lightly as she could. Gigi's steps were soundless, infused with a dancer's grace and elegance and intention. "Where are we going?"

They'd crossed the back of the auditorium, down to the farthest corner of the opera house. Gigi stood in front of a door. This space was forbidden as much as the space beneath the opera house. But Selene had never dared cross this line.

"It's in my mother's room."

"Is she—"

"A carriage from the palace arrived an hour or so ago and she left with it. I don't know how much time we have."

Gigi whispered a song into the lock. It surprised Selene that she knew it, but it shouldn't. Gigi had lived in this suite before she'd moved into the dormitories. Like Selene, she'd had a life before all this. Madame Giroux had been Gigi's mother first, teacher second. What she was now, neither of them quite knew. There was a strange sadness to the realization. Selene wasn't the only one who had lost something.

"Come on." Gigi was already inside. "We don't have a lot of time."

Selene hesitated. This felt like such a violation. But so what? Madame didn't care about her privacy or well-being. Whatever strange agenda she had, Selene didn't have the space to care anymore.

She stepped inside, shutting the door behind her.

The suite was simpler than Selene expected, tidy and stark. They stood in the parlor. To the left was a small kitchen and dining area. To the right, a study with a piano at its center and floor-to-ceiling shelves. They were almost empty, with a few scattershot books and tidy stacks of sheet music. Two doors waited like sentinels ahead. One was cracked enough so Selene could see the vague shape of a twin-size bed, a small table, and a rocking chair draped in a white cloth. Tiny ballet slippers hung on a peg on the wall, next to paper flowers pinned in clusters. This had been Gigi's room, once.

That left a single door.

It opened on well-oiled hinges. The sounds of the street drifted through the cracked window. They were far enough from the rest of the opera house that no music would permeate this space, even if there were a full production on the stage. Something about that made Selene sad. The rest of the room was stark and cold. It might as well be a prison cell.

Gigi shut the curtains and dropped onto the floor, pressing her fingertips against a knot in the wainscoting. "I was always curious about this panel as a child, so much so that my mother moved her dresser in front of it. You can see the scratches in the floor from where she moved that, again and again."

The panel slid open.

Selene sucked in a breath and dropped down to her knees beside Gigi, singing for light. There was a space here that extended down into the dark, like one of Victor's secret passageways. It was cluttered with loose papers, strewn books, a torn tapestry. A bouquet of dry flowers was half crushed by a huge, cracked wooden frame with its contents facing the wall. A porcelain doll with a split face looked up at Selene accusingly with its single, blue eye. Selene reached for a silver locket. The clasp was broken, and it flipped open. It had held a mirror once. The jagged teeth still clung to the edges.

Gigi held up a yellowed newspaper clipping.

MAGICIAN LEAPS FROM THE ROOF OF THE OPERA MAGIQUE

Hopeful in L'Opéra du Palais Renard. Lamplighters found the student after jumping off the roof of in the early hours of the
Magician is in the hospital

> morning and contacted the authorities. She was transported to the hospital and is currently being treated for substantial injuries. Monsieur Maurice de Lancret, manager of the opera house, reports that the student had been acting strangely, speaking of ghosts in mirrors.
>
> "There is an immense pressure in this competition," says de Lancret. "We are devastated by the loss of a talented magician. Our thoughts are with her as she heals."
>
> There is no statement from the student at this time.

Gigi handed Selene a second paper, pointing to a single line.

> Brigitte Giroux has been removed from L'Opéra du Magician due to injury.

"Look at the dates."

One day apart. Selene had wanted to believe this was a coincidence. But the truth of it settled beneath her skin. Madame had been the girl who'd leapt off the opera house. Madame had been the one to remove all the mirrors. Madame knew about the ghost and had tried to keep him secret from the world.

"I knew she'd gotten hurt." Gigi put the papers back where she'd found them. "But I didn't think she was the girl who jumped. She'd talked about it like it was someone else."

"It probably feels like it was." Selene shifted some of the other items, careful to note their placement.

"She's been trying to protect us from that all along." Terror shone in Gigi's eyes. "It's the ghost, Selene. It's real."

Yes, Selene thought. *He's more real than anyone else I know.*

Instead, she shook her head. "I think the manager was right. The pressure."

"Then why did she come back if not to save others from the same fate?"

Selene blew out a breath. "She said sometimes young girls make foolish promises."

Gigi considered that. She pulled out one of the books. "These are older prints of some of the history texts. Odd."

Selene leaned into the space, singing light and holding it up toward the cracked frame. The glass was spiderwebbed in the corner, casting lines over the architectural plans of the opera house. So much of the past, so much of what once was. She could use this if she found the right thing. There was a bundle of letters just beyond it. Selene recognized the handwriting before she saw her name—again and again—a thousand times over.

Oh, to stop the world and imagine a different life with that boy. Oh, to look into his mind and trace the years they'd spent apart. Oh, to have lived a life where she knew she mattered for all this time.

A door opened. The familiar sound of Madame's cane striking the wood floor echoed in the room beyond them.

Selene's heart pounded in her throat. She looked at Gigi and then back around the room. She moved quickly and quietly to the window. If they could get out fast enough, they could cling to the ledge. But the window wouldn't open any more than it already was.

That left only one option.

Gigi figured it out a split second before Selene. She was already inside the wall, gesturing for Selene to join her.

The doorknob turned.

Selene ducked inside, pulling the panel shut behind her—badly. There was a gap, small enough that Selene could just see the sliver of Madame.

Gigi reached for Selene, grasping her hand tightly.

Madame settled onto her bed. One shoe after the other fell to the floor as she let out a deep, bone-weary sigh.

Madame rolled up her sleeves, fingers tracing the constellation of scars on the back of her arms, over her fingers, her palm. A terrible knowing settled over Selene. Madame hadn't merely seen the ghost. She knew him. She had been there. She had seen his magic. She had done it with him.

Once, there'd been a girl who'd grown so frightened of the ghost she jumped off the roof of the opera house. Selene had always thought that the girl had died. Brigitte must have sung her safety out of instinct. Not enough to completely stave off injury, but enough to survive. Selene's eyes lingered on Madame's cane. Had she let the rumors of her own fall circulate to spread fear and prevent the students from going to the ghost and learning his secrets?

She wanted to scream at Madame, to beg her to let him out. But if she confirmed Madame's fear, what was to stop her from getting rid of the mirror? What was to stop her from letting it shatter?

What now? Gigi mouthed.

Selene leaned into the framed architectural plan. She could make out this corner of the opera house, this suite, which had initially been intended for guests. The trick panel was marked, as well as the space they were hidden in.

There was a passageway that connected to the main hallway. Selene committed it to memory. When she was finished, she put a finger to her lips. She took Gigi by the hand, moving gingerly down the passage. She kept her free hand against the wall, feeling for where to turn in the dark. She wished she could bleed herself a thread to lead them out. But with Gigi here, all she could do was push through the dark and hope against hope that they wouldn't be caught.

There was a click.

A flood of light.

Selene pulled Gigi around the corner a beat before Madame's voice echoed in the passage. She'd be back for the letters. She'd be back for everything if she could.

"Hello?"

Selene clung to the wall, barely moving, barely breathing.

The light faded. The panel clicked shut.

Selene had never moved so quickly in her life, twisting through the narrow spaces and around the tight corners. When they finally burst through the exit, they were both breathing heavily. Selene didn't stop in the hallway. She ran—barely caring about the sound—back to their room.

Gigi was a few steps behind her. She collapsed onto her bed. "That was close."

"Maybe we should go back." Selene wanted what was

rightfully hers. She wanted to sift through the secrets. She wondered if she'd find a name written on a scrap of old sheet music, discarded and forgotten. It would be so easy to save the ghost that way. But when had her life ever been that simple?

"Knowing my mother, all those things will be somewhere else within the hour. She works quickly."

Selene knew all too well. She put on her nightgown, ran her fingers through her hair to catch the knots and spiderwebs. The adrenaline was already running down, fatigue settling in.

Gigi's voice was edged with exhaustion. "I just wish I could talk to her about it, you know? Her life before, why she feels the need to keep it hidden. I wish I could talk to her about anything at all."

By the time Selene thought of a suitable response, Gigi's soft breaths had turned to snores.

Selene knew one thing for certain: the opera house had more secrets left for her to uncover. One of them would be the key to the ghost's freedom.

And Selene was running out of time.

CHAPTER 26

S elene slept with her music tucked against her body. This was the song her heart had longed for. This was the best thing she'd ever written.

When the sun was up, Selene tossed on a simple, marigold gown with wide pockets and a skirt above her ankles. Enough to hide her sheet music and keep her hem from dragging in the damp below the opera house. It wasn't pretty, by any means. But who was there to judge her? If things went well, she wouldn't see another person for the rest of the day.

Save for the ghost. She had to see him, had to speak Madame's name, and see if he remembered her.

But to do that, she needed to find a fragment of what once was. A piece of the past. This seemed the simplest task. Her father's watch was heavy in her pocket. She considered giving it up. No longer having the familiar weight. No longer being able to rub her thumb against the tarnished silver and imagine her father checking the time.

Not this. She'd have to find something else.

Selene pulled her hair back into a loose braid and put on her boots. All she needed was something old. She'd spend the day composing and configuring her magic.

There was a commotion in the hallway.

Selene peered around the corner. She recognized Benson's mother and father. They'd been here before. Long visits on Sunday afternoons—the one day Madame Giroux allowed them to rest. Selene had spent that time in the practice rooms, pushing herself. There was no family for her, no one to visit. More than once, Benson had bullied her into joining his family for supper. She'd been grateful for those afternoons, even though there was a part of her that hated seeing what she'd missed. Benson's family served as a reminder of a different life. One she'd never have the chance to lead.

And now Benson wouldn't have it, either.

His little sister, Marie, stood with her back against the wall, thumb tucked in her mouth. They were packing up his things. Clearing the space for someone else.

"Selene?" Marie's voice was watery with tears.

Selene closed her eyes a moment. She hadn't meant to be seen. But she needed to do this. She owed Benson that much.

There was no need to force the sadness into her smile. Seeing Benson's big eyes on Marie's face did that easily enough. She didn't ask Marie how she was. She knew.

"Marie," Selene said.

At the sound of her voice, Benson's parents stepped out to greet her. They'd separated his things into piles. Selene could pick out his most precious books, stacked haphazardly in what was no doubt the discard pile. When they were gone, she'd take the ones he'd read the most and put them in the library he so loved.

"Thank you." Benson's mother wrapped Selene in a tight hug. "Madame Giroux told us what you did."

Selene stiffened.

"It was nothing." Emotion washed over her. The look on Marie's face brought her back to moments she'd rather not remember. There was too much power in this pain. Enough to split her open and drive her into madness without a single note. "How is he?"

His mother's eyes filled with tears. "He's settling into the Asylum. We put your name down, if you want to visit."

Selene's smile could have cracked her teeth. She didn't want to visit. She didn't want to go anywhere near that place. "He will be missed."

"Was he scared?" Marie's little face was wet with tears.

"No." What was one more lie? "It was quick."

Marie nodded. She wrapped her arms around Selene's waist. Selene pressed her hand into the girl's back. If she could have, she would have told her to use this, to embrace this pain and let it shape her into something stronger. Let it burn away the impurities and forge her into something new.

"Come on, Marie." Benson's mother ushered the girl back into the room. She looked at Selene with tired eyes. "Thank you, I mean it. It could have been so much worse."

The door to Benson's room locked. The weight of that finality pressed into her chest, nearly knocking her to the floor.

Selene retreated to her room for a moment to gather her thoughts. Grief manifested in the strangest places, seeing his books stacked, books he'd never read again. She fought back tears.

Madame Giroux did not wait for permission to enter. There was a knock, and before the sound could register, she was inside.

She gave one discerning look to her splayed daughter and then focused on Selene.

"The prince has requested that you give him a tour of the opera house. I deemed it unnecessary, but he insists." Madame Giroux was clearly displeased, pinched and put out by a man who wanted to insert himself into her opera house.

"Now?" Selene's heart beat impetuoso, against her will. She wanted to feel nothing. It would be so much easier if she could expel Victor from her bones.

"Now."

"You can't wear that," Gigi protested. She propelled herself off the bed and toward the dresser.

"She can." Madame Giroux's voice was clipped and cold.

"Mother," Gigi said. If it had been possible for Madame's face to pinch even more, it would have. Gigi cleared her throat and then corrected her approach. "Madame. This is the prince. And we are afforded a unique opportunity for his patronage. If it is Selene he wants, then should we not offer him our best Selene?"

Perhaps the argument had done the trick. Perhaps Madame liked the thought of keeping the prince waiting. She tapped her cane against the floor. "Be quick about it."

She shut the door behind her with more force than necessary.

"What are you doing?" Selene hissed.

Gigi's eyes were bright with mischief. "We are performers. Shouldn't you make an entrance?"

Selene did not argue. She let Gigi rummage through her things before she settled on one of her own dresses, pulled from the pile on the floor. It was one she'd had made for a performance before she realized she couldn't move the way she liked. It was a shade off a damask rose, bleeding into a smoky plum. The skirt ended mid-calf but was full and turned each step into a drama. Intricate embroidery in green and gold traced the neckline and sleeves. Selene remembered when Gigi had it commissioned, drawing it up on the back of a piece of music. She'd worked so hard on the details, only to change her mind. Found something more suitable for the competition. The dress was all that remained.

It wasn't quite the right fit on Selene. She didn't have that slim dancer's physique or half of Gigi's musculature. She was softer around her edges, with broader hips and a rounder bust. Luckily, the back was done up with a long silk ribbon.

"Wait." Selene took her leather sheaf of music and tucked it against her skin.

"That seems a bit much," Gigi said.

"There were razors in your shoes."

Gigi yielded and fussed over the fit for a moment before she turned to her cluttered dresser. Selene reached for a lace choker and wrapped it artfully around her throat. She wasn't sure what Victor remembered and she did not want to distract him with the ugliness of the past. She would offer him only beautiful things. Save the pain for the ghost. Save the pain for the magic. Save the pain for her triumph.

Funny the way beauty could be brought out with a little color and glitter. Not making Selene any different, just a little bit more. Brighter eyes and redder lips. Like she spent her days reading in the garden, instead of locked in rooms with little light. Like her nights were spent dreaming, instead of secreting herself away to learn magic inside of a mirror.

"There," Gigi said when she was finished. "Go reunite with your childhood love."

"He's not my love," Selene said, too loudly.

"Would it be so bad?" Gigi twirled a ribbon around her finger.

"Victor?" Selene laughed, remembering the boy she knew. "Yes."

"Forget Victor, then. It could be anyone."

"I'm here to win." Selene slipped on her boots, despite the face Gigi made. "I don't have time to fall in love."

"Maybe you should make time." Gigi was gentle. "Life is short. You'll never regret the time you spent being loved."

An ache permeated through Selene. She'd thought she was nothing more than her ambition. But there was a part of her that wondered. The way she felt around the ghost, the way she'd felt with Victor last night. There was something wonderful about it. She didn't have to perform; she just had to be. Maybe when all this was over, she'd make time.

CHAPTER 27

Selene found Victor in the grand foyer. His trousers were dirty with horsehair and road dust. His hair was windswept, and his eyes were fever bright. Yet still he belonged among the golden statues and carved banisters and expansive ceiling. He was a handsome, confident man in a beautiful, opulent place. Some things never changed.

She walked soundlessly down the stairs. She caught her reflection in one of the many polished statues. What reflected back was a distortion, altered by the contours of the metal. She wondered what her life would have been, had she lived the last seven years with mirrors. Would she be as vain as Priya or as fearful as Gigi? Would her magic be sharpened by the frequent sight of her tableaux reflected back at her? Would her power be endless, with nearly seven years of shadow magic taught to her by the ghost trapped inside?

Victor busied himself with the contents of his pockets: a watch, a knife, a knot of string. She wasn't sure she'd ever get used to seeing him inside the opera house. Victor existed inside her mind, inside the palace, inside the life she'd been forced to leave behind. He was a fantasy, a ghost in his own right. One slip of light and he'd be gone.

She made a deliberate tap of her sole against the stair. Victor looked up sharply, tucking his collection of things back into his pocket.

"Miss Dreshé, how lovely to make your acquaintance again." His smile was bright as the penny on his palm.

"Your Highness." Selene dropped into a curtsy, leaning into the playful formality.

"None of that," he said in mock offense. "We are old friends, remember? If I wanted bowing and scraping, I'd be in the court with my father, instead of here spending his money."

Selene's lips tipped into the barest smile. "How much money are we talking, Monsieur? That will impact the quality of my tour."

"Victor, if you please," he said. "His Majesty will be forced to do an honest day's labor in order to make up the difference."

"Then I shall show you every part of the theater, from the ballasts to the loo."

"I've seen the loo, thank you." He cleared his throat and gestured with a flair. "This is, as you know, the grand foyer."

"I thought I was giving this tour." Selene reclined on the banister.

"You were mistaken, then. I'm here to show you exactly what I mean to do with L'Opéra du Magician."

Dread and excitement washed over Selene—stagnant and cold as the fountain water they'd once turned into a winter bath. If Victor already had his mind set on things, it would be hard to change. But maybe he was different now, just as she was different.

"You don't like the sound of that?" Victor read her the way he would a cluster of stars, picking out the light from the dark.

"This is my home, Monsieur." The playfulness of her tone fell away, the lie thick on her tongue.

"Victor," he said, this time firmly. "But it won't be your home for long. Soon you'll be a part of L'Opéra du Magician and then whisked away to some nobleman's hall."

Or yours, Selene thought, and hated herself for it.

"Or mine," Victor said. "Should you win."

Selene took a step back, as if moving away from Victor could keep him from her, from knowing her thoughts. All pretense dropped. His eyes widened with concern.

"Too bold?"

"Yes," Selene said quietly.

"Pardon." Victor took her hand, brushed his lips against it in apology. His hands were worn and calloused, not the hands of a prince at all. She remembered the feel of them on her skin, the brush of their fingers as she'd taken the nautilus shell from him. "I don't mean to overstep. The winner will, of course, take residence in the palace."

"Of course, Monsieur." She stepped back into the banter.

There was a moment when Selene thought of all the things she could say to him. She'd been making sculptures from her anger at him for years, chipping away at each corner of the stone until it was smooth and supple as skin. It seemed wrong, now that she knew the truth. He had written her letters. Hundreds of them. She wondered if she'd have been better if she had known. Or would she have tortured herself by hanging on his every word? She imagined herself reading those letters over and over until the pages were thin, the ink faded to nothing. No, she did not like that possibility.

"I would like to hear you say my name."

She wanted to say no. She wanted to tell him that—despite the best intentions—they could not go back. There was no room for him in her life. But his eyes churned like the sea and she could not refuse him.

Selene curtsied. "Victor."

His smile was radiant, light in all the dark places.

They turned into the auditorium. Selene's heart beat accelerando. She hadn't returned to this space since she lost Benson. She didn't expect the grief to radiate from the seats, the walls, to drip from the statues. The air in here was different now. The stage haunted. Selene didn't expect it, didn't know how to move through this space. It occurred to her for the first time that if she became the King's Mage, she might have to perform in the same room her father died in. The thought made the ground tremble beneath her.

"How is your friend?" Victor's voice was soft. He seemed wounded on her behalf, picking up the threads of her sorrow and sharing the burden.

"Benson is…" Selene swallowed the edges of her tears. She would not cry in front of Victor.

He brushed the back of his hand against hers, the lightest touch. He'd been so brazen when he kissed her hand earlier, yet this was far more intimate. "Is there anything I can do?"

Selene shook her head. She led him up the aisles and onto the stage. Silence trailed her like a cloak. Moisture still clung to the air, little dewdrops on the velvet curtains. There were scratches in the wood from her thorns.

"Do you remember the time we stole all the honey from the kitchens?" Victor leaned into the space between them. The curve of his shoulder blocked out the grooves on the floor.

Selene welcomed the change in subject. "I remember the time *you* stole all the honey from the kitchen."

"And His Majesty had to take his toast with jam instead." Victor chuckled.

"You were whipped for that," Selene said quietly. The image of his bloody back and the tracks from tears on his cheeks had never left her.

"Better me than some poor boy." Victor shrugged his hands into his pockets, smiling away the sudden vulnerability.

"Your obsession with whipping boys persists, I see."

"Another gruesome part of our history I wish I could make right," Victor said with a wry smile. She wondered how much he'd done to make amends, or if he counted her name among the wronged.

"Have you made amends for all that history, like you dreamed?"

"What do you think I'm doing here?"

"Vexing your father. Vexing me."

"Magic can be dangerous." Victor looked at her like he was trying to decide if he could tell her the whole truth. "And there is already far too much suffering in the world."

It was an answer to her question and not an answer. There was something he was hiding, something more to his presence here. Far too political, with a grain of painful truth. He knew the dangers of magic, had seen them carved into Selene's skin. He'd been there with her when her father had gone mad and ripped out her throat. If he was here to keep her safe, then he was here to stop her.

Something sparked within her. Just a thought, planted in

her like a seed, echoing within like an ocean trapped in a nautilus shell. She opened her palm and gestured to the rows and rows of blue velvet seats, adorned with gold.

"In a few short days, these will be full." She pointed back to the boxes that framed the stage. "You will be there, of course."

The King's Box was the second closest to the stage, with a wide balcony.

Victor smiled, a dimple forming at one side of his mouth. He pointed to the other side of the stage. There was a smaller box there. It lacked the elegance of the King's Box but had a slightly better angle to the stage and superior acoustics. "I will be there."

"You've done your research."

"I like to know what I'm getting into."

Selene took him through the side exit. "To our right is one of our rehearsal spaces. To the left is the orchestra's space. And back that way is the grand hall. Where would you like to go?"

"I need to see this place as you do. To the right, please."

It shouldn't have surprised Selene, but it did. She had taken visitors on tours before. They always avoided the dark corridors and drafty rehearsal spaces and marveled at the art and architecture of the public rooms. Everyone wanted to see the show. They seldom wanted to know what lay beneath.

"It's too dark in here. That will have to change. Electric lights. A little illumination. There might be fewer accidents if you could see."

Selene hated electric lights. They were so gaudy and without any nuance.

Victor must have noticed the slight downturn of her mouth. "You do not approve?"

"It is not my place."

"Please, tell me. This is your home, not mine."

"There is something distasteful about modern lighting. It takes away the shadows, the mystery. There is no magic like the flicker of candlelight." Selene exhaled, thoughts roiling like the dark. "There are better ways to protect us."

"Like what?"

Mirrors, she thought. The one thing Madame had made sure to remove from the opera house to keep the ghost hidden away. But she didn't want to come out and say it, not yet. It had to be his idea.

"Let me think on it."

"All right." Victor chuckled. "You shall keep your candles, then. But more of them. I would not want anyone to twist an ankle in these dark spaces."

They stopped at the door at the end of the corridor. Selene sang open the lock with three short notes.

"Why is your practice space locked?"

"A precaution," Selene said. "To keep away peeping eyes before the competition."

"Weren't you just practicing onstage?"

"Auditions." A smile tricked up her lips. "There is more to L'Opéra du Magician than one night."

The room was dark, save for the light of one high window. From the looks of the door, someone had tried to carve out the lock, to no avail. *Priya*. As if stealing her music hadn't been enough.

"If I may," Selene said.

"Please."

Selene took a step away from Victor. She breathed in deep, expanding her lungs fully. The rhythm of the familiar melody echoed in her chest. She could feel it in her bones, in the blood pumping through her veins. She let out the first note in her clear, lyrical soprano, singing the line slower than she might have if no one was watching. One by one, the candles around the room flickered and burned with warm light. She could have lit them all at once. It would have been easier. Instead, she started at the one closest to her and followed it around the room, ending with Victor.

"It is a beautiful space." Selene let her eyes trace the bare wall. "It is a shame we cannot see the magic we create reflected back, like in a proper rehearsal space. That may have been enough to save Benson."

Mirrors couldn't have saved Benson any more than they could have saved her father. But Victor didn't need to know that.

Victor's brow furrowed as he considered the room. "Why are there no mirrors in here?"

"Pardon?" She would not let the anticipation slip into her voice. He was asking all the right questions.

"This is a rehearsal space. You should be able to see yourself."

And the ghost.

If the mirrors were there, he would be, too. He would be everywhere. She imagined his prison flooded with light; the shadows kept at bay. And with the shadows away, what could he do? She imagined him reflected in all the mirrors. A hundred ways in and a hundred ways out.

"There is a ghost in the glass." Selene lowered her voice, as if she was telling him a secret. She had known Victor, years before. How to get him to do exactly what she wanted. It was time to see if things had really changed. "Years ago a girl became so frightened she threw herself off the roof of the opera house. Surely you've heard the rumors?"

Victor waved his hand in dismissal. "Sometimes I prefer the company of ghosts to people."

"Me too." Selene matched his smile.

"But the mirrors." Victor pressed his hand against the wall. There were scars on his knuckles that hadn't been there when they were children. "This is a safety issue. This must change."

"I would not do that, sir." Madame Giroux's voice echoed through the rehearsal space.

Selene winced at the way she addressed him. She tried not to let her growing disdain for Madame rise off her skin like smoke.

Victor's smile was all poison and charm. "Madame, how do magicians know what they are crafting if they cannot see?"

"You think this is about what you see?" Madame Giroux crossed her arms over her chest. "Spoken like a man who has never known magic."

"It is a performance."

"It is a competition," Madame Giroux said. "If you think it is about what you see on that stage, then you are sadly mistaken, sir." She looked sharply at Selene. "It begins before they appear on my steps, small and weak, before they crawl out of bed, before they even know the language of music."

Victor smiled easily and then started to hum. Selene knew the melody. His voice was easy and natural. He did not have the training, but there was a loveliness to it, like an uncut gem. The flames in the candles burned higher and higher, until they were bonfires, melting the wax down to the wick.

"We do not suffer fools in this theater." Madame's eyes darkened. She hit her cane against the wood, countering his melody. The candles doused. Steam wisped out of the sconces, the only shade against the shadow.

"It is a good thing I am not a fool," Victor said. "I will not bow to superstition, Madame Giroux. If installing mirrors allows your performers to recognize when they've pushed themselves too far and prevents incidents like the one I witnessed, it will be worth a little fear."

His eyes—like tea steeped to bitterness—were locked on Madame's. Selene had seen him look this way at a chessboard, at his older brothers, at the sea. Like he was trying to solve the puzzle of Madame Giroux. It was a glimmer of intensity. Not the boy from the papers, but a strategist and a leader.

Victor relaxed his shoulders, easing into one of his crowd-pleasing smiles.

"Good day to you, Madame. I'm sure we will see more of each other over the coming days."

"I shall warn you once, boy." Madame Giroux's voice was so quiet that Selene leaned in to hear. "You will bring ruin upon us all if you insist on tricks of glass and fancy."

Fear traced down Selene's spine like the brush of a feather.

"Is that a threat, Madame Giroux? Are you afraid of ghosts?"

"Just one ghost." Madame's eyes were cut to slits. She leveled her gaze at Selene. Her hands were tight against her cane. "We should all be afraid."

She gave Selene a long, appraising look and stepped out of the room.

Selene arched an eyebrow. "Do you make enemies everywhere you go?"

Victor laced his fingers together and turned them out, his scarred knuckles popping all at once. "One of my few talents."

"Like magic?"

When they were children, he would sometimes sit in on her lessons with her father. But he never sang a note. He often complained about the boredom, wanting her to go stir up trouble with him outside.

"I picked up a few things over the years."

"Offra?"

Offra had taken the last competition with a spectacular display of fireworks that turned to ice and snowed all over the theater. A complex and dangerous combination of motifs that she pulled off with ease. She had a lovely, warm alto and a smile that could have won over any audience, even without magic. Selene had watched the king put the onyx necklace around her throat. She wondered what Offra thought now that she was passing her position on to the next person, now that her tenure as the King's Mage was up.

"Offra wants nothing to do with me," Victor said. "She believes the papers. Thinks I'll try and make a plaything of her heart."

"Would you?" Selene's gaze was pointed as Madame's.

"Heavens, no. Internal organs make terrible toys." The mischief melted from Victor's eyes. "I had hoped those rumors had not been so far-reaching."

"You'd be surprised what we hear."

Victor faced her. "You know me, Selene."

"It's been a long time since we were children."

He reached forward, brushing back one of her dark curls. An acquiescence. An acknowledgment of the distance and time and what had changed between them.

"Only rumors."

"If you say so."

This had been so much easier in the moonlight, wearing masks of every kind. No matter how she wished and wanted, things could never go back to the way they were. But Selene had learned to use every opportunity, and she would not take this lightly. If that meant mirrors or the pain or a piece of the past, she'd take it. And then she'd go back to her world, and he'd go back to his. Perhaps they'd see each other in court, but she doubted it. Victor was not made for confined spaces. That's why he'd done so well in the military. Why he'd always slept with the windows open.

"Are these your only rehearsal spaces?"

She gestured down the dark hallway. "Down here, we have more practice rooms."

Victor tilted his head. "Do all of them need mirrors, too?"

Selene led Victor to the front doors the long way around, avoiding Madame Giroux's office. "We've seen everything there is to see." She couldn't help but look toward the exit.

Victor followed her gaze. "You haven't shown me the roof."

"I don't have time." Selene raised an eyebrow. "Afraid to go home?"

"Afraid that I'll stay?"

She turned away from the split of a stairway and the watching eyes of all the statues and faced Victor. For a moment, she imagined him as they had been in those last days. Thirteen and fourteen and unaware of the world's pain. They'd been on the precipice of change. There was nothing between them, nothing owed. They were nothing but a bittersweet memory. She wished things could be as easy as they had been when they were children.

She looked at him, thinking of all the things she could say. She wanted to ask him where he'd been. What had happened between the then and the now? It didn't even matter. They couldn't go back and borrow the time.

Instead, she brushed a speck of dust off the bodice of her dress and gathered her courage.

"I need something from you," Selene said. "You have to promise you won't ask me any questions."

"All right." Victor rolled his shoulders back and leaned against the closed door.

She took a deep breath. This was for the ghost, for the mirror. "I need a lock of your hair."

Victor laughed. "Is that all? Heavens, I thought you were going to ask me to jump off the building or something half as terrible."

"Why would I ask for anything like that?"

"You'd be surprised." Victor took out his dagger and cut a curl from the nape of his neck. He dropped it into her open hands. It coiled there, like a small snake. "I get asked all sorts of requests in court."

"To leap off buildings?" She tucked the curl into her pocket beside her father's watch.

"Once a woman asked me if I'd murder her husband." He sheathed his knife.

"Did you?" Selene leaned closer.

"Of course not. And I didn't murder her when the husband asked me to. Nor did I smuggle tigers, like the papers are suggesting."

"You lie to your friends, and I'll lie to mine." She crossed her arms over her chest. "But let's not lie to each other."

Victor's smile was genuine. "I've never even seen a tiger."

"Not in all your adventures?"

Victor reached over and brushed one of her curls off her shoulder again. She could feel the heat of his fingertips through the fabric of her gown. "Nothing so wild as this."

And her heart matched the cadence of his words, a tremulous rush of familiar wanting.

No, no, no.

She couldn't do this. She'd been just a girl, then. She hadn't known about broken hearts or blood or desire. She'd wanted to be at the edge of the sea with her father, singing the world into a more beautiful place. In those dreams, Victor was there, too. She hadn't understood how—she just knew she wanted him in her life, forever.

Selene was old enough to know now that dreams didn't come true. That she had to claw and bite and bleed to get what she wanted. She was old enough to know now that Victor wouldn't stay.

Victor must have sensed her turmoil. He crossed the distance between them, wrapping his arms around her. Selene couldn't remember the last time she'd been held like this. She fought the rush of her heart, trying to stay grounded in her resolve not to be pulled into Victor's orbit. But then he pressed his face into her shoulder, and she breathed in the sweet salt that permeated his clothes. She could have this. She could abandon her whole life and let Victor take her away from her dreams, her grief, her ambition. Like the dark, he could make her forget. She closed her eyes, trying to keep the world from slipping away.

He took a step away from her, hand still resting on the small of her back, fingers against her skin in between the ribbon lacing of the dress. He brushed his thumb down her jawline. She shivered beneath his touch. She could taste the sea on him—the brine and wildness of a storm and something else she couldn't quite name.

"I missed you," he said.

He rested his hand against her neck, fingers against the black lace choker she had secured there. His eyes dropped from hers, down to her lips, and back again. Oh, she could do this. She could get caught up in Hurricane Victor, let herself get swept away like she had when they were children. It would be so easy.

But this wasn't what she wanted anymore. She had her own life, her own wants. She had music to write and ghosts to save and competitions to win. Victor was a memory. She took a step away.

"I have things to do."

"You said that." Victor's smile fell into place. "Anything better than this?"

No, she wanted to say.

"Join me for dinner."

For one fleeting moment, Selene thought she would say yes.

"I have to rehearse." She looked to the stairs, to the door, to the balconies. Anywhere but Victor.

"Surely you must nourish your body, rest your soul."

"I don't have time, Victor."

"A quick dinner, then. Please."

Gods, the way he said that word. It was made new. It was a thousand symphonies folded up into that single pang of emotion. Selene remembered the thousand times she'd answered that plea. But as much as she wanted to, she couldn't give in.

"Damn you, Victor," she said. And she could see by the way his hand curled over the door handle that he had expected this answer. Resigned himself to a fate without her. He wasn't angry about it, like she was. And that's what softened the hardness of her heart. "Ask me again tomorrow."

Victor stopped, hand against the door. Hopeful. "And you'll say yes?"

"Just ask me again," Selene said.

CHAPTER 28

She stood on the stone platform, wishing she'd worn a cloak to stave off the chill. This dress was not made for lake rides and cold stone. It was made for hot stage lights and rooftop rendezvous. It was made for some other girl. She ran the lock of Victor's hair between her fingers, still tucked in her pocket. It was soft against her skin. It smelled like the sea and pitch and burst pomegranates.

"Please work."

She needed this. Selene put her hand against the mirror. Blood ran from her index finger.

The mirror gave way.

Relief cleansed her more than the swallowing dark. She kept her eyes closed, waiting for her body to orient.

The ghost's smile was a rose coming into bloom. She felt it beneath her skin, rippling through her like an exquisite bass line.

"You found something," he said, the relief visible in the slope of his shoulders and the widening of his smile.

"I did." Selene reached into her pocket and took out the lock of hair. She presented it like the strange and precious thing it was.

His pale eyes drew up in surprise. "What is that?"

"My past," Selene said, like she meant it. If she said it enough times, it would be true.

The ghost shook his head. He looked her up and down, as if to assess what else she had to offer. There was a glimmer of fear in his eyes. "There's no magic in that."

"But I came through the mirror." Selene didn't like the way he looked at her, like searching for something terrible. She could sense the shift in him. The darkness sensed it as well. The tendrils of black spun closer, ready to take.

"Then you must have something," the ghost said, desperation clinging to his voice. "A fragment of what was."

"What happens if I don't give you what you asked for?" Panic rose like bile in Selene's throat. What did she have to give?

The ghost pressed his head into his hand, mussing his dark hair. "You'll be consumed."

The dark seemed to lean in, closer and closer, hungrier for her than they were for what she brought. The ghost's face was a mask of pain, enough to remake this whole world. He reached out his hand to her. She couldn't touch him; she mustn't touch him. But if this was the last thing she would ever do, would it be so bad to end it with her hand in his?

Forcing the thoughts from her head, she strengthened her resolve. She wouldn't let it end like this. She hadn't come all this way to be swallowed by the living dark in the mirror. She reached into her pockets, pulling out the pin, a pen, and her father's pocket watch. Hoping against hope, she held out the collection of offerings.

The ghost took a step toward her. His hand stopped reaching, hovering over her palm. She took that as a good sign. There was something here. She imagined the magic was heat, warming his hand like a candle flame. His eyes lit with recognition. "This one."

"Wait—" Selene gripped the chain of her father's watch tightly. "It's all I have left of him."

The ghost pulled his hand back. He looked at her like she was the moon and he'd do anything to keep her from waning. Determined and deeply sad, facing down an inevitability. "Go, then. I'll do what I can to hold off the dark. Quickly, before you lose the choice."

"What?" Selene hadn't expected this.

"If it's all you have, leave." The ghost wasn't being cruel, even though Selene felt the slice of guilt. He knew how much this mattered to her. He'd help her find a way out. At any cost.

Selene wrapped her fingers around the watch. Already the darkness roiled around them. "And what happens to you?"

The ghost's smile was not a smile at all, but a sweet misery. "I'll let the dark have me."

Selene closed her eyes. She couldn't let him pay that price. He deserved so much more than this endless prison. And she couldn't take the thought of never seeing him again. "I can't do that to you."

She didn't want to lose this last part of her father. But she didn't know what else she had to give. She tucked her measly treasures back into her pockets. She ran her thumb over the silver nightingale one last time. Wound up the clock and listened to the metronome inside.

The oily darkness stirred. Rising to take what was not freely given. She held out the pocket watch to the ghost. He didn't reach for it.

"You're sure?"

"Yes."

And she was, she was, she was. She could give up this trinket, in exchange for what she really wanted: to follow in her father's footsteps. To sing with the ghost. To keep him safe from any more harm.

He closed his fist around the watch. The darkness shivered and pressed in. A shadow lashed out. The ghost dodged effortlessly. The darkness struck again, whirling around him. He moved with a grace she didn't know he had, like a dancer. She could watch him like this forever, if it weren't for the shadows that sliced through the air, eager to take any part of him they could.

"What are you doing?" Selene cried.

He looked up at her, still for a moment. His dark hair fell into his eye, his lip curling into a half smile. She wanted to see that smile in the light. "If it wants this so badly, let it take it."

Selene had seen what the darkness could do. "Not if it will hurt you!"

His expression shifted, softened. He opened his palm and the dark slithered out. It swallowed up the silvery bird and the sound of the clock.

"This I have asked, and you have answered." He looked defeated, like it was his watch and his father he'd given up. "I'm sorry, Selene."

"It's just a watch," Selene said, even though it wasn't. "It isn't him."

"You still carry your father, Selene. You swore on him. We swear by what matters most."

"What matters most," she repeated.

If she'd still had the pocket watch, she'd be able to measure the time that ticked between them. She counted the breaths, tasted the crisp and colorless air around them. She named the scars that moved up his arms like constellations and wondered what magic he had wrought from that pain.

"Well?"

"I'm waiting for you to guess my name." The shadow of a smile crossed his lips.

"Anthony." Selene relaxed into the familiar pattern. She ticked each of the names off on her fingers. "Vincent. Harrison."

"None of those." The ghost cocked an eyebrow. "I hope you're writing these down."

"Ten names," Selene said. "A thousand more to go."

A thousand more. Selene relished what that implied. That she'd have more time, endless time. He looked at her with a hopeful sorrow that made her heart ache.

"What is it you want?" His voice was low.

Selene didn't quite know how to answer that. Something had shifted inside of her.

It wasn't Victor. She wouldn't let it be Victor. Her whole life could not be knocked off course by a boy who couldn't button a jacket. Maybe it was the room filled with smoke, her music almost lost. Maybe it was how close she'd come to losing the ghost.

She turned away from him and worked her sheaf out of her bodice. It was damp with sweat, but the music inside was safe.

"I want to write music with you and use that song to win L'Opéra du Magician."

"This I have asked, and you have answered."

"It is my turn for a question." She tried not to think of the game she played with Victor. "Do you remember a girl? She saw you in the mirror and jumped from the roof of the opera house."

The ghost shrugged. "I don't think so."

"She—the girl who jumped—is my teacher. I think she knows of the magie du sang."

"That's not possible." His brow furrowed as the pieces of something came together in his mind. "The magie du sang is mine, a magic I created. She can't know unless—"

"Unless you taught her." Selene tried to grasp what it would be like to create magic, instead of following someone else's rules. Wasn't that what she tried to do, when she attempted a third motif? Wasn't that what she was doing now, by blending the magics?

"I would remember." He articulated each word like he was invoking something; like if he said them right then, the memories would flood in. "What was her name?"

"Brigitte Giroux."

Something lit in his eyes. The name was enough, a light in the dark. "I remember Brigitte. She was relentless, like you. She wanted to win at any cost—at first. But she didn't like the cost of the magic. She wanted to keep her pain. She was afraid."

"So afraid she jumped from the roof." Selene looked for part of him that should make her afraid. She had seen him as a monster, and yet that wasn't enough to scare her. She knew his very soul. "She's known you were trapped here, all this time...and she left you."

The ghost turned from her. "Perhaps she knows something you and I don't."

"You don't deserve this. No one deserves this."

"I have found ways to occupy myself."

Selene blew out a breath, trying to focus on something she could do. "How did you know you could do magic without music?"

"Magic doesn't need music. Music is just another tool, a form of focus, like pain. There were so many ways magic could be channeled."

"Where did it all go? That's what I don't understand. How did it all get lost in a hundred years?"

The ghost shrugged, but there was a tightness in the uptick of his shoulders. "A lot can happen in the winding of a clock."

"The effort it would take to erase that much history…"

"Improbable, impossible, and yet here we are."

He was so casual about it all, as if it was inevitable that whatever magic existed in his world could be lost in hers. Selene needed to grasp it, needed to make sense of how much the world could change in three generations.

"How did you create the magie du sang?"

He closed his eyes. "From an excess of pain. The memory is there. I just can't quite grasp it."

Selene thought of his endless scars. "Who did this to you?"

The ghost opened his mouth to speak. The darkness vibrated, pressing in around them. She had seen the dark take from him before. She couldn't witness it again.

"Don't speak. Please."

The ghost squeezed his eyes shut. "You are asking the right questions. They are merely questions I cannot answer."

Selene's skin crawled. "I'm sorry."

"You are relentless, Selene. Never be sorry for that."

The ghost pricked the inside of his forearm with his knife. The shadows writhed, forming a mass between them. The darkness seemed to fight against him for a moment. Twisting and churning and roiling like a storm-tossed sea. Had Victor been caught in storms like that, carrying the precious box with the rose he'd made for her?

He'd swept back into her life like he'd never been gone. Like he belonged there.

No, Selene thought. She had to focus. She could worry about tomorrow tomorrow.

The ghost sat down in front of the grand piano he'd crafted out of shadows and blood. It was elegant and slick, like something out of a half-remembered dream. His fingers stretched over the black keys. He played the first chord.

"Let us begin."

CHAPTER 29

It could have been hours or seconds or years. Time was a tide that ebbed and flowed with a fickle moon. Everything was melody and heartache and the impossible beauty at their intersection. Selene bled the tips of her fingers to mark the page. The ghost left smudges of blood on the keys and on the edges of the sheet music. She watched him from the corner of her eye, the cut of his jaw and the passion in his icy blue eyes. He was in love with art the same way she was. Music was more than bleeding and wanting. Each note was pulled from the ether and pressed into sound. Sung and played and felt down to the soul.

"Like this?" Selene sang the line. The ghost played the same notes on the piano. Selene ran it through a few times to solidify the rhythm before she wrote it down.

"What if the music is more, Selene?" He moved with the music. "What if instead of magic, it told a story?"

Her father had changed the world by giving magic a story. Could she do the same by adding story to the song?

Selene considered it, feeling electricity beneath her skin. She'd seen the operas, heard the sounds made popular by singers, watched every form of sung magic she could find. The tableaux were the story, every essence of entertainment focused on the magic and the loveliness of the vocals. For the most part, the songs were simple and repetitive. They had to be, for the vocalist to balance the magic and the music. Even Selene's arias were like that. She'd focused on what magic could do, instead of what music could be.

"What story?" Selene tapped her fingers against the glossy black keys.

"The only one that matters."

He played the counterpoint on the piano, the magical motif starting in the voice and then breaking and spreading between each of the parts. Selene had only ever written music with the motif contained to a single instrument. She'd start it in the voice and then let the cello or the clarinet continue the melody while she sang in the second element. Simple, easy ways to maintain the motifs. This was brilliant, using the combination of the voice and the orchestra to channel the same magics, but with a careful subtlety that allowed for endless variation. It had the power of the motif but none of the repetition. It told a story, but not just with the magic. The song was the story. It was art made new.

"Yes." The ghost's smile was a rising moon. He wrote it in his blood.

"The aria will sound like an aria." Selene suppressed a shiver. "I always wanted to push the boundaries of magic. I never considered doing it with the music."

"Anything can be magic if you make it so."

The intensity of his gaze shifted from Selene back to the piano. His fingers danced through the first movement. She hummed along, writing the notes and flourishes he added when he played. She'd always considered writing a solitary act.

Others hired coaches, worked with their friends and teachers. Besides Gigi, she'd never dared collaborate. Writing was personal, private. She didn't want anyone to hear the wrong notes or see the mess on the page.

Selene traced her fingers over the bars. The piece was lovely, nearly perfect. But she could see the gaps in what they were writing. What this piece begged for was a second voice.

"Sing with me?" Selene said.

"It would be better practice if you sing it alone."

The ghost's breath warmed her shoulder. She couldn't be this close to him without touching him. She stood up, moving to the other side of the piano. Close enough that she could still see the music but far enough that she wasn't tempted to lean into him.

"Just this once," Selene said.

"All right."

The ghost played the first chord. His voice rose like a promise, meeting hers. The languidness of the line drew her closer to him. She watched his hands fly over the keys, listened to the purr of his voice and how easily it fit with hers. Did he know how exquisite he was? From the shape of his shoulders, to the movement of his hands, to the way his lip trembled with vibrato. She'd never seen a man more lovely than music.

When she could no longer bear the sight of him in such rapturous beauty, she closed her eyes. They could be anywhere, singing like this. She could practically feel the rush of the ocean, the sand beneath her toes. She could taste the salt air and feel the sun on her face. And he was there with her, outside the mirror. They were free from all of it. From the mirror, from L'Opéra du

Magician, free from their lives. She wanted nothing more than to touch him, to be touched. She imagined taking his hand and pressing it over her heart so he could feel the vivace rush of her heart, those full lips on hers.

Singing with him was like breathing. Singing with him was like dreaming. Singing with him was everything, all at once.

He lifted his hands from the keys, their voices swallowed in the dark. He looked at her with a happiness she had yet to see on his haunted face.

"Thank you, Selene."

She pushed a damp curl from out of her face. "I should be thanking you."

"All I've brought you is a way to shape pain."

Selene shook her head. "You've changed everything."

"That final note." The ghost played the chords leading up to it. "What if you took it up to the sixth. A little dissonance, and then resolve."

Selene sang it over the piano and wrote it down. She could see the magic, rising in her mind like it would on the stage. She indicated the places where she needed pain with a breath mark.

She tried to focus on that, and not the elegant way the ghost's hands moved over the keys. Not the way it felt to sing with him, like it was the last song. Like it was the only song. Like it was her whole heart. She reached the end of a measure and realized what she'd done.

Carefully, she wrote the word *fine* in delicate script.

The aria was finished. And it was brilliant. Far beyond what she could do on her own. She'd have two sung elements, and numerous places where the melody was written in, but the magic would come by blood. Two types of magic and endless possibilities. A spectacle of ingenuity. No one else would come close to what she had created.

And the music carried the story.

"Sing once again with me," the ghost said.

She sang. The ghost played with her for a little while. Then he dropped his hands, taking out his little knife. He bled for her a quartet of shining black instruments. They took on their parts, playing each note perfectly. Selene sang louder, her voice rising above the orchestration. The ghost focused on her, hand moving from time to time to conduct. What they'd written held the continuum of the magical motifs and played so perfectly against hers. She imagined what it would be like to sing this song, with a full orchestra and an audience and the ghost out onstage with her. It would be like living a dream. The resonance and the response of the audience, the glow of the stage lights and the feel of his hand in hers as they moved to the coda. She knew each curve and line of these notes.

When she was finished, she rested her hand against the lid of the grand piano.

The open lid slammed shut. The wretched cacophony of discordant sound reverberated through the soundboard before deadening in the dark.

The ghost pressed his hands to his eyes, eyebrows drawn down. His hands trembled with memory. She could see it in the way his shoulders curved, hear it in the raggedness of his breath. She splayed her fingers against the black wood of the piano until they turned white.

"What is it?"

"There's a scrap: my hands aching and blood and teeth in new green grass. A feeling of knowing I'd done something I couldn't come back from. But nothing whole or damning." He breathed in sharply. "Not enough to warrant this hell."

"But you remembered something."

"I didn't tell you," the ghost said. "For the first time, I remembered something without you here. I remembered my mother."

The way he said it, it was like a curse.

"Was it awful?"

"She was beautiful." There was a bitterness to his voice. He put his hands on the onyx keys but did not play. "She taught me how to play the piano."

Selene sat on the bench beside him, keeping enough space between them. She played the first chord in their song. He picked out the melody while she moved through the different progressions. Already knew the memories she'd pull from. "What else do you remember?"

"One morning," the ghost said, "she dressed me up in my finest shirt and trousers and took me out near the road by the house. The sun was warm and I wanted to climb trees. She kept my hand firmly in hers. There were hoofbeats on the road. A man gave her a sack and then she kissed my cheek and sent me away. The after is hazy. But I remember being afraid. I remember knowing that my mother had traded me for whatever was in that sack. Gold or grain or wool. Whatever it was, it measured my worth."

"No one deserves that." Selene didn't know what else to say. She kept playing the next chord and the next. Music as a balm to the soul.

The ghost struck his hands against the keys. Playing out of tune and out of sync with her. A discordant, terrible melody.

"Wish I knew the rest to this tragic backstory." He kept his voice even, but she could hear the emotion that wanted to break through. "And the crime I can't remember or escape."

"I wish I knew how to help." Her voice was barely audible over the music. She had to do more. He deserved more.

"It's enough for you to be here, Selene." He slowed his reverie, ending on a final dissonant chord. "I cannot express how much it means to me."

All at once, she wished he could. She thought of Victor, and the way he'd reached for her.

"I want to see you in the light." Selene stretched out her fingers. Not touching, but close.

The ghost sang for her the smallest star. He cupped it in the palm of his hand and held it up to his face. He was so terribly beautiful. From his broken nose to the nick in his brow to the lips she could not kiss. "I'll make my own light, then."

She put her hands above his, shielding the light and casting shadows on his face. "Tell me how to get you out."

"I would if I knew."

"Before," Selene said, putting together pieces that had been scattered around her like breadcrumbs, "when you were the ghost. You said the mirrors were all around you like windows. What if I brought mirrors back into the opera house?"

"We could try," the ghost said. "But how will you do it?"

"It will be done," Selene said. "In a few days."

"Will you be in the opera house?"

Selene held very still. If Selene won L'Opéra du Magician,

she'd be whisked away to the palace. When Offra won, she'd ridden away in a golden carriage, only returning to the opera house for the annual masquerade. Then her life was something else. Selene wouldn't have time to say goodbye. And if she lost? She'd have to pack up her things and find another home. People did stay in the opera house once the competition was over. Some of them were even picked up for roles during the opera seasons. Maybe Selene could resign herself to that life if it meant more time to get the ghost out. But what would happen when it came time for her to tour? Madame Giroux might allow her to stay a week or so, but it wouldn't be enough. She would simply be gone.

"It's all right," the ghost said.

"I can get you out." Selene would, she had to. She was relentless and she would find the door. "I'll find a way to get you out of the mirror. You deserve your freedom."

The ghost kept his eyes fixed on the piano keys. There was a certain set to his shoulders, to his jaw. "There are more ways to freedom."

Selene didn't like the timbre of his voice. "What do you mean?"

"Smash the mirror. Break it into a thousand tiny pieces. If mirrors are the answer, then this, too, might work."

It felt like closing a door—something Selene could not abide.

"And risk that you'll be trapped here forever?"

"What difference will it make?" The ghost played the opening chords of their piece. "Either I'll forget you, or I'll be free."

"And what about me?" Selene said. She belonged to this place as much as he did. She belonged in this swallowing dark where the edges of music and magic warped. Where blood was the smallest price for the greatest thing. She couldn't just let him die.

"Go on with your life. Forget about me and this place of darkness. Find a way to be happy."

I can't, she thought. She should have been surprised, but she wasn't. *I don't want a life without your music. I don't want a life without you.*

She should tell him. She had to tell him what he meant to her. She wet her lower lip and looked into his pale blue eyes.

"Who killed your father?" The ghost sounded as weary as she felt.

"It was me," Selene said, her voice breaking.

The wrong answer. Again and again. She couldn't get this one right.

"This I have asked and you have answered." He sounded so disappointed.

A tear traced the curve of Selene's cheek. "Please don't ask me to wash myself in more blood."

"Blood is all we have left."

Selene pressed her hand against the black keys. Her heart was a stone sinking to the bottom of the river, tossed and tumbled and taken out to sea. She wanted to tell him how much he meant to her, why she couldn't break the mirror. Maybe it was selfish of her. Maybe the ghost wasn't a thing she could keep to herself, after years of pouring her soul into art and performance. Maybe he deserved respite in the wake of a hundred years of solitude. Still, if she could tell him how her heart ached to look at him and how he had changed her life with a song and a drop of blood, maybe it would be enough for him to stay. Her fingers brushed the edge of his sleeve.

He sprang back with unearthly speed. Shadows tore from his back. The feathers were the same glossy black as the one she'd brought him. A thousand of them stretching from black to black. His eyes had gone the reflective dark of an oil slick. Not the face of a man, but something so much worse. The shadows rippled and roiled, bubbling to the surface, hungry for Selene's transgression. She must not touch him.

"Bring me the death of a dream." The ghost's voice was distorted. A twisted, awful thing. Where was the music, the man beneath? Blood ran down his cheeks. This was the monster in the story, the thing of which she was meant to be afraid.

Selene felt no fear. Only anguish at his distortion. She stood, wishing she could go to him and make this right. The ghost made an inhuman sound, somewhere between music and pain. His great wings beat.

CHAPTER 30

Selene gasped, knees against the stone and head against the glass. The pain was sharp but forgettable. Gigi's dress was ruined; the fabric of the skirt shredded when Selene was cast out, like shadows had reached for her but not been quick enough. Selene tried to even her breathing, tried to look past her own reflection and see the ghost. She hadn't meant for this to happen. She wanted to tell him this wasn't his fault and she wasn't afraid of him.

She pressed her hand against the mirror, hoping that he could sense her. She stood to go, pressing her hand to her stomach where she kept her leather sheaf.

It wasn't there.

Her music. She'd left the music in the mirror.

She had two days before L'Opéra du Magician. She needed to practice. It was so much more complex than anything she'd sung before. She needed to be able to sing that song in her sleep.

She pricked her thumb and pressed it to the glass. The drop of blood rolled down, unaccepted. She summoned the image of her father's broken body, but the memory was fuzzy and faded, all the color gone. Even now, her attempt to draw on it again thinned the memory like water against stone, until the death mask on her father's face was just a blur.

No.

It was a memory she should have been thrilled to lose. The pain of it was too much for her to carry, and yet the loss was just as great.

Magic has a price.

Selene couldn't stop now. There was no turning back.

Instead, she remembered the crushing disappointment of her music being sung by someone else, thought of the look on Benson's face as his mind shattered, felt the warmth of Victor's body on hers.

But the mirror would not acquiesce.

Selene tried to slow her racing heart. She would have to write as much as she could from memory. Piece the song back together as best she could. That seemed an impossible task without the ghost. They'd created something so perfect; she was afraid she'd never be able to re-create it.

Her only option was to bring him what he'd asked: the death of a dream.

She walked up the stairs, her mind shuffling the possibilities of what the mirror might accept: a morning glory burst into bloom at first light, a candle sung to flame and then doused, the fragile body of a bird fallen in flight. She could argue their purpose, connect them to a dream's end. But she knew the shadows expected more. Whatever she gave up, it had to matter. Each of her offerings to the mirror had been etched with her angst, her wanting, her pain. The fight and the freedom of the feather. The endless possibilities in the seed, stolen from Madame's piano. The memories tied up in the shell. And everything the pocket watch had meant to her father. There'd been a purpose in each of them.

She'd need to find something of equal measure to win back her music and see the ghost. To get her music, to apologize for nearly touching him. She didn't want to do anything to hurt him. She hadn't meant to do it at all.

She made a brief stop in the library. Benson's table was still piled high with books. Her fingers traced over the tops of them, sending little dust motes up.

It was painful to stand so near the place where Benson had put together the pieces of his own destruction. All those late nights, writing the perfect song. For his brilliance, he'd been destroyed.

And now all that was left to remember him here was a pile of books that would soon be put away.

She made it back to her room and wrote down all she could recall on a blank page in a frenzy. It was undeveloped and completely unworthy. Frustrated, Selene peeled off Gigi's ruined dress and kicked off her shoes. She was in bed before she even had the space to register where she was.

The light broke through the window, shattering the remnants of sleep. Selene sat up, banishing the whims of her subconscious.

The room seemed wrong.

Gigi's bed had been stripped. The dresser moved out. All of Gigi's clutter and glitter and creativity were gone.

Something terrible must have happened. Selene's heart raced, trying to purge the image of the blood that poured down Camille's neck. She had to get Madame, and quickly. She grabbed her cloak from its peg and rushed out the door.

Selene should have been here. She should have checked her

priorities and watched Gigi's back. Gigi was far too trusting, far too kind. She didn't deserve any of this.

Selene had hardly crossed the threshold when she was stopped by the familiar sounds of Gigi's snoring echoing in the hall. There was a new lock on Benson's room.

Unsettled, Selene knocked on the door three times. The snores cut off.

"I'm busy," Gigi called back, her voice thick with sleep.

There was a rush of relief, followed by a deep cut of sadness.

There were two possibilities: Gigi had moved out and had not told her. Gigi had packed up her things in the secret, stolen moments while Selene was out. They'd always done everything together, but the line between friend and competitor was thin.

Or Gigi had been moved by order of Madame to isolate them. Because she knew they were stronger together, a force to be reckoned with. Because she knew what they'd done.

Selene's heart ached. Everything had gone so wrong.

Once she was back in her room, she put her trembling hand into her pocket and felt the sharpened tip of the pin. She held it up to the light. The ghost had created this magic from nothing. And here she was, weak and helpless without her music, without him. She dropped the pin onto the dresser.

She needed a way back into the mirror. That was her focus now. Where else could she go to feel safe and free from the worries of the world? She searched her too large, too empty room. She found a scrap of sheet music, a broken pointe shoe, a moth that had strayed too close to the light. Nothing was good enough, and she knew it. She couldn't feel the magic in any of it; the wonder she'd felt with the feather and the nautilus and her father's watch absent. She paced the room, looking for something—anything—she could bring the ghost. All she needed was the death of a dream.

What else could she do but take her broken heart and make it into art.

She half ran to the library, hopeful that the space would be neglected with all the preparations for the competition. There had to be something, some scrap of Benson left behind.

The magic of sleep had swept in and reordered things. The room looked pristine. All of his haphazardly stacked books put back on the shelf.

Selene sank into the chair that had once been his.

It was like he'd never been here, like he'd never even existed in this space. How easily one could be erased, swept away into the Asylum and forgotten. Maybe she could go there and take a scrap of his clothing or a cast-off piece of sheet music. She could find a way to the Asylum if she was clever enough.

Perhaps Victor could take her there.

Victor.

The rose.

There was magic in it. He'd carried that rose across the world, and for what? They couldn't make up for the lost time. So many dreams had died with that boy.

What was one more?

She had given up her father's watch. She could give this up, too.

And she'd forget about Victor. He'd take his ship and sail away. She'd move on with her life and he'd move on with his.

She made her way back up the stairs, guilt tangling around her heart. Perhaps this feeling was enough for her to be sure the magic was real. The pain already felt.

The door of her room was open. Selene approached with caution. She was sure she had shut it, locked it even. She must have forgotten in her haste.

Until she heard the sound of papers scattering against the floor.

CHAPTER 31

Selene took a moment, watching from the doorway. Priya rifled through pages and pages of sheet music. All of them blank. Not a scrap of music to be found, Selene's latest drafts tucked in her pocket.

"Where is it?" Priya pulled out another drawer, digging through Selene's scarves and stockings. She'd find no music there. She'd find no music anywhere. Selene's leather sheaf was trapped in another world, guarded by a ghost.

There was a bundle on Selene's dresser, next to the wooden box. For a moment, Selene was sure it was some new sort of sabotage. It wasn't until Priya put her fingers on it that Selene recognized what it was: letters. Hundreds of letters bound together with twine. Despite the years, the handwriting was clear and familiar. Madame had delivered the letters she'd held hostage all these years.

And left the door unlocked.

Priya reached past the bundle for the box, fingers brushing the scarred wood. Selene sang the wind, not thinking even a moment of the consequences—pushing the door all the way open and knocking Priya's outstretched fingers.

"There you are," Priya said quickly. "I was just looking for—"

"My music?" Selene continued the melody for air, letting the blank sheets rise, swirling around Priya.

Priya's eyes glittered with hate. "Why would I want anything from you? Your name will mean nothing once the competition is over. Just like your father."

"You've made a terrible mistake."

Selene sang for fire. Each of the pages of sheet music burst into flame. Fire and ash rained down. Priya was quick. She sang for air and pulled it toward herself, starving out the little flames.

"Why are you doing this?" Selene shouted when she stopped for breath.

"Getting my dream at any cost."

"It's my dream, too."

Priya scoffed. "You don't know what it's like to have no choices. You could be anything, Selene. You can have anything you want. This is the only way I can get out of my arranged marriage. I can be with Revelio, or whomever I choose. I won't be trapped."

Priya's melody shifted to a perfect imitation of Benson's aria. She ripped the water out of the air, turning it quickly into ice shards.

"That's not a good enough reason to try and ruin me."

There was poison steeped into the lines of Priya's beautiful face. Selene had less than an eighth note to think. The shards—sharp as knives—shot toward her. Priya wasn't playing.

She was going to kill Selene.

And Selene wasn't going down without a fight. She thought of the worst she could do: flowers grown in Priya's lungs choking out her breath. The wind sung into a thousand cuts, bleeding

Priya dry. A lightning strike to the heart. She could hurt Priya, or she could destroy her.

Selene sang the dark.

It swallowed the room. This wasn't the darkness of the mirror; it was merely the absence of light. And it was enough. Selene danced out of the way of the ice. It struck the wall, clattering uselessly to the ground.

Priya sang for light, but it didn't matter. Selene's darkness was stronger. Heady with power, she compressed the darkness. What would she have to do, to make it like the dark in the mirror? What would she have to do to give the darkness life? Slowly, she could feel the dark bubble. Fizzing with a new sense of autonomy, moving with a renewed purpose.

From the dark, Priya wove the melody for growth. Vines burst from Selene's drawers and floorboards and pockets. They tangled on the floor, wrapping up Selene's calf. Thorns cut into her skin.

The magie du sang came to her, unbidden, waiting for a command. Magic and magic, lifting from her blood and misery. All she had to do was to want.

She wanted Priya to stop.

Priya's song cut off.

A terrible knowing washed over Selene. She thought of the ghost and the awful things he might have done to get himself locked in the dark. Blood and teeth, he'd said, and the feeling he'd gone too far. Selene knew that feeling well, knew what she had done to protect her own life. She'd lived with that guilt for so long.

She didn't need another stain on her soul.

Selene let the darkness drop.

Priya was on her knees, hands buried in the mess of vines. She was screaming, but there was no sound. The blood vessels in her eyes popped. Her face was a mask of fear.

Selene didn't want to win like this. She wanted to best Priya on the stage, for everyone to see. She was better than this.

Undo it, she told the dark. *Give Priya back her voice.*

The magie du sang did not yield. Selene could feel its pulse and the way it pushed back, like a stuck piano key. The shadows had taken something. They didn't want to give it up.

Red ran down Priya's cheeks. Everything came back to blood.

She wished the ghost was here to tell her what to do next. If only she had a mirror, a monster, and a dying dream.

All she had was herself.

The edges of the magic were tangible, like the creases of a page. She'd always given to the shadows, never tried to take anything back. She'd fed it with her blood and misery: a piece of sky, a bloodless heart, a fragment of the past. To get what she wanted, she had to give more.

The ghost had shown her when he'd healed her. He'd given so much blood, and whatever secret pain he'd held inside. Selene brought her foot down against one of the many thorns, not allowing herself to flinch as they sank deep into her skin. She drew in a breath, centering herself around the pain.

More blood, more misery. More of everything.

She hovered around all the memories of terrible things. None of them seemed right, not enough magic for what she needed. Selene swallowed, settling into the memories of her father's voice echoing through the white marble halls of the palace. Good memories, sweet things. Worse, in a way, because she'd have to sacrifice the residual joy the memory gave her. The thought of losing her father's voice was too much for her.

They'd play this game where he would sing a line of music and Selene would try to find him. There were so many places to hide in the vastness of the palace. She'd hear the echo of music and she'd chase it down, down, down the twisting halls. He'd wait awhile before he'd sing again. She'd chase the resonance until she found him, tucked behind a suit of armor or around a pillar, gleeful at his own game. Then it would be Selene's turn.

She'd never get that back. Not the simplicity of childhood, not the sound of her father's voice, not the possibility of finding him behind a corner or door. He was gone, and the ache of him was something she'd never lose. It was endless, ceaseless, careless. She was trapped in a world without the person she loved the most and that itself was a prison.

For a moment, she felt the upside-down of the mirror. Like she had slipped through the silver into shadow. And then the pain started to fade, the image of her father's face going out like a candle flame and blurring with smoke.

What had she done?

Priya's scream sliced through the air like an arrow and then died. Replaced by Priya's sobs.

Madame's cane struck the ground three times.

Selene turned around, startled. They had an audience. Madame and Gigi and Milton and the others. Victor stood there with wide, hungry eyes.

"She attacked me." Priya's voice was a rasp, damaged by the screaming and the silence. "She lured me here—"

"Enough," Madame spat.

"They must be removed from the competition." Milton's voice was gruff. She'd never seen him look so furious and so disappointed.

Madame hesitated, devastation crossing her face between blinks. "Pack your things. Both of you."

Selene closed her eyes. Guilt pierced her, sharper than any thorn. She deserved this. Why had she retaliated against Priya? She should have walked away. What were letters compared to her father's watch? And now, so close to the end, everything she wanted was gone. She'd been given this second chance and she'd thrown it all away for a little revenge.

"I think that would be in poor form, Madame Giroux," Victor said.

Madame looked shocked, as if she hadn't known Victor was there. "This is my theater."

"It is the king's theater. And his competition." Victor kept his voice low. "I would hate to tell him that—once again—you have failed to keep *his* mages safe."

And he was right. He'd be doing the future competitors of L'Opéra du Magician a favor if he had Madame removed. Maybe he'd be doing Madame a favor, too.

"Then what do you propose we do—Your Highness?" Madame spoke through gritted teeth.

"Plant the flowers in the garden." He brushed the tip of his boot over one of the roses. "And consider how to foster a community, rather than a competition."

Madame's knuckles turned white against the head of her cane. Selene could feel that vise grip as Madame looked from Victor to Priya and back to Selene. All the blood and flowers and burned-up paper between.

Madame sang low. The vines twisted and shrank, green to brown to black. They crumbled beneath Selene's bloody feet. She crossed the room, resting a hand on the wooden box. She didn't look at Victor. Madame swept up the ashes and dust with a sharp wind. The wind pushed up Priya from the floor and out into the hallway. Selene looked to Gigi, but the dancer averted her gaze, keeping her eyes downcast. It wasn't like her at all. Of all the things that had gone wrong today, this was the worst. It was confirmation that Gigi hadn't been moved to hurt Selene. Gigi had made a choice.

"This isn't over," Madame warned.

"Not until tomorrow." Victor leaned into the doorframe, an easy, carefree look on his face.

Madame was out of the room, cane striking the wooden floor with deliberate ire. The rest of them—even Gigi—scattered.

Victor was the only one left.

"Thank you," Selene breathed.

"I didn't want to see you lose your dream." He put his hand to his forehead. "Are you all right?"

She exhaled the worst of her feelings, focusing on the pain. "I will be."

"Is it worth it, Selene?"

Selene sat down at the edge of her bed, unsure of the answer. She'd given up too much already to turn back now. "I'm not doing this for me. It's for my father. To restore his legacy."

Giuseppe wanted more for you.

Selene remembered her father's bright smile and how it had shifted over those last days. How gaunt he had been, obsessive and empty of anything except magic and music. She wished he were here to tell her what to do next.

"Do you really think this is what he wants for you?"

"You don't know what my father wanted."

Victor appraised her. "Are you happy?"

Selene was tired of all the questions. She fought to keep the irritation from her face. "It's not that simple."

"Maybe it could be. Maybe you could find out. I'd take you anywhere you'd want to go. The whole world could be yours."

"I want this."

Victor nodded slowly. "As long as you're sure."

She cleared the lump from her throat. "What are you doing here?"

Victor held up a basket. "Lunch?"

She lifted her foot. One of the thorns was still embedded in her heel. "You do realize I have to sing for your father in one day."

Victor crossed the threshold, shutting the door behind him. He took a knife from his pocket and braced the flat of the blade against her foot. He had the thorn out in a few seconds and then traced the punctures up her calf, looking for more.

Each press of his fingers was a reminder of the years that had passed between them. They weren't children anymore. He wasn't that mischievous boy; he was something else entirely. A man who'd crossed seas and earned his calluses. Still, she felt safe with him, slipping into the familiar pattern of friendship.

As far as friends went, he might be the last person she had in this world, now that Gigi was gone. She let him take care of her, just for this moment. His fingertips lit little fires in her skin.

"I thought you were singing for me?"

She thought of the ghost's fingers moving over the slick black keys. "And why would I do that?"

"I make an excellent audience."

"Unless you're putting frogs in the piano."

He winced. "There wasn't a trouble I couldn't find, was there?"

"No." She wondered what kind of trouble he was bringing to her now.

He reached into his basket, brought out a jar of honey, and peeled off his shirt. He was suntanned and salt flecked, as if he'd been to sea that morning. The muscles in his back rippled, still marred by the scars of childhood. The patterns on his back were familiar, so like the ghost's. She hadn't expected to see so much of the sun in him, to see years of earned strength beneath his skin. He wasn't just a captain, sipping rum and shouting orders. He worked alongside his crew, and he had the body to prove it.

He caught her eye, mischief gleaming in his. He'd caught her staring.

Selene cleared her throat. "What are you doing?"

"Honey promotes healing." He applied it gently to each wound, his sticky fingers moving tenderly over her punctured flesh. Carefully, he bound each cut with strips of cloth. When he was finished, his shirt was in tatters. Selene's leg tingled.

Sticky, but snug. "I've moved up in the world, ma chérie. I am now second in line for the throne."

Selene's eyes went wide. "I wasn't expecting this type of trouble. What happened?"

"Alexandre has abdicated. Thinks he'll make a better priest than king."

Alexandre was such a gentle soul. He'd spent so much of his time in contemplation, pressed like lavender between the pages of an old book. Selene had liked him enough, though she was never sure he had the will to be a good king.

"He's not wrong."

"Ah, but that leaves us with Henri."

Selene let out a breath. She couldn't think of a single kind thing to say about Henri. He'd set fire to newborn kittens when they were in the palace. Beat a serving girl so badly that she'd lost an eye. Beat Victor, too. Even at ten, he was a self-proclaimed sadist. He could not be king.

"And you," Selene said, certainty settling around her.

"I'm not cut out for it," Victor said. "Which I've tried to make abundantly clear in these last weeks. Who knew that acting the disastrous rake would actually endear me to the people?"

"So you admit it's all a ruse?"

Victor held out his hand. "Come with me and find out."

Selene's heart pounded in her throat. Everything always seemed so easy for Victor. Every moment a prize to be won. "I'm not allowed to leave."

"Is this a prison?"

Yes, she thought.

"None of us can go this close to the competition."

"And if I appeal to Madame Giroux?"

"She'll likely stab you," Selene said. "There's a sword in her cane."

"Good point. Luckily, I have incredible foresight." Victor held up his basket. "Let's get out of here."

"I can't," Selene said.

Victor's look softened out of mischief and into something a little too close to pity. He shrugged on his jacket, leaving his bare chest exposed. "Is there someplace we can go here?"

Selene's stomach ached with hunger. She could do that. "Let me get dressed first."

"Two minutes." Victor's eyes burned like the stage lights.

She shut the door behind him, pressed her back against the wood, and closed her eyes, willing the tears away. She needed a moment to process, to shake the image of Priya screaming on the floor and the feeling of the magic fighting back. To search inside herself for the sound of her father's voice. It was still there, but softer. Selene couldn't give up any more.

How close she'd been to losing everything. And Victor had stepped in to save her. But she wasn't a damsel in distress. She'd been in control. Maybe that was what Victor needed to see, so different from the lightning strike that had changed her life. She wasn't a small and helpless girl, meant to be saved. She'd grown up. Selene was powerful, indomitable. She was unstoppable.

And she wished he'd come into her life at any other point. A week earlier, a week later. Anytime but now, just as she was on the verge of something. She didn't have the time for him. Her focus was needed elsewhere, remembering her music, searching for the death of a dream, returning to the ghost.

But the room wouldn't stop spinning and Selene knew herself well enough. She needed to eat and take a breath and clear her mind. If she didn't give herself a moment's rest, she'd be useless.

Sitting down on the bed, she grabbed the only dress in reach. It was a mulberry gown with sleeves that peeled off the shoulders and tapered into fur. The wide skirt would allow her to move freely without aggravating the cuts in her leg. Gold embroidery trickled down the bodice. The high collar was lined with black fur. It was more extravagant than she needed for the day, but it would keep her throat warm and safe against the coming chill.

The door handle was sticky beneath her fingers, honey-coated from Victor's touch.

Victor stood at the top of the stairs. He'd gotten restless. Little flecks of mud from his boots traced up and down the hallway. When he saw her, his sharp inhale was audible. His tongue danced on his teeth, like there was something he wanted to say. He shook his head, thinking better of it.

She held up the bundle. "I finally got your letters."

Victor's cheeks flushed. "Oh no. Maybe you shouldn't—"

He reached for them. Selene pulled the letters back, overjoyed to catch Victor off guard.

"You think I'm going to give these up so easily?"

"Please forgive the ramblings of a lovesick teen boy." Victor rubbed his face with his hand.

"We were kids." Selene put the letters on her bed.

"And yet, I kept you like an oath."

Selene had kept him like a secret, not even telling Gigi.

"Well, now that we've gotten that mortifying truth out in the open." Victor offered her his arm. "Shall we?"

CHAPTER 32

It seemed that every room in the opera house was occupied in preparation for the competition. Servants from the palace gave them a wide berth, casting suspicious glances toward Victor.

"We could always go back to your room."

Selene shuddered. She couldn't be in that space right now. She needed to be away from her sins, away from the promise of further solitude. But what choices did she have? There was one place she was sure they would not be interrupted, but it was dangerous.

"I know a place."

She led him down the hallway, through the secret passageway to descend beneath the opera house. King Renard watched them with woven eyes. Selene flourished and pulled back the tapestry.

"Very clever. I knew you'd find the best secret places wherever you were."

She reached for the handle. It did not move.

Selene tried it again, incredulous. "It's locked. It's never locked."

"You didn't show me this on our tour."

She gave him an exasperated look. "It doesn't matter."

"It must, since it is forbidden."

Selene rolled her eyes. "Locked doesn't always mean secret."

Crouching down, she sang into the keyhole. The door did not yield.

Victor's eyebrow went up. "Not all problems are solved by magic."

Wrong. With one drop of blood and a dose of misery she could open the door. The magie du sang could solve anything. Unless the magic demanded more than she could give.

"Locks are generally the most difficult way to open a door. And conspicuous. People always check the locks. Hinges, on the other hand." He pulled out the hinge pins and swung the door open. "You see? I am of use after all."

He looked so pleased with himself. And he should be pleased. She kissed his cheek, like she'd done when they were children. He tasted like salt and tobacco and wide-open spaces, the slight stubble a rough comfort to her lips. She pulled back, surprised by her boldness. She hadn't been thinking; she'd slipped back into old patterns. Patterns from before the opera house, before her father's death, back when life was endless summer skies and pomegranate-stained fingers.

Victor looked as surprised as Selene. A smile quirked on his lips, showing his dimple. Selene couldn't bear the sight of it, standing so close to him like she'd tripped into the past. He put his hand on the small of her back, moving her incrementally closer to him.

He was going to kiss her.

She let him linger for a beat before she spun from his grasp. She twined down the stairs, unraveling with each step. She shouldn't bring Victor down here. He was far too clever, far too curious. He'd find the door and the mirror and the ghost. She could not fathom the collision of her worlds. Still she walked, each step edging her toward madness.

The darkness of the basement was familiar, calming. Selene sang the light into her palm for long enough to find half a dozen candelabras, each with three dusty, half-burned candles. Victor took them as soon as they were lit.

He cleared his throat dramatically.

Selene turned. He'd laid out the blanket in the center of the room, complete with a spread of fruits and meats and delicate pastries. He'd poured tea into fragile cups and stirred a generous amount of honey into hers. The candles cast it all in flickering shadows.

"This is too much," Selene said.

"Don't worry, I acquired this all by questionable means." Victor popped a blueberry into his mouth. "Will you sit?"

Selene folded herself down beside him, spreading out the mulberry skirt of her dress over the blanket. She made sure she was the one facing the door to the mirror. No need to pique his curiosity. The stained-glass window had been removed, all the glass and rubble cleared away. The door still blended into the stone, but there was something different.

Locks.

There were dozens of them, stacked up the frame. Locks that needed keys, combinations, and song. It would take her hours to get through. Panic crawled up her throat. Victor settled in front of the door, tilting his head.

"What are you looking at?"

He started to turn. She caught his hand, pulling him in to her. She caught his mouth with a quick kiss—just the barest brush of lips. Once upon a time, she'd dreamed of this, the heat of his breath, the sweet, salt taste of his skin. The reality was cruel, the waste of a kiss for concealment. The waste of *this* kiss. But maybe it was the flickering candlelight and maybe it was the years of wanting and maybe it was just this impossible boy—she let herself forget the world and be lost in this moment. A blink, and then she was back on her side of the blanket.

She considered decorum and propriety and decided to leave it behind. With just her fingers, she picked up a piece of thin prosciutto and popped it into her mouth. It was then her stomach reminded her how long it had been since she'd eaten. She selected a pear and bit in, letting the juices sluice down her chin. Victor cut the tops off strawberries and handed them to her, one by one. She tore into a piece of still-warm bread, smeared it with butter and honey. She drank her tea, and his, too.

Finally, she looked up at him.

"Are we going to talk about what happened?" he asked.

"The kiss?"

"That was hardly a kiss." Victor tucked a smile at the corner of his mouth. "Before that."

Selene was afraid of this. "How much did you see?"

"Enough." Victor leaned back on his elbows. The light caught the copper and gold in his curls, shimmering like a treasure.

She could only imagine what she must have looked like while wielding the swirling dark, giving it life. If only she'd grown wings made of shadow and floated above them all like a dark god, like a monster with a perfect face. "Are you afraid of me?"

"You've always terrified me, Selene," Victor said. "I've often wondered if magic could be...more."

She'd wondered the same thing, wanted to know why magic was kept as entertainment. There were so many ways they could reshape the world and make it better: an end to hunger, protection for ships from storms, rain in the worst of a drought. Magic could change lives. It could save them.

"Is that why you're here?" Selene kept her tone light.

"I'm here because my father beckoned and I came running like a good dog," Victor said. "And in turn, I'm finding a way to make cheese out of soured milk."

"What do you think magic can do for you?" Selene said.

"Anything. Everything. Pirates off the north coast have started employing mages, and the rumor is our allies and enemies are training soldiers to do the same."

The realization settled on her, thick and heavy. "You want art to be a weapon."

"Isn't it already?" Victor's smile fell away. "I saw what you could do."

"What I did was wrong."

Selene considered the rules and all the ways she was breaking them. This was the least of her sins.

"And yet it can be done. There is so much more to magic than we've been led to believe."

Selene took a deep breath. He was right, of course. Sniffing out truth and trouble in a way only he could. What would he do if he knew the extent of what magic was capable of? She didn't want to think about it. She filled her cup with tea and poured in more honey. "Did you really gamble your mother's jewels?"

"Yes," Victor said. "Though I have an agreement with the head of that particular establishment. Whatever leaves my pockets goes to the poor. It's the least I can do."

"And you trust him?"

"We served together. I trust him with my life."

Selene pressed her thumb into the side of the teacup. The heat of it sent pulses through her healing skin. "Why bother then with the spectacle?"

Victor cut the stem off a strawberry and handed it to her. The knife pressed into the base of his thumb and stained it red with the juice. "With enough shame, I was hoping the king would send me away again and I could get back to my ship."

"But with Alexandre's abdication…"

Victor's eyes were distant. "You're not the only one who can't leave."

Selene looked down at her cup. There was honey still at the bottom, viscous and golden. She swirled it around slowly.

"Do you want to see my ship?" Victor reached into his pocket and held out a thin, silver daguerreotype.

Selene cupped it in her hands, this precious thing. She turned it toward the light, the candle casting the silver into gold. She'd expected something worthy of a prince. Even in the picture, Victor's clipper looked small, with scratches and patches on the hull and sails that had been stained and then bleached out with the sun. The figurehead was the only part of the ship that seemed cared for—an only slightly chipped nightingale with wings that spread down the forepeak.

"Isn't she beautiful?"

"She's not what I expected."

"Ah yes. I'm sure you thought I'd be in one of those grand, useless ships that are only good at sinking."

"Yes," Selene said. "I did."

"I strive to be useful, Selene. I know, I know. It may come as a shock to you. I do more than drink port and spin sextants, unlike my brothers."

"I can see that." Selene traced the places where the ship had been damaged and carefully repaired. This was no ornament. For all Selene knew about ships, she could tell that this was fast and well-loved.

"She and I have been through a lot together."

There were letters, barely visible on silver. Selene held it up: *The Nightingale.*

Selene's heart beat *più mosso*. "My father used to call me that."

"I know," Victor said.

Lovesick.

She met his eyes. He had named a ship after her. He had sent letters for years. He had carried a glass rose across continents and through whatever skirmishes he had gotten into in this fast, little ship. She was far from forgotten. He had kept her on his mind since the moment they parted.

She licked her lips, the taste of him still there.

She put the daguerreotype on the saucer beside her teacup. Victor watched her as if he were waiting for admonition. Selene didn't have words for him. She clenched her hands into fists, hoping to catch the tremble before Victor saw. She stood up and leaned against a set piece, her foot pulsing with familiar pain. The magic of it called to her. She needed the space, the distance to untangle the mess inside of her.

"Do you remember the song your father used to sing?" Victor stood a few feet away from her, spinning a dusty globe. His exposed chest glistened in the candlelight.

"It's been a long time since I've sung anything but magic." She'd need this fraction of sorrow to shape her magic later. She leaned into the pain.

The wolf has lost the moon
The stars are bright as eyes
They watch the wolf weep to the north
Leedle-lie, leedle-lie, leedle-lie

The hawk clings to the trees
The wind is sharp as knives
It brings my ship back home to you
Leedle-lie, leedle-lie, leedle-lie

I wait for you til dawn
I wait for you by night
I'll never leave your side, my love
Leedle-lie, leedle-lie, leedle-lie

The wolf has the moon
And the hawk has the sky
You'll always have my heart, my love
Leedle-lie, leedle-lie, leedle-lie

Victor joined his voice with hers for that last *leedle-lie*. His voice was easy, not furrowed with concentration or the strain of opening to the magic. He had sung this song since she'd last seen him. Perhaps while he sailed his ship across the seas.

"I used to call it the waiting song."

"I always called it the wanting song," Selene said.

"What is waiting, but wanting something for more than a moment?" Victor rotated, facing her. The distance between them shrank. "The wolf wants the moon, the bird wants the skies, and I want—"

He stopped, realizing where the next words would take him.

"What do you want, Victor?"

"A little bit of everything."

"That's not an answer," Selene said. "Give me something tangible."

"I've only ever wanted one thing." Victor's voice was low. "Freedom. The freedom to choose, the freedom to be, the freedom not to be. To love who I want to love. To do what I want to do. To be who I want to be."

"You're a prince," Selene said.

"And that's precisely the problem," Victor said. "If I sail across the world, I'd still have to come back. The perch is gilded, but my wings are clipped."

"I know that feeling," Selene said.

"We could go." Victor's voice was a whisper, like candle smoke. "Leave now and cross half the world before anyone knows we are gone."

"Who will be the pirate?"

"We'll both be. We'll be whatever we wish."

"This is all I am." There was magic in the grief of her words, and something intangible, too. When had she stopped being something more?

Victor shook his head. "You could be anything, Selene."

"All I know is magic. All I have is magic. I have my father's splendid and bloody legacy. I don't know what else there is."

"Butcher."

"Please. With these delicate hands?"

"Baker."

"All that powder is bad for the voice."

"Candlestick maker."

"And make beautiful things just so they can burn?"

"That's more my style." Victor grinned. "Selene Dreshé, the King's Mage. What will you do after?"

Selene took a breath. "There is no after."

"Pretend with me," Victor said. "You've won, you've served your seven years in the palace. What happens next?"

"I'll go live by the sea," she said, after a moment. "In a house just big enough for me."

"Alone," Victor said, surprised. "Not even a lover or cat?"

She made a face. "No cats."

"A dog, then."

"No dog, either."

"A parrot," Victor said. "Something exotic and lovely that will sing to you."

She laughed. It was so easy to laugh with Victor. "I don't think so."

"Sounds lonely," Victor said.

"I could do with a measure of loneliness after all this is done."

"And what if I come to call?"

"I'll pretend I'm not home," Selene said.

"Rude," Victor said. "Though I believe I've proven myself a master of doors."

"A breaker of them."

"And fixer. I learned that trick from your father, actually."

Selene's eyebrows lifted in surprise. "My father took the hinges off of doors?"

"Just one door," Victor said. "There's a suite in the palace that used to belong to the King's Mage, back when there was just one, and not a new one every seven years. It's been locked for a century. I was doing some sneaking, and I saw your father trying to sing his way in. When that didn't work, he simply removed the hinges and went in without a hitch."

"Did you follow?"

"Of course not. That's how you get caught." Victor winked. "I went in after he was gone like any sensible rogue."

Selene leaned forward instinctually, waiting for the next part of the story. "And what was in there?"

"Dust, mostly. Whatever you father was looking for, I don't think he found it. And then a few days later..."

"He was gone." Selene inhaled sharply. "I wish I could make sense of why he pushed himself that far."

"The king gets what the king wants, regardless of who it hurts." Victor's eyes darkened. "I often wonder what would have happened if he'd released your father early, as he'd asked."

"Oh."

"I'm sorry, I thought you knew. I overheard it from one of my hiding places."

"The king refused?"

"He threatened you."

The king. He'd been at the center of everything. He'd called her father out of retirement, set them in the palace, pushed him too far. It wasn't for her or even for himself, but for the king. Her father had not sung for himself. He'd always sung for an audience.

And on that last day, he'd sung for an audience of one.

Who killed your father, Selene?

She could hear the echo of the ghost's voice and oh, how she longed for a mirror, for a dying dream to unlock the door so she could be let in. He'd asked and asked, and she hadn't understood.

Who had killed her father?

She'd only been a child. She hadn't known what she was doing; she'd only reacted. And her father was gone before the lightning strike. His mind had been drawn tight and snapped before Selene ever sang his death. This wasn't her fault. It had never been her fault.

She'd blamed herself for so long, it seemed wrong to let anyone else share the burden. But he wasn't wrong. Everything had happened in service of the king. Father wasn't even supposed to be there for a second seven years. He was supposed to be home with her. But he'd gone because the king had asked. He'd stayed because the king had insisted. And wasn't all of it at the king's whim? The competition, the magic, all of it. Selene felt like a puppet catching sight of her strings.

"It wasn't my fault," she said. Then, louder: "It wasn't my fault."

"Of course it wasn't," Victor said. And he had been there. He knew the truth of what happened. The secrets that had been swept up and stored away. He wrapped his arms around her. She listened to the staccato beat of his heart, finding comfort in the rhythm. "You were only a child. Please tell me you haven't been carrying that burden this whole time."

Selene's laugh was wild, hysteria around the edges. She broke from his embrace, unable to think. "My father's end has weighed on me since that day."

Victor opened his mouth and shut it. The corner of his lips twitched. He pressed his hand on the side of her cheek. She leaned into his touch: the warmth and the roughness of the calluses, the comfort of knowing the right answer, at long last. He brought his hand down from her face and touched the fabric around her throat.

"No more of it, then. Open the shutters of your heart and let in the light."

"What time is it?" Selene reached for her pocket watch, then remembered it was gone. She'd lost more than an hour. "I have to go, Victor."

"Can I come back tomorrow?" Victor said.

"Tomorrow is L'Opéra du Magician."

"You'll need to eat." Victor smiled.

Selene wanted to see him again. She knew tomorrow would be an endless whirl. But she wanted to know there was one person in this world who cared about her.

"We'll have to be quick," she said.

"I'll take a minute; I'll take a moment." Victor caught her hand and brought it to his lips.

And with a few steps, Selene could have closed the distance between them. Crossed the years and gone back to a time when her love for Victor was a slice of sunshine. When he was the bright spot on every day. But the night had come, and Selene couldn't remember what it was to be happy the way Victor wanted her to be happy.

"You can't be caught here."

"What's the worst that could happen?"

The ghost might sing you into the dark and you'll never want to leave, she thought.

"Let's not tempt fate."

He hastily packed up the picnic. Selene blew out the candles with a brush of wind. The wax splattered like blood against the stone floor. She took his hand and showed him the way back to the light, up the stairs and to the door.

"I trust you can find your way," she said.

"I am capable of many things."

She pulled her hand away, dropped into a curtsy. Selene escaped through the still-locked door, the hinges swinging. Her skirts moved around her like water, and she could feel Victor's eyes on her back. Once she was almost out of sight, she dared a glance over her shoulder. Victor crouched down and sang the metal pin back into the hinge. His voice was clear and easy and untrained. She could think of a dozen ways to make it better: lift the soft palate, control the breath, let the vibrato resonate through the mask of the face.

She could teach him to be a better musician, and a better

mage. But she didn't need that from him. She liked the sound of his voice and the way it felt to fall into step with him. She liked that he was here, in spite of herself. Victor Chastain had swept back into her life and she would be damned if she didn't enjoy it.

"Victor?"

He looked up, a wave of copper hair falling into his face. "Selene?"

"Thank you."

"Oh no." Victor leaned away from the door. "Don't start with that."

"Gratitude?"

"Politeness." Victor shuddered. "Can't we be friends, you and I? Without the conventions of society getting in our way?"

Selene wasn't sure if they could ever be friends, not the way they had been. There was something between them. There were so many things she might say.

"I'll be indecorous, all decorum lost."

"That's all I ask of you."

CHAPTER 33

Selene waited until Victor left through the great doors and rode down the street. She didn't have a plan. All she had was the glass rose and a way in. She gathered her sheet music and the box, desperation clinging to her skin. This had to work. She could throw together another song, but it would pale in comparison to what she had written with him. That was a remarkable piece. Anything else would be less. She couldn't take the risk.

She used the trick with the hinges on the first door and then again on the second. Victor served his purpose. With the box held against her chest, she tried not to linger on the memory of his skin and the softness of his mouth. She could give this up. She could give up anything if it meant winning. She'd already lost so much in pursuit of her art. The shadow boat took her across the water. This might be the last time she'd trace through these arches, the last time she'd see herself in the dark water. The mirror reflected the phosphorescence in all its glory. This was the moment, her triumphant return.

Selene stuck her finger with a pin and placed it against the mirror, bracing herself, the box pressed tightly against her chest.

Nothing happened.

"Please," she said. She pricked her finger again and again, squeezing out more blood. It smeared against the glass as if this was just a mirror. As if it didn't matter at all.

"He was a dream," she said. "I give him up."

And maybe it was the race of her traitorous heart. Maybe it was the barest hint of hesitation she'd felt when she first thought of the rose. Maybe it was the taste of Victor still on her lips.

The mirror did not give way.

The ghost sang from its depths, mournful and sweet. An apology. Selene thought to write it down, but the sound was strangled, muffled and far away. Like something was holding him back.

"I'll find a way," she promised.

But she already felt like a liar. And she was running out of time.

She shut the door behind her, returning the hinges as if they'd never been removed. Selene was halfway to the stairs, weaving between the set pieces, when she felt a presence. Not a ghost—she wished it were a ghost. This was so much worse. In her haste, she'd been careless and now she was caught. She turned around, bracing herself.

Gigi stood behind her. Cat's countenance, dancer's delicate steps, like her mother. Her eyes were wide with shock. Her dancer's feet moved with a skilled silence. "So this is where you've been going."

Selene was breathless. So close to being caught. "You're speaking to me now?"

"I was never not speaking to you." Gigi moved in tendu.

"You moved out of our room without telling me."

"Thought you'd be happy it was clean." Gigi smiled weakly.

"I thought we were in this together."

"We are." Gigi popped onto her toes. "We were. I know you're keeping secrets, Selene."

Selene went cold. The door—expertly locked—to the underground lake and the mirror beyond was mere feet away, guarding the lion's share of her secrets. She could tell Gigi, but then what? Gigi was afraid of the ghost. Who knew what she would do?

Selene opened her mouth, searching for some lie, some near truth she could offer.

Gigi took a step forward. "You're going to tell me everything, but not yet. I have something to say first."

"Gigi, I—"

Gigi held up a finger. "I quit this morning."

Selene's jaw dropped. "What?"

"I formally pulled my name from the competition. Or tried to."

"Why would you do that?"

"Because none of this matters to me. This isn't my dream. I don't want to be the King's Mage. I don't want to be a magician at all. I just want to be"—she cleared her throat—"wanted to be with Benson and with you and with my mother. And I realize now how foolish that all was."

"We're so close. How could you—"

"She wouldn't let me," Gigi said. "Madame said it wasn't safe for me to go yet."

"That doesn't make any sense."

"You said we were like lambs to the slaughter. Everything that's gone wrong—the razors, the stolen music, the glassed berries—it's to get us out. To save us from something worse. You have to go, Selene. You have to go while there's a chance."

Selene pushed her hair back, trying to carry the weight of this information. "Why put in all the time and effort to train us? Why make us the best only to have us gutter out into nothing?"

"There's someone else pulling the strings."

"We don't have time for this. The competition is tomorrow. We have to prepare."

Gigi's smile was resigned. "I'm not here to win, Selene."

And yet Gigi could win, like the twist of a knife. She didn't even want it.

"So you're just going to blow it off?" Selene tried to keep her words measured.

"Losing Benson changed things for me. I have no choice but to perform, but I'm not going to win. There's more to life than this."

Selene swallowed. In a beat, Gigi's dream had changed. Benson was the catalyst, a death of a dream. It seemed wrong to use his madness as a tool to further her own goals, but what choice did she have? He had said that it had to be one of them. Now that Gigi was out of the running, there was only Selene.

"Not for me."

"You're not listening to me." Gigi threw up her hands and let them fall.

"I am listening." She wondered what it would take. Some of his music, a drop of his blood, a scrap of his clothes. She would take whatever she could. Selene had to go to the Asylum. It was too late in the day now. But tomorrow. She could make this work.

"Then go. Some place, any place else. Whatever comes next, it isn't what we thought."

"You know I can't." She punctuated every word. How could Gigi expect Selene to give up everything she worked for?

Anguish and frustration lit Gigi's face. "Come on, Selene. There has to be more for you."

"Nothing else matters! Not you, not Benson, not Victor." Selene felt her voice hitch, felt the scrape of her vocal cords. She had to relax, had to preserve her voice. "I don't have a life to go back to. I have music and magic, that is all."

"You had me." There were tears in Gigi's eyes. "Until you decided to keep secrets."

"Half of my life is a secret, Gigi. You wouldn't even begin to understand."

"You're right about that." For once, Gigi was still. For once, she stood like a normal girl instead of moving through the steps of some invisible dance. "Whatever happens next, I hope you have the life you deserve."

Selene couldn't stay here any longer. She tore up the stairs and into her room, hoping to find solace in the clean, quiet space. But the room seemed wrong: too big, too empty. The cavernous expanse of the walls felt ruinous, the floor's echoing steps didn't sound like hers. It didn't belong to her anymore. Soon some other girls would share the space and stay late into the night talking about their precious, fragile dreams. Selene wished she could crush them. She wanted to tell those girls that days turn to nights and nights turn to dawns and nothing stays as it should be.

Selene took the extra sheet music and settled into her practice room, waiting for the halls to quiet so she could slink back to the mirror. Waiting, while her fingers made war with the piano and she tried to string together notes into music. Waiting, as if she had any time at all left.

CHAPTER 34

Selene should have slept. She meant to. She considered it again and again. She wrote version after version of her song, trying to remember enough from the mirror to make a passable aria. She practiced the movements that would bring the magie du sang artfully. But it wasn't right. It wasn't the same without the ghost's orchestrations. She even sang the soft lullabies of her father over and over, *leedle-lie, leedle-lie, leedle-lie*. And worse, the parade of people never ended. The halls boiled with activity, countless members of both the opera house and king's staff preparing this grand event. Selene couldn't get away unnoticed if she tried. She went back to her room sometime before sunrise and wrestled with her restless thoughts.

What would happen if she gave up L'Opéra du Magician? She could forfeit her place and then what? There was no other place to call home. It had been more than a decade since she'd seen the cottage by the sea. She wouldn't even know where to find it or if it could be hers. All she could do was step into the mirror. But then the ghost could give her a more impossible task, and she would have wasted her dream on one last shared breath. The ghost wouldn't want her to ruin everything he'd taught her on goodbye.

If only she knew how to set him free. He'd have an answer for all of this, she was sure. The mirrors were coming. That should be enough. It had to be enough.

But what if it wasn't?

He'd already released her of her vow. But she couldn't do that to him or her father. She'd sworn on his soul and that meant something.

Swear on something that matters.

The ghost had sworn on his name.

His name.

Something that matters.

Oh, gods.

She'd been going about this all wrong and all right. Guessing his name like he was some fairy-tale thing as jest while she warred with blood and magic and mirrors. This wasn't a game. She *needed* his name. That was all. The one thing that truly belonged to him.

She threw off her blankets and dressed, quick and desperate. She already knew there was nothing for her in the library and that Madame Giroux would be of no use, even if she knew. There were no answers in the opera house. She needed Victor.

Time to put on a show.

Frost formed on the glass. The last of the autumn leaves fluttered from the tree boughs. The air was metallic and cold. They'd have snow before the end of day. Selene could already imagine the dusted carriages and the luxurious furs of the spectators. She could feel the magic of beautiful things worn by beautiful people, followed by the spectacle and extravagance of L'Opéra du Magician.

The dress she chose was the churning green of the sea. She'd had this dress made on a day she missed her father too much to speak. The scalloped collar hid every scar. The silk was smooth against her skin. She did up the buttons on her back with a needle prick and a portion of blood and the memory of her father singing siren songs at the sea's edge.

Selene took one look at her dark gray cloak. It would hardly be warm enough for her breakfast with Victor with snow on the horizon. She pricked the skin between her forefinger and thumb. She cleared her mind of the thousand things that cluttered it. The shadows lifted from her skin, shimmering over the cloak, and slipping into the fabric. Selene willed herself a pair of matching gloves and new boots for good measure.

When she was finished, she twisted the black cloak over her shoulders. She'd lined it with a pale fur that was too soft to be real. The gloves were lined with the same, coming up to her elbow. Selene laced her boots and went downstairs.

"Going somewhere?" Priya's eyes were wide and predatory.

"It's none of your business," Selene said.

"I saw your pretty prince in the foyer." Priya's eyebrow arched up. "Selene Dreshé, allowing herself to be distracted by a boy. I never thought this day would come."

Selene's stomach tightened. This wasn't about Victor, but about the doors Victor could open for her. Mainly: the door outside. He was her only chance to go see Benson and get her music out of the mirror. "You should go warm up, Priya. God knows how long it will take your voice to match mine."

Priya's face soured. Selene didn't look back at her.

In the foyer, Victor leaned easily against the marble railing, looking up at the painting of his great-something-grandfather and the ghost.

Selene slid her arm into his, her eyes dragging over the face of the ghost. "Do you think history remembers the names of all those people behind the king?"

"Do they matter?"

He reached around and gripped her hand, too tight. Selene went very still, like a rabbit caught in a trap.

"What was your name again? Serena? Christine?" He looked so much like Victor. He was softer around the edges, though, like he'd never seen an honest day's work. And it was clear he put a lot of effort into looking effortless. It was the eyes that gave him away. They were dark and empty, like looking into the eyes of a shark.

"Henri," Selene hissed. "Let go of me."

"You haven't seen my brother, have you? I suppose not, since you thought he was me." Henri showed all his teeth. "I could be, you know. If I wanted."

His fingers dug into her skin, overpowering her with unsettling ease. Selene would remove him from her, crown prince or not. She started to sing, still formulating what sort of violence she needed.

Henri clapped his hand over her mouth, holding tight to her face. Selene twisted in his grip, pain sharp and bright shooting through her jaw. Spots danced across her vision. She struggled for air.

"Things are going to be very different from now on, Selene."

He brought his face close to hers, the tip of his tongue touching her ear. "You'll see, soon enough."

"Get your hands off her." Victor's voice was low and dangerous.

Henri released her, holding his arms up in surrender. Selene tilted back, trying to get her feet under her. Victor was beside her, catching her before she hit the ground. She held on to him, cold air surging in her lungs, rage burning in her veins.

"There you are, brother. I have a message for you from the king."

"Get out." Victor stood taller, straighter, one arm wrapped protectively around Selene.

"Father won't like it if you don't listen."

"Get the fuck out, Henri."

"Suit yourself," Henri chuckled. "I'll be seeing you, Selene."

Henri walked out the front doors as if he'd never been there at all.

Selene let out a ragged sob. Victor held her, brushing the blooming bruises on her face with gentle fingers. She winced, opening and shutting her jaw to make sure she would still be able to sing. She'd be sore, but she'd manage.

"I'll kill him," Victor said. "I'll kill the bastard."

"Don't." Selene wished there were water hot enough to scald off Henri's touch. "That will make you king."

"If that's what it takes to make sure he never touches you again."

She turned and pressed her face against his chest, breathing in the summer scent of him: the sea and all its promises. It was enough to calm the race of her heart, to bring her back near adagio. She looked up at him. His military jacket was open. No buttons to miss. He had leather gloves in his pocket and his boots went up to his knees, all free from mud or dust. He looked so formal, like he meant to impress her.

She'd wanted to give him up, offer him to the mirror. But the mirror had not taken him. If there was rage or disappointment, it was swallowed by the pressando of her heart.

"Please, let it go." Selene's voice was small.

"Whatever you wish." Victor's eyes were still dark, his jaw set.

Gathering herself, she looked up to the cold eyes of the ghost and back to Victor.

"Whatever I wish?" she said playfully.

"Anything."

"Take me away from here for a few hours."

"You are not permitted to leave the opera house." Madame Giroux's condemnation was scythe sharp, her mouth tight. The silence of her approach startled Selene.

"A word, Madame Giroux."

Victor walked leisurely down the hallway, not waiting for Madame to follow. It was the assumption of power, something that belonged to someone of Victor's stature. He wielded it like a sword. Madame's unchecked rage radiated from every fiber of her being.

Hoping to catch the conversation, Selene curved indiscriminately against the railing. She wouldn't look at them directly. Instead, she watched their reflection in the freshly polished gold statues. Victor looked wild with fury—just for a moment before he smoothed it away. He smiled that lazy smile and made his way back to Selene.

"You think you're saving them, but you're damning them." Madame Giroux pointed her cane as if she'd unsheathed it and could impale Victor with a single strike.

"Madame Giroux, they're already damned by your inaction." Victor had his gloves on, intent clear. He wove his fingers with Selene's. "We'll be back before curtain."

"Long before." This was her whole life sharpened to a point. Her purpose. She'd win back her father's legacy. She'd win and take her place in the palace. Selene would have everything. She'd already paid the price.

Marcus caught them by the door. He looked nervously up into the space Madame Giroux had vacated. "What time are the mirrors arriving?"

Victor's smile was pure triumph. "This afternoon. Right in time for L'Opéra du Magician."

"You're making enemies, you know."

"It will be well worth the spectacle."

Marcus shook his head and went back toward his office. There was a line of people there. So much to do before tonight.

Victor paused at the bottom of the stairs, looking up at the painting of King Renard breaking ground on the opera house.

"My father says I look like him," Victor said. "Except for the teeth."

"Weren't his pearls?"

"Yes. After a very unfortunate incident with his whipping boy."

"I thought it was an accident," Selene said.

"It was no accident," Victor said. "Though that's what the people have been told. The truth is far more sinister."

Selene exhaled, a crescendo of anticipation taking hold. "Tell me."

"No one wanted to be the hand that spanked the royal bottom," Victor said. "So some family was paid handsomely to relinquish their son as stand-in for the prince for punishment. Renard was a bit of a beast, not unlike my dearest brother. He'd get himself entangled in trouble just so he could see the punishment acted out. Well, one day, Renard took things too far. There was a girl—the daughter of a minor lord—and Renard hurt her. The whipping boy caught him. He beat Renard within an inch of his life."

"Knocked out his teeth?"

"Would have been better if he had just killed him," Victor said jovially. "But then I wouldn't exist, so I suppose I should be grateful the boy showed mercy."

Selene's heart beat steady and strong. The scars that stretched the ghost's back and his arms burned in her mind. He knew so much about pain. "What happened to the whipping boy?"

"If I had known this would be such a riveting subject, I would have brought it up earlier."

"So you don't know?" Selene rolled her eyes. "What about his name?"

Victor shrugged. "He was lost to time."

Selene breathed in deep enough to make her lungs ache. There would be records, somewhere. First, she needed her way back into the mirror, and then she'd find the one thing that mattered most to the ghost: his name.

"Are you cross with me?"

"I'm glad you're here."

"Excellent." Victor's smile was endless. "Onward!"

CHAPTER 35

Selene could not remember the last time she'd been on these steps or down this street. The air was fresh and cold, another turning of the season. The trees had shed their leaves and the leaves had been swept away by the last autumn wind. This was a breath away from winter. It was a different world than the one she saw through the windowpane, different than the night bustle of the Unmasking Ball. Carriages rolled by with little concern for what happened inside the opera house. There was something deeply unsettling in that for Selene. She'd made this place her whole life, rested her sense of self in what was achieved in these walls. And yet the moment she stepped outside, it all seemed so inconsequential. She didn't like that. The sky was bright and clear and blue in a way that made Selene long for darkness.

A crowd had gathered at the base of the steps. The tickets to L'Opéra du Magician had long since sold, and some desperate few would garner secondhand stubs at the front door for a high price. The rest lined up now to save seats to watch arrivals for the evening, to catch a glimpse at the glamorous excess that would spill out of carriages and into the Opera Magique.

"Sing for us!" one of the men shouted.

Selene turned to the man, surprised he recognized her. The

crowd cheered in agreement. Her anonymity sloughed off so easily, replaced with the confidence of knowing she was close to achieving everything. A sense of gratitude for this stranger overwhelmed her. But Selene couldn't sing now. She didn't have the time or the will to entertain.

Victor made circles on the back of her hand with his thumb. "I'm afraid she must save her voice for this evening."

The disappointment was palpable on the man's face. A murmur spread through the crowd. Far more outrage than disappointment, and it unnerved Selene. Did they think she belonged to them? Did they think they could beg her voice and have her answer?

"Isn't that the Mad Mage's daughter?"

Selene went cold. Victor carefully pressed one of her dark curls behind her ear, leaning in with a whisper so soft Selene wondered if she'd dreamed it.

"Let's give them something to talk about."

He kissed her.

It was the barest brush of lips, barely a kiss at all.

No more than she'd given him below the opera house.

And somehow it was everything. It was a breath on a spark and a wind in sails and the magic in the music. The world, still new to her, fell away.

The crowd cheered and the reality of what he'd just done struck Selene.

"You've made a grave error of judgment," Selene said.

"Have I? Tomorrow, the papers will write about what could have been mistaken for a kiss instead of you snubbing this ravenous crowd."

"Was that not a kiss?"

Victor's smile was fox-sly. "When I kiss you, you'll know."

Something trilled inside Selene, the cadence of her heart beat svegliato. She reminded herself that Victor was the means to an end. Convinced herself that the promise of *when* was just a casual turn of phrase. This was merely a distraction. A trick to quell the crowd.

Once they were down the street, on some quiet corner, Victor whistled.

A horse with a shining black coat trotted up to them. He was huge and ferocious. A creature born and bred for war. He stopped inches away from them. He snuffed at Victor and nosed his pockets.

"All right, all right. I promised there'd be sugar, didn't I?"

Victor produced three shining cubes. The horse crunched them merrily.

"Tonnerre, this is my friend, the one I've been telling you about. Selene, this is the magnificent Tonnerre."

"You've been talking to your horse about me?"

"No." Victor reached into his other pocket and fished out a few more sugar cubes. He placed them in her hand. "You've got it all wrong. He's not my horse. I'm his human." He leaned in to whisper, "He's very sensitive about it all."

"Naturally." Selene held the sugar on her palm. "Hello, Tonnerre. You are handsome."

His ears pricked up and he gave her hand a tentative sniff. His lips feathered gingerly against her gloves. With a gentleness unbefitting his size, he plucked the sugar from her palm and tossed his head.

"He likes you." Victor stroked Tonnerre's mane. The blunt edge showed where it had been cropped and had since grown out into waves of silk.

"He's stunning," Selene said. "He looks more a king than you, any day."

Tonnerre whickered in agreement.

"I don't need the two of you ganging up on me." Victor reached into the saddlebag and handed Selene a lidded mug. He cleared his throat. "Selene, there's something we need to talk about."

There was an edge to his tone, a heaviness to his gaze. Selene's stomach tightened. Not today. Whatever it was, she didn't want it today.

"Where are we going?" She opened the cup and breathed in the steam.

"Wherever you'd like."

She wanted to go into the mirror and get her sheet music. But to go back, she needed the death of a dream. She needed tangible ruin.

Benson.

It seemed wrong, like a betrayal. But it was all she had.

"Can you take me to the Asylum?"

Victor's mouth set with resolve. There was something in his eyes. "I think that's a fine idea."

The Asylum was on the other side of Songerie. The farthest edge, where the hills rolled and the trees grew tall as buildings. Selene had never been there. But she knew it was a quiet place, where magicians went and did not come back. There were a thousand dreams all gone to rot in there. She only needed one.

"We'd better go if we're going to make it back at a reasonable hour," Victor said. He swung up onto Tonnerre's back.

"I don't know how to ride," Selene said.

"Sure you do," Victor said. "I taught you, remember?"

"I haven't been on a horse since."

"It's like falling off a log." Victor offered her his hand. "Trust me."

She gripped his wrist. He pulled her up in front of him. She could feel the rise and fall of his chest against her back. The softness of his breath tickled the hairs on her neck. Oh, this handsome boy. What trouble would he get her into now? He held the reins loosely, letting Tonnerre lead.

"We're going to gallop now," Victor said softly into her ear. Selene tensed. "Don't be afraid. Move as he moves."

She took a deep breath and settled herself into his arms. Tonnerre tossed his proud mane and tore through the street. His hooves clattered against the cobblestones. The wind whipped Selene's hair. She kept her hands firmly against Tonnerre's neck at first. But then she fell into the rhythm of his movements. It was like a dance. He set the tempo, and she would follow. Loose in the hips. Steady back and straight neck.

The city blurred past them. The cramped buildings she'd seen from the roof of the opera house looked inviting, with their wide windows and flower boxes. The streets weren't so meandering. The cobblestones not so dark.

Her life was contained inside the opera house. Music and magic and the rising fear that someone might try and stop her from having either. Before the ghost, she hadn't even known that there was anything else besides ambition.

And yet there was a whole world out there. Endless and curious and promising. A world she did not have the time to indulge.

Tonnerre slowed to a trot. Selene bounced with him, no longer pressed against Victor's back, but rolling into each step.

They rode through the front gates. There were no trees here, just rows of statues. Mausoleums stood lonely against the barren background. Everything was quiet, but not quite peaceful.

This was a cemetery. Selene could make out the plaques. She recognized some of the names: famous mages and other tragic figures. Was her father buried here? She couldn't bring herself to ask. Didn't want to admit that she'd never had the courage to visit his grave, as if that would have been allowed.

"I need a minute," she said, accepting Victor's assistance off the horse.

She could sense that he was here, close and closer. She wanted to press her hand to his name, to whisper to the ground that she loved him, and that she would do her best for him today. She wanted him to know that everything she did was for him. She supposed wherever souls went, he knew. She had to believe that was true.

She pricked her forearm and hurt and wanted.

Take me to him.

A gossamer thread of shadow so thin and spindly she could barely catch it formed. She let it pull her to the edge of the graveyard. Past the mausoleums and giant statues. Past any of the places she thought he would be.

The thread ended at a simple, worn stone. It was covered in moss, the name barely legible. The seven years since her father's death had been unkind. She sang for water, doing her best to keep it from frosting in the chill. She cleared away the moss, the grime, the years.

The name on the headstone was not her father's.

She traced the worn letters, trying to make sense of it. Who had the magic pulled her to?

Dante Dumas.

"That name." Victor closed his eyes like he was searching for something. "I know that name."

It was such a peculiar moment, like hearing an old song in a new place. She'd experienced this all before, watching someone unlock a memory that had been tucked away.

"Victor?"

"The whipping boy," he said slowly. "Renard's whipping boy. Dante Dumas."

"You're sure?"

"I found a book once, in Father's study, and read the whole thing. That's where I learned the story of Dante. Some of my best scars came from reading that book." The darkness in his face was banished with a smile. "It seems I've been so much trouble that I can't keep it all in my head."

Selene's heart almost stopped. Dante Dumas was not here. He was trapped, punished far beyond any crime. She'd found his name; the name had found her.

Just in time.

"You look like you've seen a ghost." Victor gestured to the headstone.

She threw her head back and laughed. This was so much better than a collection of books. This was a library of souls, the history that could not be erased. There was magic here, pulling her through the echoes of pain left behind. But not at this stone. The ghost still lived, trapped in a mirror beneath the opera house in a prison of endless wanting. This was an empty grave. Anticipation built in her like a song.

"A tragedy." Selene stood, brushed the snow from her dress. "We should go."

Victor regarded her quizzically. "Any more graves you want to clean?"

She thought of the grave she'd meant to visit and now didn't dare, all these years grown around her heart like moss. After seeing Dante's name, she wasn't sure she was ready to see her father's in stone, the finality of what she'd done carved into more than her skin. She could face him after she was made the King's Mage, after she'd proven herself worthy of his name. She'd bring her father roses and she'd sing to him, once this was over. She'd make up for the lost time. But for now, she had no time to give.

The walk through the cemetery seemed short, the possibilities burning through Selene like a brand. Each step brought Selene closer to the death of a dream, and with it her way back into the mirror. She could honor her vow and free the ghost.

Dante, she reminded herself.

No longer nameless. She would save him. She would set him free.

The Asylum loomed before them. The limestone was stark and imposing. Sharp angles and sharper spires. Selene's giddiness replaced with dread. This was another tomb, a place where the mad mages could be stored away from the world. It was crueler and colder than she'd imagined. She could do this. She had to do this.

"Do you want me to come with you?" Victor said.

Selene shook her head. "Wait for me?"

She expected Victor to smile, that one dimple and those twinkling eyes. But his eyes were dark and serious.

"I will." He said it like a vow.

Selene took the first step to the Asylum. Her heart beat like an ambitious snare against her ribs, the sharp staccato almost painful. She hadn't quite prepared herself to see Benson. There hadn't been time to delve into her loss and what it meant to grieve for someone who was still alive. She'd continue to mourn him, unable to wrest herself from who he could have been.

Selene raced up the pathway, her heart a wild thing. Dante Dumas. Dante Dumas. Dante Dumas. She had a name for her ghost. It felt real, rife with magic. She couldn't wait to say it out loud and see his face when the memories came flooding back. She would save him, just as he'd saved her.

The roses that had been planted along the way had all gone to rot. The thorny remains seemed to reach for the hem of her cloak like skeletal fingers. The building was pale and looming, with rows of tiny windows like spider eyes. If this had once been a library, it was far from that now. Selene didn't like it here. There was a familiarity to it, and a sense that this might be the place she belonged.

If she'd sung one more note of her audition piece, she might be locked inside. She'd come so close to losing her mind, to losing everything. That was one way to fulfill her father's legacy.

Selene paused before the massive front doors. They were

ornately carved, in a similar pattern to that of the chandelier in the opera house. She rested her hand on the brass door knocker. It was cold enough to chill her through the gloves.

She knocked thrice and waited.

To her left, a smaller door opened. A woman with a round face and sweet expression poked her head out. She wasn't at all what Selene expected. This woman looked like she could smile the clouds away from the sun.

"Come in out of the cold," she said. "Those doors are for show."

She had a little brass pin on her uniform: Madame Myrtille. She was old enough to be Selene's mother. All soft edges and softer hands. She smelled like spiced plums and distilled vinegar.

"What can I help you with?"

"I'm Selene Dreshé," she said, taking off her gloves and nestling them into her pocket.

The woman's face lit up. "This way, dear. We've been expecting you."

Selene followed Madame Myrtille inside.

It was brighter inside than she thought it would be. The walls were painted a silvery white that caught the light without casting too much shadow. Selene followed her up two flights of stairs and down a well-lit hallway. There were too many doors. So many magicians who had lost themselves to the magic.

There was a wail so painful Selene could have stolen the moon with it.

"Don't mind him," Madame Myrtille said. "Don't mind any of them."

"Are they...?" Selene didn't know how to phrase her question.

"We do our best to make sure they're comfortable. Routine helps. And visitors. He hasn't had too many, you know."

Selene had assumed that Benson's family would have stayed as long as they could.

"Here we are," the woman said. "There's a bell by the door. Ring it if you need anything. There's an attendant on every corridor."

"Thank you," Selene said.

Madame Myrtille gave Selene a quick hug. Selene stood frozen, surprised by the gesture. "I'm so happy you're here."

Selene didn't know what to say. She wouldn't stay long. She turned the handle on the door.

There were flowers painted all over the walls. A little cottage, on a hill by the sea. Every inch of the space was covered in paint. A man sat in the corner of the little hospital room. Drawing bird after bird. Nightingales, every one.

Selene inhaled sharply. The sound startled the man and he spilled his water. It spread rainbows over the tile floor.

He turned.

Giuseppe Dreshé stared back at her.

CHAPTER 36

Selene counted her breaths. Tried to find a rhythm in her frantic heart. This wasn't possible. Couldn't be happening. She'd seen the smoke rise from his body, limp against the floor. He was dead. This was a ghost. The images of that day slammed back to her in the same impossibly bright colors from before the magie du sang, as if his presence had restored the memories. She hadn't quite realized how much she'd forgotten, how much the magie du sang had taken from her. Every memory she'd used had been compressed and smudged, and it wasn't until she looked at her father that she even realized how much she'd given up.

He dazzled her with a smile.

Giuseppe Dreshé was very much the same, despite the years. There was a lightness to him, a comfortable ease. She counted the differences. His hair was mostly silver, a little thinner on top. His arms were softer, not strong and cut like she remembered. He had wrinkles on his forehead and beneath his eyes.

"Selene," he said. He tapped the wall, the rhythm familiar.

He knew her.

"Yes?" She dropped down to her knees beside him.

He pulled away from her, startled, and pointed to the wall behind him.

SING THE NIGHT

Madame Myrtille stood in the doorway. She'd brought tea. "He's talking about the painting."

There it was, on the wall. A painting of a man and a girl on the beach. They were surrounded by nightingales. A murmuration of them, each of their mouths open to sing. For a moment, Selene thought there might be some order to it all. She could almost make out the music in it. But the more she looked, the more she was sure she was looking at the art of a madman. She was looking for something that couldn't be there. A weight settled on her. He remembered her, at least. He remembered something. But he didn't *know* her.

Madame set down the tray. Father got up and sat on the wooden chair. It had been painted in gold and navy, like a seat in the Opera Magique. "It's not unusual for them to gain some sense of themselves over the years. Our doctors and therapists do their best."

"I didn't know," Selene said.

"Not many people do, love," Madame Myrtille said. "They're different, not gone. It's hard for some families to adjust."

"I didn't know he was here." Selene pressed her fingers to her eyes, trying to stop the tears. Trying—and failing. Her father pulled his long legs into himself, as if he were trying to disappear.

"Oh. We thought…Never mind that." Madame Myrtille handed her a cup of tea. "You're here now."

Tea splashed onto the saucer. Selene's shoulders shook. "He's afraid of me."

"Just give it time," Madame Myrtille said.

Time, such a slippery thing.

But Madame Giroux had spoken of his death, hadn't she?

She must have known. The betrayal was a knife in so deep that Selene didn't know how to get it out.

Giuseppe leaned conspiratorially toward Madame Myrtille. "Can she see me?"

"Yes, Pippo, she can."

Her father had hated that nickname. He'd once sung a raincloud on a courtier who dared to call him that. The man had been flirting with Selene's mother. Father had soaked her silk dress but stolen her heart. He'd made a name for himself as a temperamental artist. The narrative had been reapplied to make sense of his impending madness. It was an unfair framing. This wasn't a feral madman. He was loving and gentle and kind and perfectly controlled.

He picked up his tea and sipped it carefully. "Who is she?"

"I'm Selene," she said.

"Can't." He shook his head. Tapped his foot in agitation. "Can't be. Selene is—" He put out his hand to indicate the height she had been when she'd lost him. "Not possible."

Madame Myrtille put a hand on his shoulder. "Pippo, remember when we mixed a little bit of white into the blue? It was still blue, just different."

"Two blues."

"Many blues."

"Many Selenes?"

"Yes," Madame Myrtille said gently. "And we like this one very much."

"Can she sing?"

Selene's heart was in her scarred throat.

"Why don't you ask her?"

He fixed his intense gaze on her. "Can you sing, Blue Selene?"

The sound of her name in his musical voice made her want to curl up at his feet just to listen. He was here. He was here and he was alive.

Selene smiled. "Yes, I can."

Giuseppe sat back. Waited with wide-eyed wonder. So different from the calculating way he used to watch her sing. Measuring each beat, listening to every note for perfection. Except he wasn't the brilliant man who'd remade the world magical with his voice. He was broken and small and thin and not who she remembered.

No magic, Madame Myrtille mouthed.

Selene nodded and sang his lullaby.

The wolf has the moon
And the hawk has the sky
You'll always have my heart, my love
Leedle-lie, leedle-lie, leedle-lie

"Sing it again," he said, like he used to say.

She did. And again. And again. Until she was a hole dug into the sand, waiting for the tide to ebb. She was so full. Full of magic and happiness and pain. This was her father. Still blue. Alive, after all. His death returned to her, his voice solid in her mind. All of him that she gave up she had back. He reached for her hand, holding it tentatively.

"I like you, Blue Selene," he said. "You sound like a bird."

"A nightingale?" She wanted the familiarity of those words on his lips.

"No." He scrunched up his face, thinking. "A mourning dove. Different."

He took a piece of paper from his table. It was still a little wet with paint. It was a picture of a bird perched on the chandelier from the opera house. The same scrollwork and sparkle painted in all the sunset shades and nestled in a backdrop of blue.

"For you, Blue Selene."

"Thank you."

Selene held the painting in her hands, careful not to smudge the still-drying paint. She thought she saw notes painted into the candles and all the edges of the crystal. But when she looked again, they were gone.

"It's time for him to rest," Madame Myrtille said. "But please, come back anytime."

"I will," Selene said.

"Promise?" Giuseppe said.

Selene had made promises. Promises to herself, to the ghost, to Gigi. Promises to the world when she'd agreed to sing in L'Opéra du Magician. She couldn't keep them all.

"I promise."

Giuseppe took off his shoes and put them beneath the bed. He untucked the top sheet and pulled it back. The last time Selene had seen him do that, it was for her. He lay down on his side and curled his knees up to his chest. He tucked his hands beneath his armpits.

"Tomorrow," he said sleepily.

"Tomorrow," Selene said.

Madame Myrtille shut the door behind them. Selene rolled up the painting and slid it into her pocket. She had a piece of her father again. She'd come for Benson, but she couldn't see him now, not when her whole world had been remade. Tomorrow, and those promised afters.

"Here, dear." Madame took a handkerchief from her pocket and handed it to her.

Selene was still crying. Had she been crying all this time?

"I thought he was dead."

Madame Myrtille smiled sadly. There was something in her eyes so close to pity that it made Selene want to sing for fire and burn this whole place down. "I'm sorry. We were told you didn't want to see him. Because of what happened."

Madame's eyes lingered on Selene's throat. The scalloped neckline of her dress let the scars peek through.

"Who? Who told you?"

Madame Myrtille hesitated. She looked to her right, like she was searching for a suitable answer.

"The truth." Selene stabbed the pin through her pocket and into her thigh. She wasn't sure it would work, if the magie du sang was powerful enough to coerce the mind.

"It was the king," Madame Myrtille said, compelled to honesty. There was a hazy look in her eyes. Selene should feel sick by this, should be horrified at the power she didn't know she had. "He came and told us himself."

And maybe the mad magicians here could sense the magic in the air. Maybe it was a coincidence. Maybe it was Selene's voice transmitted to all of those empty throats.

The screams echoed in the halls. Echoed in the city. Echoed in her bones all the way out.

{

Snow had dusted the Asylum grounds. Everything was white and cold and clean. New and unmarred. This was an entirely different world. As she walked down the narrow, rose-rotted path, Selene kept her hands in her pockets. She used the pressure of the pin against her skin to keep herself grounded. A few more steps and she'd be back on Tonnerre. A few more breaths and she'd be back in the opera house. A few more moments. It wasn't enough.

Everything inside her burst into music. She was singing before she could stop herself. Singing for life, for growth, for anything. The vines twisted up and up. The roses bloomed and burst and bloomed again. Petals fell around her. Red and red and red like blood on the snow.

Her father was alive.

Her father was alive and every part of her life had been a lie.

Victor sprang up from Tonnerre's side. He looked at her like he'd been the one to see a ghost, and not her. "Selene, are you all right?"

"Did you know?"

She was singing the words, but it was the roses that were talking. They wrapped around his wrists and ankles. All thorns and bite. Pinned him up against the closest headstone. A weeping angel.

Let him weep blood.

"Selene, what in heaven's name—"

She cut off his voice with the fury of her pain. The thorns twisted themselves around his throat. "My father is alive."

"Yes," Victor gasped.

She could see all the white around Victor's eyes. His own realization dawning.

"Selene," he choked. She loosened the vines around his throat. "I didn't know that they'd kept him from you. I swear to you."

She wished he were culpable. There was so much of the king in his face. If she wanted to, if she pretended, she could exact her revenge. Take away another heir. Burn this city to the ground. But he was innocent of this, and she knew it. The fury inside her turned to ash.

The vines browned and broke and crumbled.

"All of these years wasted." She fell to her knees. "Some stars burn bright; some stars burn out."

Victor was there beside her. There was blood on his wrists and throat, leaving ruby droplets in the snow. She was sorry she'd hurt him. This wasn't his fault. He brought her to his lap, his arms around her, and she tried to breathe, but she could not fill her lungs. Her chest compressed. She tried to remember what it was like to breathe. She couldn't. She didn't know how.

Victor held her. He whispered words to her, sang the waiting song. After a while, she was able to match her breathing to his. Slow and even. She felt dizzy and sick.

"You're wrong about the stars," he said gently, face nestled in her hair. "The death of a star is not a winking out of existence. When it runs out of fuel, it collapses into itself and explodes. Brighter than ever. More than it ever was. A supernova."

Selene let out a shaky breath. What did that make her? What did that make her father? His star wasn't gone. It was merely shadowed, forgotten. She had to do something to help him. She remembered the way the ghost—Dante—had bled to burn away her migraine. How much it had taken out of him. How much more would the cost be for a shattered mind? She'd pay it. She'd find a way to pay the price.

Could magic undo what magic had done? She had to hope. The ghost would know. The ghost always knew.

And now she had his name.

Victor pressed his lips to her forehead. "I'm sorry. I would have done all of this differently if I had known."

"It's not your fault," Selene said, certainty settling into her bones.

It was the king's fault. Hatred for him burned in Selene with overwhelming certainty. He was the center of everything that had gone wrong in her life.

Victor caught the tears on her cheeks with his thumb and brushed them away. For three slow breaths, Selene let herself savor this moment and the softness of his touch. There was a world in which she could be this girl: uncomplicated and savable. A girl waiting for a triumphant rescue by some lovely prince. But she didn't know how to be that girl. She broke free of him and stepped away. All of her secrets seemed so small. She didn't care about anything, except what she had to do next.

This time, it was pain, and not music. She took hold of the thorns and let them sink deep into her flesh. The blood turned to shadow in an instant. She was present in her pain, no need for memory. A force of wind strong enough to carry her up and over the city. She didn't care who saw her. She didn't care for the consequences or cost.

She crossed the sky like it was a dance floor, her cloak whipping behind her. She flew, bleeding shadows and singing a requiem for a dream.

CHAPTER 37

In the moment where misery crossed into despair, Selene knew she'd found the heart of the magic. She could use this for an endless supply of magie du sang. There was no place in her that didn't hurt. Her father was alive, and she'd wasted all these years. Her father was alive, and she'd been lied to again and again. Her father was *alive*.

The air was cold and crisp and cut against her skin. The blood turned shadows held her aloft over the city. There was little regard for the cost. The magie du sang could take all of her. She wasn't afraid. There was no room for fear. There was only rage.

The roof of the opera house settled beneath her feet. The shadows rose like steam from her still-bleeding hand. She wanted the ghost. She needed the ghost. *Dante Dumas.* Once he was out, he'd know the magic to piece together a broken mind. The mirror would let her in. It had to. She had her father's painting. And his ruined dream.

She kept her bleeding hand aloft, ready to use the flowing blood and a thousand miseries to push anyone out of her way. But the hallways were clean and empty. Selene saw no one, save for King Renard, dusty on his tapestry.

There was no time for the boat. She sang a bridge of ice,

running across it with an impending sense of finality. She didn't care about L'Opéra du Magician anymore. She didn't want to serve a king who had lied and kept her from her father. The bioluminescent creatures lit the mirror in a dazzling, dreamy blue. The mirror stood sentinel to it all, the shape of Dante behind the glass. He was there and he was waiting for her. She was afraid if she stopped to catch her breath, she'd lose her resolve.

She hit the mirror at full force, bloody hand stretched out.

There was no collision.

Only darkness.

It caught her up in its web, so close to her skin that she was sure it was taking parts from her. She sang the light of a thousand stars. But the shadows didn't burn away as they had before. They lingered, suffering the light a moment longer to stay close to her before they slithered off.

The ghost stood in a scattering of light, his eyes pale and endless as mountain ice. He looked surprised to see her, and then horrified. Maybe it was all the blood. Standing in the mirror, all her cuts started to heal. If only the mirror worked the same for the wounds inside.

"Dante," Selene said softly, tasting the magic on her lips. His eyes widened, his perfect mouth forming his own name. "Dante Dumas!"

It was like a flash of lightning. The shadows shrieked and wove around them. He was all light, his eyes brighter and brighter. He remembered. She knew, she knew, she knew. She could see the blue in his eyes blur with the force of it. He brought his hand up to his cheek. A single, shadowed tear had slipped free.

He was whole.

"Say it again." His pale blue eyes burned.

"Say what?"

"My name."

"Dante Dumas," Selene said. "You're the whipping boy."

Dante's smile was different. There was something darker to it, a hundred years of untold suffering and the life he lived before folded beneath.

"My pain to benefit the crown, always." He stared into the shadows as if he were reading them. His eyes sparked with some new understanding. "You weren't supposed to come back."

"You told me to bring you the death of a dream," Selene said.

"An impossible task."

"I'm—"

"Relentless. I remember. There are things at play here more important than promises and games played with shadow. You have to go, Selene. Now."

Selene's heart stuttered. She had to tell him about her father, about all that had changed. She couldn't leave now. She'd crossed the sky to be here on wings made of shadow.

"The prince is putting up mirrors all throughout the opera house. Enough light to banish the dark."

And set you free. Selene was afraid if she said the words out loud, she'd render them untrue.

"I don't need the mirrors." Dante's eyes went sharp and cold. "There was always another way."

There was sorrow in the pools of his ice-blue eyes. Something was wrong. Perhaps he had remembered something far too terrible to name. Maybe what she'd seen that first day had been closest to the truth—he was a monster and not a man bound in darkness.

"Do you know what you have done?" He had the oil spill knife in his hands. He was drawing lines down his arm. Cuts so deep. The blood slid into shadows almost as soon as the knife cut into the skin.

"I don't care." Desperation clung to the edge of her words. "Ask me what I want."

"Selene—"

"Ask me who killed my father."

Dante breathed out slowly.

"Ask me!"

"Who killed—"

"He's not dead. I have my father again. That's what I want. That's all I've ever wanted."

There were tears running down her cheeks. Rage still simmered inside her. All those wasted years. The lies that had been watered and fed, grown up from the ground to create a poisonous garden. She thought she could forgive that, eventually. As long as she had her father.

She waited for Dante's uproarious joy. For him to smile and tell her that everything was finally the way it should be. But he just stood there cutting moons into his skin. He looked like she'd told him that the stars had winked out of existence. Like she'd told him that he'd never be free.

"Say something," she said desperately.

"This isn't the way it was supposed to be," he whispered. He did not stop cutting into his flesh. Healing and splitting and bleeding and healing again. "Magic has a price."

Selene took a step toward him. "You have your name. I have Father. And I'm going to get you out."

"What have you brought me, Selene?" Dante said.

The question startled her. All she had was her father's painting. She reached into her pocket and pulled out the paper. It didn't hurt her in the same way it had to give up his watch. He could paint her a thousand pictures. He could paint the whole world and she'd be there with him.

"The death of a dream," Selene said.

He brought the knife to his chest and cut above his heart. He drew sigils in the blood, shapes that almost looked like music. "Whose dream, Selene?"

"Mine." She waited for him to take the paper. "I don't need L'Opéra du Magician anymore. My dream has changed. All is new."

"Damn it, Selene." He pushed his dark hair from his eyes. Smearing blood on his face. "*You* are the death of a dream. Not that paper. What I asked for, you have brought inside yourself."

The realization settled over Selene. The shadows around her rippled, pressing against the circle of light Dante cast with his blood. "But that means—"

"The magic will take you." The ghost carved the knife into his abdomen. "I am doing all I can to keep it at bay. But I cannot stop it."

"What can I do?" she cried. Desperate. She'd found her father again. She'd promised she'd be back. She'd found the ghost's name and a way to free him.

And now, all was lost.

"Nothing," the ghost said. The shadows crawled from his

skin. There was not enough blood in his body to keep the darkness at bay. He stopped, a light going on in his eyes. "I can't break this magic."

"I don't understand how this happened."

"It was always supposed to be this way," Dante said. "I didn't know it, but the magic did. The things you brought were pieces. But you were always the final piece, Selene. The magic needs someone. You're meant to take my place."

Selene inhaled sharply. Her throat was thick with emotion. "All this time you've been helping me. You were going to betray me."

"I didn't mean it—or maybe I did. I don't know. There's so much of me lost. But I don't mean it now. I know you, Selene. I could never hurt you." He kept cutting. More blood, more shadow. It wouldn't be enough.

She shouldn't believe him, but she did.

"What do we do now?"

He searched the space between them, like there could be anything there but the dark. His eyes lit with something. But it didn't matter. Selene could feel the pull of the shadows like a rip current, meant to drag her into the dark.

Dante started to sing. The feather, the seed, the shell, the watch, all pulled from the inky walls of the prison. His voice and blood carried them aloft. He made one final cut, so deep Selene was sure she could see bone. He held out the knife. The feather shifted to shadow, folding into the hilt. The seed burst into bloom, tendrils of new life shimmering into darkness and wrapping up the blade. The nautilus shell nestled into the pommel. The nightingale broke free from the watch, spreading its wings and taking its place at the cross guard. It was breathtaking, like nothing Selene had ever seen before.

Still, she wished it wasn't the last thing she would behold.

There was no escape, no hope. This was the end. She'd seen the magic and knew what it could do. Selene held her breath and looked at Dante's beautiful face. At least she wouldn't die alone.

"When you get out," Selene said. "Find my father. Heal him, I know you can. Tell him I love him and that it's okay."

The darkness moved in closer, swallowing the light.

"Not like this." Dante stepped toward her, closer than he'd ever allowed. Selene could feel the heat of him.

"Wait, what are you doing?"

He took her face in his hands and kissed her.

Selene had not dared to dream of a moment like this, of the revelation of his touch. It lit her up like a thousand little fires. This was true magic. His lips were soft, his teeth sharp beneath. She sighed into him. Breathing the wintergreen scent of him, holding on to this final thing. A kiss, a kiss at last. It unfolded in her like a piece of music. A shared symphony between them.

The shadows swirled around them, magic and misery and not enough light. Closer and closer, until Selene was sure they would take her. But they surrounded Dante like a shroud, greedy and impetuous, ready to take him, instead.

He pressed her leather sheaf into her hand. "You are the magic and you are the music, Selene. Be it all."

Inky shadows rose between them in gossamer tendrils.

And then she was torn from him.

Cast out into the dark.

It enveloped her, sucking her into a breathless nothing.

Except it wasn't the impenetrable black of the mirror space. This was a familiar darkness. Cold and tangible and wet.

Selene's lungs burned. Her feet scraped a bottom and she propelled herself upward, lighting the water silver-blue with bioluminescence.

And burst into the air of the cavern.

Her cloak was heavy with water, pulling her back down again. She unbuttoned it, kicking free and swimming to the stone platform where the mirror stood.

Where it used to stand.

The great beveled frame was empty, save for shards that clung to the edge. There was no backing, just jagged teeth in a gaping maw. She wished it would devour her.

Silver glittered up from the stone. She took one of the larger pieces, curved like a sickle moon. She saw only her own reflection. She was bleeding, bits of the mirror caught up in her hair.

"Dante," she cried.

She sang his name and listened for the response. Her voice echoed around the cave and ended in soul-crushing silence. He couldn't be gone. She could still taste the copper and wintergreen on her lips. She sang for him the song they'd written together, all the words slipping from her tongue like desperate pleas.

She waited for his voice to rise out of the darkness. All she heard was the gasping of her own breath and the shudder of things deep within the water.

He'd betrayed her and he'd saved her and it wasn't fair. None of this was fair. He should live. He'd never gotten the chance to live.

Neither have you.

She'd wanted to watch him in the sun. She'd wanted to hear the resonance of his voice outside of the mirror. She'd wanted to set him free.

And now it was over. Dante Dumas was gone.

She still held his final gift in her hands. Her sheaf of music. She opened it up. The pages remained dry. The song was perfect. She saw all the things she had forgotten. He'd written her name at the top, as the composer. And next to it, he'd signed his own: the opera ghost.

There was something else inside. The oil slick blade he'd remade with magic caught in real light. It was even more beautiful outside the mirror. The iridescences of soap bubbles and the sweetest dreams folded into the blade. She drew it across the tip of her ring finger and let the blood drip on the sliver of mirror. Nothing happened.

The memory of his mouth on hers was as sharp as the cut on her hand. He'd broken his own rules. Traded his life for hers. He'd saved her from the dark.

And now Dante was lost to her forever.

CHAPTER 38

At some point, Selene's legs crossed the ice bridge and walked her up the stairs and left her in bed. She hadn't bothered to shake the glass out of her hair or wash the blood from her face or bandage her still-weeping hand. She burrowed into her down blanket and fell into the inexorable darkness of sleep.

"Selene?"

Gigi's voice pulled Selene out of dreams. It felt so much like the mirror that she had forgotten what was real and what was not. But Dream Dante had been ever out of reach. A step too far into the shadow.

She forced her swollen eyes open. The piece of glass from her mirror was still clutched in her hand. The sky was white with snow outside.

Gigi swore in three different languages and dropped onto the bed. The movement pulled the fabric where it had dried on Selene's various cuts. She winced. Gigi froze, then moved more carefully, brushing her fingers against the wounds on Selene's face and arms.

Selene closed her eyes. She didn't know how to put it together in a way that anyone could understand. The ghost was gone, lost to her. Shattered beyond repair.

The pain was enough to remake the whole world.

She let out a sob.

"Oh, Selene." Gigi brushed her fingers over the bruise on Selene's face and the deepest cut on Selene's palm. "Let me see."

Selene held her hand very still. Gigi sighed and went to the nightstand. The song for heat rang out in her sweet soprano. Gigi returned with a bowl of steaming water. She helped Selene out of her ruined dress and into a simple shift. Carefully, so carefully, she cleaned the blood off Selene's face and arms and legs. With a gentle wind, she blew the glass from Selene's hair.

"How did this happen?" Gigi dipped the cloth into the bloody water for the last time. It was red like a rose, like a dying sun before it melted into dark.

Selene thought of all the things she could say. The secrets and the lies and the last threads of herself, pulled so taut any part of her might snap.

So she told the truth.

From the beginning to what was now the end. The mirror, the bargain she'd made, Victor, her father, and Dante. A man and a ghost and now nothing.

"All I've ever wanted was to have my father remembered for the good things he did. To rewrite his legacy and restore him as the Great Giuseppe Dreshé. I don't care about any of that anymore." Selene sobbed. "I'm sorry about yesterday. Do you hate me?"

"I could never hate you. That wasn't even a real fight. We can do much better, I'm sure." Gigi wrapped her arms around Selene. "What will you do?"

"I have to sing. He died for this, gave up everything so I could have this chance. I can't let it go to waste."

Gigi's hand rested on the folio. "I want you to be happy, Selene."

"But?"

"I don't know if this will make you happy."

Selene was out of tears. She was so tired she could sleep a thousand years and the ache would never fade. Dante had told her to be it all. What choice did she have? She had to see this through. She had to go on. She had to sing.

"This cut is too deep." Gigi turned Selene's hand.

Selene had clutched the mirror shard so hard she'd almost sliced through. The pain registered the moment she looked at it, sharp and impermanent.

With a look of determination and resignation, Gigi sang softly. Parts of the melody were familiar. Some inversion, with the motif for growth worked in. She knew the rhythm of it. Her father had tapped it on the wall, on the table, on the floor.

After a moment, Selene joined in. Opening herself up to the magic and letting it flow through her. Gigi's eyes went wide. She didn't stop singing.

The skin on Selene's hand pulled together. The heartbeat of pain dissipated. Not only her hand, but the aching in her limbs and the pulsing bruise on her face. When Gigi released her, there was nothing but a thin, white scar. Weeks of healing done in a breath of a song.

"It's never done so much before," Gigi gasped. "It's much more powerful when we're together."

"Where did you learn that?"

"You aren't the only one with secrets." Gigi pushed off the bed. She stretched her leg onto the mattress and leaned over it. Her feet were bare and unmarked. "Had to find a way to keep dancing through the blisters and bleeding toes."

Selene brushed her fingers against the healed skin of her palm, trying to find words for it. It was the antithesis of her magic. She called upon pain, needed it, leaned on it. Dante's magic—her magic—it was something dark. But Gigi, Gigi was a healer. This was more than art.

"Incredible."

This kind of magic could change lives.

She thought of her father, of Benson, of all the magicians trapped in their own minds.

"Did you try to heal Benson?" Selene said.

"It seemed like it might work, at first. I could see him, trapped inside. But then he was gone again." Gigi's eyes were bright, the seed of hope planted. "But if we sing it together?"

"Yes," Selene said. If they could heal Benson, maybe they could heal her father, too. "We'll try. We'll get every damn mage in the world to sing, if it can undo what has been done."

But not Dante, she thought. *It's too late for him.*

"Come on." Gigi picked up the box she must have dropped when she came in. "We have to get ready. Did you get your dress? I think I saw it just outside."

Selene shook her head. In her grief, she hadn't even seen. Gigi got to it first. Selene's name was written in gold ink on the outside.

Gigi opened her box and held it up proudly for Selene to

see. The dress was delicate, with flowers stitched up the bodice. The tulle skirt was adorned with ribbons. It was a meadow in spring, the epitome of all brightness and joy.

"It's gorgeous," Selene said. "Put it on."

"Get yours first."

Selene opened the box.

The dress she and Gigi had sketched out was there. Or it had been. Before someone had sliced it into pieces.

Selene held up the ruined dress, wondering if there was anything she could salvage. The skirt was shredded, but that wasn't the worst of it. Someone had taken red ink and splashed it over the collar.

Selene's hand went instinctively to her own throat and the scars there.

This was meant to rattle her. But Selene didn't care about the dress.

She put it back in the box. Standing in her chemise, she took Dante's dagger and slid it over her thumb. She thought of Dante's mouth on hers and regretted it. She didn't want to lose any part of him, didn't want the fire of that kiss to fade away. There'd be no chance to rejuvenate them or bring new memories. Selene wasn't ready to give him up. Instead, she pulled up the restored memories of her father's madness. They were bright again, the pain renewed. Even if they lost their color, Selene felt certain that she could get them back when she visited her father again.

There was a moment of doubt. Of fear that the magic would cease to exist because Dante had. But the darkness rose from her skin and wrapped around her body. The shadows thinned to sheer black that moved up her arms and shoulders, hugging her chest and waist and hips and then flaring out into the skirt. They spread down her back to form a cape that dragged and pooled on the floor. It wasn't enough. She reached deeper into her sorrow, looking at the little knife.

Threads rose from her hand, iridescent oil slicks that wove into the fabric in ornate patterns. It would have taken years to embroider something this lovely. Selene had done it between heartbeats.

She left the collar open, the pale spiderweb of scars visible for anyone to see. She was sick of hiding. She wanted everyone to know what had happened to her. She wanted the king to know what he had taken from her. And that she was here to take it back.

Let them all look at me and remember Giuseppe Dreshé. Let them know who I am. Let them come.

"That's the magic he taught you?" Gigi's mouth hung open. "He was real this whole time, and not the monster we thought."

"All I have to do is bleed," Selene said.

Gigi shivered. "I'm glad you found the ghost and not me. I would never be able to hurt like that."

"You're a ballerina," Selene laughed. "You're all pain and beauty."

Turning away to the window glass, Selene brushed the silver powder over her cheekbones and throat. Lined her eyes dark with kohl. And her lips. She painted them red. Rich and bloody like poured wine and torn-out hearts. Like handprints on the mirror, pretty and dark.

She put on her black boots. Not quite a match, but it felt right. A reminder of her sins below the hem of her dress. They felt like an option. She could heed Victor's advice and run, run, run away.

Lastly, she left her hair half up and half down. Neither wild nor tamed.

"You look like a vengeful goddess."

Selene took a breath. She could be if she wanted. She had not forgotten the flood of power outside the Asylum and how good it had felt to wield it. But tonight wasn't about that. She wanted to honor her father and show the world what a Dreshé could do. Tonight, she only wanted to sing.

Gigi dusted her dark skin with gold powder, highlighting her cheekbones and shoulders and clavicle. There were flowers in her hair. She looked like a sprite, a wood nymph, a faerie. Selene could only imagine the tableau Gigi would create.

"What will you perform?"

Selene only had one song left.

"Something new," Selene said.

Selene walked with a chattering Gigi down the stairs. She talked and moved like she hadn't found Selene in a pile of blankets and congealed blood. Like she hadn't seen Selene bleed herself a new dress. But she watched Selene from the corner of her eye the way she would watch a captured kestrel. Bird of prey, feral and frightened and so fragile. Selene didn't like it, but she appreciated it. It was a reminder that someone in this world cared for her. That someone would have noticed if she'd stayed in the darkness below the opera house.

Victor would have noticed her absence. She didn't know what to say to him after what she'd done. After what he'd seen.

Everyone was gathered in the black box. The five who would compete. And in the end, there'd be one to emerge triumphant. The King's Mage. Over a hundred years of tradition, of magic as beauty and performance and art. Magic for pleasure. A necessary, impractical art.

All of that was about to change.

"Oh," Gigi said softly beside her.

Selene looked up then.

The walls of the black box were made entirely of mirrors. Reflections that swept back to infinity. Gigi gripped Selene's hand. It might have been fear, but something was different now that she knew her fears were warranted. The ghost had been real and now he was gone. Madame Giroux stood in the center. Mouth a thin line. Knuckles white against her cane. She wouldn't look at her own reflection.

"He's not there," Selene said, only loud enough for Madame and Gigi to hear. "He's gone."

"A word," Madame Giroux said.

Selene stepped away from the half-moon of her competitors.

"What do you mean, Selene?"

"The mirror shattered. There's no ghost in the opera house."

All the color drained from Madame Giroux's face. Selene's brow furrowed in confusion. Wasn't this what Madame wanted?

"You little fool." Madame's voice was soft.

"You knew he was there the whole time. You knew he was trapped and you left him."

Madame looked at Selene's hands. The cut on her thumb

was far from healed. "You think you know what you know. You don't. You have no idea what you've done."

"Stop talking in riddles," Selene said, frustration forming a knot in her chest. Madame Giroux was her teacher, her mentor. Wasn't this why she was here? "Everything you've ever said, everything you've ever done is rooted in lies. You let me believe my father was dead. I thought I was like a daughter to you."

"And that's why I tried to get you out. The music was the least of it. But you fought and you clawed and now you're here. And thank the gods for that, Selene. I hope you win." Madame's laugh was weak. "You're like a daughter to me. But you are not my daughter."

Madame struck her cane against one of the mirrors. The glass shattered, raining shards between them, a river of broken things to divide what Selene thought she'd known.

"Clean this up," Madame said to one of the startled servants before she moved to the stage door, her limp more pronounced.

Cold understanding washed over Selene. She'd lived this moment a thousand times, the precipice between greatness or disaster. She'd always choose the dark. She'd always choose whatever was beyond her. There was no going back to the light.

Some stars burn bright, some stars burn out.

When a star burned out, it didn't wink out like a candle. The death of a star was a burst of light, more powerful than the life of a star. If this was the end for Selene, she wouldn't fade into nothing. She'd go out like a supernova.

She took her place in line. Selene could not look away from the mirrors. She searched each silvery surface for some hint of Dante. For the promise of him. If he was the ghost in the mirrors, then he should be here. She should see the scythe's edge of his smile. The cold impossibility of his eyes.

The mirrors had come too late.

"Welcome," Madame Giroux said. Her tone implied anything but. "Tonight, as you all know, is L'Opéra du Magician."

Selene took a breath.

CHAPTER 39

There was no sea of gold and blue to look over and comfort Selene. The auditorium was filled. All colors of silk and satin and soft, fine linen against the velvet seats. Fans fluttered and overshined boots scuffed against the floor. The chandelier was lit, casting a golden glow on everyone and everything. Thousands waiting to see who the next King's Mage would be.

Priya stood at the opposite end of the stage. She was dressed in shades of silver and teal. There was a little red ink on her hands. She smiled poisonously when Selene walked out, and then swallowed that poison. Selene's dress both reflected and swallowed the light. It was a living thing, like a serpent with all black scales. Like the deepest part of night, when all the fear has gone.

Selene hoped Priya would win. She'd be free from her engagement but unable to live. Trapped in the position of the King's Mage, Priya would see what it was like to serve someone other than herself. It was exactly what she deserved. Selene blew a breath of darkness and watched Priya pale.

Selene was last. The final piece, right after Gigi. She kept her eyes closed through most of the performances, listening to the rhythms and colors of the voices. One after the other. Priya abandoned her flowers, instead creating a storm big enough to carry the boom of her voice. Some of her notes were ragged from her screaming.

The rest were as Selene expected: perfect. Cameron in splendid, honeyed pitch and colors too bright to be real. Ramin's growling bass and the heat and terror of his constructed hell. Everyone at their best. The audience was enraptured, a cacophony of applause with each performance.

And then there was Gigi. She was up on her toes in a flash, the music delightful and suited best to her bubbly personality. Illusion, again. But this time, it was forest. Gigi pirouetted and dipped into an arabesque. The animals that surrounded her looked so real that even Madame Giroux gave them a second glance. Selene knew the moment she had the audience.

A unicorn stepped out of the shadow, so well-crafted he could be real. He bowed to Gigi, and the two of them danced across the stage. And then Gigi did something Selene did not expect. She stilled her feet, folded herself into the center of the stage. She let the unicorn rest its head in her lap. The orchestra went pianissimo. And Gigi sang. Not her usual whisper of melody, meant only to channel the magic and go unheard. This was a piece of Gigi's heart, vulnerable and raw. It wasn't what anyone would have expected. It was so much better.

She was incredible. Not an ounce of Priya's power and no need for it. Her voice was like birdsong, like waking up from a terrible dream. It was a reinvigoration of the magic. Something entirely new.

And when it was finished, she walked the unicorn off the stage before she released its song. She took her bow.

SING THE NIGHT

The audience roared.

Selene caught her hand as Gigi escaped into the wings. "What was that?"

"Something for Benson. I know he can feel it, even if he can't be here." Gigi kissed her on her cheek. "Go. Do your best. Be yourself. Save tomorrow for tomorrow."

Selene's dark gown caught the lights as she centered herself on the stage. She'd given the maestro her music before the first performance. She could see him replicating it on all the music stands, the notes tinged red. Blood instead of ink.

Selene was a kaleidoscope of color, dark and wild and improbable. She was the thing in the water, the shift of light in the sky. There was a rush of sound, whispers that Selene didn't care to catch the ends of. She tilted her head so that her scars were visible.

She could see Revelio, sitting behind Priya's fiancé with red-rimmed eyes. Camille was there, the seat meant to hold her murderous sister left empty. And there, in Box Five, was Victor. He was at the edge of his seat, hands tight against the banister. She would go out with the brightest of lights, like he said. His eyes were wide with anticipation. He'd done up his jacket properly this time, all the buttons neatly in rows.

She let the stage lights blur the audience into shadow. If only Dante were there, too. She wished he could hear the song they'd written together with a true orchestra. She wished he could see her on the stage. The maestro caught her eye.

Selene breathed.

She sang that first note like it was the first time, like it was the only time. Just the note. And then the magic.

Selene put her hand inside her pocket and caught the edge of her thumb against Dante's knife. The blade was so sharp. She was used to the pressure it took to make a pinprick. The cut was too deep, but that wouldn't change the magic. Nothing mattered except for this moment. She remembered the way he'd looked at her that first day, wounded and lost. How she'd wanted to help him and had failed.

Wings unfolded behind her. Little pieces of sky, shimmering and black and catching the light from the stage. She spread them out, wide, wide, wide. She stood there for a moment, an angel of music.

Then she sang the wind.

He'd made her a key and she'd make him a world.

She lifted in flight. She hung there on the stage, singing for wind, countered by an illusion, and bleeding magic. Beneath her, a forest rose up out of tiny, heart-shaped seeds. The whole of a thing, inside something so small. And from between the trees, a man.

It could have been her father. It would have been, if she still mourned him. But the Great Giuseppe Dreshé was alive. There was nothing to mourn, no legacy to restore. It wasn't his ghost that haunted her. Dante stepped out of the dark. She wished it were really him stepping into the stage lights, that he could share this moment with her. And she could give him this: a moment on the stage. He could be remembered.

She looked to the King's Box. The king leaned forward, a bottomless greed that chilled her. His lips pulled rictus.

His teeth were not teeth at all, but pearls shining in the

light of the chandelier. The curl of the lip, those dark, empty eyes. She'd stared into them while harboring secrets of her own. She'd seen his face immortalized in paint and thread and coin.

Renard.

The thought came to her and quickly dissipated. It was a fleeting impossibility. He was Renard's grandson; of course they had similarities. Victor was the same, a facsimile of the same man.

But the teeth. The teeth. The teeth?

The memory of the pearled teeth folded into the orchestra, like a misplayed note.

He'd managed to keep her father from her for seven years. What else was he capable of? What kind of monster was he?

She landed beside her ghost, letting her great, wide wings fade into shadow. She sang him all her sorrows. A requiem for all he'd lost, for the things she'd wanted, for the dreams she'd once dreamed.

She decided, then. This wouldn't just be music. If this was her finale, Selene wanted to go out like a star. She wanted the king to know what she knew.

With the power of her blood, Dante's voice met hers. She bled the sound of him, weaving it through the illusion. Rich and warm and a perfect complement to hers. This was their duet. He'd given her the gift of his magic, the majesty of his music. The trees moved through their seasons, and Selene let him have the years that were stolen from him, like the years stolen from her and her father. She wanted to stop squandering her time on the stage and go to him, make up the wasted years. It didn't matter if she could heal him. It only mattered that she had him back.

I want this to end.

But the trouble was the wanting, and the pain that came with it, and the blood flowing freely from her hand. The shadows pulled from her, measure by measure. She could feel it happening, the magic unwinding like she'd released the chains from a monster.

Her head was light, dizzy with the sensation of blood loss. The darkness unspooled from her. And Selene tried to stop. She looked at Dante. But he wasn't Dante anymore. His face was torn and twisted, a smiling monster too close to the thing she'd seen in the dark. The thing that had once been Dante. The monster, at long last.

Selene had to stop singing.

But she'd offered her blood to the shadows, and the shadows had slipped inside of her. She couldn't close her mouth, she couldn't move. Her body was a prison of its own making, no longer hers at all. She'd given up too much. She could only stand there and sing. Her voice was no longer her voice. Her breath no longer her breath. Her heart beat only shadow.

She sang through those final bars, leading up to the high note. Her eyes caught on shapes and shadows in the audience. Wisps of her blood and her will, slithering up.

The light changed. The shadows crept up the golden scroll of the chandelier. One by one, each of the flames burned black. Everything was cast into darkness. Living and breathing and free. The black spread into the veins of the marble on the ceiling, like poison.

The metal groaned.

The chandelier dropped from the great domed ceiling into the crowded audience, a shimmer of shadow and gold.

Selene's final note was a scream.

CHAPTER 40

There was a moment between heartbeats when Selene was unsure. The magie du sang had trapped her inside of her own body. Inside of her mind. She watched the chandelier shudder and fall. It would crush all these people. The fire would catch and spread. The whole opera house would be in flames in a matter of moments. Not a star at all, but a black hole. Swallowing up and destroying everything in the bottomless dark.

And it was all her fault.

Then she remembered who she was. What she was.

I am Selene Dreshé and I am relentless. A too-bright star.

There was no darkness in that. Only the endless light of truth. It was enough. She curled her fingers into fists. She had her power back. She was power.

Selene brought the knife blade over her palm and sang for light. It burst from her, illuminating the terrified faces. She could not let them die.

She sang the wind and she sang the metal and she used them to slow its descent. But the chandelier was made of more than that now. It belonged to the dark.

Selene had darkness, too.

Selene let the darkness pour through her. Not the way she'd channeled it before. She treated it like music. She was an instrument, not a well of power. She let herself be a vessel, opening her mind wider and wider. Blood and music. She needed to give a little more. Let it have a little more of her. She opened her mind and opened her veins and hoped that it would be enough.

Something cracked inside of her.

Not a breaking, just a fissure. As if through a line on a broken winter window, the magic seeped in like cold. She could taste it on her tongue, feel the dizzying expanse as more magic poured through her. But it was fine. It would be fine. She could hold on a moment longer.

Madame Giroux and Gigi and all the others were beside her, then. Singing and moving the chandelier back up. There were others, too, magicians she didn't know. And Victor. He was beside her, singing, reaching for her hand.

Selene let him take it, even though it was slick with blood. She willed the shadows away. The darkness ebbed. The chandelier was back in its place. She sang the fire back into the candles. The lights burned so bright that all the shadows were banished.

"Selene," Victor said. "It's done."

She closed her eyes, trying to catch her racing heart. It beat in rhythms she wanted to chase. Music and music and magic in the fluttering. People moved around them, water around a stone. Fleeing what should have been their doom. She had stopped her own destruction.

Not now, she thought.

She leaned into Victor. Her head swirled with music. It moved around her, like light through a prism that was the whole world, casting rainbows of music on everything. She hummed the melody. There was magic in each note. She'd given too much to the magie du sang. What had it taken from her?

Victor stiffened. "I didn't want this for you."

The king stood before them. His dark hair was threaded with gray. His eyes were so like Victor's, a touch darker, seeded with black instead of gold. Selene had pushed aside his face so often to get behind the tapestry. Something stirred in her, the ghost of a memory. Eyes the clear blue of glacial waters, blood against silver. But when Selene reached for it, there was nothing.

"That was spectacular," the king said. He brought his gloved hands together in muffled claps. "Congratulations."

"For what?" Selene said.

"Selene Dreshé, you are the King's Mage." The king looked at her with empty eyes. "Mine."

She had wanted this for so long. Imagined those words. Now it was here and this was real and the sick feeling in her stomach was real, too.

"I brought down the chandelier. I can't win."

"That's precisely why you have, my dear. That sort of power..." He closed his eyes, lips curling up like burning paper. "Let's make this official, shall we?"

He took out a gold snake pendant with a black stone and held it up to her bare throat. Selene took a step back, body pressed into Victor's. The king looked perturbed, like he hadn't expected her to refuse him.

"You have a strong will," the king said. "Like your father. No matter."

He slipped the pendant around her throat, the clasp clicking shut with an overwhelming sense of finality. The setting was striking. A snake that wrapped its way around her neck, settling around the swirling dark gem.

Something was wrong, but the knowledge of what eluded her. A note she couldn't sing. A piece of music she'd lost the melody to. *This* was wrong. She needed to get away before she lost the chance.

The remaining audience burst into applause. The mages trained for the spectacle burst her name in lights. The orchestra had all but fled; one sorrowful bassoon played her fanfare.

Her instinct to flee drifted. She relaxed against Victor.

"This is the part where you say, 'Thank you, Your Majesty.'"

Her insides burned with rage. This man was responsible for everything that had gone wrong in her life. He had kept her father from her. He had orchestrated all of this. He'd let her believe her father was dead, dropped her wounded at an opera house, bid her be taught. And when she'd stumbled, he'd ensured she would stay in the competition. He had insisted she make it to the next round. What did he want from her? She hated him. She would not give in. But then the vigor of those feelings faded, and she gave him what he wanted.

"Thank you, Your Majesty," Selene said.

"Come," he said. "We'll send for your things in the morning."

"Now?" Selene said. She was so tired. She wanted to sink into her bed, her own bed for one more night.

"My dear, after I make a request you do not ask a question. You comply."

Selene thought of her father in the cottage, in the palace, in his painted room. She understood him in a new way.

Who could say no to a king?

She couldn't even if she tried. And she tried. Every part of her fought him, fought to keep herself together against this oppressive force. She would sing the air from his lungs. She would bring the chandelier back down. She would strike lightning into his ancient heart.

Except, she couldn't.

She was frozen to this spot, waiting for his words, waiting for him to tell her what to do next. She tried to reach for the necklace and tear it off. But her hand did not belong to her.

Mine, the king said.

And there was a magic to that claim.

Victor held her fingers very tightly.

"Go," the king said. "The carriage will be waiting."

Victor tugged gently at her hand, leading her away.

"Not you," the king said. "I'd like a word, Victor."

And she could see in the stubborn set of Victor's jaw that he'd like to stay. She had no choice but to release him. The king's eyes lit at that. He smiled at her, showing his teeth.

Each one a pearl.

The Opera Magique shrank behind her. She rode in the carriage alone, as she'd arrived here. The great copper dome watched her, a single eye against the expanse of stars. They danced, forming new constellations like they had in the mirror.

It was over. L'Opéra du Magician was done and she had gotten everything she'd ever wanted.

Each dissonant thought seemed to melt away. She could not hold on to them any more than she could hold on to the sea.

The carriage rolled through the palace gates and onto the grounds. Even in the darkness, everything was green here and perfectly kept, as if carved from stone instead of a living garden. The roses seemed to whisper music to her. Selene hummed along. They bloomed redder and redder. This wasn't a melody she knew by heart. This was something else. The world had broken into a million pieces and Selene could see the magic in all of them.

When the carriage stopped in front of the palace gardens, Victor was there. He had one hand on Tonnerre—who had worked up quite a lather—and one hand on the wooden box from the opera house. He took Selene's hand.

"I didn't want to see it broken after all these years."

"Where have you been?" she said.

Victor shrugged. "You know Father, he never leaves a mark where people can see."

Selene opened her mouth. She wanted to beg him to take her away from here. Run away, as he'd said. But the words caught inside her scarred throat and slipped away.

The prince led her to the front of the palace. It was bright and white as bone. She'd wanted this for so long, dreamed a thousand dreams of this moment.

"Presenting Selene Dreshé, the King's Mage."

The great doors opened and they stepped inside. There were servants and dazzling lights and sudden applause. Everyone was here, celebrating her, chanting her name. She'd wanted this so badly she'd made it happen. Just like magic. Everything here was open and stark. Free of secrets and shadows.

She looked around for some sort of escape and saw only a mirror. Her black dress caught the lights and shimmered with color.

And for a moment she thought she saw a man who was not there. Who could not be there. With blue eyes and an angel's voice and command of the terrible dark. But when she blinked, he was gone.

The mirror was just a mirror.

And she was just a girl who had everything she'd ever wanted.

Which was like having nothing at all.

ACKNOWLEDGMENTS

While writing is a solitary act, bringing a book into the world is a team effort. Luckily for me, I have an incredible community that has supported me through the worst and best of publishing. Thank you to everyone who carried me during the cancelation and celebrated with me for this triumphant renewal. Book people are truly the best people.

First and foremost, I'd like to thank my brilliant and unflappable agent, Lauren Galit. I could not ask for a better friend or partner in publishing. Thank you for talking me off the cliff and for fighting so hard for *Sing the Night*. You're the best of the best.

To Kirsiah Depp, who read this book on her vacation and carried that enthusiasm all the way through. Working with you has been a dream come true. Thank you, Eleanor Teasdale, for making my UK dreams a reality, and Leena Oropez, Jessica Lyons, and Gina DiBenedetto, for offering the best marketing and publicity a girl could ask for. The worst thing that ever happened to me became the best because of you and the teams at Grand Central Publishing and Piatkus.

I am so grateful to the crew at 8th Note Press: Celine Wang, Allison Moore, Renata Sweeney, Bengisu Onal, and Jacob

ACKNOWLEDGMENTS

Bronstein. Even though things didn't end the way we wanted them to, I appreciate all the work you put in.

Melissa Frain, Oona Patrick, and Jill Stewart, thank you for your excellent edits. You made the editorial process delightful and taught me things about commas I didn't know. And to Mary Luna for giving me the cover of my dreams.

So much of my writing success is owed to the good people at UCR Palm Desert's Low Residency MFA. Tod Goldberg, AKA the Todfather, thank you for that first phone call and every one in between. You make a hell of a flat white and an even better mentor and friend. Agam Patel, for crossing the t's and dotting the i's, and giving me the permission I needed to stay in grad school, babies and all. Mark Haskell Smith, thanks for always calling me on my shit and showing enthusiasm for my weird faerie novel. Stephen Graham Jones, David Ulin, Mary Waters, Joshua Malkin, Betsy Crane, and Jill Alexander Essbaum Peng, thank you for raising me right.

Wendy Duren, your friendship is one of the best things that came from the MFA. Sliding into your DMs to talk about Tom Ford eyeliner has brought me a decade of joy with many more to come. Thank you for your sharp wit, kindness, and for always knowing where the best restaurants are. The bald eagles have got nothing on you.

Kathryn E. McGee, you're my literary soulmate, and I don't know what I'd do without you. Thank you for reading every draft, zooming for eight hours at a time, and writing in perfect silence beside me on retreats. We've worked so hard and for so long, and there's no one else I'd rather be with. We're poets now.

Kelsie Sheridan Gonzalez and R.J. Valldeperas, I'm so glad

ACKNOWLEDGMENTS

you guys weren't serial killers. The rollercoaster ride of publishing is worth it just to have you in my life. I look forward to waking up to 87 texts from you every morning and all the years of success.

My list of wonderful writer friends is so long that I need a whole book. You know who you are, and you know all the good you've brought into my life. Thank you, thank you, thank you. Most especially: Michelle Dominguez, Amy Joy Baumgart, Mackenzie Kiera, Lucio Rodriguez, Rebecca Thorne, Sydney J. Shields, Rachel Howzell Hall, Mary Robinette Kowal, Kendall Brunson, Katherine MacDonald, Keri Picolla, Annemarie Hauser, Darci Cole, Gina Denny, Liska Jacobs, Dara Hyde, Alex Neumeister, Heather Scheeler, Jamie Stickle Parker, Yennie Cheung, Chih Wang, Nina Lim, David Olsen, Allison Lyons, Sa'iyda Shabazz-Ryne, Madeline Dyer, Janelle Corbit Alexander, and so many more.

To my students and community at John Paul the Great Catholic University, I've never had more fun or sown more chaos. Thanks for being along for the ride.

I would need another ten pages to show my gratitude to the Jauregui family. Thank you all for enduring the Anne Shirley–level melodrama my whole life. You've been an example of strength, unity, determination, and damn good stories. A special thanks to Aunt Elizabeth for all the coffee and peanuts, and for sparking my love of stories by the cow's water. I'll stand by the fact that your Thundercats are better than any cartoon. Uncle Luke, thank you for your spiritual guidance and obscure science jokes, even though I know you'll never read this. Thanks to Aunt Ruthann for inspiring me with Silverwolf;

ACKNOWLEDGMENTS

Uncle Matt and Dad for your campfire tales and all the trauma that came from that; and Aunt Mary for showing me how to doctor a story and make it better.

Mom and Dad, your endless encouragement of my writing is such a gift. I love you for nurturing that spark and never doubting my ability to forge a future as a writer. You are the best parents I could ask for.

To my sisters: Sierra, Karly, Julia, Lexie, Jamie, and Janna. Thank you for the countless babysitting hours, for reading my books and stories, for not judging me too much when I disappeared into other worlds.

To the Eccles family, thanks for your joyful enthusiasm every step of the way. A special shout-out to Jared for your support when I was getting my MFA (and for doing my taxes). To Brie for being my sister, my confidant, and my friend.

To my sweet children: Anthony, Vincent, James, Harrison, Theodore, and Cordelia. Thanks for the endless cups of tea and delicious lattes, for keeping me fed while I'm in deep on edits, for giving me a purpose in life, and bringing me more joy than I could have ever imagined. This is all for you.

Paul, love of my life, I could write a whole book in ode to you. Thank you for being my best friend, my partner, and my soulmate. Every day I get to spend with you is a gift. Your dreams for me are as big as mine. I love you, endlessly.

Do you love fiction with a supernatural twist?

Want the chance to hear news about your favourite authors (and the chance to win free books)?

Christine Feehan
J.R. Ward
Sherrilyn Kenyon
Charlaine Harris
Jayne Ann Krentz and Jayne Castle
P.C. Cast
Maria Lewis
Darynda Jones
Hayley Edwards
Kristen Callihan
Keri Arthur
Amanda Bouchet
Jacquelyn Frank
Larissa Ione

Then visit the *With Love* website and sign up to our romance newsletter:
www.yourswithlove.co.uk

And follow us on Facebook for book giveaways, exclusive romance news and more:
www.facebook.com/yourswithlovex

PIATKUS

RAISING READERS
Books Build Bright Futures

Dear Reader,

We'd love your attention for one more page to tell you about the crisis in children's reading, and what we can all do.

Studies have shown that reading for fun is the **single biggest predictor of a child's future life chances** – more than family circumstance, parents' educational background or income. It improves academic results, mental health, wealth, communication skills, ambition and happiness.[1]

The number of children reading for fun is in rapid decline. Young people have a lot of competition for their time. In 2024, 1 in 10 children and young people in the UK aged 5 to 18 did not own a single book at home.[2]

Hachette works extensively with schools, libraries and literacy charities, but here are some ways we can all raise more readers:

- Reading to children for just 10 minutes a day makes a difference
- Don't give up if children aren't regular readers – there will be books for them!
- Visit bookshops and libraries to get recommendations
- Encourage them to listen to audiobooks
- Support school libraries
- Give books as gifts

There's a lot more information about how to encourage children to read on our website: **www.RaisingReaders.co.uk**

Thank you for reading.

---

[1] OECD, '21st-Century Readers: Developing Literacy Skills in a Digital World', 2021, https://www.oecd.org/en/publications/21st-century-readers_a83d84cb-en.html

[2] National Literacy Trust, 'Book Ownership in 2024', November 2024, https://literacytrust.org.uk/research-services/research-reports/book-ownership-in-2024